PRAISE FOR ***UNTAMED***

"Addicting and heart pounding—you won't be able to put it down until you've devoured every word."

—Christina Lauren, *New York Times* bestselling author

"Sexy, heartbreaking, and hilarious, *Untamed* is an epic emotional roller coaster. It has all the feels! If you loved Kellan Kyle, hold on tight—Griffin will rock your world! He's cocky, sexy, hilarious, frustrating, and surprisingly tender. My heart pounded for him, broke with him, and ultimately soared. Loved it from beginning to end! *Untamed* is an automatic reread!"

—Emma Chase, *New York Times* bestselling author

"No one writes a sexy rock star better than S. C. Stephens. Griffin will rock your world!"

—Kristen Proby, *New York Times* bestselling author

"S. C. Stephens does it again! Griffin is every delicious book boyfriend fantasy come to life! Stephens takes you on a wild ride of love, lust, and self-discovery that's both passionate and heartbreaking. This book was pure magic!"

—Jennifer Probst, *New York Times* bestselling author

"S. C. Stephens knows how to keep a reader turning the pages. From the first page to the last, every wiseass inch of Griffin unspooled my heart. Dare I say he's trumped Kellan Kyle? I do! Pure deliciousness!"

—Gail McHugh, *New York Times* bestselling author

"A sexy, witty, yet poignant story that will seep inside you and pull at your heartstrings. This book will make you laugh, cry, and everything in between."

—Kim Karr, *New York Times* bestselling author

PRAISE FOR ***THOUGHTFUL***

"S. C. Stephens at her best! A sigh-worthy romance you will never forget, *Thoughtful* is full of her trademark emotion and toe-curling tension. A brilliant look into the mind of one of our most beloved book boyfriends. I consumed it; it consumed me. I didn't want it to end."

—Katy Evans, *New York Times* bestselling author

"Just when you thought you couldn't love Kellan Kyle more, S. C. Stephens makes you fall in love with him all over again. In typical fashion, S. C. draws you in, makes you feel like you are part of the story, and doesn't let you go until the very last page. Emotional and addictive, it's a story you'll come back to time and again. Superb!"

—K. Bromberg, *New York Times* bestselling author

"*Thoughtful* is an emotional roller coaster ride, and Kellan Kyle is going to make you swoon and sigh in the most delicious ways."

—Lisa Renee Jones, *New York Times* bestselling author

FURIOUS RUSH

Also by S. C. Stephens

Untamed
Thoughtful
Reckless
Effortless
Thoughtless

FURIOUS RUSH

S. C. STEPHENS

FOREVER

New York Boston

This book is a work of fiction. Names, characters, places, and incidents are the product of the author's imagination or are used fictitiously. Any resemblance to actual events, locales, or persons, living or dead, is coincidental.

Cover photography by Claudio Marinesco
Cover design by Elizabeth Turner

Forever
Hachette Book Group
1290 Avenue of the Americas
New York, NY 10104
forever-romance.com
twitter.com/foreverromance

First Trade Paperback Edition: August 2016

Forever is an imprint of Grand Central Publishing.
The Forever name and logo are trademarks of Hachette Book Group, Inc.

ISBNs: 978-1-4555-8889-3 (trade paperback); 978-1-4555-8887-9 (ebook); 978-1-478-90315-4 (downloadable audio)

Printed in the United States of America

RRD-C

10 9 8 7 6 5 4 3 2 1

Library of Congress Cataloging-in-Publication Data

Names: Stephens, S. C., author.
Title: Furious rush / S. C. Stephens.
Description: First Trade Paperback edition. | New York : Forever, 2016.
Identifiers: LCCN 2016015533| ISBN 978-1-4555-8889-3 (softcover) | ISBN 978-1-4789-0315-4 (audio download) | ISBN 978-1-4555-8887-9 (ebook)
Subjects: LCSH: Motorcycle racing—Fiction. | Man-woman relationships—Fiction. | BISAC: FICTION / Romance / Contemporary. | FICTION / Contemporary Women. | FICTION / Sagas. | FICTION / Family Life. | GSAFD: Romantic suspense fiction. | Love stories.
Classification: LCC PS3619.T476769 F87 2016 | DDC 813/.6—dc23 LC record available at https://lccn.loc.gov/2016015533

To my brothers, whose love of motorcycles
helped inspire this novel

ACKNOWLEDGMENTS

I have been pouring my heart and soul into this book for more than a year—time flies when you're having fun! Creating a brand-new world has been exciting, challenging, rewarding, and yet, at times, incredibly stressful. I'm very proud of the final product and have so many people to thank for making it the book it is today.

First off, I'd like to thank my agent extraordinaire, Kristyn Keene of ICM Partners. I am so blessed to have such a patient, encouraging, hardworking person backing me up. *Furious Rush* would still be a vague idea in my head without our multiple brainstorming sessions.

My heartfelt thanks to everyone at Forever/Grand Central Publishing. Beth deGuzman for literally supporting my writing every day on her wrist. Marissa Sangiacomo for always getting me exactly what I need—I miss you already! Megha Parekh for being such a great editor, and so wonderful to work with. And most especially, a huge thank-you to Amy Pierpont. Your work on this book was extraordinary, your input invaluable. Your mind blows me away!

Virtual hugs and kisses need to go to the many people in my life who have given me their endless support, help, friendship, and advice—K. A. Linde, Nicky Charles, Rebecca Donovan, J. Sterling,

Jillian Dodd, K. Bromberg, Kristen Proby, Jennifer Probst, Katy Evans, Emma Chase, Christina Lauren, Jeanette Grey, Jay Crownover, T. Gephart, Sunniva Dee, Danielle Jamie, Kim Karr, Claire Contreras, Gail McHugh, Sam B., Becky K., Lori F., Lesa F., Rena L., Toni S., Lysa L., Denise T., Nic F., Dawn B., Jackie P., and so many more!

My biggest thank-you will always go to the fans, readers, and bloggers. I am doing what I love because of you, and I never forget that. A special thank-you to Simmi, Janet K., Christine, Katie M., Charleen R., Verna M., Glorya H., *Totallybooked Blog*, *Flirty and Dirty Book Blog*, *Aestas Book Blog*, *Maryse's Book Blog*, *The Sub Club Books*, *Vilma's Book Blog*, *The Literary Gossip*, *Southern Belle Book Blog*, *Love N. Books*, and hundreds more that I don't have room to thank!

And lastly, to my family—words cannot properly express how much you mean to me. I love you all so much! To my man, I am so glad we found each other, and so glad you accept my introverted ways with space, wine, and well-timed back rubs. Love you! To my kids, you make me laugh, you make me cry, you challenge and inspire me. I am so proud to be your mom. All my love, always.

FURIOUS RUSH

CHAPTER 1

I hated getting phone calls in the middle of the night. It was a well-known fact that being unexpectedly awoken before dawn never led to a positive outcome. As the buzzing cell phone loudly vibrating against the glass of water on my nightstand slowly woke me up, I was sure whatever I was about to find out would not be good. Icy pinpricks of fear began waging war with my sleep-induced fatigue, and I reluctantly opened my eyes. What had happened? Was everyone okay?

A part of me wanted to ignore the rising panic and return to the calm warmth of slumber. Surely everything was fine and it was just a wrong number. But I couldn't shake the concern that something wasn't right, so with blurred vision and bumbling fingers, I grabbed my phone off the nightstand and glanced at the screen. It was my friend Nikki.

"Nik? What's going on?" I mumbled. My alarm clock proclaimed the extremely early hour in large red numbers. *Ugh, somebody'd better be dead.* I instantly retracted that callous thought. *Please God, don't let anyone be dead.*

A voice far too bubbly for the early hour met my ear. "Kenzie! Oh, good, you're still awake. I have a huge favor to ask."

Nikki's relaxed tone instantly melted my worry. If something bad *had* happened, she wouldn't sound so casual. Why the hell was she calling at this time of night, though? "I'm not *still* awake, I'm *now* awake. Huge difference. What favor?"

There was a long pause before she answered me, and some of my trepidation returned. "Well..." she slowly began. "I was hoping you could drive down to San Diego with five hundred dollars. Cash." My jaw dropped as her request scrubbed the last remnant of sleep from my brain. Before I could ask her if she was crazy, Nikki filled me in. "See, I kind of lost a bet, and the people I owe money to won't let me go home until I pay them. They don't exactly take checks, you know... so I need cash."

I was so stunned, I sputtered a few times before managing to curse at her. "Goddammit, Nikki. Are you kidding me? San Diego? Now?"

"I know, I know, I suck. But I didn't expect to lose tonight, so I didn't bring that much money with me. Come on, Kenzie, your dad is going to kill me if I don't show up tomorrow because I'm stuck down here... so... can you help me? Please?"

"Ugh! You know what I'm going through right now, Nikki. The pressure I'm under. The season is starting soon. I want to make my father proud, honor the legacy he started..." I sighed as the weight of expectation firmly settled onto my shoulders. It was stifling at times, paralyzing at others. My voice more subdued, I added, "You know Dad is counting on me to do well, since things have been kind of... tight lately." My gaze flicked to the clock again. It was so freaking early. "And to do my best, I have to be at my best. Getting up at three in the morning is *not* my best, Nik!"

"I know," she groaned. "But I didn't have anyone else to call. It was either you or Myles, and once he's down and out for the night, nothing short of nuclear war will wake him up."

That was true. Our friend Myles could sleep soundly through a heavy metal concert. "So you knew I'd be sleeping when you called, but you decided to wake me up anyway... Is that what you're telling me?" I asked.

"Well, yeah... I could set my watch to your schedule." That comment made me frown, but it was also true, so I couldn't really condemn her for saying it. I liked routine; I liked predictable. It helped me race. I wanted to know that no matter where I was or what day it was, when I got on my motorcycle, it was going to do exactly what I wanted it to do. Same with my life. I wanted to know what to expect every morning when I woke up. Just another reason this phone call was irritating me.

"Nikki..."

"Please, Kenzie," she interrupted. "I wouldn't ask if I wasn't screwed. You're my best friend; don't leave me stranded with a bunch of thugs. I mean, who's gonna make your bike a lean, mean winning machine if I'm dead?"

Unfortunately she had a point. Nikki was a genius mechanic—*my* genius mechanic—and I needed her skills to do well this year. She was also my best friend, and I would never abandon her to that fate... even if she had brought it upon herself. "Fine. But you owe me, Nikki."

She breathed a heavy sigh of relief. "My soul, my firstborn. Whatever you want, it's yours." I was about to tell her that I just wanted her to make my Ducati the fastest motorcycle on the planet when she quickly added, "Oh, hey, can you grab another couple hundred from your rainy-day fund? There's another race starting soon, and I have a really good feeling about this guy."

I just about threw my phone across the room. "No! That's stup— Wait... What race? What the hell are you betting on, Nikki?"

"Krrr... sssssssshhhhh... Sorry, Kenzie... crrrrr... you're breaking up. See you when you get here! Jackson and Maddox Street, under the bridge. Text me if you can't find it!" She immediately hung up, and I closed my eyes and slowly started counting to ten.

Tossing my covers off, I forced my body out of the comfort of my bed and placed my feet on the chilly hardwood floor. Internally cursing Nikki, I walked over to my closet, where my clothes for the day were already folded in a neat pile, waiting.

While brushing my teeth, I noticed that I looked like I'd been electrocuted in my sleep. I debated whether I should spend the fifteen minutes it would take to tame the mass of unruly waves, then decided I could use the time more efficiently elsewhere in my day.

Running my fingers through the worst tangles, I cinched a band around the bottom of the mess, making a low ponytail that would easily fit under my helmet.

Regretting that I'd ever mentioned my emergency cash to Nikki, I riffled through the envelope hidden under my mattress and pulled out five hundred dollars. And that was *all* I pulled out. Nikki was crazy if she thought I was going to let her lose even more money.

Stuffing the cash into my wallet, I grabbed my jacket and my street bike keys and headed for the garage. My everyday motorcycle was peacefully resting under the fluorescent lights next to my beat-up truck. This bike wasn't as flashy or as fast as my racing bike, but my Suzuki was beautiful in its own understated way. Opening the garage door of the one-bedroom house I rented, I rolled the bike outside and started the engine purring. Such an enticing sound. It almost made up for the fact that the sun was still hours from rising. Almost.

Stifling a yawn, I closed the garage door, slipped on my helmet, and left my still-sleeping town of Oceanside, California, behind for the slightly more vibrant San Diego. The drive south only took about forty-five minutes, but I had a little trouble finding the streets Nikki had mentioned. The navigation in my phone kept trying to send me away from where I was sure I needed to go. When I finally found Jackson Street, I kept my eyes peeled for… something. But honestly, I had no idea what I was looking for. Then I spotted the bikes, and I knew I'd found the place. *Jesus, Nikki. What the hell did you get yourself involved with?*

Motorcycles were parked perpendicular to the street for at least three blocks, the occasional car or truck smashed between them. Swarms of people walked around the bikes, closely inspecting them, like they were picking out prized cattle to take home and butcher. The riders—decked out in ripped jeans and flashy leather jackets that were poor imitations of the racing leathers I wore to protect my body and promote my team—strutted around their bikes with pride-filled grins that oozed confidence. The men in charge of the betting promoted their favored racers with loud boasts and outlandish claims. Zero to one hundred in under two seconds? I highly doubted it.

Rolling to a stop in a break between the bikes, I texted Nikki: *I'm here, where are you?*

I instantly heard someone down the street shouting my name, and looked over to see Nikki jumping up and down, waving her arms over her head. With a sigh, I shut off my motorcycle and hopped off. No sooner had I removed my helmet than people started crowding around my Suzuki, inspecting the tires, the struts, the engine. A man leaned down to touch the seat while I was putting my helmet on the handlebar, and I slapped his hand away. "Me and my bike are not a part of...*this*. Don't touch her again. Or else."

Even though I had used my "scary" voice, the seat caresser laughed at me. He walked away, though, and took the looky-loos with him. Good thing, since I wasn't sure how I would have backed up my threat. I hated everything about this place, and the thought of a part of this seediness somehow coming home with me on my bike—even just a stranger's fingerprint on the gas tank—nauseated me. Racing should be done on a track, with strict rules, officiated guidance, and specifically calibrated machines. I felt like I'd just been transported back in time, or maybe zapped into some apocalyptic future, where grimy men battled to the death for a cup of clean water. I really didn't want to be here.

Nikki had made her way over to me at this point, and she was all smiles when she bounced on her toes in front of me. "Hey, you found it. Good." Nikki was of Latin American descent, and she had that perfect, golden creamy skin that didn't color with emotion the way mine occasionally did. She tried to keep the guilt out of her expression, but I saw the tightness in her lips, the worry in her dark eyes. She was afraid I was pissed. And I was. But there was nothing to be done about it now.

"Yeah," I said with a frown. "Google Maps and I are on a first-name basis now, but I found it."

Nikki's features relaxed. "Just in time too. The next race is about to start." She actually had the gall to light up at the prospect of more gambling, and the last straw holding my anger in check broke cleanly in two.

"What the hell are you doing, Nikki? Betting on street racing? That's why you dragged me out of bed in the middle of the night?" I indicated the street crammed with potential competitors patiently waiting for their shot at "glory." "You know this is illegal, right? You know Dad would probably kick us off the team just for being here, right? Hell, the ARRC could ban me from the sport for *life* if an official saw me here and thought I was taking part in this shit. What the hell are you thinking? *We* can't be here!"

Nikki cringed as she put a hand on my shoulder. "Relax, Kenzie, no one is going to see us. I mean, they'd be in trouble too if they were here, so we're totally cool. And to answer your question, what I was thinking was that I can make an easy grand tonight." She paused to mime totaling a cash register. "Ka-ching!"

Before I could remind her that the entire reason I was here was because she had *lost* money, Nikki tightened her grip on my shoulder and turned me so I was looking across the street. She pointed a finger at a guy standing beside a souped-up Ninja. "The next race is between that guy..." She twisted me again so I was looking down our side of the street, and her finger focused on a guy a few yards away. Wearing a black leather jacket and faded blue jeans, he looked calm, confident, and comfortable as he stood beside a Honda that was completely surrounded by scantily clad women. "And that guy. Rumor is, Honda Boy there is undefeated, so I'm putting all my money on the Ninja."

I turned to look at her in stunned disbelief. "What? Why the hell would you bet on the other guy? If Honda Boy is undefeated, then you should bet on him." Closing my eyes, I shook my head. "And I can't believe I just said that." Reaching into my pocket, I pulled out my wallet and handed her the five hundred dollars. "Here. Now pay up so we can leave, okay?" The sooner we got this over with, the better.

Nikki had apparently recovered from her bout of guilt, because she didn't seem bothered in the slightest as she took my money and said, "No way. We're staying. And I'm betting it all on the underdog. That other guy being undefeated just means he's due for a smackdown. It's Gambling 101, Kenzie."

Rolling my eyes, I told her, "No, it's *You're an Idiot* 101. But I guess it's your money, so…" Pausing, I stuck a finger in the air like I'd just had an epiphany. "Oh wait…No, it's *my* money." I lowered my finger to her shoulder and poked her for emphasis. "And you're not betting with it. You're paying off your debt and then we're going home. Hopefully I can still get a couple hours of sleep before I need to be at the track."

"Okay, okay…I hear you." She looked completely compliant, and I actually believed she was going to listen to me. Right up until she turned and yelled down the street, "Hey, Grunts! I got a thousand on Hayden!"

The giant of a man standing behind Honda Boy raised his thumb to Nikki, then jotted down something in his book. Her bet was logged, and I had a feeling these guys didn't allow you to have a change of heart. I pushed Nikki's shoulder to get her attention. "I said we were going home! I said no more betting!"

Nikki bit her plump lip. She shrugged, and even managed to look contrite while doing it. "Well, we're committed now…We *have* to see it through, otherwise those two guys over there will start breaking kneecaps. That's how it works. I think." I followed her pointing finger to see a group of burly-looking dudes who seemed like they'd enjoy nothing better than breaking a few body parts. Goddammit. I wanted to go home. Right now.

As I balled my hands into fists, Nikki patted my shoulder. "But you should be happy, Kenzie. I did what you asked and bet on the golden boy. Hopefully tonight isn't the night he falls from greatness…" She considered that for a second, then asked, "Just in case he does crash and burn, you have more money stashed away in your rainy-day fund, don't you?"

It took a lot of effort to not scream at the top of my lungs. "No! I don't have a thousand dollars in there! What the hell are we supposed to do if he loses the race, Nikki?" Before she could answer, I tossed my hands into the air. "Great. This is just fucking great."

The banks were closed, and I couldn't withdraw that much from an ATM. Just like Nikki, I'd have to make a late-night phone call to save my ass. Definitely not to my father, though. Maybe my sister Daphne. But she was financially wrapped up in planning her wedding; I doubt she'd be able to help me. Maybe my other sister, Theresa. But she'd kill me, then tell Dad everything. Feeling the toxic twinge of dread beginning to radiate outward from my chest, I looked down the street at the man who was going to either help get me out of this mess or completely screw me over.

Honda Boy was holding his helmet under an arm while he flirted with the girls surrounding him. He was blond, with a short, shaggy hairstyle that probably took a lot more effort to create than it looked like. I could tell from the way the girls around him were tittering like teenagers that he was charming; with seemingly little effort on his part, he had all of them eating out of his hand. When a break in the crowd gave me a clear view of his face, I realized another thing: He was smokin', someone-hold-on-to-my-ovaries-before-they-explode hot.

There was a perfect symmetry to his rugged features that made it seem unreal that he was standing just a few feet away from me. He should be plastered on a billboard somewhere, half-naked, selling overpriced cologne to men who wanted just a fraction of his sex appeal. As if he could feel my eyes on him, he turned his gaze my way. Our eyes met and locked, and I was helpless to turn away. There was something carnal about him, primal and dangerous. Exotic. I was instantly captivated, and I hated that I was. This guy was neck-deep in a world that twisted my stomach, a world that spat in the face of my sport. My *career*.

As his light-colored eyes bored holes into mine, one edge of his lip curved up in a devilish crooked grin that was both playful and promising. He was practically shouting, with just that one deadly smile, that he would satisfy my every desire, satiate every craving I could possibly have. My heart started thudding in my chest as sensations that had been dormant for far too long swirled to life inside me. Luckily for me, the big man taking the guy's bets clapped him on the shoulder, breaking our staredown. Once I was free of his steamy gaze, I instantly turned around so my back was to him.

Jesus, was I breathing harder? Ridiculous, absolutely ridiculous. I was twenty-two, not twelve.

"Damn," I heard Nikki say. "You were right. I should have bet on him from the get-go. I didn't really get a good look at him before, but he is freaking hot!"

Inhaling a deep breath, I attempted to force my body back in line with my brain. "*This* guy is undefeated?" I asked Nikki. "Really?" She nodded in answer and I had to close my eyes for a second. A face like that with racing skills to boot. Jesus.

Clearing my throat, I nonchalantly asked, "What did you say his name was again?" I could at least label the guy in the fantasy I was surely going to have later.

"Hayden…something. He's been around for a while, from what I gathered."

I risked a glance over my shoulder at…Hayden. He'd slipped his helmet on, thankfully, although his visor was popped up. The big guy taking bets had been joined by a skinny Hispanic guy who seemed to be giving Hayden instructions. Or maybe a pep talk. The little guy was acting out the race that was about to happen with his hands, complete with swerving and explosions. God, I hoped there weren't going to be explosions. While he was going through his dramatic highlights, the big guy looped a camera over Hayden's helmet.

When the two competitors were ready, they backed their motorcycles onto the street. A cheer ripped up and down the sidewalk as the hopeful gamblers prepared for another round of racing. I didn't want to feel anything but contempt for what I was witnessing, yet the energy of the spectators, the roar of the bikes—I couldn't help the zing of excitement that raced up my spine. Against my will, my mouth twisted into a wide grin, and a yell of encouragement left my lips. Hayden's helmet swiveled my way as he revved his engine. My pulse quickened as our eyes met. Then he winked at me and slammed his visor shut.

As the riders moved into position, Nikki grabbed my arm. "Come on. We can watch the action from the van."

I had no idea what she was talking about. Before I could ask her, though, she yanked me toward a black van parked on the sidewalk. The back doors were open, and a giant monitor attached to a swinging metal arm was sticking out above the hovering crowd. The screen was split in two, each half showing the footage from one racer's helmet cam. Hayden and his opponent were both looking straight ahead, and the dual feeds showed similar stretches of barren road. Looking down the street, I saw that the pair were stopped at a crosswalk, waiting for the light to change.

Returning my eyes to the monitor, I found myself holding my breath as I waited for the signal to change colors. When it turned green and the bikes surged forward, I stepped closer to the van, like that would somehow release my pent-up energy. In unison, the crowd around me started hooting and hollering. Swept up in the moment, I bounced on my toes and prayed for speed. But after watching the screen for just a few seconds, I was struck with the harsh reality of the situation I was watching. This was no closed-off track with well-defined paths. This was down and dirty, anything goes, just get to the finish line first racing.

The bikes blew through red lights like they meant absolutely nothing. The streets were fairly empty at this early hour, but they blurred past the few vehicles on the road like they were standing still; they had to be going 100 miles per hour, easy. They dodged obstacles by hopping onto the sidewalk, they fishtailed around slick corners, and they came close to colliding with oncoming traffic more than once.

I turned to Nikki with shock clear on my face. "This is insane! Someone's going to get hurt. Maybe killed!"

Nikki's face was pure elation as she watched the screens. Her expression changed as my words sunk in, then she looked at me like I had a foot sticking out of my head. I supposed it was odd to hear that type of statement coming from someone who routinely hovered around the 150 mark on the speedometer while riding, but that was a completely different kind of environment. Believe it or not, what I did was safe, relatively speaking. Millions of dollars were spent to make it that way. *This* was not safe. At all.

"They're breaking every traffic law there is," I added, feeling like a giant stick in the mud. Someone needed to be the voice of reason here, though, because everyone was clearly out of their ever loving minds.

Nikki smirked at my comment. "It's a race, Kenzie. They can't exactly drive cautiously. Why do you think this happens so late at night?"

"Because it's illegal," I deadpanned. I got a couple of odd looks from the crowd after saying that, including a particularly nasty glare from Hayden's bet collector. Maybe this wasn't the best place to be talking about the law. Shutting my mouth, I quickly refocused on the screen.

Just as I noticed a familiar section of street come into view on the monitor, one side of the screen started wobbling, then the camera showed asphalt, sparks, spinning scenery, and a rapidly approaching telephone pole. The crowd around me hushed as it became clear that Hayden's competition wasn't going to finish this race. I heard Hayden's bike rounding the corner seconds later, then Nikki was once again pulling me along like a rag doll. She shoved us into a good position to see the finish line right as Hayden's Honda whizzed past. He was alone. Cheers erupted mixed with a few groans from the people who'd bet on the other guy.

Just as I was wondering if anyone was going to go check on the Ninja rider, Nikki grabbed my shoulders and started shaking me with uncontainable joy. "We won, Kenzie! We frickin' won!"

"Great," I said, clenching my teeth so I wouldn't bite my tongue.

Releasing me, Nikki let out a squeal of excitement. "I just made enough money to pay you back *and* cover my loss. See, aren't you glad you came?"

I narrowed my eyes into poisonous daggers that would hopefully drill some sense into her. "I hate you," I murmured.

Nikki held a hand over her heart. "I know by hate you mean love, and I love you too, Kenzie. Now let's collect my winnings and go home so you can rest up. Big year this year!"

I opened my mouth to scold her with some biting remark about how I'd wanted to leave ages ago, but she turned on her heel and left me there, gaping. Just as I was forcing the muscles in my jaw to relax enough to contract, Hayden pulled up next to where I was standing on the sidewalk. It felt like the world suddenly shifted into slow motion as I turned my head to look at him.

He was still hunched over his bike, hands on the grip and throttle; the only indication that he was looking at me was the direction of his dark helmet. Then, like some freaking Prince Charming in a fairy tale, he slowly removed his helmet and tucked it under his arm. I swear the air around me condensed as his tilted smile came into view. Jesus Christ, this guy was sex on a stick.

Reaching up, he roughly ran a hand through his sweaty dirty-blond hair. The short, sexy shag he'd had going on earlier was destroyed from the helmet, but somehow after just a few scruffs of his hand, the carefree style was back to utter perfection. I kind of wanted to mess it up again, run my hands through the strands, grab a handful and clench it tight while I outlined those incredibly kissable lips with my tongue.

Whoa. No. I didn't want that.

His penetrating gaze studied my face for a moment. There was something there in his eyes that I couldn't quite grasp. Interest, sure, but almost…sadness too. Then he smiled, and the look vanished so fast, I was sure I'd imagined it. "Haven't seen you here before," he said, his voice low and easy, like he hadn't just risked his life. "I hope you bet on me. It would be a shame to see someone as beautiful as you…lose."

His grin turned suggestive, and warning signs started flashing in front of my eyes. *Danger! Do not proceed! Rocky road ahead! Turn back now!* The warnings flared even brighter when he stood from his motorcycle and began approaching me.

When he was directly in front of me, so close that I could smell the subtle spicy aroma of his cologne, my heart was hammering so hard, I was positive he could hear it, positive he could see my T-shirt lifting and releasing like a frantic hummingbird was hiding under the fabric. What the hell was he doing to me? Was I nervous or excited? Because the sensation was so similar to both, I honestly couldn't tell.

Extending a hand, he smoothly said, "Name's Hayden. Hayden

Hayes." I was just about to lift my hand and touch him—my fingers even twitched in response—when he added, "And what should I call you, sweetheart?"

Sweetheart? With those two simple syllables he had just dumped a bucket of ice water over my head and killed any fantasy I might have had about him. I lived, worked, and breathed in a world where men looked at me like I was a second-class citizen. To prove my worth, I had to work harder, longer, and with everything I had inside me, all the fucking time. I felt like he'd just tried to take all of that hard work away from me with that one demeaning word.

"Leaving," I said, walking away.

CHAPTER 2

The sun was rising by the time I got home from my little fun-filled adventure in San Diego. I parked my bike in the driveway instead of the garage, since I would just need it again in a couple of hours, and wearily shuffled to my front door. Once I was in my entryway, I put my keys in the basket reserved just for them, put my boots in the empty slot of the shoe cubby, and hung up my jacket on the coatrack. Then I debated what to do—go back to sleep and risk being very late to the track, or admit defeat and start my day now. With a sigh, I traipsed to the kitchen to make myself something to eat. The first race of the season—Daytona—was only a little more than a week away. As much as I wanted to, I couldn't sleep in today. There was too much to do.

After my quick, protein-packed shake, I headed to the bathroom to finally do something about my hair. Since I had some time to kill now, I might as well untangle the snarls. My coffee-colored waves were a gift (or perhaps a curse) that I'd inherited from my mom. No one else in my family had hair like mine; my two older sisters were blond like our dad. The visible reminder of Mom was nice, though. She'd passed away when I was four. Car accident. A drunk driver had crossed the center line and hit her straight on. She'd died instantly and painlessly, from what I'd been told. I couldn't remember much about her, except that she'd loved my long, wavy hair. Although it was a pain in the ass to maintain, and even harder to stuff into a helmet, I kept it long because of her. The connection, however meager, was all I had.

When it was time to go, I pulled out my jacket, boots, and keys again and headed back outside to my bike. I was so tired and groggy that for the first time in a long time, I wasn't looking forward to training. But this was it—my first year racing as a professional. Now wasn't the time to start slacking.

I'd been riding motorcycles since I was three years old, but I'd been around them since birth. My father was a god in the sport of professional road racing. When my peers spoke of him, they uttered his name with such awe and reverence that it was almost as if Jordan Cox had created the sport and founded the ARRC—the American Road Racing Championship. The fact that I was his daughter placed a mountain of expectation on my shoulders. It wasn't just my own personal goals on the line when I raced. No, my entire family legacy was at stake. And that legacy had been going through a hard time lately.

Running a business like ours was expensive, and finding top talent who could win championships was tricky. Cox Racing hadn't placed in the top five since Dad had retired. My father was excited that I was finally ready to race, not just for me personally, but also because he needed a win. He needed sponsors, needed notoriety, needed endorsements... and frankly, he needed money. And while I wasn't the only potential winner on the Cox Racing team, I *was* the only one with blood ties to a legend. To say a lot of eyes were on me this year would be an understatement.

When I got to my family's practice racetrack, I noticed my dad at the inner gate, arguing with a heavyset man with thinning hair and muttonchops leaning against a metal arm crutch—Keith Benneti. My dad's hands were balled into fists as Keith pointed up at the sign over the gate: COX RACING/BENNETI MOTORSPORTS PRACTICE TRACK. An aggravated groan escaped me as I headed their way. Dad and Keith fought over that goddamn sign at least once a year, and their squabbles never ended well.

My father and Keith had been teammates and best friends when they were younger. Both hotshots on the track, they'd each won multiple championships. Eventually they'd decided to form a racing team of their own—Cox Benneti Racing, or CBR for short. The power pair had purchased the practice track together to use as a base of operations, and had gone on to win several more ARRC championships. CBR soon became as legendary as the two men behind it. But the good times hadn't lasted. I wasn't entirely sure what had gone wrong, but Keith and Dad had had a nasty collision during a race; the footage of the crash is absolutely horrifying. They both survived the incident, but Keith never fully recovered; he still needed his crutch to walk.

In the blink of an eye, Keith's career was over, and to this day, he still blamed Dad for what had happened out there. But in my opinion, what Keith had done to Dad in retaliation was a thousand times worse. A hundred thousand times worse. I still had trouble believing it, and I couldn't bear talking or hearing about it. Let's just say Keith took advantage of my mom during a *very* low point in her life. He'd overstepped every moral boundary there was, and very nearly ended my parents' marriage.

When Dad found out about…the affair…he'd brought in a lawyer and terminated CBR. The two teams had been separate ever since, but they were still bound to this mutual racetrack. It was the last lingering remnant of their better days, and a constant source of irritation to my father. He wanted full control of the track just as much as Keith did, but each man was too stubborn to part with his share, so, reluctantly, they co-owned it. And that was working out about as well as could be expected. The ongoing tension between Benneti Motorsports and Cox Racing was so thick, you could almost see it shimmering in the air above the course, like a vaporous cloud of deadly gasoline, just waiting for a spark to ignite it.

Not wanting that explosion to happen today, I stopped my bike beside my father and lifted my visor. "Everything okay, Dad?"

Dad unclenched his fingers in a concentrated effort to remain in control. My father was famous for his self-control, and his opinion about its importance was quoted in racing magazines around the globe. I'd had the adage drilled into me since birth: *The person who wins the race may or may not have the best bike or the best crew or be the most talented rider, but one thing they will have is absolute control over their emotions. Winning is about schooling yourself as well as your equipment.*

Dad was my hero, and yet he was almost as unreachable to me as he was to any aspiring racer wishing to meet their idol. Emotional distance was an unfortunate side effect of always reining yourself in, and that fact didn't change just because he and I shared DNA. When I was here at the track with him, I was Jordan Cox's employee first, his daughter second.

His gaze still firmly locked on Keith, Dad told me, "Everything is fine, Mackenzie. I was simply explaining to Keith, yet again, that we don't need to spend thousands of dollars redoing the sign so that Benneti is listed first. It's a waste of time and money." While Keith narrowed his eyes, Dad turned to look at me. Every day Dad seemed a little older, like stress was aging him faster than time. His hair was more gray than blond now, and even his eyes seemed a weaker shade of blue. They were still bright with intelligence, though, and steely with authority. Being around my father was a lot like being around the principal at school, or a police officer, or a drill sergeant—someone whose presence commanded respect. I tended to stand straighter when I talked to him.

Nodding at the gate, Dad told me, "Why don't you go inside and get started. I'd like you to get a few laps in before noon." That was when our allotted time on the track was over, and Benneti's crew took control of it.

"Yeah, sure."

Keith's gaze drifted from my dad's face to mine. There was anger in the dark depths, and I knew it wasn't just because Keith was ticked about the sign. He always seemed upset when he looked at me, and I supposed if he'd had any feelings for Mom at all, then that was why. I was a living, breathing reminder of the fact that Keith had lost Mom to Dad in the end. They'd stayed together after the affair, and she'd cut all ties with Keith.

"Good luck this year, Mackenzie," Keith said in a low voice. "You're going to need it."

His words made a rush of anger bloom in my chest, but I forced myself to ignore the sensation. Keith was an asshole, always had been. I didn't need luck to do well. I had skill, top-of-the-line equipment, and the blood of a champion running through my veins. That trumped luck any day. I hoped. I'd never been tested on this level before, and I was a little nervous about living up to the expectation.

Slapping the visor closed on my helmet, I rode my bike through the open gate and into my home away from home. The bulk of the space was devoted to the practice track, where we tested our skills and pushed our motorcycles for performance. Counting all the twists and turns, the track was a total of three miles long, with movable cement walls that allowed us to change the course periodically. While memorizing the track was a sound strategy, we all wanted to be able to adapt to anything that was thrown at us.

On opposite sides of the course, about as far away from each other as they could be positioned, stood the office buildings and garages of Cox Racing and Benneti Motorsports. While Benneti's side was bright and flashy with new paint and neon signs, the Cox side had seen better days. There were dings in the garage bay doors, chunks missing from the siding, and the paint was flaking off in large pieces that littered the ground like snow. Fixing up the place was on Dad's to-do list, but first he needed to start winning some races.

I drove straight to the Cox garages and parked my bike outside one of the rolled-up doors. The walls of the garage bay were lined with toolboxes holding just about every tool known to man. There were three garages like this on the Cox side, and they stored all the bikes and equipment for the team. Directly above the garages was the team's gym and the offices for management. A symphony of sound met my ears as I stepped inside—the clanging echo of metal banging on metal, the high-pitched whine of power tools—and the smell of oil, grease, and gas permeated everything. Everywhere around me, some mechanical beast was being torn apart or pieced back together, and the familiarity of the chaos lifted my spirits, my irritation at both Nikki and Keith instantly forgotten. This place was a gearhead's paradise, and it was my favorite spot in the whole wide world. Besides the racetrack, of course.

Sticking to my normal routine, I warmed up by running three miles on a treadmill, then I changed into my racing leathers. When I reentered the garage, I ran into Myles. "Hey, Kenzie. Are you ready for this year? Racing in the big leagues is a hell of a lot more intense than what you're used to."

Myles was currently the second-best racer on the team, almost always finishing top ten. My father had high hopes for his future and loved him like the son he'd never had. I wasn't jealous, though. I loved Myles like the brother I'd never had.

"I was born ready, Myles," I answered back, spouting a confidence I didn't entirely feel. Dad had won his first rookie race, and while he hadn't said it, I knew he expected the same result from me. I poked a finger into Myles's chest and boastfully added, "You better enjoy your superstar status while you can, because after this year, you and Jimmy will no longer be the jewels of the Cox Racing crown." Jimmy was currently Dad's number one racer. He'd finished in sixth place overall last year and was looking good to break Dad's slump of not having a top five racer.

Myles's dark brown eyes lit up with a devilish playfulness, and he rubbed his hands together like he was warming them. "Superstar, huh? I like that. I should start using it." He held his hands out to his sides like he was addressing an audience. "Hey, ladies. Wanna hang with a superstar?"

I was about to smack him when he was suddenly struck by an empty motor oil container. Looking over my shoulder, I saw that Nikki had finally shown up—she was never on time for anything, something her late-night antics probably hadn't helped with. "Don't get cocky, Kelley. You're bad enough as it is."

While Nikki was a genius mechanic and nobody touched my bike but her, I was still pretty miffed at her for being the reason I'd gotten only a handful of hours of sleep last night. Nikki gave me a sheepish grin as she took in my irritated expression. "So... sleep well?" she asked.

I glared at her in answer, and Myles leaned forward to study us. "I missed something, didn't I?"

Turning to him, I snipped, "Just Nikki losing her firstborn to me."

Myles smiled as he straightened. "I have got to hear this story."

"Later," I said, grabbing his elbow. "We need to get some laps in before the track changes into enemy hands."

Glancing at the clock on the wall, Myles nodded. Every day it seemed like noon came quicker and quicker. "Right, let's go."

Leaving my friends for a moment, I stepped over to my one true love. My *only* true love: my Ducati 848. Adorned with my racing number—twenty-two—she was blue and white, sleek and beautiful, and faster than any motorcycle I'd ever ridden before. Sitting on the back of her, going full bore, felt like being strapped to the top of an airplane during takeoff. She was coiled power, waiting to test my limits, waiting to push me further. She was my ticket to impressing my father.

Wishing Myles and me luck, Nikki waved us off before heading to her station, where she was working on my backup bike, another Ducati 848. Slinging my helmet onto the edge of the handlebar, I pushed my bike out of the mammoth rolling door; Myles was a step behind me with his own bike, a flashy blue-and-white Yamaha YZF-R6.

As Myles and I approached the entry point of the racetrack, I saw that there was a red-and-black Honda out there, whipping over the concrete, the number 43 proudly plastered on the front. When I'd been upstairs working out, I'd overheard the crew saying they'd changed the track today, but you wouldn't know the course was completely foreign to the person gliding through the corners; the maneuvers were so fluid, so seamless, that the bike almost seemed sentient, like it instinctively knew where to go and all the rider had to do was hang on.

I knew all the Cox and Benneti racers by sight and racing style, but I didn't recognize this guy or his machine.

Twisting to Myles, I said, "It's not noon yet, right?" Myles shook his head and I racked my brain trying to remember if Dad had mentioned hiring anyone recently. He hadn't. Not to me, anyway. "Do you have any idea who this guy is, and why the hell he's on our track?"

Myles tilted his head as he thought. "Don't know, but if he's on the track before noon, your dad must have hired him. The Bennetis know not to break that rule. Not after what happened last time."

The last time a Benneti stepped foot on our track before they were allowed to, that Benneti had found himself duct-taped to the flagpole in the middle of the track. Naked. Of course, the Benneti team had gotten us back by breaking all the windows in the garage doors. They were still boarded over, since we couldn't afford to fix them yet. For the sake of our bank account, Dad had ordered every Cox racer not to continue the paybacks, no matter how warranted they were.

Ignoring Myles's chuckle, I renewed my inspection of the racer. The new rider was fast, and ridiculously good—his setup on the corners was perfectly timed, and he kept his body low, hanging off the bike so that nothing was over the center line but his outside arm and leg; his "triangle of daylight"—the space between his inside knee and the bike—was so beautiful that Dad would probably photograph it and hang it on his office wall. Considering the furious competition at the professional level—races were won or lost by mere seconds—and considering how much time, energy, and resources were spent on training new riders, I wasn't too surprised this guy was top-notch. With the upcoming racing season so close, any person Dad brought onto our team would be impressive. Dad wouldn't settle for anything less than amazing; he couldn't afford to. Yet another reason I was feeling a profound pressure to perform. There was no free ride for Jordan Cox's daughter; I had to earn my place, same as everyone else.

When number 43 finally finished his set and slowed to exit the track, Myles let out a low whistle. "Not bad. He reminds me of you." Frowning, I peeked up at him. His dark eyes sparkled with amusement. "No guts, no glory, balls-to-the-wall racing, like you have something to prove every time you go out there." He raised a dark eyebrow at me, but I remained silent. Having to prove myself was a daily occurrence, and Myles knew that.

The rider exited the track at the same place where we were standing with our bikes. He slowed to a stop directly in front of us, shut off his motorcycle, and removed his helmet. My jaw dropped to my chest, and my eyes bugged out of my skull. No. It was not possible. But the long-dulled desires starting to tingle back to life at just the sight of him told me it *was* possible. The man who was proudly wearing the number 43 was the same drop-dead-gorgeous man who'd won the street race early this morning. What the hell was he doing here—on *my* turf—looking for all the world like he belonged?

In the bright sunshine, I could see that his eyes were actually a light shade of green. There was a devious glint in them that silently promised that every day with him would be even more intriguing than the last. Add that to his dirty-blond hair, rugged jawline, perfect bone structure, athletic build, and perfectly full lips that hinted at a treasure trove of untold pleasures, and you got a man who attracted a lot of attention everywhere he went—as I'd witnessed last night by the swarm of groupies surrounding him while he'd been *illegally* racing.

No way. There was no way Dad had hired this guy!

Hopping off his bike, the stranger ran a hand through his sweat-soaked hair. The shaggy strands were sticking up every which way now, and the chaotic hairstyle was too damn appealing. A small groan slipped from me in my shock. *Get it together, Kenzie.*

His emerald eyes swung my way, taking me in, and I held my breath and stood a little straighter. Did he recognize me like I recognized him? Did I want him to? Damn it...what was his name again? And why the hell did he have to have such incredible eyes? Green with flecks of gold, penetrating and intense, like when he was looking at you—truly looking at you—nothing else around him mattered. I could easily picture him studying the track with that unrelenting gaze. I could also picture him studying my curves with that superheated stare. Goddammit, no. This couldn't seriously be happening.

The air between this stranger and me seemed to crackle with tension as we stared at each other. I was sure only a second or two had passed, but it felt like hours. What the hell was he doing here? It made absolutely no sense. Before I could ask him, Myles stuck his hand out. "Myles Kelley. Nice riding out there, man. You new to the team?"

Tearing his intense gaze from me, the guy looked over at Myles and shook his hand. "Hayden Hayes. And yeah, today's my first day."

"That's right," I mumbled as the pieces clicked into place. "Hayden 'Undefeated' Hayes..." Both men twisted to look at me and heat flushed my cheeks. Damn it, I hadn't meant to say that out loud. But still, regardless of his record on the street, Dad wouldn't have brought Hayden onto his team. My father didn't Dumpster-dive for talent.

Shaking my head, I firmly informed Hayden, "You're trespassing. You're not supposed to be here."

Myles's eyes widened in shock that I'd say that to the new guy, but Myles didn't know what I knew. "Kenzie..." *You're being a bitch.* He didn't say that last part, but it was heavily implied.

Looking up at him, I shook my head again. "This guy's a thug, Myles. Dad would *never* hire him."

Myles gave me a look that clearly said *And how do you know that?* I'd tell him about Nikki's gambling problems later; right now I wanted this intruder—however hot he was—to get the hell off my property. He'd probably snuck onto the track. We should be calling the cops.

Hayden's eyes hardened as he studied me. "Easy there, princess. I have just as much right to be here as you do."

The anger simmering inside me instantly transformed into a boiling pool of volatile fury. "*Princess*?" I sputtered.

Ignoring my indignation, Hayden continued speaking. God, I really hated it when he opened his mouth. "If you don't believe me, go ask your dad. I'm sure Keith would be more than happy to show you the contract I signed."

I felt like his words had covered me in a layer of filth that would take weeks to wash off. "Keith? Benneti? You think he's my...Oh God, I feel sick." And I did. I even had to put a hand over my stomach.

Myles's expression turned serious as he pieced together what Hayden had just said. "Wait, you signed with Benneti Motorsports? Then she's right, you're trespassing. You shouldn't be here."

Hayden looked more confused than ever as he flicked his eyes between us. "Why the hell not? It's a *practice* track. I'm *practicing*," he stated, his face firming into a hard look. Sweet Jesus...he was even more attractive when he was angry.

Clearing my throat and shaking the image of his furious face from my mind, I told him the track rules, since he clearly didn't know them. "Cox Racing has exclusive rights to the track until 11:59 a.m. Benneti has the track until 11:59 p.m."—a fact that annoyed my father, since it gave Keith's team better practice hours; just one more thing they bickered about—"Since you're a *Benneti*, you're not allowed to be here until noon."

There was an unstoppable sneer in my voice when I said his team allegiance out loud. I couldn't believe this insanely attractive yet talented *asshole* was going to race for my family's bitter rival. Well, I guess it made a lot more sense than him racing for our side. Keith wouldn't hesitate to scoop someone out of the gutter.

Hayden laughed, then looked surprised when we didn't laugh with him. "Wait, you're serious? That's actually a thing? Some of the guys mentioned it...but I thought they were just being dicks." He frowned like he'd been on the receiving end of his teammates' poor humor one too many times already. I sympathized. *With them.*

"Yes, it's actually a thing," I coolly told him. "You're breaking a very serious rule, and you need to leave. Right now."

Hayden calmly smiled in response, like he didn't give a rat's ass about the track's rules. He would when Keith cracked down on him. It wasn't just a Cox rule. "Good to know, sweetheart."

"You're not welcome," I snipped. "And my name is Mackenzie. Mackenzie Cox, daughter of Jordan Cox, and racer for Cox Racing. Not 'babe,' not 'darling,' not 'sweetheart,' and definitely not '*princess*.'" I stressed the word like a hissing snake.

Hayden lifted an eyebrow once my rant was over; there was a faint, intriguing scar line through his brow that screamed of some unknown recklessness. If he wasn't more careful, he'd soon be getting another one to add to the collection. "Wait, you're the daughter of Jordan Cox…the *owner* of Cox Racing?" His eyes scanned my Ducati before returning to me, and with a scoff he added, "That explains a lot. So…Daddy lets you race, huh? Sweet, but stupid. This isn't a game, something you can do on a whim. This sport is dangerous. If I were your dad, I would have encouraged you to stay on the sidelines…maybe pushed you toward modeling. You're attractive enough. And every rider needs their own personal umbrella girl." Leaning forward, he grinned and said, "It gets hot out there."

Umbrella girl? Was he fucking kidding me? "Good thing you're not my dad, then," I snarled, as the bubbling inferno of fury inside me started churning into molten rage. Too dangerous for a girl like me? Bullshit. I knew exactly how dangerous this sport could be—I saw the evidence of that whenever Keith limped across the parking lot—but the risks didn't matter: racing was my life. Always had been, always would be.

As Hayden slowly shook his head at me, my hand balled into a fist. I'd never been angry enough to hit someone before, but I was now. I was going to slug him, then impale him to the track, then run over him with my bike a few times, until he fully understood that I was his *equal*. With the words "You're attractive enough" dancing through my brain, I cocked my arm back in preparation. *I hope this doesn't hurt too much.* The pain would be worth it, though.

Before I could take a swing at him, Myles grabbed my forearm. "Don't, Kenzie." Pulling back, he ducked down so he could look me in the eye. "Remember what your dad always says: Control is power. You're better than this guy. Don't let him win."

Hayden laughed again, then slowly shook his head. "You two are both a little tightly wound, aren't you?" Locking eyes with me, he purred, "I could help you thaw out, Ice Queen. And who knows, chipping those blocks off your shoulders might even help you go a little faster... if you're still gonna insist on giving this racing thing a try. Personally, I think you should stick to ponies."

I wasn't one to completely lose it, but I swear my vision turned red. "Let me hit him, Myles. Just this once."

Myles sighed as he held on to my arm. "You know I can't let you do that, Kenzie. And you also know we shouldn't even be talking to him. He's a *Benneti*."

He whispered the word like it was a curse, and I understood why. Sticking to our allotted times for the practice track wasn't the only rule around here. Both teams had a ban in place, and fraternizing in any way, shape, or form with a member of the opposite team came with severe repercussions. Just last year, a pair of racers—one on each side—were both terminated because they'd been watching football games together in their spare time. On this one point both Dad and Keith agreed, and we'd all been warned on numerous occasions that getting caught hanging out with Bennetis was cause for immediate termination.

Myles looked over at the Benneti side of the track before returning his gaze to me. "And besides, it looks like he's got company coming anyway."

From the other side of the track I could see a pair of Benneti riders coming this way to collect their lost sheep. Hopefully they smacked some sense into Hayden when they got here, since I wasn't allowed to. While I nodded at Myles, he put on his helmet, flashed a quick glance at Hayden, then headed out onto the track.

I was just about to join him when I felt Hayden grab my arm. Fire and ice sizzled through my chest as I twisted to glare at him. He had no right to touch me. Face serious, green eyes dark with intensity, he quickly said, "I would appreciate it if you didn't mention to anyone... where you've seen me before."

Heat in my eyes, I inspected his face; being so close to him was doing strange things to my insides. I felt like I was pulsing with energy. "So you *do* recognize me."

One side of his lip curled up, sending bolts of electricity through my arm where his hand was still wrapped around my jacket.

"You're a hard one to forget... '*Leaving*.'" Blood rushed to my cheeks as I remembered callously dismissing him when he'd asked for my name.

Yanking my arm free, I gave him a threatening look that should have been unmistakable. My expression didn't incite the terror I'd hoped it would, however. He simply smiled wider.

"Why should I protect *you*?" I snapped.

He shrugged. "Because it looks just as bad for you as it does for me. Unless your dad doesn't mind you gambling on illegal street racing?" He lifted an eyebrow and I had to close my eyes to scrub the enticing visual from my head. *That face does not belong on that personality.*

"I wasn't... I don't..." Opening my eyes, I stopped trying to defend myself. He was right. I shouldn't have been there. And neither should he, not anymore, not if he was genuinely a part of the ARRC now. "Are you still... doing that?"

While I watched, transfixed, his lips curved into a smooth smile, the kind of smile a devious man used often to get out of trouble. "Still street racing? Of course not. You were lucky enough to witness my final race. I retired from that life last night." With a wink he added, "I'm many things, but stupid isn't one of them."

"That's debatable," I murmured.

His grin turned amused. "True. But I'm fully aware that the officials will ban me for life if I'm still... a part of that world. And I'm not anymore. This is what I want now." His voice hardened and his face grew sterner. He almost looked like he was trying to convince himself.

"Fine, whatever. I really don't care anyway," I said, quickly turning to my bike. His crew was almost here, and the last thing I wanted was to be surrounded by Bennetis.

Slamming on my helmet, I started my motorcycle. I could feel Hayden's eyes on me. They were like laser beams running across my skin, and everywhere I thought he might be looking began to tingle with excitement. I wished my head would tell my baser instincts to stay in the backseat where they belonged, because this guy was not an option. He was everything I didn't want, rolled up in one undeniably sexy package. A package I had no intention of opening.

Needing to get away from him as quickly as possible, I peeled out and sped away. Dad was going to kill me for leaving tread marks on the track, but I didn't care. I needed speed. Speed was safe. Hayden was not.

CHAPTER 3

The next day, when I got to the track, I noticed a handful of people hovering around the open garage doors. I wasn't too surprised to see that I wasn't the only early riser this morning. With Daytona right around the corner, people were fired up, eager to get out on the track. But I could instantly tell that this wasn't a positive, *We're gonna raise hell this year* meeting. Something was wrong. There were too many scowls on the faces I could see, and Myles looked like he wanted to punch a hole through the wall. Wondering what was happening, I parked my street bike near the doors and quickly hopped off to join him.

"Hey, Myles," I said, walking over. "What's going on?"

Myles indicated inside the garage, where Dad and his second-in-command, John, were talking to the number one racer on our team, Jimmy Holden. "Jimmy just quit. Said he took a job with Stellar Racing. Idiot. Everyone knows Luke Stellar is an asshole to race for." With a sigh, Myles ran a hand through his piecey dark hair. "But the real sucky thing is... Jimmy's taking LDL Motor Oil with him. Jerk not only quit, but he fucking stole a sponsor too. Asshole."

Icy shock ran through me as I watched John and my dad doggedly trying to convince Jimmy to stay. From the look on

Jimmy's face, it was a futile attempt on their part; I knew determination when I saw it. He was leaving. He was our best bet for a top five win this year, and he was taking sponsorship money with him. This was more than just a personal blow for the team, this was potentially *disastrous*. It would be up to Myles and me to fill the void of his departure, since out of the four remaining racers, we were the best. Or at least, I hoped I would be among the best. I felt like a tiny fish being dropped into a shark tank and told that the entire world was doomed unless I somehow survived. The pressure to do well had just increased a thousand times over; I felt sick.

Clearly not swayed by Dad and John's quiet words, Jimmy picked up a duffel bag and started shoving personal items inside it. Myles blew out a long breath. "I can't watch this crap. I'm gonna go upstairs and lift weights. Or punch a bag. I need to hit something."

I felt like joining him, but I was too stunned to move. We'd given Jimmy his start; my dad had shown him the ropes. Maybe it was wrong of me to feel betrayed—this was just business, after all—but I felt Jimmy owed us some loyalty for everything we'd done for him. Especially now, when we needed him more than ever.

Unable to stomach watching this a moment longer but unable to walk through the garage to get to the gym upstairs, I stalked over to my street bike and climbed back on. I would come back later, when the traitor was gone.

Not sure where I was going, I sped away from the garage. Benneti's garages loomed on my right, casting my bike in shadow like some evil phantom. I wished I could blame Jimmy's departure on Benneti. It would be easier, and far more understandable. It wouldn't surprise me in the slightest if Keith had placed the bug to leave in Jimmy's ear, though. One way or another, this had to be his fault.

Avoiding the enemy's base, I headed for the gate. Since I couldn't take my street bike onto the track, and I didn't want to be anywhere near the garage, I'd blow off steam in the parking lot. Scanning the lot, I saw a clear track in the pattern of the parked cars. Smiling for the first time today, I revved my engine, leaned over the gas tank, and let the bike loose. My street bike wasn't as fast as my racing bike, but I took advantage of the slower pace to really work on my form. Time was only wasted if I allowed it to be.

After doing the circuit twice, I was in the zone, completely focused on what I was doing. That was when I noticed a motorcycle blocking my path. Cursing, I skidded my bike to a stop and ripped off my helmet. "What the hell are you doing?" I yelled at the idiot who easily could have caused us both a world of pain.

As the rider unbuckled his helmet, I realized the bike looked familiar. When the helmet was completely removed, I knew exactly where I'd seen the bike before. It was Hayden smugly smiling at me as he sat on the Honda he'd illegally raced the other morning. Wonderful.

Tilting his head at me, he calmly said, "I'm stopped in a parking lot. What are *you* doing?"

Irritated at both him and my thudding heart, I snapped, "Isn't it obvious? I'm practicing."

His lip curled up in amusement. I really hated amusing him, but man…that smile could launch a thousand ships, I was certain. My heart started thumping erratically for a completely different reason. "Call me crazy," he slowly intoned, glancing at the sky, "but isn't it well before noon? You have complete control over the practice track, if I'm correctly recalling the rules."

Setting my helmet on the handlebar, I quipped, "Yes it is, and I'm surprised you remembered."

Hayden's smile dropped and his gaze drifted to the ground. "Yeah, well, I was encouraged to remember…I don't think I'll be forgetting anytime soon." I might have just been imagining it, but I swear he rubbed his side and cringed. Had his teammates gotten rough with him? I knew he was an asshole, but beating him up over breaking a rule seemed extreme. Unless *I* was the one doing the beating, of course. Then it was perfectly reasonable.

Looking up at me, Hayden smiled again. It looked forced. "I swear everyone around here is just as high-strung as you and that Myles guy. Must be something in the water."

Not liking the thought that his teammates had hurt him, and not liking that the idea of him being hurt bothered me—what the hell did I care if his teammates beat him to a pulp?—I straightened in my seat and concentrated solely on the almost-insult he'd just given me. I was not high-strung. Jerk. "I know it may seem stupid to you, but there are rules for a reason."

He let out a humorless laugh as he edged his bike closer to mine. When we were side by side, so close our thighs were almost touching, he stopped. His eyes were liquid fire, like emeralds simmering in molten lava. "I never said rules were stupid, sweetheart. If there were no rules… well, then, it would be impossible for me to break them, wouldn't it? So in a way, you could say I value rules more than most."

He'd dropped his feet to the cement while murmuring those words to me, and our knees were touching now. The slight contact sent a shock wave straight up my thigh.

Reaching down, I pointedly pushed his knee away from mine. "That makes absolutely no sense at all." I really didn't know whether I was commenting on the sudden emptiness I felt or what he'd just said. *He shouldn't make me feel this way.*

Hayden bit his lip as he studied me. The move instantly drew my attention to his mouth… a spot I really didn't want to focus on. "You seem more surly than usual. Something wrong?"

His comment, or the fullness of his lips—God, I bet they were soft—provoked my agitation. I was *not* about to discuss my problems with him. "You don't know anything about me," I snapped. *And you never will.*

He shook his head, his expression instantly transformed into one of contempt. "And you know so much about me? You called me a thug after seeing me *one* time. So… let me just take a stab at what's eating you. Daddy won't buy you the latest and greatest to race with? What? Your *Ducati* not good enough for you anymore?"

Just the snotty tone of his voice would have been enough to set my teeth on edge, but *what* he'd said was ten times worse. I wasn't some rich-bitch spoiled brat who was racing because I was bored—I'd been doing this my entire life. I'd researched what bike I'd wanted, then I'd gone out and gotten it—*myself*. My father couldn't afford to provide bikes for all of his racers, so to help take some of the burden off his shoulders—and because I'd wanted the best bikes around—I'd stepped up and purchased my own. Or partly. I'd taken a loan out for some of it, a plan my dad had argued against. He hadn't wanted me to be up to my eyeballs in debt, but it was a small sacrifice to help out the family business. I was not about to explain any of that to this douche, though. And besides, I was right calling Hayden a thug. That was exactly what he was.

"Get the hell away from me...before I tell *Daddy* you were messing with me. He has no patience for Bennetis. Or assholes." While it made me feel like I had a thousand splinters sticking out of my skin to let him keep thinking I was some pampered heiress who had no right to be here, I wasn't in the mood to explain myself or justify my actions. Not to him. Let him think what he wanted; I knew the truth. And besides, what did he know about sacrifice anyway? He'd probably never had to earn a damn thing in his life. He'd probably stolen everything he had, including that shiny Honda he was straddling.

Hayden worked his jaw before responding to me. The heat in his eyes was an equal match for mine, and for a minute, I couldn't tell if the sparks flying between us were anger...or something else. His tone pure ice, he bit out, "Sure thing...princess." Then he opened his throttle and zipped away from me. It was only then that I realized I'd been holding my breath.

When I got back to the garage, things were calmer, and Jimmy was gone. Nikki was there now, looking around at all the glum expressions with confusion on her face. She approached me the minute I stepped inside.

"Why's everyone acting like they're at a funeral?" Before I could answer, she asked a different question. "Why were you racing through the parking lot?" I opened my mouth, but again, she didn't let me get a word out. "And is what Myles told me last night true...that Benneti hired some hotshot named Hayden, and that the asswipe totally insulted you?"

I paused to see if she'd let me speak. When she didn't ask another question, I nodded. "Yes, he did, and yes, the guy was a douche." *Yesterday and today.*

Nikki's eyes widened and she suddenly looked really nervous. After making sure no one was within earshot, she quietly said, "Did he mean Hayden-Hayden...as in street-racing, undefeated, golden-boy Hayden? *That* Hayden?"

Rolling my eyes, I nodded again. "Yeah...same Hayden." *Unfortunately.*

Nikki scrubbed her hands on her coveralls, like she was sweating. "Jesus...what are the odds that it's the same guy? Do you think he's still doing...that? Because he'll get banned from the sport if someone finds out."

For a second, I debated whether I should tell her the truth. Then I shrugged and said, "How would I know?" I didn't want to admit that I *did* know, because that would be admitting that I'd talked to him. And that would lead to questions like, *Why are you talking to him?* and *Why is he talking to you?* and *Do you want Myles and the guys to set him straight?* On second thought, maybe I should tell her. No, Hayden's teammates were already setting him straight...Why was that still bothering me?

"Yeah, guess you wouldn't know..." Nikki murmured, sounding distracted. Looking around again, she lowered her voice even more. "I noticed you haven't said anything to Myles about the whole illegal gambling thing. You're not going to, right?" Her expression turned pleading. "Because he would seriously kill me, and then he'd probably let it slip to someone, because he blabbers when he's stressed, and then your dad would find out and fire me. And I *really* love my job, Kenzie."

I had to shake my head at that. Myles wasn't the only one who blabbered; unless the secret was hers, Nikki couldn't keep quiet to save her life. "Of course I won't say anything." While I really didn't care if Hayden's secret got out, I would keep quiet for Nikki's sake. And my own, I supposed. Because Hayden was right. Even if I was only there to help Nikki that night, it looked bad for me too.

Nikki's glee was immediate, and the bright smile that spread across her face was almost contagious. Almost. "But we have bigger problems today than your poor judgment," I muttered, changing the subject. Her face scrunched in annoyance and I quickly explained. "Jimmy quit, and he took LDL with him."

Her dark eyes widened in shock. "He...what?"

I sighed. "Yeah. I gotta go talk to my dad, make sure everything's okay. We'll catch up later, all right?" She mumbled something that sounded like "Okay," and I started walking away. Pausing, I turned back to her. "Oh, and Nikki, if I'm going to keep silent for you, then you need to stay away from that world." She immediately opened her mouth to answer me, but I cut her off before she could. "I'm serious, Nikki. Stay away from it." Her expression fell, but she nodded, and I felt a little better as I left to go see my father.

As I trudged up the stairs to my dad's office, my heart grew heavier with each step. My father didn't often confide his financial troubles to me, but I saw signs all around that were pointing to a downward spiral. In addition to the general lack of upkeep to the property, the mechanics were using tools that should have been replaced ages ago, our supply of spare parts was disastrously low, and two of our team's backup bikes didn't run at all. Even worse than that, though, my oldest sister, Theresa, had recently told me that Dad had refinanced his house. Again. I felt like this season was it—a make-it-or-break-it year for Cox Racing—and I wasn't sure if I was up to the challenge ahead of me. I'd like to think I was, and I'd tell anyone who asked that I was ready to take on the world...but doubt was seeping in, and fear was following closely on its heels.

The heavy door to my dad's office was closed when I got there. I briefly knocked on it, and Dad's gruff voice immediately answered. "Come in."

I opened the door to see him sitting at his desk, poring over a messy stack of invoices. He was frowning as he ran a hand through his close-cropped hair. As I stepped inside his office, I saw that many of the bills in front of him had the word OVERDUE stamped across them in bright red ink.

Dad flipped some of the papers over when he saw it was me. "Mackenzie, good to see you. Have you been on the track yet?"

Frowning, I told him, "No, not yet."

He sighed like he was disappointed with my answer. Great. Two seconds in and I was already letting him down. "We leave for Daytona in a week. Now isn't the time to slack off."

"I know, and I was..." I stopped talking and shut my mouth. No matter my intentions, goofing around in the parking lot wasn't training, and there was no way to make my dad see it as anything but a waste of time. Changing topics, I said, "I saw what happened with Jimmy."

Leaning back in his chair, Dad studied his hands in his lap. "Ah, yes. That was... unfortunate, but nothing to be done about it now." When he looked back up at me, there was a weariness in his eyes that never seemed to really go away anymore.

"Unfortunate?" I said, stepping around his desk to stand beside him. "Dad, it was a bit more than unfortunate. He was our best rider."

"But not our *only* rider," he answered, standing. Locking gazes with me, Dad put a firm hand on my shoulder. "I have faith in you, Mackenzie, and I know you'll do *exactly* what you need to do this year." From the sternness in his voice and the glint in his eyes, it was clear that anything less than my absolute best would not be tolerated. It was mild praise hidden under a mound of responsibility. How the hell was I supposed to stand a chance at succeeding when the bar was already set on the top rung?

I swallowed the sudden anxiety tightening my throat. "Of course, Dad. I *am* a Cox, after all." Which was a blessing and a curse. Would I ride faster without the weight of his legacy on my back? That was one question I would never know the answer to.

A half smile formed on Dad's face. "I'm glad to hear it. Now get out there and work on your laps. I need you to be ready for Daytona, and you're not quite there yet. As I've told you before, you need to work on endurance. You can't let yourself ease up when your muscles start to fatigue. Work through the pain, Mackenzie. And watch your speed on the corners. You're going to lose control one of these days." He clapped my shoulder, then returned to his chair, and I knew I was being dismissed.

Visualize the victory, and it will be yours. Dad used to say that to me when I was younger, racing on dirt bike tracks with a bunch of other five- and six-year-olds. Back then, it had just been about having fun. Some of that magic had faded now that so much was riding on my success. Remembering another piece of his oft-repeated advice—*Your attitude will forge your future*—I told him, "I'll be ready, Dad. I've got this."

Dad gave me a curt but pleased nod. "I certainly hope so. There are no second chances out there, Mackenzie." The sudden bleakness on his face gave me the chills. No, I supposed there weren't any more second chances for Cox Racing.

I left my father's office feeling bolstered, worried, and also a little dejected. I wanted to do my best, but I was scared my best wouldn't be good enough, and I was worried that Dad would push me away if I failed. Not intentionally, of course, but his priority was the team and making sure all of us reached our peak performance. He had a lot on his plate, and I couldn't be both a daughter *and* a rider to him. Not when so much was on the line. I was fine with that most of the time, but sometimes...I just wanted him to be a dad and nothing else. I wanted him to forget about the business for five seconds, forget about the never-ending stress that came along with running it, and just be proud of me.

Even if I lost.

* * *

I was an anxious ball of energy when we arrived in Daytona one week later. I'd been there several times before, helping out and watching the event with my father, but this time I was competing, not observing. I was practically bouncing off the walls with nerves; the excess energy coursing through me was so chaotic and frazzled that I could barely sit still as I met with fans and signed autographs. It was a little surprising that I had fans at all, since this was my rookie year, but there were dozens of young girls coming up to me with stars in their eyes and their dreams plain as day on their faces. It made me happy that at least in this one small way, how I finished the race didn't matter—I would still be an inspiration to these girls even if I was dead last. *Oh God, please don't let me come in dead last.*

As fate would have it, Benneti Motorsports was given the spot next to ours for the prerace publicity, and while I tried to ignore the models and giggling girls fawning all over Hayden and the rest of the team, bursts of laughter kept drawing my attention to their stall. The latest batch of laughs was coming from a group of preteens. Hayden was doing some sort of complicated handshake with one of them; he seemed perfectly at ease around kids.

Hayden noticed me looking his way, and my breath locked in my throat. With more effort than I cared to admit, I pulled my eyes from him and focused on the girl in front of me. Holding one hand to her chest, she said in a rush, "Cox Racing is my family's favorite team. Your dad is seriously a legend; you must be so excited to race for him!" I was about to answer her when she leaned forward and whispered, "But why didn't your dad hire Hayden Hayes? He is soooooo hot! I don't know how you're going to race against him. I would be too distracted." She used her photo of me to fan her face and I—very carefully—yanked it from her fingers.

"I'll manage somehow," I murmured as I signed my name over my face.

When the social part of the day was over with, I decided to explore the grounds; I was still way too wound up, and I needed to calm down before race time. *Control, Kenzie. Control.*

I instantly regretted my decision to sightsee when I heard a familiar voice shout, "Hey, princess!"

Before I could stop myself, I snapped my head around to give Hayden a bone-chilling glare. "That's not my name," I hissed.

Hayden's smile was cocky as he jogged to catch up to me. "Are you sure? It fits you."

Shaking my head, I trudged forward, determined to ignore him. No good could come from me engaging this man in conversation. And I shouldn't be talking to him anyway. He was a *Benneti*. If someone saw us...I'd be fired. Hayden would be sacked too. But even with all that running through my head, it was surprisingly hard to ignore Hayden when he was only a few inches away from me. Like a shadow blocking the sun from my eyes, or a fly buzzing around my head, his presence was just too intrusive.

"So…did Daddy prepare you for this? Because it's nothing like squirreling around the track in the backyard, sweetheart."

With fire in my eyes, I spun around to face him. He hadn't expected my sudden movement, and we ended up colliding. Stubbornly, I refused to step away. "What the hell do you want, Hayden?"

His face was mere inches from mine now, and I could clearly see every perfectly crafted detail that made him so frustratingly attractive: the light stubble along his jawline, the subtle yet sexy scar through his eyebrow, and the random streaks of gold and blue that highlighted his emerald eyes. My chest was rising and falling against his at an ever-quickening pace, and I could feel my heart pounding against my rib cage. A crackling energy was zipping through my body, faster and faster. It was an oddly familiar feeling, like I was about to start a race. Experiencing that sensation because of him was disorienting. I wanted to pull him closer; I wanted to shove him away.

His eyes locked on my mouth and he licked his lips. "I just… there's a hairpin turn in this one. It comes up fast…be ready." He almost looked confused after he said it, like he wasn't sure why he had. But odder still, there was genuine concern in his expression. Was he actually worried about me? Ridiculous. He didn't like me, I didn't like him. That was our…thing.

The thought that he might be worried about me was unsettling. It was strangely sweet, and that was something I was *not* used to from him. But it was also slightly condescending; he thought I couldn't hack it. I was still buzzing off the energy between us, and having all this extra crap tossed on the fire was not helping anything. Not sure how to take what he'd just said, I spat out, "I know, asshole. I've already done the practice lap."

Hayden's face immediately hardened into stone. Good. I'd rather have him be angry. Turning around, I immediately stalked off toward the Cox Racing camp. I needed to get out of here.

Thankfully, Hayden didn't try to follow me. He couldn't let me go without getting the last word in, though. "Relax, Ice Queen. It was just a tip."

I almost flipped him off, but my body was still churning with opposing desires—*closer, farther*. Hayden was a bad idea, a horrible idea. But...standing right in front of him, touching him like that, it had kick-started something in me. A prickly rush of adrenaline, screaming at me that I was about to do something crazy, dangerous...and exciting. It was a damn good feeling, like competing. And while I looked forward to that flood of endorphins before every race, I could not feel that way about Hayden. No, I *wouldn't* feel that way. I would ignore it, and it would go away.

* * *

It felt like forever, but finally it was time to race. With the sighting and warm-up lap completed, the group of us were all lined up in our grid boxes. This was it, my first official race as a professional. My heart started pumping hard, and my breath sped up. Dad was expecting a lot from me; I needed to be amazing today. Trying to control the adrenaline—control *myself*—I took a deep breath in, held it, then let it out in ten long counts. It helped. Somewhat.

I'd had a really good qualifying round, and I was sitting in the tenth position. Hayden was a few spots in front of me, one position below Myles. Focusing on him relieved some of the pressure I was feeling, but it irritated me that I hadn't bested his time. I consoled myself by keeping in mind that it was the actual race that mattered, not the qualifier. As soon as possible, I was going to slip around Hayden and stay in front of him. My backside was all he was going to see all race long. I hoped.

No, I *could* do this. One of the greatest things about a new season was the fact that everyone started over, which meant a rookie like me had as much of a chance to win as a seasoned pro who'd won five times in a row. All I had to do was stay focused, stay calm…stay in control…*Please let me get a win today.*

Heat waves rose from the pavement, making the ground before me seem to shimmer, like I was hallucinating or something. This was real, though, and my lifelong dream of competing at Daytona was about to come true. Knowing I only had a second or two until the bank of red lights shifted to green, signaling the beginning of the race, I flashed a glance at Hayden. Surprisingly, his black-and-red helmet was focused back in my direction, not straight ahead like everyone else's. Why was he staring at me like I was the starting line, like I was the prize? I was no prize for him to win.

I was just about to point a finger in the direction Hayden should be looking when he suddenly nodded his helmet and peeled out. As he streaked away from me, it took me a second to realize the race had begun, and everyone was moving…everyone but me. Spitting out a vile curse, I hurried after the pack. Goddamn Hayden Hayes.

Thanks to my delayed reaction, I ended up leaving the grid closer to the back of the group than I'd wanted to be. I noticed a familiar bike streak past me—Jimmy the traitor—and wondered why he was so far back in the starting line. As I picked up speed and sailed past riders, I forced myself to remain calm, in control. This was an endurance race, the only endurance event in the series, and in preparation for this day, I had specifically trained for distance: countless times around the track, endless laps in the pool, hours of surfing wave after wave, and miles on the treadmill. I'd taken my father's advice to heart, and I was in tip-top shape; I was ready for this.

Ignoring everything around me, I focused on the roar of the bike, the vibration of the engine connecting me to the rhythm of the road, and only let one thought permeate my brain—*Find Hayden*. Fear and worry melted away as every molecule in my body dialed in on absolute concentration. The sound of my breath echoed inside my helmet, mixing with the rush of air from the vents, while the near-nauseating blur of movement in my peripheral vision amplified as I accelerated to exhilarating speeds. God, I loved this.

My motorcycle was top-of-the-line and perfectly crafted for me. Almost as if it were alive and could sense my wishes, it responded to my every command. It took me mere seconds to find the sweet spot on the bike for straightaways—low and light, tucked in for optimum aerodynamics, the peak placement for efficiency and speed—and before I knew it, I was zooming past other racers like they were standing still.

Unlike in car racing, the track curved both left and right, adding to the difficulty. I had to concentrate on the now but maintain a keen awareness of the future. The turns were tight and deep, with my body hanging off the bike and my knee and elbow hovering just inches above the concrete that was ripping past me at breakneck speeds. One wrong move and I'd disrupt the bike's balance, sending me and the motorcycle skidding across the track.

I kept the back of Hayden's bike in my crosshairs as I blurred past other racers. There were more than forty of us in this fifty-seven-lap race today, but only one rider mattered to me right now. When I finally gained position so that I was right beside Hayden, my thighs were throbbing from keeping my muscles tense and tight for so long. I embraced the pain as I tossed a victorious glance his way. *You tried to delay me, but I caught up to you, asshole.*

As if he felt my glare, he flashed a glance my way. Then he did a double take. I nodded my helmet up in the same arrogant way he had at the start of the race. Hayden hunched over his bike and, amazingly, found some acceleration. I frowned as he pulled directly in front of me. *Oh no, not today, Hayes.*

Shifting my weight, I pressed for speed. Some part of my consciousness was aware of the racers we were passing, of the laps that were accumulating, but the bulk of my concentration was purely on Hayden. For a moment, everything else slipped away, and following his path was my only focus. I hated to admit it, but chasing him gave me a rush. *You're going down. Whatever it takes, I've got you.*

I could tell by the feel of my bike that I needed to head to the pit soon. I wasn't about to go in before Hayden, though. I was physically incapable of leaving the course while he was still on it. Luckily for me, Hayden was due too, and after two more laps, he pulled into the pit lane.

As I rolled to a stop in my stall, my crew was already on their way to me with fresh tires and much-needed fuel. While they worked on my bike, my father approached me. "Keep it together, Mackenzie. This is where you tend to slack off."

One of the crew gave me a thumbs-up that my bike was done, and I tossed out, "I know, Dad!" Not wasting any time, I started the bike and sped away. Jesus. That was really not the kind of encouragement I needed right now. How about "*You're doing great*" or "*You've got this*"? That would have been much better than being reminded that even with all my training, the last part of the race was still a struggle for me.

Hayden had a really quick pit stop, and ended up pulling out right in front of me. Much to my annoyance, his rear was, once again, the focal point of my view. Shifting to look back at me, he lifted off his seat for a second, showing off the backside women fawned over. Then he gave himself a quick smack in the ass. Cute. Jerk.

Right before we reentered the track, I looked over at the boards. In the thick of racing, the other riders on the course had almost slipped my mind—Hayden was the only one I cared about—but I was curious where everyone was currently sitting in the event. I nearly stalled the bike when I spotted my number. I was right below Hayden. We were duking it out for fourth and fifth place. If I could hold on, I could easily finish in the top ten, and that was a record on this track for a female rider.

Pushing aside the potential history I could be making today, I refocused my attention on Hayden. Triumphing over him was enough to think about right now.

Lap after lap, I did my best to skirt around him, but as if he had a sixth sense for my location, he maneuvered his bike in such a way that I couldn't slip by him. It was as infuriating as it was invigorating, and I knew that my inevitable win would be that much sweeter because of the challenge. And then, finally, on the very last lap, he made a fatal mistake: he left me an opening.

He was taking the turns slightly tighter than before, and there was a decent amount of room between him and the outside of the corner. If I increased my speed instead of easing up on my acceleration, I could scoot around him. It was risky. I would be going way too fast for the curve, and then I would need to hit it even harder after the turn, or else Hayden would just accelerate from the inside and cut me off. Staying full throttle like that, I could easily lose control of the bike and slide out. It was my only chance, though. Victory wasn't for the faint of heart.

Halfway through the lap, as we approached the last hairpin corner, Hayden slowed as he set his body up for the turn. My heart started to race as I went against my natural instinct and increased my speed. My head was screaming that I was being stupid, that I should be braking as I swung my knee into position, but it was too late for me to listen to reason. I could finish in fourth place if I moved around him. Fourth! It was a too great a temptation to resist.

Committing myself to the action, I edged past Hayden in the space he'd left open. Praying that my bike stayed on the track and that I stayed on my bike, I leaned into the corner, slightly increasing my speed. Everything was exactly how it should be: My body was perfectly balanced as I hung off the inside of the bike, my tires were holding in the sweet spot, and the road was rushing beneath me like an asphalt river; it was so close, I could reach down with my hand and stroke the smooth surface with my gloved fingers if I wanted to. But then…I passed the point of no return, slipped over the razor-thin line of control. Before I could make a correction, I felt the bike's weight shift, felt the tires lose traction and position, and saw the raging river of concrete rushing up to greet me.

My bike fell onto its side, pinning my leg to the ground. My shoulder, arm, and hand quickly followed suit. The blow stunned me, but luckily my leathers absorbed a lot of the impact, and, even more important, they absorbed the friction from the road; without them, my skin would have been ripped to shreds. The momentum of the bike dragged me toward the outside wall. I had just enough time to see it coming before I smacked right into it. The breath left my body and my vision hazed to black. No…I could *not* afford to pass out right now.

When I stopped moving, I blinked rapidly, trying to reboot my body back to alertness; I didn't have time to fall into the oblivion of unconsciousness. Even now, rider after rider was passing me, taking my hard-earned spot. Feeling nauseated, I gathered up every ounce of willpower I had and forced myself to stand, forced my shaky limbs to right the bike. I was dazed and a little delirious; it took an enormous amount of concentration just to point my bike in the right direction. My limbs felt on fire, I tasted the tang of blood in my mouth, and my entire leg was throbbing. Ignoring the physical pain and the pair of corner officials asking me if I needed help, I restarted the bike and made myself complete the damn race. Hayden was not crossing the finish line without me.

CHAPTER 4

While I usually loved the exhilarating relief that came with finishing a race, I was bone-tired, dying of thirst, sticky with sweat, and filled with crushing disappointment. My head was pounding and every muscle ached so much I was a little afraid I was going to split apart like overripe fruit. I was also limping a little, since putting all my weight on my ankle hurt; I was mildly concerned about that. I could not afford to get injured this year. *Cox Racing* couldn't afford it.

I just wanted to turn my bike over for inspection and find a nice ice bath somewhere. But then I saw Hayden. He was pumping his fist in the air, playing to the crowd like he'd just won the whole damn thing. He'd only come in fourth, for God's sake. I really couldn't stomach the fact that he'd placed higher than me.

Once I was inside the assigned Cox Racing garage bay at the track, I hopped off my bike and eased it onto its mat. Taking off my gloves, I shoved them into my helmet and tossed the entire bundle across the room. My helmet landed on the concrete and spun, out of control, into the corner of the garage. It reminded me of my epic failure at the end of the race, and that pissed me off even more. I was ready for this entire goddamn day to be over.

"Great race, Kenzie! Thirteenth! For your first Daytona, that's amazing!"

I looked over to see Nikki entering the shop. I couldn't help but cringe at her praise. "Amazing? Did you happen to miss my epic crash on the last turn?" Anger and disappointment darkened my voice. "I wouldn't exactly call that amazing." More like incredibly foolish and amateurish. I should have known better than to attempt something like that. What the hell had I been thinking? I was going to agonize over my decision all night long; it would be a miracle if I even slept tonight.

Nikki grimaced. "Oh, yeah...that...Are you okay?"

Ignoring the head-to-toe ache, I shrugged. "Right as rain."

Her eyes shifted to my bike resting on its mat. "And the Ducati?" Her worried expression settled into one of deeper concern as she surveyed my motorcycle. She looked so much like a mother hen inspecting her injured chick that it was almost comical. Her dark eyes roved over the surface, lingering on the spot where I'd scraped the cement. I could tell she really wanted to walk over there and assess the damage, but the rules stipulated that the bike couldn't be touched until after the postrace inspection.

Almost as if to distract herself from the temptation sitting in front of her, she wrenched her gaze away and said, "You hear what happened to Jimmy?" Her expression brightened as she began to indulge in her second-favorite thing to do on the track: gossip about the riders.

"No. The officials forced him to start at the back of the grid, but I never heard why." Even though Jimmy was a douche for leaving, he was way too good to start at the back of the pack. What he could have possibly done to get the officials on his ass was a mystery to me.

I removed the band holding my hair in a ponytail and attempted to fluff the waves back into shape. It was difficult, since my head was so sweaty; I looked like I'd just taken a shower. Nikki handed me a towel so I could dry off my face. "He had a battery charger plugged in while refueling his bike after the sighting lap. Can you believe it?"

I understood her dumbfounded expression. Doing something as stupid as committing a safety infraction was almost unheard of for a racer of Jimmy's experience. Rules like that were drilled into us constantly by John and my father, but even if they hadn't been, it was common sense: Gas fumes plus a spark from a battery charger equaled a huge explosion. Weird, and yet…kind of karmic. He should have stayed with us. "Wow…stupid mistake. Where did he end up?"

Nikki's expression was amused, like she was thinking it was cosmic payback too. "Twenty-fourth. He just never recovered. Must have plagued him all race…" Biting her lip, she eyed my bike again.

I clapped her on the shoulder as I headed for a chair; I really needed to rest my ankle. "Leave the bike. We don't need to be hampered by some stupid penalty like Jimmy." As I sat down, I added under my breath, "My mistake was bad enough."

Turning around, Nikki put her hands on her hips. "Thirteenth isn't a horrible finish, Kenzie. In fact, I think it's pretty outstanding for your first time on this track."

Yes, I supposed it was, but that opinion wasn't very comforting at the moment. I'd almost had fifth wrapped up in a bright, shiny bow. I opened my mouth to tell her that, but my father walked in and beat me to it. Giving me a stern look, he told Nikki, "Thirteenth isn't fifth, which is where she would have ended up if she'd done her job correctly."

As Dad turned his gaze to me, I quickly clamped my mouth shut before I said something I regretted. My father's steel-blue eyes studied me, and his jaw was set in a rigid scowl of disappointment. He didn't need to verbally admonish me when he had a disapproving jawline like that, but I knew he would. Jordan Cox didn't let things go. There would be no pat on the back with a "better luck next time" for me; too much was at stake for that. I was going to hear about this race all season long.

After a deep inhale, I began the pointless process of attempting to defend myself. "I'm sorry…but it *is* a points race, Dad. I can still get to the top."

"Winning the race is the easiest way to get there, Mackenzie, and you know how much we're counting on you to…" Dad sighed and looked away. The family crest above his heart, proudly displaying our racing logo, was a prominent reminder of the legacy I'd been born into. At the moment, I felt unworthy to carry the Cox name. Dad was right, thirteenth wasn't good enough. *I should have done better.*

"I'm sorry," I whispered. I really hated how weak I sounded, but what else could I say? I'd fucked up, and we all knew it. Dad had won his first race, and I hadn't even cracked the top ten. There was nothing to be proud of here.

The steel in Dad's eyes returned as he looked at me again. "I'd just like to know what you were thinking, trying to pass on the outside of a turn like that. Accelerating instead of braking? You should have known you wouldn't be able to hold it." As he shook his head, I could see the bewilderment in his eyes. "Know your limitations, Mackenzie. How many times do I have to tell you that?" He threw his hand out to indicate my damaged vehicle; Nikki sighed.

"I thought I could do it," I said through clenched teeth. Embarrassment and shame washed over me in waves. Why couldn't we be alone for this conversation? "I'd noticed that Hayd—that number forty-three was leaving more room than usual on his turns, so I thought I'd take a chance and go around him. No risk, no reward…you tell me that a lot too."

Dad sighed. "Normally I would agree with you, but in this situation, Mackenzie, it was the wrong call. And to be quite frank with you, I'm shocked that you made it. I thought I'd taught you better."

Anger and guilt combined in my chest, flaming my cheeks bright red and stinging my eyes with pinpricks of shame. I choked back tears. I was not about to cry in front of my dad. "It was one bad call in an otherwise perfect race. Don't I get any credit for what I did right today?"

Dad shook his head. "No. When the stakes are as high as they are, you don't get kudos for losing a half dozen places for a mistake that you haven't made since you were eight years old. You need to be better than your best now that you're in the professional league. Better than *everyone's* best. Impress me, Mackenzie."

I pressed my fingertips tight against my thighs as his words shrank me; I felt about an inch tall under his gaze. "That's what I'm trying to do." My words wavered with emotion, and I hated it. I wanted to face Dad proud and tall, with nothing but conviction and confidence in my voice, but when his eyes turned stern and his stance turned authoritative, I reverted into that eight-year-old child once more. Always falling short of my father's expectations.

Dad's eyes narrowed as he watched me struggle with the shame, disappointment, and anger. "Control, Mackenzie; you still need to work on your control. You let this new Benneti racer get under your skin, let him force you into a rash decision. I don't know much about this number forty-three, but I know Keith. If he brought this guy onto his team, he did it for a reason. Keith looks for arrogance, overconfidence, do-anything-to-win hunger. He hires time bombs about to go off, and I'm guessing this…Hayes kid is no different than the rest of his reckless teammates." With a sigh, he shook his head. "Don't let them get under your skin, Mackenzie. Focus on the race, not the individual riders. I know it's difficult, but pretending that the Benneti team isn't racing beside you is the best thing you can do this year."

I opened my mouth to tell him that pretending no one was on the track *but* Hayden had actually driven me to race better than I ever had before, but I knew my father wouldn't understand, so I stayed silent. Hell, *I* barely understood why racing against Hayden had sparked something in me.

Dad examined me before continuing. "I know you think I'm being overly hard on you, but it's only to get the best performance from you. You're too good for slipups, and you're better than what I saw out there." His words were delivered softly, but they stung just as hard as the asphalt. "I'm going to push you hard this year, but it's all for your betterment, you'll see. We *need* a victory, Mackenzie…you know that." My emotions somersaulted as I stared at him. Yes, I did know that…I was painfully aware of that.

By his expression I could tell Dad was waiting for a response; I gave him a stiff nod, since that was all I could do at the moment.

Pointing to my side, he said, "You landed pretty hard. Go have one of the track doctors take a look at it, then report to the trailer for debriefing. We have a lot more to talk about."

With that, he turned and walked away. I couldn't stop shaking as I watched him leave. My hands were balled into tight fists, and my eyes were stinging with tears that I refused to let fall. He was right. I'd made a stupid decision out there and I'd paid the price for it. A hefty price. My bike was damaged, my body might be damaged, and most important, I'd missed my chance at landing a record-breaking position that would have had every racing sportscaster talking about me and Cox Racing. But instead I'd slid into a wall at almost sixty miles an hour, and while that moment was sure to be replayed on ESPN over and over, it wasn't the kind of exposure my family needed right now.

Looking over at Nikki, I mumbled, "I'm gonna go find a doctor. See you later." My voice came out with a lot more warble to it than I cared to hear, and Nikki's gaze was instantly sympathetic; it only made me feel worse.

Even though my entire leg was beginning to pulsate with pain now that the adrenaline was wearing off, I took the long way around to find a doctor. My meandering walk took me past the Benneti garage bay. Being so close to the enemy's headquarters gave me a sick feeling, like I was walking past a leaking nuclear power plant. I didn't want to look, but my eyes disobediently swept the room. Hayden was by the open garage door, celebrating his glorious fourth-place finish. Or...I thought he was celebrating—his teammates were on the other side of the room, laughing as they opened a bottle of champagne. Hayden was standing by himself, ignoring them. Still no love between them, then. Odd. I would have figured they'd have bonded over Hayden kicking my ass.

Hayden's helmet was off, his gloves were gone, and only his boots and riding leathers remained: red and black, like his soul. I did my best to ignore him, to act like I hadn't spotted him, but with a sinking feeling in my stomach, I saw his green eyes flick to me as I passed by. And then he did the unthinkable. He *followed* me.

Great. After being reprimanded by my dad, I was really not in the mood for Hayden's crap.

"Nice race today," he said as he walked along at my side. I quickly looked around, but no one from the Benneti camp seemed to have realized he'd left. Thank God.

Wondering if Hayden had meant that sarcastically, I threw him a glare. Surprisingly, the expression on his face seemed genuine—had he meant it? He also looked impressed, like he really hadn't expected me to be able to hold my own. Asshole. Had he actually believed that I couldn't race, couldn't keep up, couldn't do my job? Did he really think my father had handed this life to me? Even though I didn't care what he thought, that surprisingly hurt.

Glancing down at my side, he asked, "How are you doing after that slide out?"

Again, I couldn't tell whether he was blatantly mocking me for my poorly executed attempt to pass him—my multiple failed attempts to pass him, if truth be told—or if he was actually concerned, which would be absurd. He couldn't truly be concerned about me. This was a mind game.

Stopping suddenly, I spun to face him. Glancing around to make sure no one who knew us was close, I snapped, "What the hell do you mean by that?"

Looking at me like I'd spoken another language, he slowly said, "Um…I thought I was being pretty straightforward. How. Are. You. Doing? What else could those words possibly mean?" He cocked a puzzled eyebrow, then his lip curved up into a half smile. "Are you just pissed that I beat you?"

Trying very hard not to notice the way his damp hair was sticking up in that messy, carefree look that only Hayden could successfully pull off, I snipped, "You were being a jackass and getting in my way at every opportunity. No, what could possibly piss me off about that? Did you miss the fact that I wasn't the only rider out there, or were you just too mesmerized by me to notice the forty-plus other racers on the track?"

His mouth popped open in disbelief. "Oh my God…Are you seriously angry at me for racing defensively?" he snarled. Leaning in toward me, he added, "That's the name of the game, honey, and if you can't handle it, then I suggest you find another line of work. Maybe something where you won't have to worry about breaking a nail."

He finished with a smirk that was both infuriating and tantalizing. We were standing so close to each other that a flash of tingles ran across me, like his gaze had physically touched my skin. God, why the hell did racing against *him* have to feel so... good?

I stepped away from him, hoping to break the kinetic energy between us. It didn't help. My voice was shaking when I finally found some words that were kind of civil. "For the hundredth time, don't call me honey, sweetheart, baby cakes, or sugar pie. My name is—"

"Mackenzie Cox, of the elite Cox family," he interrupted with a roll of his eyes. "Yeah, I know exactly who you are, and exactly why you're really sore at me. Daddy can give you all the best gear and all the best bikes, but he can't hand you a win, can he? *That*, Twenty-Two, you still have to earn." There was fire in his eyes as he spoke, and heat in his voice. The combination did nothing to squelch the squirming sensation of anticipation that was flaring within me. *Cat and mouse. Give and take. Run and chase.*

"Fuck you, Hayden," I spat, then I turned and stormed away.

As I was striding off, I heard him shout, "Just pick a time and a place, princess, and I'll scratch whatever itch you've got!"

* * *

The track doctor took entirely too long to see me, but once I was done, I was given a clean bill of health. Bruised, raw, a few scratches, yes, but nothing broken and only minor swelling in my ankle. That made me a vision of health in my book, and well enough for the doctor to send me off with just a bag of ice, a bottle of over-the-counter painkillers, and instructions to take it easy for a few days.

As I slowly walked back through the motor homes, semis, vans, and campers to the Cox Racing area, where my father was most likely preparing his speech for me, I came across Myles. He'd had an exceptional day today, finishing third, right ahead of Hayden; funny I hadn't even noticed him in front of us the whole time.

"Hey, Kenzie," he said, smiling brightly. "Great race today. Harsh fall, though. How's your leg?"

Lifting my foot, I swiveled my swollen ankle for him. It only mildly ached. "It's totally fine, Myles. I can take a little bashing."

He grinned like he'd just had a dirty thought. "That's good to know." I was about to tell him to stop being such a guy when the light faded from his dark eyes. "Did I see that Hayden guy giving you crap after the race?"

My heart started thudding. Had he seen us? I rolled my eyes, and it was only partly for effect. "Douche had to rub it in that I wiped out. Told me Daddy couldn't buy the race, I had to earn it..." Even though repeating the words felt like barbed wire digging into my skin...Hayden was right, in a way. Equipment would only get me so far. Skill had to get me the rest of the way.

Myles's normally jovial face hardened. "Asshole. If he bothers you again, Kenzie, just let me know."

Biting my lip, I nodded. The thought of Myles getting into an altercation because of me didn't sit right. And the idea of him getting into it with Hayden...bothered me for reasons I didn't even want to think about.

Annoyed that there was some speck of concern for Hayden buried *anywhere* within me, I shook my head and told Myles, "I gotta go see my dad. Catch up with you later, okay?"

"You bet," he said, clapping me on the back.

When I returned to the Cox Racing area, I hung out with Nikki instead of going to see my dad right away. She was in the garage, working on my backup bike. Per my doctor's orders, I leaned back in a chair and put my foot up on the workbench. I needed to ice my ankle anyway. And put off seeing the disappointment in my dad's eyes again. Not that I could do either for very long.

My cell phone rang while I was resting, but before I could even curse the fact that I was going to have to get up to answer it, Nikki rummaged through my bag near her toolbox and handed it to me. I thanked her as I glanced at the screen. It was Theresa. "Hello?"

"Oh my God, Kenzie, I saw you crash into the wall on TV! Are you okay? Is anything broken? Do you have a concussion? Have you passed out or vomited? Because I heard that's bad..."

Hearing the stress in my sister's voice made me smile. She could be such a worrywart. "I'm fine, I promise."

"Are you sure? Have you seen a doctor? What did they say; tell me every single word." With a sigh, I relayed everything the track doctor had told me. When I was finished, Theresa was silent for a solid ten seconds. Then she quietly told me, "Dad's crazy for pushing you to race. You could be killed out there."

I gritted my jaw before responding. "I *want* to race, Theresa. All of this is my choice. Always has been." Even though we'd all grown up in this world of racing, my sisters didn't understand my need to be a part of it. They had both given up riding motorcycles when they were young, but I was more like Dad. Racing was in my soul.

Theresa let out a wistful sigh. "I know... Just be careful, okay?" As I assured her that I was as careful as I could be, I heard someone eagerly whispering something in the background. Theresa let out an annoyed grunt, then snapped, "I'm not asking her that, Daphne! She said she was fine."

"What does she want?" I asked, removing my boot.

"She wants to know if you're going to be in a wheelchair for the wedding, and if you *are* going to be, she wants to know if she is going to have to find someone to push you, or if you've got someone in mind."

Daphne had gotten engaged recently, and her upcoming wedding was all she ever talked about now. Shaking my head at my obsessed sister, I told Theresa, "I'm fine, and I'll talk to you guys later," then I disconnected the phone. God, I really wished they hadn't been watching today.

Nikki's dark eyes shifted from the bike to me once I was off the phone. "So you're not hurt badly?" She inspected me from head to toe, as if she could visually assess me the way she did my bikes.

I shook my head. "No, I'll be fine. I just need... rest." And to forget about Hayden. And to race better. Damn it, I needed to *be* better.

Nikki eyed me for a moment, then said, "Hey…about what your dad said…He's just stressed, Kenzie. Thirteenth is great. Your mom would be so proud of you."

Just the mention of my mother made hot tears spring to life and a cold void close around my heart. "Thank you," I said, placing the bag of ice on my ankle as I swallowed back the telltale moisture in my eyes. I didn't like wearing my emotions on my sleeve. My feelings were personal, private, and while some people tossed theirs about for everyone to see, I kept mine close, guarded, protected. The painful ones, anyway.

Nikki thankfully ignored the turmoil in my voice and returned to her work. Closing my eyes, I let myself relax for a moment. Things were so simple on the track. Gas, brake, turn, more gas, repeat. I could do that all day. But dealing with people, feelings… drama…that was so much harder.

CHAPTER 5

A few hours later, after a mandatory dinner with my father and the crew, I was finally back at the hotel. Collapsing onto the bed, I wondered if I had ever been this exhausted in all my life. Trailing my fingers along the pattern sewn into the quilt beneath me, I debated shutting off the light and trying to make a genuine attempt to sleep; if I wanted it bad enough, I could make it happen…right? The light switch was so far away, though, and there was no way I'd be able to stop replaying the video of my slide out that was running on constant repeat in my head. Whether it was light or dark in the room didn't matter if my brain was wide awake. It didn't even matter that my limbs were heavy with fatigue and all of my muscles were tired and aching. My brain wouldn't stay silent, so there would be no real rest for me.

Letting out an annoyed groan, I managed to find the remote on the nightstand. Flicking on the TV, I prayed I might be able to find something that would partially entertain me, or at least distract me. Nothing did, though. All I could think about was the race. I wanted to be home, in my bed, surrounded by my things. Maybe if I were back to my regular routine, I could stop the never-ending replay of my body smacking the concrete, my bike hitting the wall.

We were leaving bright and early tomorrow morning to head

back to Oceanside. I was ready to go home, yet reluctant too. I felt like my failure would be the talk of the track for a long time to come—both sides of the track—and I really didn't want people talking about me, especially about my screwup. But I *did* want to get back to work; I wanted to begin preparations for the next race, in Wisconsin. God, I hoped that race was better than this one.

After flipping through every available channel at least six times, I turned the TV off. I needed something more engaging to keep my mind from drifting into dark, anxiety-ridden places. Forcing myself to get up, I grabbed my bag from where I'd flung it and dug around for my cell phone. Pulling up Nikki's number, I texted: *Can't sleep. Are you up?*

Her response was immediate. *Yep! Just heading to the hot tub. Meet me in 20!*

Frowning, I texted back: *I didn't pack a suit.*

She responded exactly how I thought she would. *So? Go commando.*

Laughing, I shook my head as I texted her that I'd see her soon. Her parting words were *Bring wine!*

Rolling my eyes, I looked over at the items available for purchase on top of the minibar. There was a bottle of wine among the chocolate, nuts, condoms, and toiletries. This hotel thought of everything. Shrugging, I grabbed the bottle of wine, a corkscrew, and a couple of glasses. I didn't usually drink, but I might have a half glass tonight. Maybe a few sips would make me tired enough to go to sleep. Setting the wine on the bed, I debated what I could wear into the hot tub. Skinny-dipping wasn't exactly my idea of relaxing. Grabbing a robe from the bathroom, I decided my bra and panties would suffice. They covered more than a lot of bikinis anyway.

We were staying at a hotel near the ocean. It was a pretty nice place, with beachside fire pits and saltwater pools, but my favorite thing about it was the ultra-private pool and hot tub on the roof. With the crashing waves of the surf nearby and the twinkling lights of Daytona in the distance, it was a spectacular display. Just what I needed to unwind. Hopefully the hot water didn't aggravate my scrapes too badly. It would be worth it, though.

Clenching the wine bottle in one hand and the glasses and corkscrew in the other, I made my way up to the roof. When I got there, I looked around for Nikki, but she was nowhere to be seen. Not too surprising.

Figuring she'd get here when she got here, I headed for the hot tub. I could almost feel the stress releasing from my overtaxed muscles as I spotted the softly lit tub nestled in the corner of the rooftop oasis. As I approached the steaming water, I noticed a dark head just barely above the surface. Wow, guess Nikki had beaten me here after all.

"Hey, girlie," I said, setting down the wine and shucking off my robe. "I brought some wine for you, as requested. And just so you know, if Dad chews my ass out for the room service bill, I'm totally throwing you under the bus."

The wet head swiveled around to look up at me and my heart sank. It wasn't Nikki. A slow smile spread across Hayden's face as he sat up higher in the water, eyeing the lacy bra and underwear I was using as swimwear. Thankfully, they were black, and not a pale color that would show him way more than I ever wanted to. I quickly scanned the rooftop, but we were alone. Horribly and completely alone.

"Well, look who it is," he mused. "Lucky number twenty-two. Are you here for that scratch, sweetheart? I'm a little worn out after today, but don't you worry, I'm sure I can still give you what you so politely requested." He added that damn aggravating wink on the end that made me want to dunk him under the water and hold him there a few minutes. Just until he passed out. I swear.

Flustered and caught off guard, all I could think to say was, "You're not Nikki." I felt my cheeks flame as his gaze lingered over my curves, but I stubbornly refused to cover myself up. I worked hard for my sport and it showed in my body. There was nothing on me that I had to be embarrassed about... plus, I'd shaved earlier today, so it was all good.

Hayden seemed amused by my response. "No, I'm not." Bringing his arms up to the edge of the tub, he turned to face me. As he propped his chin on his arms, water droplets beaded and ran down his skin like little racetracks. There was something about steaming water and an attractive man that was exceedingly erotic, but Hayden was *not* what I wanted to be looking at right now. This was supposed to be relaxing girl time.

"So..." he said with a smile. "Do you and Nikki often meet up for lingerie hot-tubbing after a race? If so, I'm going to have to stay at your hotel more often."

Familiar irritation pricked my skin, but I somehow managed to keep my expression even. "I didn't realize you were staying at this hotel. I figured you'd be at some sleazy motel that charged by the hour, along with the rest of the Bennetis. Seems more your speed than a *nice* place like this."

His jade eyes darkened, and I knew I'd struck a nerve. Good. I shouldn't be the only one annoyed, and if he was going to make me sound like a spoiled princess, then I would make him sound like he was fresh from the gutter. And considering where I'd first met him, I probably wasn't too far off the mark anyway.

Hayden opened his mouth to speak, but I didn't wait for him to get even so much as a sound out. Making sure we were still alone and no one was here to witness me sharing a could-be-intimate moment with a Benneti, I gingerly placed a foot into the water opposite him. He wasn't going to chase me away from here with vile words, no matter who he raced for—I needed this too badly after today.

If Hayden had been about to say something, he clearly changed his mind; he was silent as stone as he watched me sink into the water. The searing heat was heaven on my chilled muscles, and even though the raw places stung, a soft groan escaped me. Closing my eyes, I laid my head back on the tile surrounding the tub. Hayden cleared his throat, and I heard soft splashes in the water as he adjusted his position. Cracking an eye open, I saw that he was intensely studying me, and in the silence of our staredown, that crackling energy began to resurface. In a heartbeat, the water suddenly became an extension of him, and the gentle waves were like his fingers caressing me all over, all at once. It was heady and intoxicating, and it made my breath quicken and my body tingle in delicious anticipation. *Damn.*

I was a millisecond away from getting out of the water… but…the near-boiling temperature was so incredible, I didn't want to give up the luxury yet, not for my cold, lonely hotel room, where the ghosts of my failure were ceaselessly haunting me. I needed this break. For the first time since the race had ended, I actually felt at peace. Almost. Hayden's absorbing gaze was too intent for full relaxation; shivers that had nothing to do with my body's adjustment to the blazing heat of the water were flashing across my skin.

"What?" I snapped, hoping to sever the connection, to diminish the pinpoints of excitement that were starting to work their way through me. Inch by inch. Ripple by ripple.

Hayden's gaze shifted to the bubbling water before lifting to mine again. "Can I ask you a serious question?"

I was shocked. Our conversations had never gone much deeper than trading insults, and even though I was curious, instinct made me answer him with, "No."

With a frown, he ignored my answer and asked me anyway. "Did you…did you feel it today…while we were racing?"

My heart started pounding in my chest. I knew exactly what he meant. That fire, that drive, that feeling that we were alone, even when we were surrounded by thousands of people. It had been the most intense race of my career because of that sensation, but I wasn't about to admit that to him. I couldn't. It would be like admitting weakness, and I couldn't ever appear weak in front of this man; he'd pounce in an instant, ripping me to shreds. "I have no idea what you're talking about, and I said you *couldn't* ask me a question."

He pursed his lips, annoyed, but then he leaned forward in the water. His sudden movement caused tiny waves to come my way, and I instinctually pulled back from them. The sensation that we were connected, even though we weren't, was bad enough without him coming closer. "You didn't feel that…I don't know…that connection? Like it was just the two of us out there? You must have, since you made that crack about me ignoring everyone else and focusing only on you."

He tilted his head and a water droplet rolled down his cheek and curved around his neck. Watching it made my toes curl. The intimate lighting out here was playing tricks on my senses, making him too appealing. But the mood-setting couldn't alter his personality, so I focused all of my energy on remembering the fact that he was an asshole who could never seem to get my name right. Plus he raced for a despicable man who would do just about anything to see my father brought down.

"Like I said, I have no idea what you're talking about." I indicated the swirling water between us. "I think you've been in here too long. Your brain cells are beginning to boil." *I* was beginning to boil. *I should leave...*

Hayden smirked, then began sliding through the water toward me. As he cut into the frantic bubbles between us, my heart began shifting into overdrive. *I should* definitely *leave.* But Hayden's gaze was locked on mine, holding me in place. I couldn't look away. A familiar surge of adrenaline was building inside me, telling me that something incredible was about to happen.

On your mark...

"I don't believe you." His voice was low, and his eyes were boring holes all the way through my soul. I unintentionally sucked my lip into my mouth, and his penetrating gaze dropped to study the movement. God, what would his smoldering skin feel like against mine?

His eyes slowly shifted back to mine. "You know exactly what I'm talking about, and you can't deny that competing against each other, one on one like that, pushed us both." He stopped right beside me, and our legs touched under the water. His were warm, hard, unyielding, and I had the sudden horrible image of having them wrapped around me. Owning me, claiming me.

Get set...

"I've never raced that well before, and I don't think you have either. I've watched you practicing on the home track a few times, and I've noticed something. You worry when you ride, worry about all the people you might be letting down. I get that. But focusing on your fear will only hold you back." Shock ran through me, temporarily icing the heat. How did he know I constantly stressed about the weight placed on me? And who did he worry about letting down?

Voice soft, he added, "But during the race, I could tell that you let all those expectations go. Because all you were focusing on was me. You raced better when I was out there with you, and I raced better when you were out there with me." He shifted his position under the water, coming closer until his chest brushed against my arm, and it was like a bolt of electricity struck me. I was tingling all over, ready…wanting. How did he know these things? How could he see inside me so accurately?

Hayden's gaze flicked over my face, alternating between my eyes and my mouth. He looked torn, like he didn't know what he wanted to do, but then he gently placed his hand on my leg. While his eyes searched for approval or rejection, his fingers began sliding up my inner thigh, igniting me with passion, burning me with desire. My breath was suddenly coming fast and furious. *Yes, touch me.*

Hayden's lips parted as he studied my every reaction, and I could see his chest rising and falling as his own breaths quickened. His palm was barely inching across my skin—I was going to explode soon if he didn't move faster. The glorious anticipation of where his fingers might go was killing me. But then, with a pained look on his face, he stopped moving. *Damn it, just do it. Feel me, touch me, take me…free me.*

With obvious restraint, he slowly leaned forward and pressed his hot lips to my ear, making me shudder. "We're magic together, Twenty-Two," he breathed. "Just admit you need me…and we can take this up a notch."

Need him? Take this up a notch? His audacity enraged me. "Get your hand off of me," I seethed.

Hayden pulled back to study my face for a moment, then he lifted his hand from my thigh and retreated. Raising both hands from the water like he was surrendering, he told me, "Fine. Whatever you say, princess." He swallowed a few times after he said it, as if he was trying to calm himself down.

Furious at him for going there, furious at myself for not stopping him sooner, I shot up out of the water. The steam lifting from my skin matched my mood, but that was nothing compared to the heat of Hayden's eyes as he hungrily took in every inch of my dripping-wet body. *Enjoy what you see, asshole, because this is the last time you'll ever see it.* Stepping from the tub, I grabbed my robe, tied it tight around my waist, and stormed off.

* * *

I allowed myself exactly one afternoon of rest once I returned home from Daytona. Then I got right back to my routine, and headed to the practice track bright and early the next morning. Spring was right around the corner, and the crispness in the air was occasionally softened by gentle, warm breezes. The sun had only been up a few hours, but it was already a beautiful day to be outside, and I thanked my lucky stars that I lived in such a picture-perfect place. Southern California just couldn't be beat.

I took my time driving up the coast to where the Cox Racing/Benneti Motorsports track was, and my eyes drifted to the choppy ocean beside me as I rode. Dad said visualization was one of the major keys to success, but all I was visualizing as I alternated my gaze between the road and the pounding waves buffeting the shore was Hayden in the hot tub. His words were running through my brain over and over. *I've never raced that well before, and I don't think you have either. We're magic together.* As much as I hated to admit it, he was right. We *were* magic together. Dark magic.

Several minutes later I was pulling onto the road that led to the track. I screeched to a stop when I noticed the sign next to the highway. Someone had spray-painted over the word "Cox." It now said "Sux Racing"…real mature. I'd have to tell Dad about that. Then he'd tell Keith to fix it, then they'd fight about the sign. Again. Sometimes I thought Dad should just sell his half of the track and move on. Fresh start. But he couldn't afford to buy another track on his own, and besides, I hated the thought of losing this place—my childhood had happened here. But Keith and my dad wouldn't fight so much if we left, and I wouldn't have to worry about running into Hayden. That thought made me sigh in frustration as I continued on toward the gate in the fence surrounding the complex. *Damn Hayden.*

Every time I thought about the electricity between us in the hot tub, I broke out in a cold sweat. That had gone way too far, gotten way too intense. A part of me wanted to tell someone about the encounter, but I couldn't. It was too horrifying—I had willingly climbed into a hot tub with a Benneti...and he'd touched me...and I'd *liked* it. Scrunching my face in disgust, both at myself and at the memory, I stopped at the card reader beside the gate.

Frustrated and annoyed, I slammed my key card into the reader, punched in the four-digit code, then yanked the card out. The gate slowly started creaking open, and I edged through the instant there was room for my bike. Even with my helmet on, I could hear the sounds of the track—engines whining at full capacity, tools buzzing, people shouting. The familiar sounds were comforting—I was *home*.

Riding my bike through the parking lot, I made my way to the inner gate that led to the racetrack and garages. As I passed through, I happened to notice that this sign had also been tampered with. It now read COX RACING/BLOWS ASS MOTORSPORTS PRACTICE TRACK. Guess someone on our side had already gotten Benneti back for defacing the highway sign, although not as poetically. Great. Keith was going to lose his shit when he saw that, which was going to make Dad extra prickly about our guys not retaliating; everyone was going to be on edge today.

The buildings gleamed in the early-morning sunlight and the anticipation of breakneck speed started filling me. My ankle was fine, my scrapes were healing, and my bruises were slowly fading—I was ready to go fast again. Crazy, balls-to-the-wall fast.

Ignoring the Benneti side of the track, like I always did, I headed over to the Cox side—the right side, as we called it. Perpetually late Nikki wasn't in the shop below the offices, but a few other members of the crew were there, along with two other racers—Myles and a guy we'd lovingly nicknamed Ralph, because he always threw up before a race.

Myles was standing beside one of his bikes. I waved at him when he looked my way, and he nodded his head in greeting. Then a devilish smile played across his lips and his dark eyes sparkled with playfulness. "Good timing. Daphne is here. She's upstairs with your dad. Going over fabric swatches." He raised one eyebrow in a knowing smirk.

An amused grin stretched across my mouth. "Seriously? This I've gotta see." Myles laughed and I cast a quick look around the garage, looking for evidence of recent spray paint abuse. "You notice the signs?"

When I looked back at Myles, he crossed his arms over his chest. Anger instantly replaced the levity. "Yeah, those dicks. Sux Racing…I got somethin' they can suck."

Studying his expression, I asked, "You see *both* signs?"

A slow smile spread over his face. "I have no idea what you're talking about."

With a small laugh, I held my fist up to Myles and he silently bumped it. I doubted he had actually been involved with the sign—that just wasn't his style—but his loyalty was endearing. Myles would never leave us, never jump ship for greener pastures with another team. He bled blue and white.

Setting down my stuff, I was about to go upstairs to see my dad and Daphne when Myles started making an odd lasso motion with one hand.

"Ready to get your cowgirl on tonight?" he asked.

I knew he wasn't propositioning me; he'd known me too long for crap like that. "Umm…what are you talking about, Kelley?"

He stopped moving and frowned. "Didn't Nikki text you? We decided to celebrate St. Patrick's Day by riding fake bulls, and you're coming with us." He grinned, like this idea they'd concocted was genius. Now I was frowning.

"Oh, and when did you and Nikki decide this?" I tapped my finger against my jaw, like I was thinking. "Maybe after Daytona, when you hijacked Nikki and then you both abandoned me at the hotel hot tub to go clubbing? Thanks for texting me the change of plans, by the way. Oh wait, you didn't." No, Nikki had texted me an apology the next morning. Bitch.

Myles scratched his head in an adorable expression of guilt. "Right... We were totally going to text you when we got to the club to check it out... but there was foam. We got distracted... Sorry."

I rolled my eyes at his answer. It didn't take much to distract those two. "You're both assholes."

Myles cringed and grinned. "So you'll let us make it up to you tonight then, right?" I opened my mouth to tell him no, that I needed to focus on racing, but as if he'd read my mind, Myles lifted his finger and countered my unspoken argument. "One drink... surely your diet allows for that. And a motorized bull, Kenzie... Just think of the core work! It's like being on a motorcycle that bucks. Where else can you get that kind of training? And it's a team thing, a bunch of us Coxes are going. And you're the best Cox... you have to be there. It's mandatory."

The cute look on his face would have most women agreeing to do whatever he asked, and I was no exception. I laughed as I caved. "Fine, one drink. But I'm not staying out late."

This time *he* rolled his eyes. "I know that, Kenzie. It is *you*, after all." Then he started rubbing his hands together, like an evil scientist scheming to take over the world. "This is gonna be great. Nikki will pick you up tonight. And make sure you wear something green. Wouldn't want you to get pinched."

He winked and I lifted a finger in warning. "If you even think about it, Kelley..." He raised his hands like he was the most innocent person in the world. I didn't buy it for a second.

Shaking my head at Myles, I left him with his bike so I could go upstairs and witness the hell my sister was putting Dad through; I was dying to see him elbow-deep in wedding magazines. Even though Dad would rather do just about *anything* else for her, Daphne had decided to make him her wedding planner; she ran every aspect of the ceremony past him. And I mean *every* aspect. Just last week they'd been going over fonts for the napkins. I think Dad only put up with it because he was the last parent left to us, and he felt obligated to give Daphne the wedding of her dreams—even if it was costing him enough to purchase a small island in the South Pacific. Daphne wanted the best of the best, and Dad just couldn't tell her no.

I lightly knuckled the door, then waited for my dad. He answered with a weary "Yeah," and I gleefully stepped inside.

What I spotted was absolutely priceless. Daphne had turned Dad's desk into a mosaic of pastel delight. Every frothy, tutti-frutti, bubblegum shade of femininity was duking it out for a place of prominence on Dad's overflowing workspace. Peppermint blues competed with seafoam greens, cotton-candy pinks, lilac lavenders, and sunset tangerines. As Daphne handed Dad swatch after swatch of minutely different shades of peach, his face contorted into a pained expression of helplessness. He reminded me of someone who had endured countless hours of slow, methodical torture designed purely to destroy a person's mind and was on the tipping point of losing the last shred of his sanity. It was great.

The second Dad saw me, his spirits lifted. "Mackenzie, thank God you're here."

I held a hand up to stop the request I heard coming. "I can't stay long. I'm working on the track today, like you asked." I wanted to be subjected to examining Daphne's endless color palette about as much as Dad did.

Daphne finally noticed my entrance and smiled at me. "Hey, Kenzie!" She grabbed two pieces of pink fabric and held them up. "What do you think…Summer Nights or Raspberry Parfait?"

I shook my head. "They look exactly the same to me, Daph, and neither one looks like its name, so I say screw them both. I mean, Summer Nights? Aren't nights inherently dark? Hence the word 'night'? So shouldn't that color be black? Or really, really dark blue? It just makes no sense to me."

With a groan, Daphne tucked a long blond lock behind her ear. "You're about as helpful as Dad. If I asked you two to choose between Kawasaki Green and Yamaha Yellow, you'd probably have no problem."

At the same time, Dad and I both said, "Kawasaki Green."

Daphne groaned again while Dad shot me a smile. We didn't always get along that well, but I think Dad found it easier to connect with me than with my two older sisters. It was no great secret in my family that Dad had wanted sons, but fate had blessed him with all girls, and I was the only one who'd followed in his racing footsteps. My sisters wouldn't even ride anymore. I think Dad had died a little inside after each daughter had given the sport up. But then I'd become the son he'd never had. Only, I wasn't a boy and I'd never be a boy. I couldn't help but feel like I'd never entirely be what he wanted me to be.

Turning back to Dad, Daphne said, "So, like I said, I need your help picking out coordinating colors for the wedding." She handed him a clipboard with a spreadsheet that looked to be about thirty pages thick. "I've gone through and listed all of my favorites and the reasoning behind them. I want you to go through the colors and pick out your top twenty favorites, along with your reasoning for each choice, then I'll merge the two lists and see if we agree on any color combinations."

Dad took the clipboard from her, but it was with clear reluctance. "Couldn't your fiancé help you with this?" he asked her, pain in his voice.

With a smile bright enough to power Oceanside, Daphne shook her head. "Nope. This is a family matter, and Jeff's not family. Yet." She winked, then spun on her heel. "I'll give you some time alone to ponder your decisions. Call me if you have any questions. See you in an hour!"

She waggled her fingers over her shoulder as she walked out the door. Once the storm had passed and the office was calm, Dad's weary eyes found mine. "Please do me a favor and never get married."

"Not a problem," I murmured, looking over his homework assignment. "Dad, did you see...?" The expression on his face made me pause. There would be time to tell him about the signs later—he had enough on his plate right now. "Never mind. You've got a lot to do here, so I'll leave you to it. I'll be on the track if you need anything. Anything *not* wedding related, that is," I added with a laugh as I started backing away.

Dad sighed and shook his head. "So much pink," he muttered, studying his desk. Still laughing on the inside, I hastily began my escape. I was halfway through the door when I thought I heard Dad whisper, "Vivienne... how could you leave me here alone with so much pink?"

I froze at hearing Dad mention Mom's name. He didn't talk much about her; I could list the number of times he'd brought her up in the last several years on one hand. The grief was heavy in his voice, though, and feeling an enormous amount of trepidation, I slowly looked back at him.

"You... okay, Dad?" I asked, tense. Dad and I didn't discuss things like this. We discussed racing, or my crazy sisters, or how evil the Bennetis were. We didn't talk about feelings, didn't delve into emotions. Not like this.

Dad's face immediately transformed into a stoic mask of professionalism, and I relaxed. Stern, controlled, and powerful I could handle. Cracked and needy, not so much. "Of course I'm fine." He pointed a stern finger at me. "I want to see your practice results the second you're done."

I gave him a curt nod, then darted out the door. Potential emotional crisis averted. Thank God.

When I got back downstairs, Nikki was finally there. She was busy working on my main bike, getting all the dents and dings out of it. By the look on her face, she'd been dying to get her hands on it since we'd gotten back to California. I thought of pestering her about not texting me the change of plans in Daytona... but I didn't want her to ask what happened at the hot tub, so I simply waved a greeting at her and left her to her work.

Grabbing my bag, I headed to the locker room to put on my leathers. Once I was done, I felt a surge of nervous, pent-up energy coiling in me. I tried to contain it, control it like my father always said, but it was like I was coated in doubt. I'd messed up so badly in Daytona. I needed to show Dad that I was back on track, unstoppable. With a long, slow exhale, I pushed my backup bike toward the course entrance. I could do this.

Ralph was out running his laps when I got there, so I waited, somewhat patiently, for him to finish. I bounced on my seat, testing the suspension; flexed my gloves, keeping my fingers warm; and wiggled my toes in my boots. I wanted to go, wanted to impress Dad.

While I was waiting, someone else pulled up beside me and shut his bike off. I looked over to see Hayden straddling his red Honda. Damn, he looked good on his bike, like a Greek god resting on his chariot. His lips started curling into a smile, and I immediately returned my eyes to studying the racer on the track. He couldn't affect me if I didn't look at him. Hayden wasn't about to let me ignore him, though. "Hey, sweet cakes, want to practice together? You know you ride better when you've got a nice view."

I looked over in time to see him nodding at his backside. Rolling my eyes, I shook my head. "Don't flatter yourself...sweet cakes." My words came out with the acerbic sting of pure venom. Why couldn't he ever call me by my name? And what the hell was he thinking? We couldn't practice together. He couldn't even step foot on the track for a few more hours.

Undeterred by my frosty tone, Hayden leaned his bike toward me. "Come on, ride with me. It will be like Daytona again, only better."

I didn't want to give him the satisfaction of engaging him, but I couldn't help but ask, "Better? How?" Just acknowledging his ludicrous idea was stupid. I shouldn't be standing next to him, let alone talking to him. Discreetly glancing around, I made sure no one was looking our way.

His voice brimming with eagerness, Hayden said, "With just two of us racing, one of us is assured the number one spot. And I'm pretty sure you know who that will be...and that's why you're really scared to race me."

I knew he was just saying that to get to me, but I couldn't help my reaction. "I'm not scared of anything," I bit out, staring him down.

"Good," he stated. "That's exactly how you should feel before you enter a track, not nervous, like it's your first time." I could only gape at him; how did he always see right through me? While I pondered that, Hayden popped on his helmet, leaving the visor up, and started his bike. Over the roar of his engine, he yelled, "Race me or chase me, Kenzie."

And with those words, he lowered his visor and shot forward onto the track. Shock held me in place, and I wasn't sure what I was more surprised about, the fact that he was actively breaking the track rule—again—or the fact that he had actually used my name.

Letting out an annoyed curse, I slammed on my helmet. Caution held me in place for a few precious seconds. *I shouldn't race with him, not like this. If someone sees us... if my dad finds out... And Ralph—where did he go?* I scanned the track, but I didn't see my teammate anymore. All I saw was Hayden's retreating form as he owned what was supposed to belong to me. Narrowing my eyes, I started my bike. There was no way in hell I was going to let Hayden get the best of me on *my* track.

Throwing caution to the wind, I shot forward. I was right behind Hayden in record time, and as much as I hated to admit it, he was right: I rode better when I was chasing him—more relaxed, more fearless, like racing was just about having fun and not about proving to the world that I belonged. My balance was perfect, my shifting was seamless, and my handling was flawless. I felt invincible as my front tire inched ever closer to his rear tire. *Chase you or race you, huh? Well then, get ready for the race of your life.*

We ripped around the track over and over and over. Neither one of us gave up much ground for long. I'd sneak around him, hold him for a few heartbeats, then he'd snake around me and do the same. In the back of my mind, fear and worry were trying to punch a hole through the joy—*Someone could be watching, someone could see, someone could think I'm willingly fraternizing with a Benneti.* And wasn't I? But I wouldn't let the anxiety win—not until I had him. All I would allow myself to focus on was getting around him, gaining ground on him, not giving him an inch. I was nearly there too... and then my bike started acting funny. It was losing traction and losing power.

That was when I noticed the condition of my tires, and my gas gauge; I was almost coasting on fumes. Hating that I was going to have to retire while Hayden was in the lead, I slowed down and started making my way to the exit. Hayden glanced back, saw I was leaving, and pumped his fist into the air in victory. Pompous jerk. I hoped he stayed out there too long and completely fried his bike. Let him explain that to Keith and his teammates. They'd probably give him another lesson on respecting the rules. Oddly, that thought made my stomach feel like it was cramping. Or maybe I was just nervous that I'd get taught a similar lesson.

My heart was thudding in my chest when I returned to the Cox Racing garage bay. *Act cool, act cool. I didn't do anything wrong.* I mean…it wasn't *my* fault Hayden had crashed the track. When I eased back to the bay, several Cox Racing members were standing outside, staring at something. My already racing heart threatened to stall on me. *Oh God…they know.* As crew members stared at me, I pulled up next to Myles and Nikki and said the one word that would certainly be my doom. Removing my helmet, I asked, "What?"

Nikki pointed up at the testing screen, used to measure lap times. Shit. The board, I'd completely forgotten about the board. Chips on the bikes logged our lap times…and displayed them right next to our racing numbers. Hoping against all hope that the board had malfunctioned somehow, and that Hayden's bike number wasn't plastered next to mine, I glanced back at the screen. My jaw dropped when I saw what had my teammates in a daze.

"That's my best time…ever," I muttered, stunned. The board listed the last several laps I'd made, and all of them matched or exceeded my previous record. Some of them, when I'd really hit my stride, beat my best time by quite a bit. And even more shocking…Hayden was nowhere on the board. Either it really had malfunctioned…or he'd removed his tracking chip. I was dazed by what I was seeing—and what I *wasn't* seeing. While having fun with Hayden, I'd smoked my previous times, and *no one* seemed to realize who I'd been racing against.

From the looks on people's faces around me, it was clear none of them had been watching the track while I was out there—and that wasn't too surprising; everyone had stuff to do, and unless my dad or John was actively critiquing someone's form, we generally just glanced at the lap times when the rider was done. I looked around for Ralph, since he might have seen me with Hayden as he was leaving the track, and spotted him near the back of the room; he was already halfway through his lunch, and seemed more concerned about his sandwich falling apart than about anything I was doing.

All smiles, Myles clapped me on the shoulder. "Way to go, Kenzie! I think you even beat my best record. Your dad is gonna flip when he sees this!"

Yes…he *was* going to flip when he saw it. But he would come completely unglued if he knew what I'd done to earn it.

CHAPTER 6

Nikki frowned at me when she picked me up that night. "What are you wearing? And why don't I see any green?"

I was in comfortable black cotton lounge pants and a black Cox Racing T-shirt, while Nikki looked like the epitome of St. Patrick's Day in her green leggings and shamrock-covered oversized sweater. Her hair was perfect and her makeup was flawless. Maybe because she spent so much of her day being dirty and greasy, or maybe because she was currently single and searching, Nikki made sure she looked like a million bucks whenever we went out. But honestly, now that she was here to get me, all I really wanted to do was close the door on her, grab a book, and head to bed. It had been a confusing day, and my mind was still reeling. Making a fool of myself on a mechanical bull was about the last thing I wanted to do. Good core exercise or not.

As if Nikki could tell that I was about to bail on her, she grabbed my hand and pulled me forward. "Doesn't matter. Myles is waiting, let's go."

It was all I could do to snatch my purse and turn the lock on the door before she had me outside with her. Nikki yanked me all the way to her tiny two-seater smart car. Once I was seat-belted in place, she gave me a bright smile. "This is gonna be great, you'll see!"

A groan escaped me and I rolled my eyes. Nikki gave me an odd look as she started the car and backed out of the driveway. "I know you're not thrilled about this, but what's up with the gloomy 'tude? You should be high on life after your amazing practice today, but instead, you look like you're choking down a piece of my mother's infamously horrible meat loaf. What gives?"

"I'm just...processing today," I told her, while I studied the darkness outside for a palatable answer to the problem that was plaguing me. Why did racing beside Hayden feel so good? And why did I do so much better when I tuned the world out and focused solely on him?

Nikki thwacked me on the shoulder. "What's to process? You made that track your bitch! Now, just do that when it counts, and you'll be golden. Cox Racing will be the talk of the town!"

Yeah...do that when it counted. Like it was so easy. But out there with just Hayden and me on the track...it *had* felt easy.

When we got to the bar, Myles was waiting outside with a couple other members of the Cox Racing crew—Ralph; our other racer, Eli; and Myles's mechanic, Kevin. Myles was standing under the entrance, wearing a Kiss Me, I'm Irish T-shirt. Pointing up at the gigantic bull horns attached to the building, he proudly exclaimed, "Those are going home with me tonight!"

Laughing at him, I waved at the group. The guys all gave me friendly nods. Eli let out a low whistle as he shook his head. "Man, Kenzie, you sure killed it today."

I gave him a short "Thanks" in response, since I really didn't want to talk about it, but Nikki wasn't about to let it go without a little more fanfare.

"Yeah, she did!" she exclaimed. Then she mimed a shotgun shooting the horns above us. Myles was the one who acted like he'd been shot, though. Clutching his chest, he started weaving left and right like he was drunk. Hams.

I gave Nikki a shove toward the door to get her moving. Myles and the guys fell in line behind us. Once we were all inside, I looked around for the famed entertainment here. Didn't take me long to find it. In the middle of the bar was a sunken floor surrounded by a tall railing and piled high with thick safety mats, and right smack in the middle of the padded area was the rectangular "bull" covered in black leather and topped off with a saddle.

Nikki took one look at it and squealed. "Let's do that first!"

Myles shook his head and pointed at the bar. "Beer first, bull second. It's part of the rules."

Kevin looked around for this elusive list of bull-riding rules. "It is?" Seeing a warning sign on the fence surrounding the pit, he jerked his thumb at it. "Are you sure? Because all that says is that the bar isn't responsible for...well, for anything, really." He swallowed, like he was unsure about just standing in this place. Kevin was kind of the wuss of the group. He often told Myles he was a mechanic for a reason; he'd rather go 60 miles per hour in the safety of a fully enclosed car than 160 with nothing between him and the world but open air.

Myles shrugged. "It's more of an unspoken rule."

Nikki laughed at the look on Kevin's face, then clapped him on the back. "To the beer then! 'Cause who are we to break rules?"

I had to raise an eyebrow at that statement as an unfortunate early-morning phone call ran through my mind. A phone call that had—in a way—started this whole mess with Hayden. Nikki cleared her throat and started making a beeline for the bar when she noticed the look on my face.

At the bar, Myles ordered two pitchers of green beer. We found a table that would fit all of us, and as we sat down, I reminded him that I was only having one drink. "Don't try refilling my glass or beg me to help finish the pitcher. One and I'm done, Myles."

He lifted a hand to his chest like he was morally offended. "I am *not* an alcohol pusher, Kenzie, and I respect your discipline. Admire it, really. If I had just a little more self-control of my own...I might have been able to say no to the Donnelly twins last year," he finished with a wink.

Kevin, Eli, and Ralph all dropped their jaws simultaneously, then started clamoring for details. Nikki rolled her eyes as she looked over at me. She made an obscene gesture with her hand that instantly had both of us on the verge of tears, we were laughing so hard. With a smile on his face, Myles flipped us both off.

Nikki excused herself to go to the bathroom, and while she was gone, our pitchers arrived. After the waitress finished passing out glasses of frothy green beer and left the table, we heard a loud crash, followed by the sound of breaking glass. Tracing the noise, I spotted a group of guys about to get into it on the other side of the bar. A scrawny guy stood next to a hulk of a man; both looked familiar to me, although I couldn't place where I'd seen them before. They were both staring down another guy, who was red in the face and dripping with what had to be alcohol. A frustrated waitress was standing next to the trio of testosterone, and there was an upended tray of drinks scattered across the ground—the source of the disturbance. The waitress's look of exasperation and the wet guy's expression of pure venom spoke volumes about what had just happened. And about what was *going* to happen.

"Ohhh, someone is about to get the shit kicked out of him," Myles said, laughing.

I had to agree. Even with his burly bodyguard standing behind him, backing him up, the little guy—who had clearly dumped the tray all over the wet guy—was going to get hit at least once. And sometimes once was all it took.

Cringing, I waited for the inevitable strike...but then, before chaos erupted, something incomprehensible happened. Hayden freaking Hayes stepped between the men, arms outstretched, like he was some goddamn referee. What in the hell was he doing here? Playing peacekeeper of all things?

I felt like *I'd* just been struck by a set of meaty fists as I watched Hayden fluidly disarm the situation. Then, even more shocking, when he was finished with the men, he walked over to the waitress and handed her some bills—paying for the mess and clearly smoothing things over with the bar. Why the hell would he do that?

From beside me, I heard Myles say, "Wow, I did *not* see it going down that way. What the hell is Hayden doing here?"

I was just about to tell Myles I'd been thinking the same thing when I noticed that Hayden had walked over to a woman. She was a slight girl, with dark hair and dark eyes, and she was clearly upset over the almost-altercation. While I watched, Hayden pulled her in for a warm embrace, then he kissed her temple. It was tender, sweet, and full of familiarity. They clearly weren't strangers…but they seemed too intimate to only be friends.

Something dark and insidious wrapped around me like cold steel, hardening *and* chilling me. Jesus, did Hayden have a girlfriend? With the way he'd been acting around me—in the hot tub, at the track—I'd just assumed he was single. But what if he wasn't? And what the hell did it matter if he *did* have a girlfriend?

As if he knew I was staring, Hayden's eyes suddenly found mine. I wanted to turn my head, ignore him, but I couldn't. I was trapped. He held my gaze with an unnerving intensity, and even though we were in a crowded bar, surrounded by people, and even though Hayden had his arms around another woman—a woman who was probably his girlfriend—that feeling of the world narrowing down to just him and me started to simmer in the air between us.

The girl noticed that Hayden was preoccupied and turned her head to look at me. There was an innocence to her large dark eyes that was surprising, and her tiny frame made her seem fragile, breakable. They were an odd pairing. It wasn't like I'd expected any girlfriend of Hayden's to be a skank, but…yeah, maybe I had. This girl just seemed too…nice for him.

She looked back up at him and he finally stopped staring at me. Glancing down at her, he shook his head, then gave her another quick hug before letting her go. A whirlwind of fury swirled within me. Had he just told her I was nobody? That what we had was nothing, and she shouldn't worry? But…that was true, wasn't it? We didn't have anything, we weren't anything, and I didn't *want* us to be anything.

Then why was my breath shaky, and my pulse racing? Needing a distraction, I started chugging my beer. It was completely unlike me, and Myles's eyes were wide as he stared.

Nikki returned and sat down in the seat beside me. Glancing around the table, she asked, "Did I miss anything?"

Eli was about to answer her when I interrupted. "We should go, Myles."

He glanced at Hayden, then back at me. "Because of him? He doesn't scare me. If he even tries to start anything with us, we can take him."

Nikki looked over to see who we were talking about. "Hayden is here? And is that…?"

She didn't finish her sentence, but by the look on her face, it was clear she recognized the guys Hayden was with, and she didn't want to talk about them. And if she didn't want to talk about them, it was because she didn't want to talk about how she knew them, which meant…damn it. Everything instantly clicked into place, and I suddenly knew exactly where I'd seen the ginormous and minuscule guys—the street race Nikki had dragged me to. The muscular man had been taking the bets while the little Hispanic guy had been talking to Hayden before the race, like he'd been coaching him. Why were they here? Why was Hayden still hanging out with them? And did Nikki know Hayden's gal pal too? A part of me wanted to ask her, but it was none of my business. And…I didn't think I actually wanted to know the answer.

Myles looked like he was about to question Nikki, so I distracted him with what I hoped sounded like logic. "He's a Benneti; we can't be seen with him or we'll be fired."

Myles instantly looked agitated. "We're *not* with him." Then he let out a forlorn sigh. "A bull, Kenzie…come on, I've always wanted to ride a bull. And so far as I know, we'd have to actively be fraternizing with him to get canned. We're just…in the same place at the same time. I doubt Hayden even realizes we're here." He must have missed Hayden drilling me with his eyes then…eyes that were still secretively watching; I could feel his gaze on me like rays of sunlight on a cold day. He should really be paying attention to his girl, not staring at me.

Eli nodded. "Yeah, we'll be fine, so long as he stays over there with those guys." He leaned forward, like he was about to divulge top secret information. "Hey, you guys hear the rumor floating around about him yet?" He tilted his head to indicate Hayden.

Like a student in class, Nikki raised her hand. "Oh, I heard it! Don't know if I believe it, but I heard it." All of us twisted to look at her and Nikki chomped down hard on her bottom lip, like she regretted speaking and was trying to eat her words.

I wasn't too surprised Nikki had heard a rumor about a rider—she lived on gossip—but I was dying to know what she'd heard about Hayden, and I wondered where she'd heard it. Although if Eli had heard it too, maybe it was common knowledge. Sometimes I got so caught up in racing, I missed the obvious. My heart started speeding up as numerous scenarios leaped through my mind.

"What rumor?" I asked, hoping I sounded casually curious.

Nikki twirled a strand of hair around her finger as she looked around the table. "Yeah…the rumor I heard…at Daytona." Eli nodded, like that was where he'd heard it too, and Nikki's expression visibly relaxed. Getting into it now, she placed her elbows on the table, a giddy grin on her face.

Before she could start in on her secret, though, Eli interrupted. "So, the rumor is, he started his career *street* racing." Eli sneered the word "street" while Nikki made a tittering sound as she flicked her guilty eyes at me. "Anyway," Eli continued, "they say he was undefeated on the road…because he made *sure* he was undefeated."

Eli lifted an insinuating eyebrow at us, but I wasn't following what he was implying. "What does that mean?" I asked.

Focusing his gaze at me, Eli said, "It means he fixed the races. He messed with bikes, messed with riders, did whatever he had to do to win. And now he's here…racing against *us*…and we should all be watching our backs."

Messing with bikes? That was the biggest crime in our sport—taboo, sacrilegious, detestable. It endangered everyone, not just the rider who was sabotaged. The reason we all felt comfortable enough to put our lives on the line whenever we rode was that there was a thin layer of trust between all the racers, even those who hated each other. Just suggesting that someone would do it, could do it, or *had* done it was a sinister accusation. I couldn't believe anyone was capable of sinking that low. Not even Hayden. "Oh, come on, Eli, not even a *Benneti* would tamper with bikes."

Eli shrugged, like he hadn't just said something scandalous. "Are you sure about that, Kenzie? You know Keith wants to squeeze your dad until he breaks. What if he brought this guy on *just* to make sure we fail?"

I wanted to object, but I wasn't about to defend Keith, so I shut my mouth. And besides...Eli made a good point. What if Keith *had* brought in Hayden just to mess with us? Given that he blamed my father for ruining his career, I wouldn't put it past him. But would Hayden really stoop to that level to win? I had no idea, and that made my stomach tighten for an entirely different reason.

Not wanting to think about Keith or Hayden, I nudged Nikki for help. She glanced at me, read my expression, and thankfully changed the subject. "Well, this night just took a ride through Downer Town. How about we turn things around and start having some fun now? Bull, anyone?"

All the boys were on board with that idea, and they quickly slammed the rest of their beers. I thanked Nikki by clinking glasses with her and took another long gulp of my beer, finishing it. Even though I'd only had one drink, I was a little light-headed when I stood up. Yep, lightweight was my middle name. It was just one of the many reasons why I didn't indulge in alcohol often.

Myles got in line to put our names down while I watched a female rider giggling as she positioned herself on the saddle; she was wearing a low-cut tank top and a short green skirt—not a great outfit choice for bull riding, but the men in the room seemed to appreciate it. The guy controlling the bull had an indecent smile on his face as he started the machine. The woman was laughing so hard, she almost fell off as soon as the bull began to move in a slow circle. She held on, though, and then the motorized beast started doing things that instantly pricked my indignation.

The fake bull was behaving in a way that no real bull would. Instead of the standard circles and bucking, it was...shimmying. It shook and jostled in such a way that the poor girl almost bounced out of her shirt, and I was beginning to believe that was the point;

she was tipped forward at such an angle that everyone in the bar was getting a pretty spectacular view of her bright-pink bra. The woman didn't seem to mind, but I sure minded for her. It irked me even more when I noticed how differently the male riders after her were treated.

While I waited for my turn, I watched five more riders take theirs. Three men and two more women. All the men got the standard, realistic bull-riding experience. All the girls got jug jiggling. It ticked me off.

Myles slung his arm around my shoulder while I watched yet another girl get vibrated to the ground; the men nearby cheered when she hit the floor. "Ready? Our group is up next."

I shot him a look that clearly said I'd rather lick the bottom of my shoe than ride *that* bull. "I'm out."

He looked at me like I'd just shot his puppy. "What? No, you have to." I raised my eyebrows at his comment. Aside from kick ass at the next race, I didn't *have* to do anything. Understanding the heat in my eyes, he changed his tone. "Please? We're all doing it, even Kevin." He jabbed his thumb at Kevin, and the shy mechanic waved.

With a frown, I ignored him and pointed at the girl currently walking out of the corral, rubbing her ass. "No. It's degrading."

Using his fingers, Myles forced my lips up into a smile. "It's fun. Remember fun? You used to have it on occasion, if I recall. That might be someone else I'm thinking of, though."

Yanking his fingers from my face, I shook my head. "I would rather drink shots all night from a stranger's belly button than ride *this* bull."

Myles pursed his lips, like he was thinking. "I could probably arrange that…"

He started searching the room and I shoved his shoulder back. Asshat. Turning to Nikki, I said, "I think I'll just get a cab and call it a night." Public humiliation of *any* sort was not my idea of a good time.

They all groaned at me, Nikki and Myles the loudest, but I held up my hand in farewell and started walking away before they could come up with arguments for me to stay. With this group, a quick retreat was best.

I was speed-walking back through the waiting line for the pit when I heard a familiar voice say, "Are you leaving, sweetheart?"

Looking to my right, I saw Hayden standing there at the end of the line, watching the show while he waited for his turn. He was alone. For now. I opened my mouth to tell him to go to hell, but he leaned in and words instantly left me. God, he smelled good, like a sea breeze on a warm summer night.

His face was incredibly close to mine now, and my eyes could clearly pick out the intriguing mixture of dirty-blond, dark brown, and fiery red in his stubble; I wanted to study the varying shades for hours. I never wanted to see it again. *He's taken... and I'm not interested.* When Hayden spoke, his voice was so low I almost thought I could feel it vibrating against my rib cage. "Did the bull scare you? You really shouldn't let fear win..." He blinked, then pulled back and said, "Besides, I have a feeling it's been a while since you've had a good... buck."

That loosened my tongue. "Wouldn't you like to know," I purred, stepping into his side. My goal had been just to torment him with something he could *never* have, but as soon as our hips pressed together, that familiar heat from the hot tub resurfaced, and everything but the two of us dissolved from my consciousness. Just like when we were racing, I suddenly had tunnel vision, and *he* was all I could see.

Hayden was breathing heavier and there was heat in his eyes as his lip curled into a devilish one-sided grin. "Maybe I *would* like that," he whispered, almost too low for me to hear. And as if he had dragged a mild electric current over my skin, my entire body started buzzing with energy. The fact that his date was somewhere nearby made his comment ten times more inappropriate, but my body didn't seem to care, and when he sucked his bottom lip into his mouth, I swear the room started spinning. Jesus, I couldn't get drunk on one beer, could I?

Abruptly, Hayden took a step back and shook his head like he was clearing it. The loss of contact was like waking from a dream—sounds around me got louder, the smell of the bar became more pungent. Hayden's smile turned smug as he studied my face. "But it's probably better if you leave. Watching you walk away is far more enticing than anything you'd do on that bull." He ended his comment with a wink. Philandering, flirtatious asshole.

Looking over my shoulder, I saw that my teammates were just starting to ride the bull, and luckily everyone was preoccupied watching Eli get tossed around. Since Hayden shouldn't be getting any sort of satisfaction from seeing my ass walking away from him, I turned sideways and inched my way back to where Myles and Nikki were waiting. Hayden's chuckle followed me the entire way.

When I returned to Nikki's side, she did a double take, then hugged me. "Oh good! You changed your mind!"

I gave her a halfhearted smile, then scowled at Myles. "You owe me for this, Kelley." For good measure, I finished my statement by flicking his nose with my finger. He rubbed it as if he'd been stung by a bee, and I finally smiled fully.

Nikki went on the bull after Eli, and of course, she loved every second of the gratuitous display. Ralph and Myles laughed the entire time; shy Kevin respectfully turned away. Ralph went next, and he was surprisingly good at it. I had to wonder if he had some real-life experience bull riding. Maybe he was a cowboy in his spare time. That image brightened my mood for a moment. Until Myles turned to me and said, "You're up."

Internally I cringed. Damn it. Since it was too late to back out, I decided to throw on a bright, carefree smile and fake it. "Excellent. Can't wait."

Myles patted my arm. "Good luck!"

Lacing my voice with confidence, I told him, "I'm a professional road racer. I don't need luck with this bucking bike wannabe." *Please don't let me fall off in the first five seconds.*

I had to walk past the bull's controller to get to the padded circle where I was about to meet my fate. On a whim, I slapped my hands on his table and leaned over the top of his control board. The guy looked up at me with wide, startled eyes. He had to be about my age, but he seemed around fifteen as I stared him down.

With my most intimidating voice, I told him, "Look here, buddy. You're going to give me the ride you give the *men*, or I'm going to come back over here and use you as my personal stress relief ball. And I've got a lot of pent-up frustration. Do we understand each other?"

The guy blinked at me as he nodded. Hopefully I'd get a regular ride now, and not the jiggly kind. I did *not* need that kind of embarrassment tonight.

Feeling determined, I climbed onto the saddle and decided to own this bull just as hard as I'd owned the track earlier. If I could rocket along the concrete at over 150 miles per hour, then I could handle this stationary piece of machinery. This should be easy in comparison.

Flashing the bull operator a final warning look, I settled in for the potentially wild ride. When I gave him the go-ahead, he played with some switches on his board, and the bull slowly came to life. Clutching the pommel with both hands, I tried to get my bearings as the bull started rotating. It was a strange rocking, circling movement, one I definitely wasn't used to. Damn it, I could not get thrown off this bull. I had something to prove.

Once I felt comfortable with the motion, I let go of the pommel with one hand and leaned back, copying every bull riding movie I'd ever seen. It was easier said than done, but after a few seconds, I felt like I actually had the hang of it, and found it wasn't as difficult as I'd feared. There was something strangely sensual about the movement of the machine, and the memory of my hip pressed against Hayden's only amplified the sensation. I tried to ignore the spark of tingling desire, but the more I tried, the stronger it became.

As I spun and bucked, my mind drifted into fantasy. I knew it was wrong on multiple levels, but I started imagining that Hayden was with me on the bull, in front of me, facing me, and every forward movement had me crashing into his body. I once again felt the world retreating, and it was just imaginary Hayden and me left in the bar, striving toward a common goal. *I shouldn't indulge in this... but it feels so good.*

Closing my eyes, I concentrated on the intense ache beginning to form in my core, begging for release. I imagined Hayden putting his hands all over me, his warm mouth traveling across my skin, his body sliding in and out of mine, and the embers of desire started churning into a passionate fire. Knowing who was turning up the heat inside me almost squelched the raging inferno, but the continual rocking motion of the bull quickly pushed me past the point of no return; I couldn't have cared less at that moment that I despised Hayden. In fact, it only made the visual that much sweeter, turned the sensuous movement into something erotic and forbidden. Unknowingly, Hayden was driving me toward something wonderful and amazing, something he wouldn't *ever* be able to partake in. It was my own form of victory.

Just the thought of climaxing right here, right now, with everyone watching, was enough to have my heart racing. The thin cotton pants I was wearing made it easy to focus my energies on the desire cresting within me, and if I could get just a little more stimulation, I knew I'd fall apart almost instantly. God, it had been way too long since I'd felt this…

The ride was getting wilder, making it harder to hold on, but I really didn't care about that anymore. I was close to feeling something epic, I just needed a little more to get me all the way there. As subtly as I could, I leaned forward on the bull, so all my sensitive spots were grinding against the saddle. The bull crashed down at just the right time, with just the right pressure, and I instantly hit the wall. *Oh… my fuck. God… Yes, Hayden… Yes…*

I was barely done riding out the waves of orgasmic bliss when the bull suddenly stopped moving. I was panting and my heart was racing, and I had no idea what the crowd around me had seen. Because of how long I'd stayed on the bull, they were all cheering and clapping—even the guy controlling the beast looked impressed—but Jesus, had any of them noticed I'd just had an orgasm? On a freaking bull? Thinking about freaking Hayden Hayes? God…I felt dirty. I wanted to scream in frustration, I wanted to hit something, I wanted to run and cry. But I had to act completely normal, just in case by some miracle they had missed that performance.

As I hopped off the bull, I nonchalantly scanned the crowd. No one seemed shocked, no one seemed scandalized, and no one seemed stunned. In fact, no one seemed to have noticed anything strange about that bull ride at all. Were they all really that oblivious? Even Myles and Nikki only seemed happy that I'd been successful on the bull. Damn it…way too successful. My heart soared with glee at the thought that I might have perfectly hidden the euphoria that had pounded through me. Then I accidentally looked over at Hayden, and my bubble of relief instantly popped as our gazes locked.

From the frenzied look of wild desire in his eyes and the fact that his hand was discreetly squeezing the front of his jeans, I knew he was fully aware of what I'd just done. While he stared at me with heavy breath and parted lips, I was suddenly struck by an undeniable rush of attraction.

I desperately wanted his hard, naked body wrapped around mine, wanted to feel the softness of his skin under my fingers, and wanted him to taste the inevitable wetness he inspired. Then I wanted him to drive into me, to give me another mind-blowing release, and I wanted us to work together to achieve it. I wanted to jointly reach for something bigger than ourselves…And wanting that from him freaked me the fuck out.

Not this guy—he's taken, he's trouble, he's not what I need right now. I have too much to do, too much at stake, too much to prove…too much to save.

CHAPTER 7

I needed to get out of this bar. Glancing back as I cut through the crowd, I saw Hayden still standing alone at the end of the line. His emerald eyes were glued on me, and the second our gazes connected, I felt a flash of heat burn up my spine. My breath caught and I almost stumbled. Just the heat in his stare made me want his hands, lips, and body all over me. God, if just the fantasy of being with him gave me that much of a shuddering release, what would climaxing *with* him actually be like? What would his kiss taste like? What would his skin feel like? What would he sound like when he came…?

The sudden tingling rush of desire that immediately followed that thought made me want to run. Run, and never stop running. *He's not an option.* Once I was outside, I gulped down the fresh air, hands over my knees like I'd just finished a marathon. *Control, Kenzie. For fuck's sake, work on your control!*

"Are you leaving?"

The familiar voice sent a spike of ice through my heart. Oh no. Not now. Bolting upright, I spun around to face him. Hayden's gaze raked over my body and his lips formed a smile that was entirely too sexy; what would his girl think if she saw him giving me a grin so seductive, it should be illegal.

"I was wrong," he murmured. "So very, very wrong... That was far more appealing than watching you leave, and now... I really don't want to ever watch you leave again." His eyes seemed to glow with heat as he approached me, like a jungle cat stalking its prey. Without meaning to, I backed up a step. *I'm no one's prey.*

"Well, I hate to disappoint you, but I have a cab to catch." Unintentionally, I added, "And you have *friends* to get back to."

His brows scrunched together at hearing the acid in my voice. As best I could, I schooled my features. Let him figure that one out himself; I certainly wasn't going to remind him that he had a girlfriend.

Hayden closed the distance between us, but I stubbornly refused to retreat again. He was so close to me, I was practically straddling his thigh. It brought back the moment on the bull. His scent consumed me, that intriguing blend that reminded me of pounding surf, scorching sand, hot rays licking my skin. Goddamn Hayden Hayes. What the hell happened to me when he was around? It was like my head went one way while my body went another. Right became wrong, up became down.

"I've never met anyone quite like you. You're more than I thought you were, so much more," he said, stepping even closer. If he pushed any farther into my space, certain body parts were going to line up... and that could *not* happen.

"Back up," I hissed, still refusing to move. I hadn't meant to engage him, and I clamped my lips together in regret. Not another word would escape my mouth.

"When you let go... you're amazing on the track. Fast, tight... perfect curves." His eyes drifted down my front, and I inhaled a deep breath. Was he flirting or complimenting me? Both were unnerving at the moment. I just wanted him to go away. "You really *can* ride, Kenzie," he said with raised eyebrows, like I'd surprised him.

Seeing yet another man doubt my skills because of my gender doused the flames that had been flickering, and I broke my mental promise to not speak again. "Yeah, shocker of the year. I'm not just a pretty face. I actually *earned* my place on the team."

For a half second he managed to look properly chastised while he absorbed my comment, but then his lips shifted into a charming smile. "No, you're definitely not just another pretty face…but I meant that as encouragement. Sometimes I think you forget you're as good as you are."

Gathering my willpower, I took a step back, then quickly turned around to leave. He wasn't inside my head; he couldn't possibly know that. He was just messing with me. Hayden grabbed my arm, stopping me. "Wait, Kenzie. I just want to talk to you. Nothing more, I promise."

"Yeah, right," I muttered, yanking my arm away. I'd already seen the desire in his eyes. There was a lot more he wanted from me than conversation, and I had no intention of giving it to him. I shouldn't even be talking to him. What if one of the guys came out here looking for me and saw this little…exchange? What if his girlfriend spotted us? I didn't want to be fired *or* yelled at tonight. I needed to leave.

Eager to wipe this evening from my memory, I pulled out my cell phone as I stormed through the parking lot. The quicker I called a cab, the sooner I could get out of here.

Because Hayden was a stubborn asshole, he hurried after me. "Wait, Kenzie." When I didn't stop walking, he yelled, "Goddammit, wait!" Catching up to me, he grabbed my arm again and spun me around; I instantly jerked myself free. He was *not* allowed to touch me. Breathing heavier, he panted, "Would you relax and let me talk to you?"

Keeping my expression even, I calmly said, "There, you just talked to me," and started searching for cab companies on my phone.

Hayden grabbed my cell from my hand and held it behind his back. "Why are you such a bitch?" he asked, his eyes intense.

Something in the air started sizzling between us. Sparks were flaring to life with an almost audible crackle, and I felt the kinetic energy vibrating through every pore, every cell. In some sick, twisted turn of fate, just being around him fueled me, fed me, sharpened my senses. What would it be like if I caved, if I lowered my defenses? Not just some lust-filled daydream, but the real thing? No…he was the last person I wanted to be with.

"Give me my phone back," I seethed.

"No. Not until you stop being stubborn and talk to me." His tone was so commanding, it instantly enraged me. Who the hell did he think he was? My father?

"Talk to you about what?" I asked, clenching my hands into fists. If I pushed him away would he leave me alone? *If I pulled him into my body, would he stay?*

Eyes hot with passion and desire, he snarled, "Well, how about this *thing* between us, for starters." His gaze slid down my body, and I knew he was referencing the heat that seemed to hover in the air whenever we got close. Even now, I could feel it pulsing against my skin. The fantasy of him had helped bring me to release, but my body was thudding a message deep inside—*it wasn't enough*. His eyes inspecting my every curve was only making the dull ache grow stronger with every passing second. *No, he's a Benneti. He's a thug. He's taken. He's not for me.*

"I have no idea what you're talking about," I said flatly.

With obvious effort, Hayden pulled his eyes back to my face; the loss made a shudder run through me. He smirked, then said, "Right, your go-to answer. So would you just like to stick a pin in that and move on to the next topic—the fact that we race better when we're together. And there's no point in denying *that*, so don't even try. I *know* I race faster when you're beside me, and I know you race faster when you're beside *me*. We should be practicing *together*."

Just the thought of hopping on a bike and going full bore against him had my heart beating quicker and my mind spinning with need for a different kind of excitement. Yes, I loved racing him; I felt more secure, more confident, and more relaxed with him…more like the racer I was supposed to be. And I hated that I felt that way; I didn't want anything from Hayden, especially the thrill he gave me when we were going all out. Knowing I needed to end this pattern before it even began, I told him, "There is no way in hell I can practice with you. It isn't possible for the two of us to be on the track at the same time. We'll both be fired, and you know it. So you're just going to have to grow up and get better on your own."

His eyes darkened. "You're better when you're going up against me. If you want to make a splash this year, get people noticing you, talking about you, talking about *Cox Racing*...then you should train with me, and *only* me." He stepped even closer, so his body was flush with mine. The growing desire I'd been struggling to extinguish shifted into a raging inferno at his nearness. I felt delirious with the need for more, yet furious that he was the one making me feel this way.

"Don't tell me what to do," I said, shoving him away from me. "I'm not a child."

He stepped forward until we were toe-to-toe again. His breath was heavy, and I was shocked to find that mine was too. "Are you sure? Because sometimes you really act like one. I'm just trying to help you. I'm just trying to help us both. Is that so wrong?"

Yes. In our case, it was. Helping each other was forbidden. Besides, rumor had it he only helped himself. And while I wasn't sure about the plausibility of the bike tampering, the helping himself part of the story I completely believed—him being out here flirting with me while his date dutifully waited inside the bar was proof of that. All of this was only about Hayden helping Hayden.

Hayden's chest was heaving, and when I glanced down, I could see an inch or so of skin at his waist as his shirt lifted and lowered. Even knowing what a bad idea this was, seeing his bare skin was torture; it called to my fingertips, urging me to touch, to explore. I wouldn't cave, though. Not to *this* man. Lifting my jaw as I refocused my resolve, I told him, "I'm a grown woman, a daughter of a legend, and I don't need your help. Now give me back my phone."

Hayden stared at me for a full thirty seconds before he did anything. Then he slowly handed my phone back to me. "All right, fine. There you go...princess."

Anticipation energized the air, a lightning storm building, about to explode. He'd just thrown the ball in my court. Now what the hell should I do with it?

Control. Dad would want me to show control.

With my phone tightly in my hand, I turned around. I would leave him standing there, watching me go. My backside was all I would give him.

Unfortunately, that wasn't enough for Hayden. Before I could completely turn away from him, he said, "Wait…one more thing before you go." Then he reached out, grabbed me, turned me toward him, and pulled me into his body.

His arms wrapped around me, holding me tight and pinning my arms in place. Panic and desire surged through me. What was he going to do to me? What did I *want* him to do to me? "Let me go," I hissed, squirming.

His face was just inches from mine, so close I could feel his breath on my cheeks, taste the whiskey he'd been drinking. His mouth moved toward me and my heart started pounding in my chest. Jesus, he was going to kiss me. His lips were so full, so inviting, so powerful and confident…Being someone's side action was *not* okay with me, and being with a *Benneti* was even farther down the list of acceptable acts…but…despite it all, a part of me really wanted what he was offering. *Yes…kiss me.*

Before our mouths collided, though, his hands slipped down my backside and pinched. Hard. I let out a surprised, pained yelp, and with a deep laugh, he let me go. Rubbing my ass, I glared at him with eyes hot enough to melt glass. Inwardly, though, I was relieved. Had I honestly wanted him to kiss me? What the hell?

Pointing a finger at me, he stated, "That's for not wearing green." Without waiting for a response, he turned and walked back to the bar. I was so stunned, I couldn't move. Who the hell still pinched people on St. Patrick's Day? And why had I been expecting—no, *wanting*—so much more?

* * *

The next morning, Nikki wasn't in yet when I got to the garage bay, but Kevin and Eli were there. They waved a greeting when I walked through the doors, and I prayed they didn't ask me why I'd disappeared last night. Luckily, they just went back to work when the pleasantries were over with; we all had a lot to do before Wisconsin. I couldn't wait for the next race. Daytona had *almost* been amazing. Wisconsin was *definitely* going to be.

After changing into my leathers, I headed to my main bike and inspected it for any sign of damage. You'd never even know I'd dragged it across the concrete, though. It looked brand-spankin'-new, thanks to Nikki's meticulous care. I inspected the brakes, the shocks, the air intake, the oil, the gas. Nikki would keep everything in race-ready condition, of course, but I liked to know my bike, right down to the minute scratches in the paint. This wasn't just a piece of machinery to me; it was an extension of my soul, and it was yearning to soar.

"Almost, baby," I cooed, patting the seat.

"Talking to inanimate objects, huh? That's the first sign of mental illness, you know."

Hearing Myles's voice, I looked up to see him walking toward me, looking sleepy and disheveled, like he'd just rolled out of bed. "You're here early," I said with a smile. "Lose a bet or something?"

He frowned, then reluctantly looked around the shop. "Actually... yeah. And now I have to sort all the tools. Nikki won't care if I just throw things in there, will she?" he asked, hope in his eyes.

Keeping my expression even, I replied, "Have you met her?"

Myles sighed and groaned, sitting on a swivel stool. "This sucks. That woman is evil. Pure, vindictive evil."

Laughing softly as I grabbed my helmet off a nearby table, I asked him, "What was the bet about?"

He swished his hand like he didn't want to talk about it. "A glass. A quarter. The details really aren't important."

As I rolled my bike away from its resting place, I clapped him on the shoulder. "Well, you're a true man for following through on the deal. I wouldn't have."

He smiled up at me. "That's 'cause you're not a man. And you're not scared of Nikki like I am."

"True on both counts." I laughed again.

I was about to leave him to his tedious task, but his expression turned puzzled. "Hey, what happened to you after the bull? Nikki and I looked everywhere for you when we were done, but you were just... gone."

Yeah, I know. My phone had exploded when they'd started searching for me. I'd already texted my excuse to them, but clearly Myles wanted the expanded version. "It was just like I said. Riding the bull made me nauseous, so I called a cab and went home. After throwing up in the bathroom a couple times." That lie made me want to throw up, but I couldn't tell my friends the truth. Word would spread that...*something*...was going on with Hayden and me, and then Dad would have no choice but to fire me. The Benneti Ban allowed no mercy, not even to the daughter of Jordan Cox.

Myles shrugged and nodded, like he thought it was weird but he was letting it go. With a long exhale of relief, I started rolling my bike toward the garage bay door. "Mackenzie, going out to practice?" Dad's voice behind me made me stop and look back.

He was walking my way, sheets of statistics in his hand. "I was just going over yesterday's numbers. Very impressive, you bested everyone's times. Try and duplicate that again today. Being consistent is what activates muscle memory. And that's exactly what you'll need for a win at Road America."

He patted my shoulder before he left, and I stared after him in amazement. That was kind of a compliment. For my dad, anyway; he rarely gave them. Unfortunately it was competing against Hayden that had gotten me those great times. Honestly, I wasn't sure if I could repeat the performance without him, and that worried me. I had to try, though. I had no other choice.

That night, I met up with my sisters to go dress shopping. Watching Daphne try on an endless number of wedding gowns was about the last thing I wanted to be doing, but I'd promised her I'd participate in the bonding ritual. And besides, Daphne was making Dad go too, and watching him squirm was always entertaining.

"It's perfect, Daphne, let's get it." Daphne was twirling her latest find in front of Dad; a pained smile was on his face, one that clearly said, *Someone please get me out of here.*

Stopping her swirling motion, Daphne rested her hands on her hips and scowled at him. "You said the exact same thing about the last three. You can't have liked them all." With a sigh, she sat down on the white padded bench beside him. "Where's your journal? Let's see your notes."

Theresa and I snorted, earning us both glares from Daphne, and I quickly turned around to examine the mannequins in the front window. Leaning into me, Theresa whispered, "I can't believe she's making him take notes on every single dress she tries on. Dad's never going to survive this wedding." I had to agree with her assessment. But unfortunately it wasn't just our sister's bridezilla tendencies that were going to kill him. Every dress Daphne had tried on was at least four figures.

Wishing my sister had less expensive tastes, I told Theresa, "Just wait until she starts on shoes." Theresa tried to contain her laughter, but a few giggles squeaked out, making me laugh too. But then I spotted something outside, and my good mood instantly faded.

Hayden was across the street, casually walking down the sidewalk with that woman from the bar. Definitely his girlfriend. Bile filled my throat as I watched the two of them. They looked so damn cute together, comfortable, like they'd been with each other for years. But what was even more shocking than seeing them together again was the young girl, maybe seven or eight, walking between them, wearing a big, fluffy hat. Hayden and the woman were each holding one of the girl's hands, swinging them back and forth like they were all some picture-perfect family. *Oh my God…does he have a kid too?* Jesus. So despite the heat between us sometimes…it really was just about the racing with Hayden. His interest was somewhere else. I was just a tool that he wanted to use to perform better. And that was just fine. I didn't want him to be interested in me.

"Hey, you okay?" Theresa asked, laying her chin on my shoulder. "You know that guy or something?"

"No," I said, slapping on a smile and turning back to my family. I really didn't.

* * *

Before I knew it, it was time to pack up and head out to Elkhart Lake, Wisconsin, for the second event of the season. I was itching to go—completely healed, and completely ready to blast my finish of thirteenth place out of the water. The entire way there I hoped for no mistakes this race. I needed to be the epitome of the perfect Cox racer. I needed to go all the way to the top this time. The family business wouldn't magically get better on its own. It was up to me to be the miracle my father was praying for.

Friday morning, I arrived at the course as early as they would allow me to be there. Except for the qualifying round and the practice round, we weren't allowed on the track, but I liked to study the road and visualize the race. I was standing on the hot side of the pits, staring out at nothing as I envisioned myself twisting low through corners, flying at heart-stopping speeds through the straightaways. I was completely absorbed in my vision when a face suddenly appeared in my line of sight, distracting me.

As I blinked in confusion, my mind's eye evaporated and Myles's smile came into view. "Howdy. Whatcha doing?"

In my fantasy I'd been passing Hayden to take the lead and win the race. Hopefully that was exactly what would come to pass this weekend. My solo practice times hadn't been anywhere near where they'd been when Hayden had lured me into a few laps with him, a fact that was seriously messing with my head. Along with the fact that he had a kid. What the hell? "Just picturing my win," I told Myles, feigning a relaxed smile.

Dark eyes bright with encouragement, Myles nodded. "Good. You know what your dad says about success."

"You have to see it before you can have it," I automatically spouted.

Myles clapped my shoulder in friendly camaraderie, just as a group of eager reporters walking down pit lane approached us. "Myles Kelley, Mackenzie Cox. Would you mind giving us a few words?"

Making sure my back was to them, I made a sour face at Myles. I hated talking to reporters, especially TV reporters with imposing cameras like this group. Not only was being recorded while trying to have a conversation with a stranger incredibly awkward, but every single one of them only seemed to want to know what it was like to be Jordan Cox's daughter. If only I could give them real answers to those questions... *"How was it growing up with such a huge role model?" Fine, until I started racing and discovered just how massive his shadow was, something you guys love to remind me about. "At what age did your father tell you you'd have a place on his team?" Meaning the only reason I'm on the team is my DNA? Thanks, asshole. "Do you think you'll ever be able to win a championship like your father did?" Oh... right. Because I'm a girl, so I don't actually have a chance of coming in first. Well, screw you.*

Myles grinned at me before turning to face the reporters. "Of course we don't mind," he told them. He pretty much had no choice but to say that, though. The officials insisted that all racers be courteous to the press and answer any and all questions presented to them. Positively, of course. They wanted to attract the public's attention to the sport, but only in the most flattering light. Riders who spouted negativity to the cameras were fined and penalized. So were riders who ignored the cameras altogether.

With an internal sigh, I followed suit and smiled brightly at the awaiting journalists.

"Myles, how are you feeling about the race today? Any concerns?" A man extended his microphone out to Myles, and Myles instantly turned into the flawless professional that he always was when cameras were involved. His ability to bullshit always made me a little jealous. I tended to turn into an unintelligible idiot when reporters asked me questions.

While I listened to Myles giving the group a slew of intelligent, well-thought-out answers, my heart started racing and my stomach started twisting. The weight of my name was crushing during moments like this. I felt like the world expected profound theories and concepts to come out of my mouth every time I opened it, ideas and attitudes that would forever change the face of the ARRC—because that was what my father had done. His speeches had rewritten rules, influenced the sport. But I couldn't be him, I could only be *me*. If the penalty were only a fine, I would have walked away and left Myles to answer for both of us, but unfortunately, grid placement was also a penalty for not speaking with the press, and I couldn't risk starting at the back of the lineup.

As I silently ran through what I'd say when asked about the upcoming race, I suddenly noticed that Myles had stopped talking and silent tension was filling the air. Myles was staring at me with raised eyebrows, and when he saw that he had my attention, he flicked his gaze toward the awaiting reporters. That was when I understood. Damn it. They'd asked me a question, and I'd completely missed it. I already looked like a fool.

Clearing my throat, I said, "I'm sorry, what was that?"

A reporter who looked annoyed at having to repeat himself said, "So, Mackenzie, being the daughter of racing legend Jordan Cox, you must have a lot of pressure to do well this season, especially with the rumors of your family's financial troubles. Can you tell me, was your father pleased with your results at Daytona, or was he disappointed with that unfortunate slide out on the last turn?"

I opened my mouth, but no words came out. What the hell was I supposed to say to that? What I ended up saying probably wasn't the most diplomatic answer. "I'm not my dad, so I can't answer that. You'd have to ask him how he felt."

The reporter smirked, just a tiny bit, then said, "I guess I will. What about the news that your fellow rider Jimmy Holden dropped his contract with Cox Racing at the start of the season to join Stellar Racing? And that he took one of your biggest sponsors with him? That must have been quite a blow to your already shaky circumstances. Any thoughts you'd like to share on the matter?"

His questions infuriated me. My family's hardships were private, not fodder for the news. Speaking without fully thinking it through, I told him, "I'm not sure where you're getting your information, but our circumstances are just fine. And Jimmy's the one who decided to turn his back on the team that raised him up from nothing. I'd say the crappy finish he got at Daytona was fate paying him back for his ingratitude. Karma is a bitch, after all."

The reporter's eyes widened and Myles put a warning hand on my shoulder. Jesus. I'd just cursed in an interview, after insulting another rider. "Don't suppose I could get you to leave that part out, could I?"

Like he understood he was completely in control of the situation now, the reporter said, "Maybe...One final question, though. Being a woman in a male-dominated sport has to be difficult. Do you feel pressure to be...at a certain level? Or are you comfortable with where you're at?"

Wasn't that a loaded question? So how to answer it without getting myself into even more trouble. After a moment's consideration, I said, "I know what I'm capable of, and I know I haven't gotten there yet. And I also know that I will get there because of *who* I am, not what I am. So no, I don't feel pressure to win because I'm a woman. I *want* to win, because I'm a racer."

My voice got a little passionate at the end, and I really hoped the reporter took it as fervor, not as an insult. With a politician-worthy smile, the reporter looked between Myles and me. "Thank you both for your time," he said, making a cutting motion to the cameraman behind him. All grins, the group stalked off to find someone else to harass.

Groaning, I dropped my head in my hands. "Oh my God... they're going to air that debacle, aren't they? I'm so screwed."

Myles placed a comforting hand on my shoulder. "It will be fine, Kenzie. Totally...fine." I peeked up at him with narrowed eyes, and he added, "It could have been worse, right?"

"Not really." Staring after the reporters, I shook my head. "Dad was so good at talking to the press when he was racing. He had them eating out of his hands. I can barely string two sentences together, and when I do, it's all crap I shouldn't say in public." It was just one of the many, many ways my dad and I were different.

Myles gave my shoulder a sympathetic squeeze. "You're alike where it counts, Kenzie. On the track. And that's all that really matters."

I peered up at him, wishing that were true, but we both knew there was more to this world of racing than being good on a bike. You needed charm to schmooze sponsors and a sparkling personality to win over the fans, and I wasn't sure if I had either of those things.

As I nodded at his comment, I happened to see the flock of reporters pouncing on Hayden. They were practically salivating at the opportunity to talk to the photogenic, charismatic new member of Benneti Motorsports. Hayden had his arms wide, and the reporters were visibly hanging on his every word. His ability to charm the press was yet another thing about him that irritated and frustrated me, and a small spark of doubt ignited in the back of my mind. Was I truly cut out for this life? The racing yes, but everything else…

I forcefully threw a bucket of water on that ember of unrest. Yes. I was *absolutely* cut out for this. It was all I'd ever wanted to do with my life.

Tuning out Hayden's annoyingly resonant voice as he answered questions about his triumphant debut at Daytona, I resumed imagining my success. *Dad is counting on me, my team is counting on me, the business is counting on me…I can do this.* Closing my eyes, I saw the course in my mind, saw myself starting at the back of the pack. Then I pictured Hayden, and imagined slipping around people to get to him. I felt my body relaxing as I visualized myself grabbing an opportunity and sliding around him. In my mind, the visor on his helmet was clear, and I could see his shocked expression as I outmaneuvered him. My heart started beating harder as I imagined myself squealing away from him, crossing the finish line with him right on my heels. I pictured myself stopping my bike and looking back at Hayden with a challenge in my eyes. He screeched his bike to a stop right beside me, jerked off his helmet, and looked me over with desire clear in his features. Suddenly, my helmet was off, and he was grabbing the back of my neck and pulling me into him, claiming me for his victory since I'd stolen the race from him. Oddly, even with everything between us, I wanted to let him. My breath picked up and that familiar tingle of excitement shot through me as his mouth closed over mine.

What? No! The last thing I wanted to do was have another sick, twisted, erotic daydream about Hayden. I forced my eyes open, and did a double take when I saw the *actual* Hayden standing right there, staring at me. I was still sort of worked up, and had to take a deep, calming breath before I could speak to him. Even then, my voice came out strained. "What are you doing here, and why are you staring at me like that?"

He glanced over his shoulder to where the reporters were catching up with other racers before returning his eyes to me. "Meditating?" he asked with a smirk.

"Something like that." My vision of kissing him had rekindled the memory of that heated moment between us outside the bar, when I'd been mentally begging him to put his lips on mine. Now all I could think about was his mouth. I needed out of here before I did something I regretted, like make that fantasy a reality.

"Well, don't psych yourself out about tomorrow," he smoothly responded. "You'll do fine."

His insight into the dark, doubt-filled part of me I hid from everyone was infuriating, but oddly, it only made me even more attracted to him. *He gets me.* "We can't be seen together like this," I said, walking away from him as quickly as I could. I wasn't even sure where I was going, but I knew now was not a good time to be alone with him. Especially with all the potential witnesses around us. I needed to keep walking until the thought of his tongue brushing against mine completely left me. Bikes. I needed to think about bikes. Or the race. Or my father. Anything but Hayden. *He has a girlfriend, he has a kid. Stop fantasizing about him.*

"Kenzie, wait." Hayden jogged until he caught up with me, which only made me want to run. I didn't, though. There was no point. History told me he would just follow until he'd said his piece. When we were more or less alone, he glanced around and said, "How'd you do with the reporters? Kill it, or get killed?"

Why the hell did he care? "I don't want to talk about it." Darting into a break between two garage bays, I looked around for a food vendor. I needed water. And maybe a cold shower.

Hayden, as always, didn't listen to what I was saying. "Got killed, huh? Did you stick to team statements? That's what you should do next time. The media loves crap like that. When a camera is on, just say stuff like, 'I owe it all to my crew, I'd be nothing without their support, I couldn't do what I do without the people behind me…' Do it next time, you'll see what I mean."

I had to wonder when he had become such an expert on all this. His *one* race in Daytona? Seriously, he was a freakin' street racer who had walked into this world from nowhere while I'd been immersed in it my entire life. Stopping beside a camper, I dug my nails into my palms. "I didn't ask for your advice. Go. Away."

He stared me down for a solid ten seconds before he said anything, and I swear, the air between us started smoking in the silence. When he finally spoke, his voice was that sensuous low tone that went straight to my libido. "When you get all fiery and defiant like that, it just makes me want to pinch you again."

My mind screamed at me to back up a step—this was quickly going somewhere I couldn't let it go—but my body refused to listen. "You wouldn't dare," I seethed, inadvertently leaning forward.

A small smile twitched his lips. "I love a good dare."

My breath picked up as we stared at each other, and I was rigid with tension, waiting for him to do…something. I wasn't sure what I would do when he finally did. I also wasn't sure what I would do if he didn't. Good or bad, right or wrong, I *needed* something to happen. The waiting was going to make me implode.

Hayden's breath had quickened as well, and his hands twitched, like he was restraining himself from grabbing me and dragging me into the camper beside us. Some perverse part of me wanted him to cave into temptation and do it. *Yes, take me in there, throw me down, and show me how well you handle a different set of curves.*

The back of his hand brushed my thigh, and I tensed. Was he actually going to do it? A gasp escaped me and his bedroom eyes grew even steamier. He wanted to do a lot more than pinch me, and I wanted to let him do it...and I felt horrible for feeling that way. *He has a family.*

"Say it," he murmured as his knuckle swept back and forth across my jeans. Every pass made me want him all the more.

Like we were mentally connected, I knew exactly what he wanted me to say. I leaned forward until our chests were completely touching. "I dare you." I elongated the words, made them low and sexy. My heart was pounding. *What am I doing?*

Hayden's eyes widened at the challenge. Desire clouded his features as he grabbed my ass and pulled me into his hips. A soft groan escaped me when I felt just how badly he wanted me. *Screw the pinch, just take me.*

"Oh, Kenzie, good, there you are. Your father is looking for you."

At hearing Nikki's voice, I shoved Hayden's hand away from my backside and spun around to face my friend. Shit. Had she seen Hayden copping a feel? How could I possibly explain that? How could I explain being in this random, out-of-the-way place with him? We shouldn't be together like this. We shouldn't be together at *all*!

Nikki was looking between Hayden and me with a baffled expression, like she was witnessing an impossibility that went against every law of nature. And it did. Bennetis and Coxes didn't hang out by strange campers together. Not if they wanted to keep their jobs. *Calm down, Kenzie. Act natural.*

Apparently, I didn't seem natural enough, and Nikki rapidly came to the conclusion that Hayden's attentions were unwanted. She wasn't too far off the mark. "What the hell are you doing with my girl, Benneti? You better step off before I call an official down here and have you arrested for badgering a witness! Er, I mean rider."

Cringing, I shot Nikki a look. She watched way too many lawyer dramas. Hayden smirked at her as he casually ran a hand through his hair. "I'm pretty sure they won't arrest me for *talking*...but I was just leaving anyway."

"Good," Nikki said. Then she stepped between the two of us like she was my bodyguard. Hayden shook his head as he walked by; Nikki glared at him the entire time. Once he was gone, she turned to face me, and her expression was a picture of concern. "You okay? What did he do? What did he say? Did he give you anything? Something to eat, something to drink? Did he touch you? Any skin-to-skin contact?"

Just thinking about the skin-to-skin contact I'd been hoping for had my cheeks hot. God, if she only knew, she'd flay me alive. "It was fine, Nikki. He was just giving me interview tips."

Nikki gave me an odd look and I instantly realized my mistake. I shouldn't have defended him. "Tips? Any tip from that guy is probably the exact opposite of what you should be doing. And have you heard his interviews? *No real competition for me out there, the only one I'm racing against is myself.* Conceited jerk."

My eyes widened at hearing that. No real competition? *Oh, we'll see about that.* Nikki nodded when she saw the heat flare in my eyes. "Yeah, and you know why he thinks that."

No, I wasn't sure that I did. "No... why?"

Nikki rolled her eyes at me. "Remember what Eli was talking about at the bull riding bar? The rumor floating around about Hayden? Well, what if it's not just a rumor?"

That night, it had seemed like Nikki hadn't been entirely sold on Eli's conspiracy theory. "I thought you didn't buy into that."

"Well, I might have played it down." She cringed. "I didn't want the guys to know about the street racing stuff—which I've stopped doing, just like you asked, so you can quit giving me the stink eye. But I don't know, Kenzie... there *were* some questionable crashes, some really odd malfunctions, and he *was* undefeated for a really long time. I just... I don't know. All I *do* know is that he's bad news. Be careful out there, okay?"

I gave her a stiff nod in response. It was all I could do.

CHAPTER 8

It was a beautiful day in Wisconsin, perfect for racing. Road America, the historic track at Elkhart, was the longest one in the series, with each lap coming in at just over four miles, but that meant we only had to do twelve laps to complete the almost fifty-mile sprint. It made the race feel even faster than it was.

I was itching to go by the time the race was due to start. My father gave me his ever-practical words of wisdom about control, then said, "You're building steam, but you need to maintain it to make it all the way up the mountain." Basically, what he meant was *Don't fuck up today, okay?*

I nodded at him, then shoved my helmet down over my head. His words made a heavy weight settle in my stomach. I didn't plan on fucking up, but things that were beyond my control happened in races…what if I didn't handle them properly? Inhaling a deep breath, I forced myself to focus on one idea that was much more satisfying—kicking Hayden's ass so hard he'd beg me for mercy.

When we were all positioned in our grids, waiting for the light to change, my grin grew so large, I thought my cheeks might split open. I had qualified to start in the top ten—a fact that thrilled me—but I was still a few spots below Hayden. That didn't please me so much. Even still, I had never been quite so pumped for a race before; the rush of being seconds away from racing Hayden again was rampaging through my veins like thousands of tiny charging bulls. I almost jumped the gun, I was so eager to start, but the light happened to turn at just the right instant, and I was free to be released. Hayden wasn't taking away a second of my time *this* race.

Excitement and energy ripped through me when I surged forward, and as I relaxed into my riding, only one thought pounded through my brain: *Catch Hayden*. The crowds in the stands morphed into an incoherent blur in my peripheral vision, and the other riders on the track became nothing more than numbered obstacles blocking my path to him. Where was he?

When I spotted him a few places in front of me, I pushed my bike to its limits. Passing him was my only concern. The road seemed to rise up to meet me on the corners, giving me the illusion that I was standing still and the course was moving. The rhythm of my bike's hum was perfect, my positioning as I hung low off the inside of the bike was flawless, and I was soaring with hope. As I shot past other riders like they were stationary, a tiny thought exploded to life. *There's no reason why I can't win this.*

It wasn't long until I was right on Hayden's tail. As if he could feel me behind him, he miraculously found more speed. But lap by lap, I gained on him. And once I got past him, everything else would fall into place. This race was mine.

As if the universe heard me, well over halfway through the race, one of the bikes in front of Hayden and me started spewing toxic black smoke. I looked over just in time to see the motorcycle shimmy and wobble, then the rider lost control; at the speed he was going, there was no way to get it back. The bike tumbled and flipped over and over down the center of the track, throwing the rider onto the concrete.

A warning flag immediately popped up, but it was too late for those of us following just a few seconds behind him. I dodged debris the best I could and tried not to look at the carnage. I wasn't sure which racer had fallen, but I hoped he was okay.

The red flag went up next, and it was quickly changed to a checkered flag. They were calling the race. My jaw dropped as I slowed my bike. No! I was so close to taking Hayden, so close to beating him. As worried as I was about the rider who'd crashed, I couldn't believe this was how today was going to end.

By the time we were all ushered into pit lane, I was steaming. I wanted the officials to help the rider, then clean up the track and let us go again. The race was unfinished, and I felt unsettled. But I knew they wouldn't let us compete anymore today. The race had been past the magic 80 percent mark—too close to the end to restart.

After hopping off my bike, I stormed into the cold pits. "I almost had him! A lap and a half! That was all I needed!" I violently chucked my helmet across the room. Thankfully, one of the nimbler crew members caught it; my dad hated it when equipment was damaged due to temper tantrums. Actually, he wasn't a big fan of temper tantrums altogether. *Keep it together, Kenzie.*

I was about to apologize for chucking my stuff when I noticed the tension in the air...and I didn't think it was because of my outburst. It felt like everyone was holding their breath, waiting for something. It made the hair on the back of my neck stand straight up, made my gut feel like I'd swallowed a handful of marbles. The fallen rider. He must be hurt pretty bad for everyone to be on pins and needles.

Everyone was focused on the TVs that showed various areas of the track, so I turned to look at them as well. An emergency vehicle was on the field, and three or four medics were surrounding a body lying on the ground. I couldn't tell who it was.

Over my shoulder, I spotted Nikki gnawing on her knuckle. Working my way back to her, I asked, "Who was it? Who crashed?" I'd been so focused on Hayden during the race, I had no clue who had gone down.

When Nikki turned her head my way, I saw that her eyes were watery. She looked on the verge of a complete meltdown. The discomfort in my stomach instantly shifted into sharp spears of pain. *Don't say it.*

Nikki swallowed before she spoke, and a single tear rolled down her cheek. "Myles," she whispered.

No. It couldn't have been Myles who wrecked—he *never* wrecked. Not like that. But now that I was revisiting the moment without Hayden foremost in my mind, I could see the blue-and-white jersey, see the number 12 on his bike as it toppled out of control. Shit…it *had* been Myles, and I hadn't even noticed. What the hell was wrong with me?

Panic and fear tightened my chest. "Is he…okay? What's going on?"

Nikki shook her head. "Don't know. Your dad is heading over there now. John is on the headset, listening for news…We just don't know anything yet, though. But…congratulations on your finish, Kenzie," she said, giving me a pat on the shoulder. "Eighth place is amazing. And you tied the record for a female finish on this track."

I'd been so preoccupied with the race being called that I hadn't checked my placement. I felt a little light-headed, like I should lie down. "Eighth? Tied the…" I was sure there was some coherent sentence I should be forming, I just couldn't get the words out.

Nikki let out a soft chuckle, then gave me a hug. When her arms wrapped around me, she started sobbing, and I instantly remembered *how* I'd ended up eighth. *Myles. Please let him be okay.*

Unable to just sit around and wait for news anymore, Nikki and I decided to go to the first aid station, where the ARRC kept a couple of doctors on staff. If they were going to take Myles anywhere once he left the track, it would be there. Unless it was his back or his neck—then an ambulance would take him straight to the hospital. I fervently hoped he came here first. *Please don't let it be serious.*

The garage bay being used as a makeshift doctor's office was pretty busy when we got there. Staff were treating dehydration, a nasty road rash, and even a gushing gash that was definitely going to need stitches. Every single one of the riders being cared for looked annoyed to be there. Riders preferred the walk-it-off treatment, but crew chiefs tended to disagree.

We heard Myles's name being spoken by a guy on a cell phone and we followed him to the corner of the room, where an exam table was being prepared. When Myles arrived on a stretcher, I breathed a sigh of relief—*Thank God, not a spinal injury*. There was a flurry of activity as he was brought into the garage, and my chest constricted at seeing my friend in pain. His neck might not be broken, but something was definitely wrong.

"Myles! Are you okay?" I surged forward to help, but staff members held me back.

A woman in a pristine white jacket folded her arms over her chest as she blocked our path. "I'm sorry, but unless you need treatment for something, you'll have to wait outside."

For a moment, I considered pretending that I'd reinjured my ankle, but then I thought better of it. Dad might actually believe me and make me stay off it for the next few days. "I just want to know what's happening with Myles Kelley, the Cox Racing rider who went down at the track. Can you tell me what you know?" I could hear Myles grunting and groaning in pain as he was moved to the exam table. The sound tore my heart, and it killed me that I couldn't do anything to help him.

The lady looked over her shoulder, where Myles was being helped out of his racing leathers. Turning back to us, she said, "When we know something, you'll know something. Until then, please wait outside."

I was about to argue when I happened to spot Dad. He was one of the people helping Myles undress. Stern-faced, he indicated with a jerk of his head that Nikki and I should leave, then he pulled a curtain around Myles's bed, shrouding them in privacy.

With a sigh, I started pulling Nikki out the garage door. If the nurse wouldn't tell us anything now, Dad certainly would later, and being in the way wouldn't really help anybody. Nikki was frazzled when we got outside, though, restless. Her manic energy was starting to infect me too. Watching her pace made me feel like a legion of ants were scurrying under my skin. "Hey, if you want to go work off some steam, I'll text you info as soon as I get it."

Nikki paused in her pacing to look at me. "Yeah, okay. I'm gonna go back to the garage…see if Kevin has heard anything about Myles's bike." We both knew the officials would be examining the bike first—for hours, probably—but Nikki needed something to do, so I gave her a hug, then let her go on her way.

Dad emerged from the first aid station about fifteen minutes later. He looked worn to the bone as he scrubbed his face with his hands. "How is he?" I hesitantly asked.

Dad sighed. "It looks like his leg is broken, possibly his collarbone too. They'll be taking him to the hospital soon. We'll know more then."

So many feelings hit me at once—sadness, guilt, relief—that my vision swam. Broken? No wonder he'd been in so much pain. Damn it, he'd been lying on the track in agony, and all I'd cared about was that the race had been called early. And now... Myles would need time off to rest. But how much time? How many events would he miss? Even if it was only one race, he was going to be crushed. "How long will he...? I mean, if it's broken, can he still...?" I couldn't even say my fear out loud.

Understanding my real question, Dad shook his head. "Most likely, he'll be out for the rest of the season."

The *entire* season... His year had just started, and it was already over. Myles... God, he was going to be devastated.

Dad put a hand on my shoulder, refocusing my attention. "You had a decent race today, Kenzie, even tied a record. But unfortunately... decent isn't enough anymore, *tying* isn't enough. I need you to step it up next race. With Myles out, you're our best shot for a win now. Don't let me down."

It was like he'd launched a wrecking ball of disappointment right at my gut; the hit almost made me double over. "Decent race"? "Not enough"? That was the encouragement I got for tying a record that had been in place for six years? I knew I shouldn't be disheartened—abundant praise wasn't Dad's style—but still I was hurt. And scared. *I'm the only hope for Cox Racing now? So, if I fail...*

I couldn't speak, so Dad must have figured we were done. He started moving past me, and I spun on my boot to face his retreating form. Really? That was it? *The future of the business rests on you... don't fuck up.* Was that supposed to inspire me? "Is that really all you have to say to me?" I sputtered.

Dad stopped and looked back. "Was there something else you wanted to hear?"

I lifted my hand, then let it drop back to my side with a heavy thud. "I tied a record, Dad. That means something. How about 'Congratulations'? 'Nice work'? 'Great racing out there'?" *How about "I love you, no matter how you finish"?*

Dad's brows knitted together, and I could see that I was irritating him by asking for a compliment. Embarrassment and discomfort crashed through me, and I wanted to be anywhere other than here. I shouldn't have opened my mouth; I should have let him walk away. Dad hated pity parties, and he'd made it well known that he wasn't in the business of placating whiners. He made *racers.* That was what he did. And I…respected that.

"I'm not here to hold your hand, Mackenzie. You have friends for that. I'm here to forge you into a better rider, and I'm sorry to tell you, but when I watch you race, I see *a lot* of room for improvement. I can't afford to give you superfluous praise when I know you're better than what you're showing me. I'd be short-changing you, and this team. When you *win* the race, or better yet, when you win *multiple* races, then I'll ease up and congratulate you. And maybe that seems harsh to you, but that's the reality of our situation. *Everything* depends on you now, and I won't let you be satisfied with eighth place, not when you have the potential for first. Now, if you'll excuse me, I have a statement to make."

With that, he turned and left. Rage, sadness, and understanding battled within me as I watched him go. He was right; he wasn't here to baby me. But on the other hand, I *was* his baby, his youngest child. Where was the balance? It was all work with him, all the time. Maybe that was the real reason both of my sisters had quit riding. They had known what I was only just beginning to understand: Dad couldn't be a leader *and* a father. He just wasn't capable of wearing two hats at the same time.

Wiping tears from my cheeks, I twisted back around to go check on Myles. After I turned, I noticed someone unexpected watching me. Hayden. And from the blank expression on his face, he'd witnessed that entire incident between my father and me. Great. I really didn't want to show weakness in front of him, especially family weakness. *Yes, the legendary father-and-daughter Cox Racing team isn't perfect.* What on this earth was?

I didn't want Hayden to see me like this, and I really didn't want him to talk to me while I felt like this. I wasn't sure if I would rip him to pieces or fall apart in his arms. He was examining me with concern on his face; it was an expression I wasn't used to seeing on him, and it made me uneasy. I think I would have preferred him looking at me like he wanted to rip my clothes off.

Hayden's eyes shifted to where my dad had gone. "Hard to please," he stated.

Sometimes I felt like he was impossible to please. "He has his reasons," I said, my voice sharp. I felt my eyes stinging with traitorous tears. No. I would *not* cry in front of him. "What are you doing here?" I asked, blinking as quickly as I could.

Hayden had a speculative look on his face as he studied me, like he was seeing things in a different light. It was frustrating; I didn't want him to see me in *any* light. He was silent a long time, so long I thought he wasn't going to answer. Then he said, "Be happy you have him. It's harder with no one." His voice was quiet, understanding. I wasn't used to either of those things from him. It made my heart beat faster, and I wasn't sure why.

Just when I was about to ask him what he meant by that, a voice behind him shouted, "Hey, shit stain! Keith wants to see you. Now!"

Ice froze my chest. *No.* Someone had spotted us. Well, we weren't doing anything…just talking, and barely talking at that. Immediately after the chill came a flash of heat. *Shit stain?* Had they seriously just called him that? And why did it bother me?

Hayden and I turned to see a pair of riders wearing Benneti jackets strutting our way. Their faces were picture-perfect portrayals of cocky self-assurance. Even though I'd never personally talked to them before, I recognized them from the track—Maxwell and Rodney. Assholes extraordinaire.

When Maxwell reached Hayden, he shoved a finger into his chest. "Whatcha doing? Fraternizing with a Cox? Interesting…if you grab us some beers on the way back to Keith, we just might fail to mention this to him." Looking over at me, he winked, "Hey there, gorgeous."

Hayden cracked a smile, but his eyes grew ice cold. "Watch it, Maxwell. She bites, especially when douchebags call her pet names."

Maxwell's face turned to stone. "After you're done with Keith, smartass, you can wash the bikes. All of them. Unless you want us to mention your little rendezvous, of course." Rodney grunted and punched Hayden in the arm, hard, then the pair of them walked off. They high-fived each other as they strutted, like they'd actually done something worth celebrating. Jerks.

Hayden's face was even, emotionless, but that had to have upset him. Maybe that was what he'd meant by *harder with no one*. "Hard to please?" I asked, trying to lighten the mood.

He smirked, and the icy void around him lifted. "Yeah, like your dad, they're dicks. Doesn't matter, though, I'm not here to make friends."

Clearly not, since he just insulted my dad. *You don't know anything about him.* As anger churned within me, Hayden's proposition to practice together raced through my mind, along with the memory of him walking down the street with his girl and his child. No, Hayden was definitely only here to win. Whatever heat I felt coming from him was just a ploy to get me to agree to training.

"I should go check on Myles—" I began, frost in my voice. Before I could finish my goodbye, I noticed someone near the bushes hissing to get Hayden's attention. And unless I was mistaken…it was the little guy from the bar. And standing a few feet behind him, not even bothering with discretion, was the big guy from the bar. What the hell were they doing here? "Um…I think someone else wants to speak to you." Was Hayden's family here too? Great. What was I doing talking to him?

Hayden turned to see where I was looking. When he saw the two guys, he sighed. "Right. I should take care of that." He looked back at me. "Good race today, Twenty-Two."

My mood fluctuated again at the sincerity I heard in his voice.

"Thanks..." Not liking the butterflies in my stomach as I thanked him, I quickly blurted out, "Your teammate jerks won't actually say anything to Keith, will they?" God, I hoped not.

Hayden didn't looked worried, though. "I'm not about to get fired. I'll do *whatever* I need to do to make sure they keep their mouths shut. You have nothing to worry about."

His answer was what I wanted to hear, but it still made a flash of unease go through me. "Yeah...okay. Well, see ya around, Forty-Three." Wait, what? *Why did I say that?* I wasn't going to see him around. I didn't plan on crossing paths with him ever again if I could help it. Watching him walk away, I saw him meet up with his friends. The little hyper one was pointing at his watch and gesturing over his shoulder. Hayden nodded, pointed toward the Benneti camp, then patted his friend on the shoulder and started walking away. His friends looked a little irritated as they watched him leave, like they'd thought he'd immediately go with them or something. I wondered what they'd been talking about, then I wondered why I cared. None of this had anything to do with me.

Annoyed at my own curiosity, I stepped into the first aid station to talk to Myles. The mood around his exam table was heavy. The staff had carefully crafted expressions on their faces; just by looking at them I could tell things with Myles were bad. He was staring up at the ceiling when I reached the side of the table. His face was strained, like he was trying to bottle up the pain.

"Hey, Myles," I said, lightly squeezing his arm. "How...are you?"

"So long as I don't move, I'm great," he said through clenched teeth. His eyes flicked over to mine; they were laced with agony. "How did you do?"

With a sad smile, I shook my head. "Your leg is broken, and you're asking how I finished?"

Myles shrugged, then sucked in a sharp breath. "Well, it beats thinking about how *I* did," he grunted.

Grief and guilt squeezed my heart. "I'm so sorry, Myles," I whispered, shifting my stance as an uncomfortable emotion settled between us.

I hoped he would say something funny to dispel the awkwardness, like he usually did in situations like this, but instead his eyes grew dark with anger. He looked around to see if we were alone, then tried to move in closer. Shifting was obviously causing him pain, so I leaned down to help him out. When I did, he snarled, "That wreck wasn't natural, Kenzie. Somebody messed with me."

His statement shocked me to the core. This was no small accusation he was making. "Myles, you can't seriously be suggesting that…" I couldn't even say it. "Wrecks happen. It sucks, but it's a part of racing, you know that."

He pressed his lips together. "Not like that. You don't know what it felt like before I went down. I didn't hit an oil patch, didn't lose control, didn't slam into somebody. No, something popped on the bike…and there was a flash of light…then all of a sudden, it started vibrating like it was shaking to pieces. You know how well Nikki and Kevin maintain the bikes. There's no way it just…broke apart."

I wanted to tell him that of course it was plausible that it had just broken apart, the very act of racing was hard on the equipment, but I knew he wouldn't listen to me right now—he was in shock, in pain, and most likely wishing he were knocked out. "Myles, you should rest—"

Lifting up slightly, Myles hissed, "You heard what Eli said. Hayden will do *anything* to win. I think Eli was right, and I think Hayden put something on my bike…"

His eyes fluttered closed and he fell back onto the table with a thud. Staff rushed around him, pushing me away. I was so stunned, I let them. I wanted to write off the crazy talk Myles was spouting—it had to be the pain talking—but something he'd said was making a warning light flicker in the back of my brain: *Hayden will do anything to win.* That sentence was quickly followed by Hayden's ominous words of encouragement. *I'll do* whatever *I need to do…*

Right. And what exactly did that mean?

CHAPTER 9

Sitting up in my bed back at home, I gave up on the sleep that wasn't happening. My mind was too full to rest. Instead of checking the clock to see what time it was, I looked out my bedroom window. Darkness was still clinging to the countryside, but a faint glow from the east was just beginning to caress the sky. It was way too early to drive down to the family track, but it wasn't too early to head out to the ocean to ride some waves. Maybe being on the water would help clear my head.

Getting out of bed, I plodded to the closet and grabbed my swimsuit and wetsuit; I might live in California, but the ocean in the springtime was still chilly, even here. Once I was dressed, I made my way to the opposite end of the house. It didn't take long. The place I rented was small: just one bedroom, one bath, a small living room, and a kitchen. It was only me here, though—I didn't even own a pet to keep me company. I liked to keep things simple, efficient. The hallways were bare; the bathroom only had a toothbrush and a handful of toiletries, all neatly arranged. The only photos in the house were in the living room—my parents' wedding picture, a holiday picture of my dad and my sisters, and me on my very first bike at my very first event. That was about as much as I did for decoration. I just wasn't here all that often. If I wasn't traveling to an event or at the track practicing, I was at a friend or family member's house. My home was really just a place to sleep at night.

Once I was in my garage, I bypassed my bike and headed to the old beat-up truck that I'd purchased from Myles. While riding a motorcycle was my preferred method of travel, it wasn't always a practical option.

My surfboard was resting in its place, on hooks along the garage wall. After taking a minute to secure the board to my truck, I headed out. It was peaceful outside this early in the morning. Calming. No hustle, no bustle, no traffic. Just silence. And as dawn crept ever closer, more yellows, oranges, and reds painted the sky, turning it into a masterpiece so perfect, it would surely make even the greatest artists in the world weep.

Despite the beauty around me, I couldn't keep my mind from returning to the track. Ever since returning from Road America, my times had slipped. Hard as it was to admit, my laps were nowhere near as fast as when I raced against Hayden. It was like being on the track with him gave me a shot of adrenaline that nothing else seemed to replicate.

Spotting the turnoff to my favorite local beach, I carefully drove down the bumpy dirt road. Occasionally other vehicles would be parked in the small patch of weeds that the locals used as a makeshift parking lot, but today it was just me.

Removing my board from my truck, I picked my way through the grass to the rocky shore of the beach. The rhythmic sound of the waves instantly calmed me. Sliding my board into the water, I waded in. Once I was waist-deep, I dunked myself, then slicked my hair back. The chill made me shiver, but it didn't take long for me to acclimate.

I worked my way past where the waves were breaking, then straddled my board. Taking a deep, cleansing breath, I glanced around the quiet cove. Dawn had turned the sky a restful shade of pale pink, and the shore was clearly visible now. It was a perfect day for surfing. The birds were awake, chirping their greetings, and the scent of seawater permeated the air. Oddly, the smell reminded me of Hayden.

Finding a potential wave I liked, I quickly paddled to the edge, then hopped up on both feet. The rush it gave me when I hit the sweet spot wasn't quite as satisfying as the thrill I got from racing, but it was pretty close. Smiling ear to ear, I balanced on the precipice of potential disaster, almost all the way to the shore.

For the next hour, I enjoyed the waves as the ocean and I got to know each other on this idyllic morning. All thoughts of the pressures of living up to my family name, of Myles's season-ending wreck, his startling pronouncement of Hayden's possible involvement in said wreck, the many mysteries surrounding Hayden, and all the unnerving yet enticing things I felt around him when we found ourselves alone slipped my mind. There was just me, the board, and the surf. Heaven.

Unfortunately, heaven couldn't last forever, and before I was truly ready to part with my peace-filled solitude, it was time for me to get to work.

After doing a quick parking lot wardrobe change, I drove my truck to the track. Dad's truck told me he was already there, along with Kevin, Eli, and Ralph. Surprisingly, Nikki's smart car was there too. I think I could count the number of times she'd beaten me to the track on one hand. She was really torn up about what had happened to Myles. I think she blamed herself. She wasn't Myles's primary mechanic, but she always looked over his bike before he went out; she was convinced she'd missed something.

Parking next to my dad, I locked up my truck and headed to the garage. Like they had been the last several days, Nikki and Kevin were scouring the bits and pieces of Myles's bike, looking for clues. After it had tossed him to the ground, the bike had rolled, flipped, tumbled, and ripped apart. It wasn't repairable, and neither Dad nor Myles could afford to replace it right now. One more problem resting on my shoulders as the last hope for Cox Racing.

Nikki cast a glance my way when I walked in. "Hey," I said. "How's it going?"

She sighed as she wiped her hands on a towel. "It shouldn't have just fallen apart like that, and it's such a mess now, I can't tell why it did." She tossed her towel onto her workbench in frustration.

"I'm sure you guys will figure something out," I told her, trying to be encouraging.

She gave me an appreciative half smile. "Thanks. Oh…I should tell you…" The smile completely fell off her face. "You know the interview you did at Road America? The one they keep replaying nonstop? Your dad just got off the phone with the officials…they've decided to fine Cox Racing for what you said about Jimmy. They're considering it slander. Sanctimonious assholes." She rolled her eyes.

A sick feeling started knotting up my stomach. "That jerk said he'd trim that part."

Nikki cringed. "I know. No one's even talking about the fact that you tied the record. They're all caught up on that stupid interview. And Myles's wreck. They won't shut up about that either. It's sickening. Makes me want to…" She smacked her fist into her hand for emphasis.

I smiled at her attempt to defend Myles's and my honor, but Nikki wouldn't hurt a fly and we both knew it. And besides, there was no one to hurt here. Just bad fucking luck and my loose tongue. "I better go smooth things over with Dad. He's probably pissed."

"It's hard to tell with him; he always seems the same, but yeah…with Jimmy leaving, Myles out for the count, and your sister's wedding getting more and more expensive by the day—did you hear that she wants doves *and* butterflies now? Diva. Well, on top of all that, this was about the last thing he needed." She sighed, then her eyes went wide. "Not that it's your fault or anything. I would have answered the same way; that interviewer was a total douchebag for airing it."

I thanked her for trying to cheer me up, then headed upstairs to face my dad. It felt good hearing Nikki defend me, but I knew exactly whose fault this one was.

As soon as I stepped into my father's office, I could tell by the stern look on his face that I was in for a lecture. To buy myself some time, I tried to throw him off guard with a fact I knew he wasn't thrilled about. "So…I hear Daphne wants you to pick a father/

daughter song for the reception. Have you considered 'Butterfly Kisses'? It's a little sappy, but easy enough to dance to."

The steel look on Dad's face melted into a grimace. "Don't remind me…" Like clearing an Etch A Sketch, he shook his head. "I take it Nikki told you about the fine?"

I nodded. "And the doves. Does Daphne really want her guests pooped on?" Dad crossed his arms over his chest and I sighed. "I know, I know. I'm sorry. You know I'm horrible at interviews anyway, and they caught me by surprise, and whenever I think about Jimmy I just want to…" Lifting my hands, I started choking Jimmy's imaginary neck.

Dad cracked a smile. It quickly faded. "I understand the instinct, Mackenzie, but you need to control your tongue just as much as your body. Perhaps more. The fine wasn't large, but it was enough to leave a mark on our bottom line. And with Myles out…" He ran a hand down his face. "Ready or not, I need you to be exemplary right now."

"I know, Dad. I'm—"

He didn't let me finish. "Then please explain why your lap times have been slacking since Wisconsin—considerably slacking. You're better than this. What's going on?"

You placed the fate of the entire business in my inexperienced hands, and I'm stumbling under the weight. That's what's going on.

Unable to point out the pressure I was under so bluntly, I shrugged and gave him the most pathetic answer possible. "I don't know. I'm trying, Dad, it's just…not happening for some reason."

Dad's lips curved into a hard-edged frown. He hated getting half-assed answers. He wanted facts. My time sucked because of A, B, or C. Period. Vagueness didn't sit right with him. "Mackenzie, now is not the time to start falling apart. Barber will be here before you know it."

Barber. My favorite track as a kid, and I was finally going to be racing on it. I should have been over the moon with excitement, but my eagerness was coated with dread. What if I couldn't get it together in time? What if I failed? Swallowing my fear, I told Dad, "I'll be ready." Somehow.

As if he didn't believe my confident statement, Dad let out a weary sigh as he sat on the corner of his desk, which was, as usual, littered with paperwork—invoices, from what I could tell. "I don't understand. You were on pace to break records, but now...I just don't understand."

I bit my lip to hold in the truth: that I just couldn't get anything under control anymore. What was wrong felt right, what was right felt wrong, and the only way I seemed to be able to push myself to greatness was by chasing Hayden.

Still not able to speak my true thoughts, I said the only thing I could. "I'll do better."

Frustrated with my inability to pinpoint the problem, Dad said, "Is this because of what happened to Myles? Are you worried? Upset? That I could understand, at least." Pressing his lips together, he shook his head. "Myles told me his theory about his bike...that he saw something go off...that he's positive someone messed with it. He wants me to have the race officials open an investigation."

Chilling shock coated me with fear. I didn't want to believe Myles was right—about the tampering *or* about Hayden's involvement. It had to be a random accident. An official looking into it...might prove otherwise. *But isn't that a good thing?* If Hayden was guilty, he should be punished. Severely. "Are...you going to?"

Dad sighed again. "No. Whatever was done to the bike, there isn't enough evidence after the crash to prove wrongdoing. It's just conjecture at this point, and it would only aggravate the officials to bring it to them. And they're annoyed with us enough as it is..." He flashed a glance at me and I cringed before schooling my features. *Yeah, because of my stupid interview.*

Heat in his eyes, Dad briefly peered out the window overlooking the track. "If Myles says he saw something, felt something...then I believe him. And I definitely wouldn't put it past Keith to pull crap like that. There's not much he won't do to win. And hiring that Hayden kid to do his dirty work...well, it wouldn't shock me. Rumor is, Keith found him on the street. Did you know that?"

I kept my expression very even. "I just don't know if I can believe that anyone, even Keith, would sink to that level, Dad. There must be another explanation for what happened." *There has to be.*

Dad's face clouded over as he gave the window one final glare. "There is *nothing* I wouldn't put past Keith." As he looked over at me, his brow softened with concern. "Just be careful out there, Mackenzie. If someone *has* sunk that low...I don't want you getting caught in the cross fire. I know I don't need to tell you this, but be wary of the Bennetis. The *entire* team."

Swallowing a tight lump in my throat, I told him, "I will," then I quickly turned to leave his office.

Before I could escape, Dad called my name. When I looked back at him, his face was once again the stern visage of a disappointed leader. "Whatever is going on with you, Mackenzie, I need you to figure it out, and I need you to fix it. Fast. Whatever it takes, just...fix it. For me. For the team." His eyes grew heavy from the weight of his inner burdens. "Please. We need you."

His plea stung, and nodding, I quickly left the room. Dad was counting on me to carry the glory of his name, and I was letting him down. He was right, bit by bit, day by day, I was slipping. If I didn't change something—*now*—I was going to completely fail my father. Possibly send him into bankruptcy. Or worse. There was only one thing I could think of that might potentially prevent that from happening. And it was also something that would instantly get me fired if Dad knew about it.

Damn it. For better or worse...I needed to train with Hayden.

I needed to feed off his competitive spirit. I needed to let go of everything holding me back, tune out the entire world and focus on nothing but him. I needed that fire I felt when we were together. That fire would blaze me to a glorious finish. My family's legacy depended on it.

But how? Hayden and I couldn't practice together on the track. We couldn't even *be* on the track at the same time; Hayden's little chip-removal had worked once, but that wouldn't be enough every single time. Eventually we'd be spotted. The track was too busy. And Jesus...was I really considering taking him up on his offer? Hayden? The former illegal street racer? The potential saboteur who might be the reason Myles got hurt? The guy whose friends started bar fights? The guy with a kid and a girlfriend. The guy I knew next to nothing about? Was that who I wanted to get *even more* involved with?

Did I have *any* other choice?

Jesus, this was a horrible idea. But it was the only one I had left.

As I went to the gym to lift weights, I considered how to contact Hayden. We needed to talk, that much was clear, but we needed to do it privately, and that was exceedingly hard to do inside the racetrack complex. My father couldn't know the secret to my success, especially now, when he suspected Keith had hired Hayden to mess with riders. Dread settled over me as I considered the fact that the man I was hoping would help me hone my skills might also be setting other people up for failure. If that was true... would I be next? God, that put a whole new spin on this dangerous arrangement I was about to make.

Since I didn't have his phone number, I couldn't just text him to meet up, so I did the only thing I could think of. I hovered around the practice track and waited for him to show. Once twelve o'clock hit and all the riders going into and out of the track were Bennetis and not Coxes, I got a lot of crap for being at the track entrance. "Go home, Cox, you're not welcome here." "You lost, little girl?" And my personal favorite, "Aww, did you break your bike? Or break a nail?" Asswipes.

"Hurry the fuck up, Hayes," I muttered. The longer I waited for him, the worse I felt: light-headed, yet anxious too.

A voice off to my right answered my disgruntled muttering. "Sorry, didn't realize I was late." I snapped my head around to see Hayden walking his bike my way. His gait was slow and steady, and his long, lean body was enticingly defined by his tight racing leathers. All my favorite things were on display, and it was really hard to not allow myself to appreciate them.

When he was so close to me I could smell the unexplainable scent of summer on his skin, he asked, "What are you doing here after noon, Twenty-Two? Or did we have a date I wasn't aware of? If so, this probably isn't the best place to get to know each other. What with the no-fraternizing rule and all." His green eyes sparkled with playfulness as his mouth curved into a one-sided smirk that would defrost even the iciest libido. Lord knows it was making *my* heart beat harder. *No. That's not what this is about.*

"We need to talk, but not in the open like this. Meet me here... at this beach." I quickly handed him a folded piece of paper with directions to my favorite hangout scribbled on it. My cell number was also hastily written across the bottom of the note. *I can't believe I'm actually doing this.*

Hayden's eyebrows crawled farther and farther up his forehead as he took the note. "I must have fallen asleep in the sauna, because there is no way you seriously just invited me to meet you somewhere?" he whispered, looking around for anyone who might be close enough to hear us. Luckily, we were alone. We wouldn't be for long, though.

"Tomorrow morning, dawn. Don't be late." With those words, I started walking my bike away. Considering every red flag between us, it was surprisingly hard to move away from him.

From behind me, I heard him say, "Can I ask what this is about?"

"No," I said, not turning around. "Not here."

* * *

I packed my surfboard the next morning, thinking I might unwind while I waited for Hayden, but I was so riled, I wasn't sure if even surfing would relax me. Asking for help with anything was difficult, but asking for help from *Hayden* was going against the laws of nature. Impossible. But I didn't have a choice; I couldn't let my team down, my father down. I *refused* to be the weakest link, the one who put the final nail in the family business's coffin.

When I arrived at my hidden beach, I immediately saw Hayden sitting on his motorcycle nestled in the weeds. All thoughts of surfing away my tension vanished. *Here we go.* Parking next to him, I took a nice, long, cleansing breath. This was nothing. Simple.

Taking off his helmet, Hayden started walking my way. His every movement was fluid, sensual, like he commanded the laws of physics instead of following them. He walked in front of my truck, and the headlights splashed over him, highlighting his blond hair and making his eyes flash bright green, like jewels in the early-morning light. In an instant, one of my steamier fantasies leaped into my head—racing him, chasing him, his hands, his mouth, his body over mine…

God, I bet he would feel good. But just because he might feel good didn't mean he was good for me. Besides being an asshole on a team solely comprised of assholes, he was deeply involved with someone—*bad idea* was practically stamped on his forehead. I had to be careful, had to keep this on a very narrow path. Even still, my breath was quicker when he stopped outside my door, my pulse even faster. A dark part of me craved a slipup, a tiny moment of connection, something scintillating to add to my mental movie. *No, stop that. Mind over matter. Control. Stick to the plan.* These were my mantras as I shut off my truck and stepped outside into the cool morning air.

When I was as close to him as I felt comfortable getting, I stopped. His eyes inspected every inch of me, and I no longer felt cold; I was a little surprised steam wasn't rising from my skin.

"You wanted to see me? Alone? Are you finally going to tell me what this is about?"

"You…were right. I'm better with you." Those words were surprisingly painful to say. Hoping my cheeks weren't flaming red, I kept my back straight and my chin lifted. I probably looked like a goddamn military recruit, I was so rigid, but somehow being stiff made me feel like my pride was more or less intact, even if it wasn't.

"Yes…you are." Hayden's grin shifted into something a lot more sensual. The way his eyes gleamed and his lips curved spoke to the most basic part of me, ignited senses that I could never quite keep dormant around him. My body was whispering dark and sinister thoughts to my brain. Thoughts like *Look at those lips. Picture them all over your body. What harm could it do?*

No. It could do a lot of harm to a lot of people, and I wasn't about to let that happen. It took some willpower, but I firmly squashed the insane words that were rattling my attention-starved sex drive. I was here to ask him to practice with me so I would perform better at the next event. Nothing more. "Whatever you're thinking, just back that thought right up. I was talking about racing together."

As if he heard my internal debate, Hayden's smile grew wider. "So was I."

Irritated that this wasn't going as planned, I spat out, "Look, my family is in trouble, and I'm the only one who can get us out of it." My eyes widened when I realized what I'd just confessed to him. I hadn't meant to say anything other than I'd changed my mind and I wanted to race with him. I hadn't meant to give him details.

His expression softened as he gazed at me. "What kind of trouble?"

Stalling for time, I considered making something up, something less horrible than the truth. Our financial woes were no great secret, though, and he'd probably already heard some rumors. Still, it wasn't something I was comfortable talking to a stranger about, and my throat locked up like someone had frozen it shut.

As if he knew what I was struggling with, Hayden ducked down to make eye contact with me. "What trouble, Kenzie?" he softly repeated.

Something about the tone of his voice loosened my throat. "Our best racer left this year, taking a huge sponsor with him. And with Myles breaking his leg and being out for the rest of the year, plus my sister wanting this insane celebrity-level-type wedding and my dad seemingly unable to tell her no... well, this might be Cox Racing's last year... unless I start winning. Or at least garner some attention that's not negative. We need sponsors, we need advertising deals, we need... wins." Having told him so much about my problems was making my palms sweat and my heart surge, but inhaling a big breath, I mentally prepared myself to throw it all out there. "My times without you are nowhere near my times *with* you, so... if I'm going to save the family business... I need you. To practice with," I quickly added before he could get any lewd ideas.

Hayden's eyes drifted over to the surfboard strapped to my truck as he considered what to say. There was a stern seriousness to his expression when he looked back at me. "This year is important to me too, Kenzie. Maybe for different reasons… but it's just as…" He snapped his mouth shut, while my mind raced with questions—I knew what *I* was fighting for, but what was he after? Glory? Riches? More women to knock up? Yeah, probably.

"Okay, Twenty-Two," he said with a smile. "No one can know we're working together, though. We'll have to keep everyone completely in the dark. *Everyone*. I know you're close to your team… are you comfortable with that?"

He lifted the eyebrow with the alluring scar through it while he waited for my answer. God, was I comfortable with *any* of this? But he was right. No one could know we were conspiring together. "Yes," I whispered; my voice refused to go any louder.

Hayden ran a hand through his hair as he thought. It was distractingly attractive. "We'll have to meet at the track at night. It's the only time we can be alone there."

Alone. Just the word made me shiver. Was this a horrible mistake? "The garages are locked at night," I said, frowning. "And I don't have a key." And if I didn't have one to my family's garage, I doubted Hayden had one to Keith's.

He flashed me a grin, though. "Don't worry about that. I'll get us in."

An uncomfortable feeling started hardening my gut. Who exactly was I getting into bed with? Figuratively speaking, of course. "Okay… but my dad is usually there until ten or eleven. We'll have to meet around midnight. That work for you?"

Hayden looked up in the air, like he was checking his mental calendar. Really? He had plans that late at night? Maybe with his girl… Nodding, he finally said, "Yeah, that will work. See you there, Twenty-Two."

"Yeah…" Our eyes locked, and as if the green depths of his irises were swirling with magical hypnotic powers, I couldn't look away. I felt him draw nearer, and a rush of anticipation surged through me. Every sense sharpened, coming to life like a flower unfurling in the sun—the cool breeze tickled my skin and the sound of the surf dozens of feet away pounded my brain. All I could see, though, was Hayden. His eyes, his skin, his lips as they inched ever closer to mine…

He tentatively raised his hand, then softly cupped my cheek. The contact shocked reality back to my system, and every reason I didn't want him touching me came flaring back to life. *Not him.*

Raising my hands to his chest, I shoved him back. "Hey! Just because I agreed to race with you doesn't mean I agreed to do anything else with you." The shock on Hayden's face made me stumble over my words. "I mean…you're with that girl, and…you have a kid, for God's sake. You shouldn't be…" I wanted to crawl into a hole and never come out. This was not a conversation I wanted to have with him. What he did and who he did it with didn't matter. At all.

"What the hell are you talking about?" he asked, confusion clearly written all over his face.

Well, shit. Now I was going to have to explain that I'd kind of been keeping tabs on him. "The bar…that woman…I saw you in town with her and a little girl, and you all looked so…" I squeezed my eyes shut, mortified, then cracked one open. "She's not your girlfriend?"

Hayden's gaze shifted over my shoulder for a second before returning to mine. "Wait, are you talking about Izzy? You saw me with her daughter and you thought…" His confusion shifted to amusement so suddenly that I instantly knew I'd gotten it all wrong. *Okay, not his baby momma then.* "No, there is nothing going on between Izzy and me. She's like my sister," he said with a laugh. "And Antonia is *definitely* not my daughter. I'm completely single, Kenzie, if that's what you're asking." A devilish gleam brightened his eyes.

Feeling embarrassed, self-conscious, and so uncomfortable I wished I could run to the beach and slip under the waves for an hour, I blurted out, "Did you have anything to do with what happened to Myles?" I checked on him as often as I could, and he was still convinced Hayden was the reason he crashed.

The amusement on Hayden's face winked out in a flash; it was replaced with cold, hard steel. "What? Why would you ask me that? Why would you even *think* that?"

This was better. Being the source of his anger was much easier to deal with than being the source of his mirth. "Rumor is, you were so good at street racing because you made sure you'd win. Rumor is, you'll do anything to get to the top."

A vein in his neck began to pulsate as his mood darkened. "And you believe every rumor you hear?"

The heat in his eyes was making my heartbeat quicken for a completely different reason; how was he still this attractive when his blood was boiling? "No. But I believe our mechanics don't know what happened to Myles's bike. I believe he's too good of a rider to lose control for no reason. And when he says he heard a pop and saw a flash of light before his bike started rattling to pieces…well, I believe that too."

A strange expression flickered across Hayden's face, and his eyes were speculative when he looked away. Was that surprise on his face? Or guilt? His features were smooth again when he looked back at me. "I left the streets for a reason, Kenzie, and I have no desire to go back. I'm trying to start over, and the last thing I want to do is mess that up. Believe me or don't, but I didn't touch Myles's bike."

I really wasn't sure whether I could believe him. But sadly, I needed him too much to walk away.

CHAPTER 10

Around eleven, I almost had myself convinced that I'd dreamed the early-morning meeting with Hayden. I hadn't actually done that, had I? Gone behind my team's back and made a peace treaty with the enemy? But like it or not, he *was* the key to our future. Within him was the power to unlock what was within me.

As time mercilessly ticked forward, I paced my living room. Getting ready to go to the track at this hour felt all wrong. I should be fast asleep, resting and recharging my batteries, not planning to disobey every single rule my father had all in one fell swoop. Wearing a path in my light-blue carpet, I debated just not showing up at the track. After a couple of hours, Hayden would get the message that I'd changed my mind. But then…what would I do? Accept my falling times with grace? Fuck. That.

Raking my hands through my hair in frustration, I begged my mind to shut off, to relax, to take the night off. *Let instinct take over for once.* Just as my brain was telling me where I could shove instinct, my cell phone chimed.

With a sigh, I walked over to the coffee table and picked it up. The number wasn't one I recognized, but the message made it clear who it was from. *See you at the track in twenty minutes, 22. Don't be late.* Damn it. Why the hell had I given Hayden my number again?

After programming his number into my phone under the name Major Asshat, I tucked my cell into my pocket and grabbed my coat. Might as well get this over with.

A little while later, the headlight of my motorcycle was splashing across the recently repaired Cox Racing/Benneti Motorsports Practice Track sign. It was odd to be arriving here at night. Even odder to be meeting up with a Benneti…with Hayden, a very single Benneti. It was almost easier when I'd believed he was taken. That mystery woman and her child had put some sort of buffer between us, and now that it was gone, I felt exposed. Being alone with him here was such a bad idea, but desperate times…

I couldn't stop looking around as I drove the short distance to the outer gate; I felt like my father could somehow see me, could possibly even feel my betrayal. *You won't understand, Dad, but I'm doing this for you.*

Using my key card, I punched in the code to open the gate. No problems there, unless my father decided to check the log. Everyone used the same code, though, even the Bennetis, so all he would know was that someone had stopped by at an odd hour. I drove my motorcycle through the parking lot to the inner gate, where I could see Hayden sitting on his bike, waiting for me. This gate, like the garages, was locked with a key.

While I rolled to a stop at the first obstacle blocking us, Hayden removed his helmet and walked over to the padlock keeping the rolling gate together. He flashed a too-damn-attractive grin at me, and I again cursed fate for putting us in this position. Why couldn't he be happy and committed to that girl? It would make being around him so much simpler.

Squatting down, Hayden looked at the underside of the lock. "If you break it, they'll know someone was here," I warned. The track didn't have cameras, but it might soon if this went badly.

Hayden looked back at me with an expression that clearly said, *I'm not an idiot.* It also said, *This isn't my first rodeo.* The former was amusing, the latter…disturbing.

Reaching into his pocket, Hayden pulled out some tools before returning his attention to the lock. He got to work picking it, and I shook my head in disbelief. "Left the streets behind, huh?" I muttered.

With a cocky grin on his face, he looked over his shoulder. "I said I'm *trying* to leave them behind. But sometimes the streets are the only way to get things done." His smile shifted into a frown as he returned to the lock.

Before I could ask what he meant by that comment, the lock sprang open. With a triumphant expression, he slipped the hook around a loop in the chain-link fence and pushed the gate open. Then he held his arm out wide and bowed, like he was welcoming the princess to her palace. Jackass.

I drove my bike over to the Cox garage and waited for Hayden to catch up. I couldn't believe I was about to let him pick the lock to my father's building, but unfortunately, it had to be done. Pulling up behind me, he hopped off his bike and got to work breaking the law. As he knelt in front of the main door to the garage, his leather jacket lifted, showing a little skin above his jeans. Watching the alluring movement was distracting me from the B&E taking place right in front of my face, and he was done before I knew it. He spun around while I was still staring at his backside, and the shift in my view snapped my eyes to his face. Damn it. I hated getting caught. This already wasn't going well.

Hayden's grin said everything he didn't. *You like that view, don't you?* No. Not really. Maybe…

With a groan, I entered the garage and flicked on the lights. Hayden took a look around with a nod of approval. When his eyes settled on me, he said, "I'm going to head over to Keith's garage. Meet you at the track?"

I nodded and he turned and left. And damn if I wasn't captivated by the way his ass moved when he walked away from me. Jesus. Why couldn't I focus when he was around?

After quickly changing into my leathers, I grabbed my Ducati and went through my prerace check. When she was all set to go, I opened the garage doors and rolled her outside. "Ready for a little late-night fun, baby?" I cooed, patting her side.

The track lights flared to life as I approached the entrance, then the lap board flickered and brightened. The silence was eerie. I was used to noise and chaos here, but it was so quiet now, I could hear the electricity buzzing through the lampposts. A few minutes later, I could hear the hum of Hayden's bike approaching in the unnatural stillness. I looked over as he pulled into view. Just seeing him decked out in his red-and-black leathers, sitting on his red-and-black Honda, made excitement churn in my belly. It was like *he* was the red light about to turn green, and I couldn't wait to surge forward.

Hayden's smile was huge when he popped up his visor. "Ready for this, sweethear— Kenzie?"

His obvious attempt to curtail calling me by a pet name made me smile. So he *was* capable of learning. Good to know. Because I was about to teach him a thing or two.

"I've never been more ready," I stated. "Whoever is ahead after twenty laps wins?" I asked. When he nodded, I immediately took off, leaving him in the dust. Maybe it wasn't fair of me to not wait for him, but I really didn't care about fair at the moment; I cared about beating him.

I felt Hayden catch up to me before I heard him. It was like my body was supernaturally attuned to his location. When he was right on my back tire, I pressed my bike to go faster. *No.* If he never caught me, then he'd never pass me, and I was determined to win this. The world swirled by in a rush of blended colors, and the bike beneath me hummed and vibrated in harmonious rhythm with the road. Even though I was pumped full of adrenaline, a sense of peace washed over me. Racing against Hayden helped me find my center even more effectively than surfing did. The world froze, my thoughts froze, and all that was left was instinct—and this type of instinct my mind was more than happy to let me have.

Hayden eventually pulled up beside me, but I wasn't about to give him another inch. My heart thudded in my chest as I pushed my bike even harder, and a huge smile broke over my face as I crossed the last lap ahead of him. Finally! I'd beaten him.

As we slowed down to exit the track, I thrust my fist into the air. Victory! We stopped the bikes in the entrance lane, and I hopped off. Unstrapping my helmet, I tossed it onto the ground and held both hands in the air. "Yes! I got you!"

Hayden slowly shook his head, then carefully removed his helmet. His expression was amused as he watched me celebrate. "Wow, Twenty-Two…try to act like you've been there before," he said, getting off his bike.

His words did nothing to stop my jaunty jig of in-your-faceness. I even did a little rodeo roping maneuver, just to tease him. His eyes widened, and his smile twisted into a ridiculously attractive grin before he started laughing. I didn't care. I'd just proven something to myself. Two things, really. One: Racing with him really did improve my time—the electronic board beside the track was proof of that. And two: I *could* beat the god of racing, and if I could beat *him*, I could beat *anyone*.

Hayden tilted his head at me; there was a surprising smile on his face, considering I'd just creamed him. "Nice racing, Cox."

His praise was unexpected, and an odd warmth began expanding from my chest, curling outward to every extremity. *Nice racing*. Such simple words, yet ones I rarely heard. Feeling compelled to say something nice in return, I told him, "Thank you, I seriously needed that." My grin was uncontainable. I felt like I could do anything. Be anything. *Win* anything.

Hayden was staring at me in a way that was making me a little uncomfortable—but it wasn't completely unwelcome. The warmth and good feeling in my chest was shifting the tingling fire I usually felt for him into something warm and pliable, taffy that could be stretched, molded…shaped around my heart. It was a dangerous feeling to let myself have. There was no future here. No potential *us* to romanticize. Even if he wasn't taken like I'd originally thought, he was still a Benneti, and I was still a Cox. Anything between us would severely alter both of our careers and forever damage my relationship with my father. Just meeting like this was bad enough; anything more…was impossible.

"No, thank *you*," he whispered, taking a step toward me.

The sincerity on his face made my heart thud in my chest, made me feel winded, like I'd been running, not racing. "For what?" I asked, unconsciously stepping toward him. God, he was so much more desirable when he wasn't being an asshole. It made me want to forget all the obstacles between us.

Before Hayden answered me, he slipped his gloves off and tossed them onto his bike. There was a sparkle in his eyes from the track lights, making them even harder to resist staring into. "For agreeing to race with me," he finally said. "And for being so damn beautiful, it's almost physically painful to look at you."

Surprise made my lips part. "I…"

Reaching out for me, Hayden gently tucked a piece of hair behind my ear. His smile was soft as his fingers brushed across my cheek and over my bottom lip. I sucked in a sharp breath. I felt like he'd just lit a fuse inside me, and in about ten seconds, I was going to explode. *I should leave. I should run. I should invite him home…*

"Mackenzie?" he asked, his voice quiet.

"Yes?" I murmured. *Shouldn't I be saying no?*

"Do you—?" Before he could finish his question, the cell phone tucked in the pocket of his racing leathers started making a wailing siren noise that sounded like a bomb warning. Hayden cringed, then looked up at the time on the lap board. "I gotta go, but same time tomorrow, right?" His eyes were alive with hope that I would say yes. And I wanted to. Almost as much as I wanted to know who was calling him this late at night…and what he'd been about to ask me….

"I'll be here." *Waiting for you.*

* * *

I was later than usual to the track the next morning—I had to get *some* sleep, after all—but I didn't feel tired. Quite the opposite. I felt energized, alive, ready to take on the world. My mind was telling me to be extra cautious when I entered the Cox Racing garage, to be on alert for any clue that someone had discovered what I'd done, but my soul just wouldn't shut up long enough to listen to my head.

Racing with Hayden had opened something inside me, and I

couldn't stop thinking about it. Or him—his praise, his fingers on my skin, his lingering question...I couldn't wait for the sun to set so I could experience it all over again. I was getting addicted to the rush of competing with him, or maybe it was just *him* I was developing an addiction to. *I should stop before it's too late. It already* is *too late, dummy.*

A voice startled me out of my thoughts. "'Bout time you showed up. I was just about to send a search party out for you."

I looked over to see Nikki kneeling by my bike. The residual adrenaline flowing through me instantly froze into a solid lump of ice as Nikki inspected the bike's engine. I'd refueled, changed my tires, and made the bike just as perfect as I'd found it, but if anyone would notice something was off, it would be her. Jesus, what would I say if she spotted something weird? *I couldn't sleep last night, so I broke in and did a few laps.* Yeah. She knew me too well to buy that. Even if it was mostly the truth.

While I waited on pins and needles for my betrayal to be uncovered, Nikki absentmindedly said, "I dragged Myles out of his house and made him go out last night. He's been a hermit since the wreck. Says he can't drive so there's no point in going anywhere. I told him that's why he had friends with cars. He bitched the entire time, but I think he had fun. He got a lot of sympathy shots anyway. I texted you to join us. Where were you?"

"Sleeping," I automatically answered as I sat on a stool next to her. Had I screwed the gas cap on as tightly as she normally did? She wasn't acting like she was concerned with the bike, though, so I relaxed. It was fine. She didn't know anything. A flash of guilt followed that thought. She was my best friend, and she didn't know anything...

"You okay?" she suddenly asked, her brows furrowed in concern.

I forced a smile. "Yeah. How do you think Myles is doing? He always seems so...depressed when I see him. I keep waiting for him to bounce back, but he's not." Even more guilt flashed through me after that realization. I should be doing more for him. But I needed to focus on racing. My friends were beginning to fall to the wayside in my pursuit of excellence, and I hated it. There were only so many balls I could juggle, though.

Nikki opened her mouth, then shut it. Shaking her head, she said, "I'm actually kind of worried about him. All he talks about is Hayden."

A long sigh escaped me. "Yeah, I know..." And even worse, I knew Myles might be right about his suspicions. *I shouldn't see Hayden again.*

"Myles is so sure Hayden caused the wreck, even though there's no proof of anything..." Nikki shook her head before continuing. "I told him he's starting to sound just like Keith does when he blames your dad. He needs to let that shit go before he winds up like Keith too." She looked around the garage to see if anyone had heard her. Just speaking Keith's name out loud was a fast track to getting on my father's bad side.

Her dark eyes shining with worry, she said, "Can you talk to him, Kenzie? Convince him he's just pissed he got hurt, and he's looking for an excuse?"

"Yeah, of course. Maybe I'll swing by his place tonight or something." I wasn't meeting up with Hayden until midnight. I had time.

Looking relieved, Nikki stood and gave me a swift hug. "Oh good, I hate to see him like this. He should be taking us cockroach racing, not planning Hayden's downfall."

I froze with my arms around her. "His downfall?"

Sighing, Nikki pulled back. "Yeah. It's getting bad, Kenzie. The sooner you get over there, the better."

Reassuring her that I would, I put talking to Myles in the number one spot on my mental to-do list. Hayden's downfall would lead to my own, and I couldn't let that happen—too much was at stake.

After working out—an hour of weights and an hour on the treadmill—I did a few laps around the track so my father would know I was still giving him my best effort. And much to my surprise, my times were better than they had been the day before. Not as great as my late-night run with Hayden, but better. Dad even gave me a nod of approval when I was packing up for the night. So, all in all, it was a great day.

I drove to Myles's duplex after leaving the track. All the lights were off, but I couldn't believe he was asleep already, and I doubted anyone but Nikki could have successfully gotten him out of the house, so I walked to his door and pounded on it. "Myles? It's Kenzie. Open up."

No answer. I tried again and waited a few more minutes. When nothing happened, I squatted down to look at the lock. Was I seriously contemplating taking a page out of Hayden's playbook and picking the lock? Maybe if I had his tools…and any clue how to use them.

Just as I was debating whether I should try jimmying the lock with a credit card, the door opened. I peeked up to see Myles staring down at me. "Kenzie? Uh…drop something?"

I instantly stood up and slapped on a carefree smile. "Hey…no, I just wanted to check on you. How are you doing?"

Myles pushed the door open wider and indicated inside his dark house. He looked like he'd just woken up—or hadn't gone to sleep in days. His eyes were bloodshot, his hair was a disheveled mess, and his clothes were rumpled. His fractured leg was fully casted, and he was using a crutch under one arm to get back to his couch. "I'm great, Kenzie. Awesome, really."

He sat down in the dark living room like it was perfectly normal to not have any lights on. The small space was littered with takeout boxes. At least he was eating; that was an improvement from the last time I was here. Turning on a light, I joined him; he cringed at the sudden brightness. "Come on, Myles, don't do this to yourself. Your leg will heal, you'll be back next year."

He turned his weary eyes my way. "You really think there will be anything to come back to?"

My jaw hardened as I locked eyes with him. "I won't let the team go under. I promise."

Myles sighed, then patted my arm. "I know you won't." He said it like a parent trying to make a child feel better, like he didn't truly believe what he was saying. A stab of pain ripped right through me. *He doesn't think I can do it.*

I choked back the hurt while Myles sighed again. "The leg's not really the issue anyway. I fractured my collarbone. That's the one that's gonna cause me problems. They did the best they could, but it might always bother me…"

The grief on his face dissolved the sting from his words. *He's hurting, depressed. He needs me.* I put my arm around his shoulders. "It's gonna be okay, Myles. Nikki and I will help you get through this. Whatever you need, we're here for you. *I'm* here for you."

He looked over at me, his expression suddenly stern. "Do you mean that?"

"Of course," I immediately answered.

He gave me a curt nod. "Then help me get Hayden back."

Tension tightened my body. "Myles…" How could I convince him that Hayden didn't have anything to do with his wreck without sounding like I was defending Hayden? I couldn't, and I really didn't know if Hayden had been involved or not. All I knew was that I needed Hayden to help my racing improve, so I was going to have to convince Myles that he would be worse off going after Hayden than leaving him alone. It made me feel sick that I had to. "Dad doesn't tolerate retaliation. If you mess with Hayden, you'll start a chain reaction with Benneti that will escalate into something…truly ugly. And if Dad pinpoints it back to you, you'll be fired. For the sake of your career, just…leave this one alone. Please?"

Myles glared at me for a moment, then sighed. "Yeah…maybe you're right."

Hearing him agree with me made me relax a little, although the guilt of why I really wanted him to leave Hayden alone didn't lessen any. "Of course I am. Now how about we turn some more lights on, I'll make a real meal, and we'll watch a movie or something?"

He was grimacing at my suggestion. "Uh, everything sounds great except the dinner part. I can't eat that diet tofu crap you live off of."

Rolling my eyes, I said, "Well, how about spaghetti then?"

His jaw dropped. "You're *voluntarily* eating carbs? I'm the one who got their head knocked around, but you're the one acting different."

Frowning, I socked him in the arm. "No, I'm not." Not really. Maybe.

The hours I spent with Myles seemed to drag. I hated that they did—I loved hanging out with my friends—but I had somewhere I really wanted to be, and a certain pair of jade-green eyes kept invading my thoughts, along with the words "so damn beautiful." They replayed in my head over and over. I couldn't even remember what movie Myles and I watched, but as soon as it was over, I faked a yawn and said good night to him.

When it was finally time to go meet Hayden, my heart started beating out an increasingly fierce rhythm that reminded me of a locomotive gaining speed. I couldn't wait to see him. No, I meant I couldn't wait to *race* him.

He was in the parking lot when I got there, waiting on his bike with his helmet under his arm. The lights in the lot made his dirty-blond hair shine, but that was nothing compared to the seductive gleam in his eyes. "Hey, Twenty-Two. Miss me?" he asked, his lips curling into a slow smile.

Yes, oddly enough…I had missed him. Not that I would ever admit that to him. "I've missed kicking your ass," I teased.

His smile broke into a warm laugh that made butterflies swarm through my stomach. "Ready?" he asked, tilting his head toward the locked gate he was about to pick. I eagerly nodded. *Yes, I've been ready for you for a while.*

My oddly passionate thought made me pause. No…I wasn't ready for him like that. I wasn't ready for *anything* like that, and I never would be. Not with him. I wasn't sure if I knew anything real about him…or if I believed half of what I did know. And that made all of this so much worse.

Hayden tilted his head as he studied me. "You okay?"

God, I needed to school my face better so people would stop asking me that question. "Yeah, let's do this."

Hayden's eyes were glued to mine. The connection was so great, I couldn't have looked away if I wanted to, and I wasn't sure I wanted to, because with every second that our eyes remained locked, it felt like some part of my body was coming to life—my hands, my face, my chest... my heart.

Finally he broke the spell and moved over to the gate. "Come watch. I'll show you how to do it."

I had to raise an eyebrow at that. "Why would I ever need to know how to pick locks?" Damn it. Hadn't I just wished I'd had the knowledge over at Myles's place? Before Hayden could respond with some clever quip, I squatted down next to him. Might as well take the opportunity to learn a new skill.

Hayden laughed, then started talking me through everything he was doing. Once the gate was open, he showed me the trick again at the Cox garage. I wasn't sure if I could do it on my own, but I thought I understood the concept.

When the lights were on and everything was ready, I asked Hayden how many laps we were shooting for this time. "Want to go for twenty? Or maybe fifty, really make it challenging."

Broad smile on his face, Hayden shoved his helmet on and pushed the visor up. Looking up at the lap board, he thought for a second, then said, "Let's make it thirty." When he returned his eyes to mine, they were brimming with playfulness. "And just for fun... how about we put a little wager on the race. If I win, you have to answer a question. Honestly."

My insides tightened at just the thought of an intimate Q&A with him. What did he want to know? And would I be able to tell him? Opening up wasn't my strong point, especially when it came to feelings and emotions. Acknowledging the heat between us wouldn't help us race better, but then again, maybe I was just scared, and that didn't sit right with me. I didn't want to be scared of anything. Clenching my jaw, I pushed aside my concerns and asked, "What do I get if I win?"

He leaned his bike my way. "What do you want?" His eyes were burning with intensity now, and my breath caught in my throat.

God... that was the real question, wasn't it. The answer was both extremely simple and profoundly complicated. I wanted to earn my father's respect. I wanted to be a champion. I wanted to win. I wanted to save the family business. I wanted Hayden to…help me do it.

I felt a part of me ripping open as a simplified form of the truth leaked from my mouth. "All I want is to race." True, yes. The complete picture…no. *What the hell do I want?*

Hayden stared at me a second longer, then flipped down his visor and started his bike. A rush of adrenaline filled me as I did the same. Yes, I loved this part—the anticipation of release. We rolled onto the track, then got into position. I leaned over the handlebars as Hayden held up three fingers. A bliss as sweet as climaxing filled me as I started counting backward. Yes, just a few more seconds, and then I could let go of this pent-up energy.

When my mental clock reached zero, I punched it, same as Hayden. We flew away from the starting line with a jerk of speed that had me clutching my bike to hold on. A giggle escaped me as I relaxed my brain and focused only on soaring down the track with him. I lived for this, so much more than I cared to admit. As we raced through the course, taking hard lefts, steep rights, and as we moved around each other, jockeying for position, everything between us fell away. There was no tension, no secretive past or mysterious future, no heated passion boiling under the surface, and no worry. There was nothing but the all-encompassing, all-consuming joy of the pursuit of victory. And when I crossed the finish line just a heartbeat behind him, I knew this was right. For some reason that I didn't fully understand, Hayden was my center. I needed him to maintain my balance, and without him…I was lost.

We were both smiling wide when we exited the track. Helmet resting on his handlebar, Hayden gave me a look that was both curious and cautious. "I beat you…You owe me an answer."

Unease instantly choked my good mood. "No, I never took that deal," I said, taking off my helmet.

With a smirk, he shook his head. "You raced me. Acceptance was implied." He ended his sentence with a playful wink. Damn loophole. And damn Hayden. His hair was that rumpled mess that looked so good on him, and beads of sweat dotted his neckline. And I would much rather lick them off than answer his question.

Seeing my uncertainty, Hayden shrugged and added, "If you don't want to give me a truth, you could always do a dare." From the way his smile turned suggestive, it was perfectly clear just what the dare would be.

Feeling desire starting to cloud my senses, I quickly spat out, "What is it that you want to know?"

He chuckled at my quick reaction, then his expression grew serious. My heart started racing in anticipation. Shit. He was going to ask me something I didn't want to answer, I just knew it. But what? I had to get out of this; I was starting to feel a little faint.

With a soft smile on his lips, Hayden shook his head. "Hey, relax, Kenzie. You're not about to ride your bike off a cliff…it's just a question."

Taking a deep breath, I forced a smile to my face. He was right. It was just information…and I didn't really have to answer him if I didn't want to. When he saw I was calmer, he asked his question. "I just wanted to know…why did the idea of me being with Izzy bother you so much?"

My teeth ground together as embarrassment washed over me. "What makes you think it bothered me?"

Pulling off his glove, he leaned over and brought his finger to my forehead. "You have this little vein here that pops out when you're mad. I just can't figure out why that made you mad."

He didn't remove his finger until he trailed it along my brow line. The loss of his touch was like a blow to my chest. God, why did the tiniest things affect me so deeply around him? And what would it be like to get lost in that feeling? Shaking those thoughts out of my head, I told him, "I don't know what you're talking about. That didn't bother me at all. You can sleep with whoever you want to."

Hayden smirked at my answer, like he knew I was full of crap. Then his smile widened. Looking up into my eyes, he purred, "*Whoever* I want?"

The intensity in his eyes was heating the air between us; I could feel the warmth of it on my face. Damn…he meant me. "Yes…" I murmured, not meaning to. Shit. Had I just said that out loud?

Hayden's eyes widened as his lips parted. He ran his tongue over his bottom lip, and I had to stifle a groan. "Kenzie..." he murmured, leaning his bike even closer. Unconsciously, I found myself being drawn into him. His head angled toward me, mine angled away. We were perfectly aligned; all we had to do was keep moving forward. *Kiss me.*

He was so close I could feel his breath on my lips. Then his goddamn cell phone cut the silence in the air. Again? Really? Like last night, we'd been here over an hour, and it was getting pretty late. Who the hell kept calling him at this time of night? Hayden instantly pulled back. His eyes flashed to the clock on the lap board before returning to mine. "I'm sorry...gotta go. Continue this tomorrow?"

"Called away twice in two nights. You have standing plans with someone besides me?" I asked, my voice tight. I knew I shouldn't care, but it really bothered me that I wasn't the only one who got his late-night time.

Hayden smiled in answer, but his eyes were guarded. "You're so cute when you're jealous."

My defenses went up so fast I heard a distinct slamming sound in my head. "I am *not* jeal— See you tomorrow, Hayden. For *training*." I emphasized the last word as hard as I could, so Hayden would have no doubt about what was happening between us...and what wasn't.

CHAPTER 11

After a month and a half of night racing with Hayden, I finally saw my day times catch up to my evening performances. It was exhilarating to see that, slowly but surely, training with Hayden was working, and I was becoming a more confident racer. I wanted to shout it to the world that I'd found the secret to my success. But unfortunately, it really was a secret.

Seeing Hayden almost every night was oddly intoxicating. The simmering heat between us hadn't dissipated any. In fact, it was so much worse. When we were standing close together, staring at each other, and his hand brushed my thigh, it was almost painful to ignore the desire to grab him and pull him into me. But I refused to cross that line with him. I was fully aware that he was only using me to help himself…and I wasn't about to let him use my body as well as my racing skills.

But sometimes it was hard to remember that, because sometimes being around him felt a little too…familiar. After his little truth or dare game, we started talking more, and I was getting more comfortable around him. I still wasn't entirely positive what he was up to, but he'd become such an intrinsic part of my life that I couldn't imagine not meeting up with him anymore. And when it was just us on the track, I tended to forget about who he was and what he represented, and what he might or might not be doing, and I just enjoyed being with someone who pushed me to be my best. I was beginning to feel very…free…with him. And that terrified me. It helped that he still got called away almost every night. He never said why, and he deflected whenever I asked, and that kept some very important space between us. Because freeing or not, he wasn't someone I could trust.

While my double life was helping my career, it made me feel really guilty around my teammates. Especially whenever they praised me on my improved times. Dealing with Dad was the hardest, though. A couple of weeks into late-night practices with Hayden, he'd told me, "Your times are getting there, Kenzie. A lot more in line with Road America. Hit the gym a little more often, and you might be able to get that extra boost you'll need to tackle Barber." He'd even patted my shoulder after he'd said it. Sure, it wasn't glowing, superfluous praise, but it was something, and it made me want more, made me want to work harder, push myself…step even farther out of my comfort zone.

With the memory of Dad's praise on my mind, I was grinning ear to ear one beautiful June morning when I walked into the Cox garage. Nikki was there, working on a bike. Myles was with her, which was a welcome sight. I'd been visiting him most nights since that bleak drop-in. He was slowly letting go of his depression, and his fun-loving personality was beginning to return. That wasn't to say he'd released any of his anger toward Hayden. No, *that* he was holding on to as fiercely as ever.

Nikki straightened from the bike when she saw me. "Well, I guess coming in a little later really is paying off for you. Not only are your times better, but you're looking exceptionally peppy today. Maybe I should start sleeping in," she joked to Myles.

Giving her a playful scowl, I retorted, "I'm peppy every day. Cheery is practically my middle name." My lips wouldn't hold the frown, and a smile erupted on my face. God, I *was* peppy today.

Nikki rolled her eyes, then cast an incredulous look at Myles. His expression was completely blank as he stared at me, then he started laughing. He laughed so hard he put a hand to his collarbone and started muttering, "Ow, ow, ow." Wiping tears from his eyes, he chuckled, "Cheery…that's a good one, Kenzie."

I tried to glare at him, but I couldn't even pretend I was angry. Laughing, I left them and went to put on my leathers.

Minutes later, I was zipping around the track at breakneck speeds. The course hadn't been changed since last week, and since I was practicing on it twice a day, I knew it by heart. My mind started to wander as I rode low through the curves. I started thinking about going through these turns with Hayden just inches in front of me, or sometimes a foot or two behind me. I thought of how it made me laugh every time I passed him. And then I thought of afterward, when we'd stop at the entrance to the track and he'd remove his helmet as he hopped off his bike, and his eyes would lock with mine…

After our hour or so of practice, we usually talked for a little bit before we called it quits for the night. For the most part, Hayden asked me questions about my family—where I'd grown up, what happened to my mom, what it was like having sisters. He was less of an open book. The only thing I'd gotten out of him so far was that he was an only child, and his favorite color was blue. I never pressed too hard for more. I think I was scared to find out something I didn't want to know. I was having enough difficulty with the horrible realization that not only was I insanely attracted to him, but I kind of…liked him. If I found out that he was every bit as bad as Myles and my father said he was…well, I just wasn't ready for this bubble to pop yet. I still needed him too much.

As I worked on my practice laps, I glanced over at the Benneti side of the track. I was on the long turn closest to their garage, and I could see a group of people standing around outside it. That piqued my interest. Was that Hayden there in the back? What had he been up to since we'd parted ways late last night? And where did he go when his mysterious caller pulled him away…?

I was almost through the corner when I saw something that jarred me so hard, I slammed on the brakes. My bike protested the sudden change of velocity, and I almost cartwheeled the damn thing before getting it under control. Coming to a rest, I looked behind me to where the Benneti garage could be seen over the low wall surrounding the course. There were four guys out there, and three of them were clearly ganging up on one—the monkey in the middle was being shoved around by the trio of bullies. I couldn't breathe when I saw that it was Hayden being surrounded. I knew his teammates didn't like him, but surely it wouldn't come down to violence. They'd stop short of that. They'd laugh at Hayden's expense, then leave him alone.

I could tell right away that wasn't going to happen, though. While I watched in horror, two guys grabbed Hayden's arms, trapping him, and the third guy socked him in the gut before he could break free. I was off my bike in an instant, and just about to run over there and do something to help him when reality washed over me like glacial water. *I can't help him.* He was neck-deep in Benneti Land, and I couldn't step foot outside of the track wall. I shouldn't even be watching so blatantly, in case someone noticed, but I couldn't avert my eyes. *Get out of there, Hayden*, I thought, ripping off my helmet.

Hayden was desperately trying to get free, but the thugs on either side were holding him tight, and the nonstop blows to the stomach weren't allowing him to catch his breath, let alone fight back. The guy in front of Hayden was screaming things as he pummeled him. "Think you're better than everyone else 'cause you're Keith's little pet project? Think you're hot shit 'cause you live above his garage, ride his bike, eat his fucking food? You're nothing, worm! He found you in the trash, and when he's done with you, you'll go back to the trash. But whether you're Keith's lapdog or not, if you ever touch our fucking bikes again, we'll fucking kill you!"

Shock at what I was hearing froze me solid. What had he done to their bikes? And wait…he lived with Keith? The icy surprise melted into rage as they continued beating him. Regardless of what he'd done, they had no right to touch him! Just when I couldn't stand another second of seeing Hayden in pain, just when I was about to throw away my job to help him, Hayden finally yanked one of his arms free. Within seconds he was slugging the guy who had his other arm pinned. Then he was a whirling storm of fury. Before I could close my gaping mouth, he had all three guys down on the ground, panting and spitting up blood.

Hayden kicked the guy who'd been attacking him in the stomach, then leaned over him and growled, "If you ever fucking touch me again, I'll break every fucking bone in your body."

I wanted to be disgusted by what he'd done…but I wasn't. As I watched him saunter back into his garage, a smile broke over my face. *Holy shit…Hayden's a badass.* And for some reason, it made him that much hotter. But what the hell had he done to make them so angry in the first place?

When I got to the parking lot of the track later that evening, Hayden was already there. Helmet resting on his bike, he was standing by the inner gate, flipping his leather pouch of lock-picking tools into the air. His smile was relaxed and breezy as he absentmindedly caught the tools. He didn't look at all like he'd been in a fight earlier. He just looked…gorgeous. "Hey, Twenty-Two. I think tonight is your night."

Lifting my visor as I pulled my bike up next to him, I asked, "My night to do what? Win? Yeah, I already knew that." I flashed him a teasing grin and he laughed.

"No. Well, maybe, but what I meant was *this*…" He handed me the tool set as his sentence trailed off. His face was eager, as if he found leading me to the dark side enjoyable.

Working my lip, I shook my head. "No thanks. I'm good for the year on illegal activities."

He raised an eyebrow. "You've actually committed an illegal activity before?"

Looking around, I said, "You mean besides *this*? Well…I sped in a school zone once."

He started laughing so hard, he bent over. "Oh God…you're so damn cute."

Wanting the warmth in my chest to fade away—and also wanting to embrace it with every fiber of my soul—I yanked the tools from his hand. "Fine. I'll give it a try." Anything to stop him from saying stuff like that.

Taking off my helmet, I squatted down in front of the lock. I'd seen him do this more times than I could count by now, but I'd never tried it before. Hayden pointed out which tools to use, all while explaining the logistics of how locks operated. I had it popped open before he finished. "Wow, you're a natural," he said, pride in his voice.

Rolling my eyes, I handed him back his tools. "Well, don't think I'm going to help you in your next burglary or anything."

I thought he'd laugh, but he frowned instead. "I'm not a thief."

The indignation in his eyes was so severe it caught me off guard. "I know," I murmured, although I wasn't sure if I truly knew that or not.

As if nothing I'd just said had bothered him, his expression instantly shifted into one of amusement. "I *am* pretty amazing at practical jokes, though. Just ask my old high school principal. My friend and I once gathered up three dozen snakes and locked them in his office. None of them were dangerous, of course, but he had a really bad phobia. He wouldn't go back into his office for weeks, started working out of the janitor's closet."

A small laugh escaped me at the thought of Hayden wrangling snakes. "What? That's so mean..."

"So was he," Hayden said with a shrug.

Shaking my head, I asked, "Did you and your friend get caught?"

Hayden's smile was huge; it made me want to make him smile like that all the time. "Nah, Felicia was super paranoid for a month, but Mr. Dixson never had a clue who did it. I think he wrote it off as some weird infestation."

My mood dropped a smidge. "Felicia?"

Hayden shifted his gaze to the ground. "Yeah...girl I used to..." Returning his eyes to me, he was silent for a second before saying, "We were close for a time...but she's gone, and that's that. Are you ready to ride now?" he asked, not-so-smoothly changing the subject.

A mixture of compassion and jealousy ripped through me; I quickly beat back the latter and embraced the former. He was protecting himself with vagueness—and I understood not wanting to say too much, understood hiding in silence and misdirection. This Felicia person had meant something to him, I was sure of it. "She hurt you, didn't she?"

He immediately averted his eyes. "She dropped out of my life a while ago, so I don't see how it matters."

There was sadness on his face that suggested that it did matter, he just didn't want to talk about it. "I'm…sorry it didn't work out." And yet, I was grateful too.

The expression on his face melted into a smile. "Don't be. It was a…toxic relationship." Tilting his head, he eyed me up and down. "You sort of remind me of her."

My eyes widened and my cheeks heated. "I'm toxic for you? Well, thanks. Just so you know, the feeling's mutual," I finished with a smirk.

He laughed, then shook his head. "No…you're nothing like her, it's just…you look… " His eyes turned reflective as he studied me. "It's damn uncanny how much you look like her," he muttered almost too quietly for me to hear.

His gaze was suddenly so intense, my heart started racing. "We should…get going," I whispered. "We're burning moonlight." He blinked, like some spell had been broken, then he nodded and we started heading toward the garages.

When we got to the Cox garage, I tried my hand at picking the lock again. Surprisingly, it was easy for me. Guess I really was a natural. Not that I was ever going to do anything with the skill—other than break into my family racetrack every night. Jesus. My father would die if he could see me right now. Literally have a coronary and die.

While I got my bike ready, Hayden went over to his garage and prepped his motorcycle. We met at the entrance, same as usual, only I noticed Hayden was holding his stomach. Not obviously—he just looked like he was casually wrapping his arm around his side—but I knew why he was doing it; I'd witnessed the entire attack. I wanted to ask him about it, but before I could, he leaned over his handlebars and said, "On your mark. Get set…"

The second he said, "Go," I shot out of there like cops were on my tail. The rush and euphoria filled me to the brim as I led Hayden on a wild chase through the twists and turns of the track. The fear of getting caught was always in the back of my mind when we came here, but right now, it was a far-off concern. Letting go of everything and being in the moment with Hayden filled me with joy, peace, and an uncharacteristic excitement. I could feel myself getting swept away by the eroticism of it all—the giddiness of being in front of Hayden, the hum of my bike, the speed of the concrete flying underneath me. My body's reaction was mystifying. Racing had done many things for me over the years, but before Hayden, it had *never* turned me on.

I rode that delightful high all the way to first place. And then I popped a wheelie in celebration. God, that had felt good. I almost wanted to go again just to keep the buzz alive.

Coming up beside me, Hayden laughed at my display. Slipping off his helmet, he said, "One of the greatest things about racing you, Twenty-Two, is watching you enjoy your victory." Then he cringed. A slight move, but one that reminded me that he wasn't exactly at his best tonight. Some of my high faded with the realization that he was in pain.

Removing my helmet, I debated whether I should ask him about the fight. Maybe I was still high from the race, maybe it was because he'd opened up a little, but I suddenly wasn't afraid of depth. I wanted something real, wanted an answer to another one of his many mysteries…wanted to risk popping the bubble. "What happened today? With your teammates?" I clarified. "I saw the fight…"

Hayden's eyes grew so wide, I thought they might pop out of his skull. "You saw that?"

I nodded, my jaw tight. "I've never felt so helpless. I wanted to do something, but that damn ban…I was completely stuck there, staring like an idiot." Shit, why had I confessed that? It felt way too personal, way too intimate, and yet, as I took in the stunned look on his face, I was glad I'd said it.

"You wanted to *help* me?" Hayden asked, his voice soft.

Staring into his deep green eyes, I couldn't answer right away.

It was like every cell in my brain had simultaneously turned into thick Jell-O from the power of his gaze. Hayden's smile loosened my tongue. "So what happened?" I asked. "Why'd they go after you?"

His eyes turned steel-hard as he retreated into his memory. "Keith left early for the day. Doctor's appointment or something. Anyway, when he leaves, the team sort of turns into…well, have you ever seen the movie *Lord of the Flies*?" When I nodded, he gave me a wry smile. "I'm the newest fly, the easy target, so it's only to be expected that they'll turn on me whenever they can. It's okay, though, I can handle those assholes. I'm not defenseless," he added with a wink. No. Definitely not. Just alone and outnumbered. He shouldn't be with the Bennetis; he didn't belong there. *So where does he belong?*

That pesky thought made me frown. "Still, it's not right. You should tell Keith how they're treating you." Wow, was I really promoting Keith as some sort of father figure for Hayden? I guess it wasn't that much of a stretch, since they already lived together. Damn it, just the thought of Keith influencing Hayden made my skin crawl. And made the rumors around him even more plausible.

Hayden let out a harsh laugh. "You want me to tattle? No thanks, not my style. And besides, do you honestly think that would make things any better?" He paused to shake his head. "Trust me, eventually they'll get bored and move on. I just have to power through until then. And if there's one thing in this world I'm good at, it's powering through crappy situations." Even though he was smiling, there was age-old pain in his features; it was difficult to witness, yet impossible to turn away from. *What happened to you?*

Too curious to resist, I asked, "Is that how you learned to fight like that? Crappy situations?" I wanted to reach out and touch him, stroke his face…but I stopped myself.

Hayden shrugged, like it didn't matter. "Foster care kid. I got bounced around a lot, so I learned to adjust."

"Oh…I'm sorry." That must have been so lonely. I'd always had family close to me. I couldn't even comprehend having no one.

His expression softened as he smiled. "Again, don't be sorry.

Sure, it sucked…but I wouldn't be where I am now without my past. And I kind of like where I am…now." Seductive half smile on his face, he stepped even closer to me, so that our legs were touching; his eyes blazed with heat, and I knew he was referring to this *exact* moment. *Here…with me.*

God, this was the most I'd ever gotten him to say, and there was so much I wanted to know. But the desire to help him was even more compelling than my curiosity. Hayden had made talking slightly more bearable for me; I wanted to make it easier for him too, but there was one more question I needed answered. "Hayden…what did you do to your teammates' bikes that pissed them off so much?"

Anger instantly filled his eyes, and he immediately stepped away; the loss chilled me. "I didn't do anything to their fucking bikes," he snapped. "That damn rumor, the one you asked me about…those dicks all believe it's true. So when one of the mechanics forgets to change the spark plugs on Rodney's bike and he has engine problems, naturally it's *my* fault. God, I thought I'd left all that shit behind, but I guess not." He avoided looking at me after his speech, and his hands flexed into fists as he let out heavy breaths. Clearly this was something that really bothered him.

"You okay?" I asked, not sure if he would answer.

He looked over at me with a forced smile on his face. "Yeah, I'm fine. It's just, I…" He hesitated, and I could see the debate in his eyes; he wasn't sure if he could trust me either.

I smiled, in what I hoped came across as encouragement. "It's just what?"

Closing his mouth, he looked away before returning his eyes to me. "Do you want to get out of here? Maybe go to a late-night diner and get something to eat? I feel like I could eat half the city, I'm so hungry."

I was momentarily disheartened that he'd changed the subject, but his suggestion to go out caught me by surprise. Even more surprising, I wanted to say yes. Hayden had revealed more about himself tonight than he ever had before, and I didn't want to part ways with him yet. But recalling that this was usually around the time when his phone went off made me respond differently than I wanted to. "You mean there are no late-night plans you need to rush to?" I snipped. "The bat phone's not about to go off?"

There was a lot of bitterness in my voice, but Hayden only gave me a soft smile as he stared at me. "No, you're my only rendezvous tonight."

Relief zipped through me so fast, my breath caught in my throat. "Oh, well…I guess I could eat, then."

Hayden seemed shocked that I'd said yes. That made two of us. "Great. I'll turn off everything and meet you in the parking lot."

Now's your chance to get out of this. Just tell him you're not feeling well and you're going to go straight home. "Okay, see you in the parking lot." Jesus, what the hell was wrong with me?

I felt like I'd recently suffered a blow to the head as I put my bike away, painstakingly making sure it was exactly how I'd found it. Why was my body taking control and pushing away common sense? Was it because I'd seen a crack in the tough-guy façade? Because there was so much more he wasn't showing me? Because he kept calling me beautiful, talented, cute, and funny? Because I needed the positive feedback so much more than I'd realized? God, was I really that pathetic? Well, it was only food I was agreeing to. This wasn't going any farther than a Denver omelet. And besides, I could take the opportunity to try to get him to open up to me again.

Rolling my street bike to a stop just outside the inner gate, I sat and waited for Hayden. As I fantasized about fluffy eggs—because that seemed the only safe thing to think about—I saw something strange on the highway in the distance. The bright beams of a car's headlights were slowing down just before the turnoff to the track. My heart sank to my stomach when the lights turned down the road that would bring them directly to *us*.

Panic surging through every pore, I shut off the headlight on my bike. *Shit! Shit! Shit!* Turning my head, I lifted the visor on my helmet and shouted over my shoulder, "Hayden! We're about to have company!"

Luckily he was close and heard me. Zipping his bike up to mine, his headlight already dark, he peered down the long road to where the lights of a pickup truck were slowly and surely inching closer. Was that my dad's truck? I couldn't tell. Goddammit.

Letting out a curse, Hayden quickly ran over to the inner gate, slammed it closed, and replaced the lock. Seconds later, he was back on his bike. "Follow me," he said, then he sped off. Zipping away from the main entrance leading to the highway, he raced along the parking lot that surrounded a good portion of the track. I immediately chased after him.

The parking lot eventually shifted to plain, unmarked concrete, then shifted again to bare dirt. The wall surrounding the racetrack was high enough that once we got on the far side of the inner gate, whoever was approaching the track shouldn't be able to see us. My heart hammered in my chest as I tried to calculate whether we were visible. If we were spotted here at this hour—*together*—we were both done for. Fired. Possibly even arrested for trespassing. My career with Cox Racing would be over in the blink of an eye. Eli or Ralph would have to save the team…fat chance of that. Nikki would be heartbroken, Myles would never talk to me again. How would I ever be able to look Dad in the eye? Face my family? And Hayden…he'd probably have to go back to the streets. Would anyone else give him the chance Keith had?

Shaking off those dire thoughts, I focused instead on what was actually happening, not what might happen. We were near the back of the track now. Just as I was wondering what phase two of Hayden's getaway plan was, he pointed toward the fence that ran around the entire facility. Unless he had a bolt cutter in his back pocket, I wasn't sure what good it would do to head toward the chain-link barrier. Personally, I thought we should stay as close as possible to the track wall. We'd be invisible unless whoever was here decided to do a perimeter sweep—and that was highly unlikely. Unless it was John. He was anal about security and always bugging Dad to install motion sensors. *Fuck*.

Kicking a spray of dirt behind us as we sped along the ground, we finally made it to the fence. Hayden hopped off his bike and started looking for something. When he found what he wanted, he paused, then he started removing links of chain. What the hell? Who had made a door in the fence, and how had Hayden known about it? Feeling a little violated, I watched in stunned silence as he pulled back a segment large enough for our bikes. Hayden ushered me through, then once he was out, he returned the missing links. Unless you really scrutinized the fence, you'd never know a makeshift door was there. He had his own private entrance to my sanctuary? *You've got to be kidding me.*

I couldn't stop staring at him. When he got back on his bike, he shouted, "Beach!" and motioned for the highway. Now wasn't the best time to question him, and I knew that. We couldn't stay here; parts of the highway were visible from the track, especially from the offices on the second floor of the garage. Understanding where Hayden intended us to end up—the hidden beach that I had shared with him—I sped away, kicking up rocks as I went. My heart didn't begin to settle until I was on the highway, heading back into town. That had been too close. Much too close.

Hayden was nipping at my heels on the dark, empty road. Then he started inching around me. *Oh, I don't think so.* Without even thinking about it, I leaned forward and increased my speed. *Race me or chase me, 43. Let's see what you've got.*

It didn't take Hayden long to react to my prompt. He was beside me an instant later, and our speed picked up as we fought for ground. Somewhere in the back of my mind, I knew that what I was doing was dangerous and stupid, but it was late at night and the road was clear of traffic, and besides, I was too far gone in the rush of trying to beat him to stop.

I was so caught up in the curves of the highway that I almost didn't spot the turnoff for the beach in time. My bike slid a full half circle in the dirt as I made the too-tight corner. Hayden darted into the parking area a hairsbreadth behind me. *Yes, I got him!*

Hayden's face was practically radiating energy when he took off his helmet. "Holy shit, Kenzie. Holy fucking shit!"

My heart still pounding, I unfastened my helmet and slipped it off. "I know…that was too damn close." The rampaging adrenaline coursing through me came out in a series of small chuckles.

"Thank God you knew about the fence. And how the hell *did* you know about the fence?"

Hayden chewed on his lip before answering me. "Let's just say I used to practice there before I was given a key card." He gave me a grin that was supposed to be endearing, but I couldn't believe what I'd just heard.

"You practiced...? Wait...did you ever break into the Cox garages and ride our bikes? Did you ever ride *mine*?" The look on his face spoke volumes, and my blood began to boil with rage. My earlier feeling of violation was nothing compared to this. He'd ridden my baby! "Oh my God, Hayden, *did* you ride my bike?"

He gave me a sexy grin. "A gentleman never tells."

Hopping off my motorcycle, I chucked my helmet at his chest; he easily caught it. "Gentleman, my ass. I can't believe you rode my bike. Don't you know how wrong that is?"

Setting my helmet down, Hayden climbed off his own bike. Hands in the air, he walked over to where I was standing with my hands clenched into tight fists. I knew it was just a bike, but I was ticked. He'd ridden her without my knowledge. Or consent!

"Look, whatever might or might not have happened on your bike...I apologize. It was a long time ago, and I was...a different person then." He laughed, then quickly stopped when he saw I wasn't amused. "It's not like I knew you at the time and did it intentionally to piss you off, Kenzie. It was just a hot-looking bike that I wanted to take for a spin."

My eyes turned into steely daggers. Was that the way he saw me too? Something fun to practice on? Or just a tool to practice with? "My Ducati is a high-speed work of art, not a toy for your racing pleasure." *And neither am I.*

"I know that," he murmured; his voice was so soft and sensuous, my sudden spike of anger started fading. He stepped closer to me, making my insides squirm with anticipation. "I'm sorry about your bike, but...I don't want this night to end yet. Do you?"

Oh God...what was he asking? "No...but it has to eventually. And it's late...I should go home." *Before I do something stupid... like invite you over.*

Reaching out, Hayden grabbed my hand; his fingers were still cold from the windy ride, but his touch made me feel like I was standing too close to a fire and about to get burned. "Wait…we could still get something to eat. I have a feeling that after that scare we both need food. And alcohol. And pie."

Memories of our near-discovery that ended with that dangerous flight down the highway rushed through my head. That had been so stupid of me, but at the time, it had felt completely right. "I don't drink all that often. And I definitely don't eat pie." I glanced down at our fingers. Why hadn't I pulled away yet?

Hayden stepped closer to me; his face was just inches away now. "Are you sure? You seem to be doing a lot lately that you probably thought you'd never do. Maybe you need to reevaluate just where your guardrails are."

God, right now I wasn't even sure I had any. *Take me over the cliff. I'll tumble all the way down with you.*

His eyes scanned my face. Could he tell I was breathing harder? "You're gorgeous in the moonlight," he murmured. "I wish the lights on the bikes were off and the moon was the only thing on you." From his tone of voice it was clear that he meant that literally. Naked under the moonlight. *With him.* Desire flared inside me, electrifying me. That sounded…amazing.

Running his tongue across his bottom lip, Hayden started leaning toward me. Slowly. Like time meant nothing. His fingers came up to cup my cheek, drawing me in. My lips parted, ready. And just before we touched…his fucking cell phone blared that goddamn annoying siren ringtone, breaking the magic of the moment.

Gritting my jaw, I hissed, "If you don't change that goddamn setting, I'm chucking your phone into the goddamn Pacific."

Hayden pulled back, and reality rushed into the void of his absence. What the hell had I almost let him do? I couldn't kiss him, and I definitely couldn't let him kiss me. There were too many unanswered questions hovering around him—including who was calling him every night. And why didn't he ever answer the call? Or even look at the phone to see who was trying to reach him? That ringtone was obviously for *one* specific person, and I really wanted to know who it was. "Who keeps calling you at this hour anyway?" I asked, quickly taking a step back.

Reluctantly letting his fingers drop from my cheek, Hayden shrugged. "A…friend."

Yet another mysterious friend. He seemed to have no other kind. "At almost two in the morning? Is something wrong?"

Hayden gave me a smooth smile. "Of course not, Kenzie. Everything's fine. I will have to take a rain check on pie, though." After he cancelled our plans, he suddenly leaned forward and lightly pressed his lips to my cheek. Before I could catch my breath, he whispered in my ear, "Good night, Twenty-Two."

CHAPTER 12

My nerves were on overdrive when I arrived at the track the next morning. I found myself walking around with my shoulders bunched up around my ears, like any second the shit was going to hit the fan. But Hayden and I had closed everything, turned everything off, locked everything up...no one should know what we'd done.

I didn't begin to relax until the afternoon, when everyone still appeared to be clueless of my crimes. When our track time was up I decided to go for a run outside instead of on the treadmill; a little fresh air was exactly what I needed. Throwing my unruly hair in a ponytail, I grabbed my tennis shoes and headed out.

When I got to the entrance of the course, I noticed Hayden was doing practice laps out there. Pretending I was tightening my shoelaces, I stopped to watch him. His times were good, but not the best I'd seen him do. *Looks like he needs me too.* As I watched him, I wondered about all the mysterious questions that had popped up last night—who was always calling him, and was he involved in Myles's wreck, and what had happened between him and this Felicia person that he didn't want to talk about, and what had being bounced around from home to home been like for him, and...was he happy?

Maybe I was wrong about him. Maybe he'd fought tooth and nail for everything he had in his life and that was why he'd looked down on me when we'd first met. I really must have seemed like a spoiled princess to him, handed everything on a silver platter. The paths that had led us to this point were certainly very different—I'd had easy access to all I'd ever needed, and Hayden had clawed through the mud to get where he was—but maybe the two of us were more similar than I'd originally thought. We were both struggling for respect, we were both fighters, we were both underdogs.

I felt like Hayden and I were teammates, in a way, and wished I could grab my bike and go out there on the track with him. For the first time in my life, the ban between Cox Racing and Benneti Motorsports seemed absolutely ridiculous to me. And besides, Hayden wasn't really a Benneti…he just didn't have anywhere else to go. We were being punished because of Hayden's limited options, and it wasn't right. I'd never convince Dad of that, though. Keith either…

Straightening, I started to move away, but I was captivated by the way Hayden moved over his bike. His rage about the rumor surrounding him filled my mind as I studied his flawless transitions. He'd been so upset that people believed he'd mess with bikes. That passion had to mean he was innocent of what Dad and Myles suspected him of, right? He was trying to change; he'd said so himself. So why would he throw all that away? To win, that was why. To succeed. To get out of the gutter for good. *I left the streets for a reason, Kenzie, and I have no desire to go back …*

"Kenzie, what are you doing here?"

Startled out of my thoughts, I spun around to see Myles standing there, leaning on his crutch with a deep frown on his face. "God, you scared me, Myles. I was just…on my way outside… going for a run." I gave him a cheery smile, but he didn't return it. My heart started thudding. Was it suspicious that I was so intently watching a Benneti rider?

Reaching into the large pocket of his cargo pants, Myles pulled out a piece of paper. It looked like lap times to me. "I think you forgot this last night. Luckily I was the first one in the control room this morning, and I spotted it resting in the printer." He handed it to me and my chest seized. It *was* lap times. Hayden's and my lap times from last night. We'd forgotten to clear the computer, and it had automatically printed the report at the end of the hour, just like it always did when it was on. It had logged our bike numbers, the date, the time…everything. Shit.

Flicking the piece of paper, Myles sneered, "Want to tell me what the hell you were doing here in the middle of the night? With *him*?" He tilted his head toward Hayden.

My palms instantly turned clammy as I crumpled the evidence. "Don't tell my dad. Please…I don't want to be fired." I began frantically looking around. We were alone, right? No one could hear us?

Myles looked like I'd just asked him not to breathe. "Then tell me why you were with him. *Him*. Of all people." Pointing over his shoulder, he added, "Jesus, Kenzie. You can pull the knife out of my back anytime."

Glancing between Hayden and Myles, I desperately tried to think of something that would save me. Only the truth would. "Because…for reasons I don't even understand, he makes me a better rider. And I *need* to be better. I need to be the best. You *know* what's at stake."

Closing his eyes, Myles shook his head. "I know you're making a mistake." When he opened his eyes, they were hard. "And I know he's changing you. Breaking and entering, going behind your dad's back, hiding things from your friends…This isn't you, Kenzie. He's corrupting you, not improving you."

Panicking, I tried to smooth out the paper. "Look at my times, Myles. Just look! This is proof that he's helping me!"

He snatched the paper out of my hands. "He's a crutch you don't need." Sighing, he put a hand on my shoulder. "You can do this on your own. You *have* to."

I felt ice pooling in my gut. That sounded like a threat. "What does that mean?"

Myles gritted his jaw, fortifying himself to swing the wrecking ball. "It means end it with him…or I tell your dad everything."

Once his verbal blow was dealt, he turned and started walking away, the evidence of my deception still clenched in his hand.

"Myles...please!" He didn't respond in any way, just kept shuffling back to the garage. I wanted to fall to my knees and scream in frustration. No. This could *not* be happening. Barber was this weekend. I needed Hayden to keep me on my toes. I absolutely could not afford to end things with him now...even if that meant actively lying to one of my best friends.

* * *

When we arrived at Barber Motorsports Park, just outside of Birmingham, Alabama, I felt more relaxed than I had been in days. I was recharged, ready to take on the world, and ready to make a dent in the history books. It probably helped my nerves that Myles had stayed home and I didn't have to directly lie to anyone for a few days. Hanging out with Myles every night, trying to convince him that I'd seen the error of my ways and cut things off with Hayden, which I hadn't, was almost a full-time job. The guilt was excruciating, but my end game was worth it. That was what I told myself, anyway.

As we were staging our area at the historic racetrack, I was so pumped full of energy, I could barely contain myself. I felt like I was going to vibrate out of my skin at any moment. It was almost time. *Finally.*

"Do you need a sedative, Kenzie? Because I'm sure I could get somebody down here in an instant to give you one." Nikki's face was twisted in annoyance as she watched me pacing where she was trying to set up her stuff.

"No," I retorted. "I'm perfectly fine. I'm just...I'm ready to go," I said, clapping my hands together. "I want to be out there already, making my mark." Waiting around a solid day to get on the track was going to kill me.

"You know I love you, and I'd do just about anything for you, but you're driving me up the fucking wall." Picking up my bag, she shoved it into my chest. "Go to the hotel. Drink. Dance. Meet a guy and bump uglies. I don't care. Just let me work in peace. Please."

I was about to protest her choice of suggestions, but she seemed really stressed and really tired; the dark circles under her eyes were plain as day. My dad was a taskmaster *and* a perfectionist, and he expected the same out of everyone on his payroll—especially now, since there were so few of us left and so much was on the line. And since I was the top rider now, and I couldn't do well unless Nikki did well, Dad was probably riding her pretty hard. Probably about as hard as Daphne was riding Dad about the wedding; she'd given me strict orders before we left to make sure Dad stopped procrastinating and helped her pick a cake flavor for the wedding shower. She was unrelentingly focused.

Compassion filling me, I told Nikki, "I'm sorry. I would go somewhere, but I don't want to leave you hanging. All hands on deck, right? I'll try to control the excess energy...just tell me what to do." I set my bag down on a workbench and accidently knocked off a tray full of tools. The loud clang got everyone's attention, and earned Nikki a seething glare from John. With a groan, she picked up my bag and shoved it into my arms again.

"The best thing you can do for me is leave me alone!" she snapped. Closing her eyes, she took a deep breath before reopening them. "Please," she added, in a much calmer voice.

Knowing I was only making things worse, I nodded. "Okay, I'm out of here...Sorry." Feeling like a gigantic horse's ass, I made a beeline for the parking lot. *Now what do I do to burn off energy?*

As if fate knew I was yearning for activity, my cell phone started ringing. Pulling it out of my pocket, I glanced at the screen and smiled when I saw MAJOR ASSHAT on the display. Then I frowned and quickly glanced around. I considered silencing the call and not answering, but I was too curious to let it go to voice mail. Keeping my voice quiet in case someone somehow knew my code name for Hayden, I told him, "You shouldn't be calling me."

"I know, but I'm about to crawl out of my skin. I need a

distraction... and I bet you need one too." The low tone of his voice sent a chill down my spine.

Just the idea of being alone with him had my skin buzzing, but Hayden's team was set up at a different hotel than mine, and I could *not* walk into the lobby of the hotel where every Benneti racer was staying. "You know I can't come over," I said, approaching my rental car. "Too many witnesses." And besides, I wasn't sure if the two of us being around a bed was a good idea...

"Actually, I was thinking we could meet somewhere neutral. You have a car?"

"Yes," I said, unlocking the door of my rental. Damn, was I really considering meeting up with him here? Away from the track, away from racing, away from every excuse that made our get-togethers back home somewhat acceptable? Yes... I was.

"Good. There's a lake south of here. Meet me at the boat launch." He rattled off directions while I stepped into my car and shut the door. When he was done telling me how to get to the lake, he murmured, "See you soon, Twenty-Two."

"See ya, Forty-Three," I responded, starting my car. Putting my phone down, I paused with my hands on the wheel. What the hell was I doing?

I pulled out of the parking lot and made my way to the lake Hayden had mentioned. I beat him there, but just by a few minutes. Parking in the lot, I wondered what the hell we were going to do at a boat launch. And oddly, I didn't care. Just hanging out with him would occupy my time and help settle my excitement for tomorrow. And that was why I'd said yes, wasn't it?

Hayden pulled up beside me in a sporty two-seater coupe that looked super fast. A trickle of jealousy seeped into me as I closed the door of my safe and reliable Ford Focus. Dad wouldn't let us rent flashy cars when we traveled; he didn't want us getting into an accident before the race. Not that the company could really afford to rent a car like Hayden's anyway.

When he opened the door, he was wearing khaki shorts, a Benneti Motorsports ball cap, and a black T-shirt featuring the name of the bull riding bar we'd been at what felt like ages ago. Before the day was done, both of those last two items might have to be burned. With a relaxed, laid-back smile on his face, Hayden seemed more like a man who'd been enjoying a poolside barbecue all afternoon than someone who was stressed over an upcoming race. And as if the sun had reappeared after days of being hidden behind clouds, just the sight of him—the small curve of his smile, the sexy gleam in his emerald eyes—made me feel warm all over. Why did he always have to look so damn good?

"Hey," he said, his smile pleased.

Wishing he didn't have such a strong effect on me, wishing there were some other way to work off my nervous energy, and wishing we didn't have to hide everything we did, I walked over to him. "Hey," I answered. It felt weird to be alone with him like this. Weird…and wonderful. "So…what do you want to do?"

Hayden's lips twisted into such a seductive smile that my heart skipped a beat. Reaching into his back pocket, he pulled out a flask. "How about we start off with a drink?"

I automatically shook my head. "I don't think so."

Rolling his eyes, he extended the flask to me even more. "One sip won't kill you, Kenzie, or mess up your day tomorrow. It will just relax you…and to be honest, you look a little wound up. I think you need this."

Snatching the flask out of his hand, I unscrewed it and took a long draw. It was whiskey, and it burned like battery acid going down. I didn't react, though, just smiled and handed it back to him. Hayden chuckled, then took a sip himself. Looking around, I absorbed the beauty surrounding us. A few boats were on the water, enjoying the beautiful day, and off to the side in a grassy area, a couple was having a picnic. It was idyllic and calming, and a great place to spend time with…a friend.

Hayden indicated the dock. He handed the flask back to me while we walked toward it, and I took another sip as I sat down on the weathered wood. It actually was unwinding me…not that I was high-strung. Just anxious. Eager. Ready to go.

Somewhere on the other side of the lake I could hear dirt bikes ripping through the woods; it made a shiver of excitement wash over me. *Soon.* I was handing the alcohol back to Hayden when he suddenly asked, "Did you ever consider dirt bike racing instead of street bikes?"

I smiled. "Yeah. I even started out on dirt bikes when I was little. Dad wouldn't let me continue, though. He thinks dirt bike racing is…beneath us. He says it's a bastardization of the nobility of our sport, and a child of his will never compete in it." Hayden's eyes widened and I laughed. "I think it just scares him. Going fast is one thing; going fast over big-ass jumps is something else entirely."

Hayden nodded. "Makes sense."

As he took a swig, I softly asked him, "Did you ever consider that route?"

He didn't answer immediately after swallowing his drink, and for a moment, I thought he might not answer at all. Then he said, "Until Keith found me, I hadn't considered *any* career, much less racing. He gave me…" Hayden stopped and I was sure he was done talking. Disappointment flooded through me; I desperately wanted him to open up again—just a little bit. Because how would I ever really trust him if I didn't get to know him? Although did I need to trust him…?

"He gave you a place to live?" I ventured. "I heard your teammates say that you live above his garage…" A fact that placed another huge obstacle between us.

I saw the war in Hayden's eyes as he studied me. I wanted to tell him he could talk to me, even about Keith, but before I could, he quickly said, "Yeah. He lets me crash with him, shares his food, his bikes…everything. It's just another reason why those dicks hate me, but I don't care what they think. Before I met Keith, my life was just about…surviving. Keith gave me a goal, a dream…he gave me hope. And where I come from, that's one thing that's in very short supply. So my teammates can suck it…because I'm not going anywhere."

He was staring at me so intensely, with such a passionate fervor in his eyes, that I almost couldn't breathe. I wanted him to lean toward me, make a connection with me. *I could save you too. You don't need Keith.* But how could I possibly compete with someone who had plucked him from obscurity and given him everything he needed to get a leg up? Shit. His devotion to Keith went so much deeper than I'd realized. A cold wash of darkness swept over me as I thought about just what Hayden might do for Keith, the man who had given him a direction, a future...given him that elusive hope. He would probably do anything for him, same as I would for my father.

Feeling like I shouldn't be here anymore, I tore my gaze away from Hayden. His fingers found my jaw, pulling me back. "What?" he whispered.

I didn't want to answer, but with his penetrating eyes boring into mine, I couldn't stop myself. "Keith hates my father, blames him for killing his career. He seduced my mother, took her away from my dad for a time. I *hate* him so much for that, and you...you're saying he's some sort of hero or something, and I...I just can't..." I was surprised by the emotion in my voice; it was warbling so badly I could barely understand myself. But everything I'd said stung with truth and pain...and I was so sick of holding on to it.

Hayden grabbed my face and held me just inches from his mouth. Eyes locked on mine, he heatedly said, "I'm not him, Kenzie. I know he's not perfect. I know he's only helping me because it helps him too. And I'm okay with that." I tried to look away, but he held me in place. "I'm not telling you that you should forgive him. Fuck that. He screwed your mom; you *should* hate him. But Kenzie...*we're* not them. Their issues don't have to be our issues."

My lips parted as a flood of desire rushed through me. His words spoke to me, soothed every tender spot, calmed every trickle of pain his loyalty had sparked. I held on to his assurances with everything inside me. *Yes. We're not them. Their issues aren't our issues.*

Suddenly, Hayden was springing to his feet. "There's too much seriousness on this dock. I say we rectify that." He held his hand out, and, grabbing his fingers, I slowly stood up. "Do you trust me?" he asked, coyly raising an eyebrow.

That was the real question, wasn't it? But he'd shown me another glimpse inside himself, and I was feeling closer to him than I ever had before. "Yes," I whispered.

Squeezing my hand, Hayden pulled me off the dock; his palm in mine felt like fire against my skin. He led me along the shore, where a bunch of kayaks and canoes were resting by a building. Pointing at the kayaks, he said, "Race me."

"In the water? With those things?"

Smiling, he nodded. "Being on the water helps me relax."

That filled me with warmth. We had something else in common. "Me too."

"Great," he said with a grin. "Then help me get these into the lake."

I shook my head. "They aren't ours."

"I know, that's why we should do this quickly," he said, indicating the water. I frowned and he cupped my cheek with his free hand. "Please, beautiful girl. I need to see you smile."

A part of me wanted to reprimand him for the almost–pet name, but the rest of me was too taken aback by what he'd said. God, he was kind of…amazing. *You need to see me smile, and I need you to kiss me. Please.* My lips parted again, but I quickly sealed them shut. No. That would only make ending this harder, and there was no future here. Their issues might not be our issues, but they absolutely dictated our lives. For now.

"Okay, fine." I couldn't believe I was actually agreeing to this.

Hayden released my hand and pointed to a kayak for me to take. Looking around, I grabbed it and a nearby paddle and rushed to the water as quickly as I could go with my load. My heart started racing as the thrill of doing something spontaneous and crazy filled me with lightness. How did Hayden talk me into these things?

He was seconds behind me. We splashed into the water, our shoes and ankles getting wet as we worked our way into the small crafts. I was laughing by the time I grabbed the paddle and started pulling myself into deeper water. From beside me, I heard Hayden say, "Yeah, that's what I wanted to see."

We spent more than two hours on the lake, racing from one end to the other. Hayden won twice, then I won twice, but after a while, we stopped keeping score and just enjoyed having fun together. I was a little sad to see the sky darken to a point where we had to leave.

After returning the boats where we'd found them, we slowly walked back to our cars. I knew I was going to see Hayden tomorrow at the race, but I really didn't want to say goodbye yet.

"So, I guess this is good night," he said as we'd reached our cars.

"Yeah…" Whether or not I wanted more, I couldn't have it. He had to go back to his world, and I had to go back to mine. It was as simple as that.

Hayden took a step toward me, arms slightly outstretched, subtly asking if he could touch me. My breath sped up as I took a step in his direction. That was the closest to saying yes that I could get. He wrapped his arms around me, and my eyes fluttered closed. God, he felt good. And smelled good, spicy and forbidden. I nuzzled into his neck so I could smell him better. Our cheeks rubbed together and I almost groaned. His mouth was so close, just a twist of our heads and I could touch my lips to his. Or he could take mine…I could surrender to him, body and soul.

"Mmm, you make it hard to say goodbye…"

"You do too. I wish…" *I wish I hadn't said that. I wish we didn't have to hide. I wish this could actually go somewhere.*

Hayden pulled back to look at me; hope was in his eyes. "You wish what?"

"I…wish you well tomorrow," I stated. "But not *too* well, because I still plan on kicking your ass."

His expression dropped, just a little, but then he grinned. "Right. I guess we'll just have to see about that."

Stepping away, he leaned down and kissed my hand. It was a sweet way to let me go, and yet it was a nod toward his royalty comments back in the beginning of our…whatever we were. Ass.

Before I could change my mind, I forced myself to get into my car. Hayden seemed to be forcing himself as well, as he stiffly shuffled to his vehicle. Once we were both inside, cars running, Hayden revved his engine. It sent a message straight to the section of my brain that craved speed. *Game on, Hayes.* Throwing my car in reverse, I spun around and zoomed for the exit. Hayden was a breath behind me.

My little reliable car couldn't hold him back for long. He pulled around me on a straightaway; it really pissed me off to see his taillights in front of me, mocking me. It was so natural for me to race him that I wasn't even consciously aware that I was doing it until we hit traffic. When he started weaving around cars—and I shockingly followed suit—a warning started gonging in my brain that I was being stupid, that I was taking this too far, that I should slow down and let him win.

Screw that.

I kept on his tail as close as I could until he pulled into a parking lot. I was so proud of my little car for keeping pace that I didn't realize where we were until I got out of my car and saw Hayden's hotel looming behind us. Shit. I'd followed him home. I shouldn't be here.

Smiling, Hayden came up to me and wrapped his arms around me again. All coherent thought left me. I had nowhere to be but in his arms. "You almost had me!" he exclaimed, pulling me tight. Pushing me back, he looked down on me with adoration in his eyes. "That was amazing. *You* are amazing. Come inside with me, Kenzie. I'm not saying anything has to happen, I just don't want to say good night yet."

It sounded so right, he felt so right, I couldn't object. But I could voice a concern. "Someone might see me."

Hayden shook his head. "I'm on the ground floor. I can let you in the back slider." His thumb ran over my cheek, and warmth radiated outward from the point of contact. "No one will see you, Kenzie. I promise."

I was nodding before I realized it.

Hayden led me around to the back of the hotel; both of us were hunched over, looking for people we might know. We couldn't have been more conspicuous if we tried. But nobody was nearby, and we successfully walked through the berms behind the hotel with no one the wiser.

Hayden was inspecting the surroundings, looking for some clue he was near his room. When he spotted something that confirmed it for him, he stopped us. “Okay, this one is mine. Stay here, and I’ll go in and unlock the slider. Ten seconds, I swear.”

Feeling very open and exposed—and crazy for doing this—I laughingly said, “What? Can’t pick a slider?”

“Not without breaking it.” He smirked.

He was just turning to run back to the lobby when the sliding glass door leading to his room suddenly opened. Hayden and I exchanged startled glances, then Hayden protectively stepped in front of me.

A familiar-looking skinny Hispanic guy stepped out of the room and Hayden let out a relieved sigh. “Jesus, Hookup. What the fuck are you doing in my room? You scared the shit out of me.”

Hayden’s friend…Hookup—what the hell kind of a name was Hookup?—was snacking on a bag of hotel peanuts. “What the fuck are *you* doing out here? Skulking in the shadows. I thought you were about to get robbed, dude. I was savin’ the day.” He looked around Hayden and locked eyes with me. His eyes widened, like he recognized me. Stepping closer, he said, “Holy shit…Felicia? Where the fuck have you been, girl?”

I felt the little hairs on the back of my neck stand up. This guy knew Felicia?

Hayden adjusted his position in front of me, hiding me even more. “She’s not Felicia,” he said, heat in his voice. “Now are you going to tell me what you’re doing here? I thought we were…” He stopped talking and glanced back at me, his expression guarded.

Hookup shrugged. “Something came up. Thought we’d…go over it.” He leaned to the side so he could look at me again. “Sorry, Felicia lookalike, but Hayden will have to fuck you another night. Boys gotta talk. You understand, sweetheart?”

Understand? The only thing I understood here was that this guy was an asshole. Maybe sensing my prickly mood, Hayden spun around and put his hands on my shoulders. His expression apologetic, he cringed as he said, “I am so sorry.” His jaw tightened, and I could see the tick of his pulse pounding beneath the skin. “For everything. But I'll see you tomorrow…right?" The plea in his eyes was palpable.

Wow…really? I had been about to enter his *bedroom* and he was blowing me off? For this…thug? Guess he hadn't completely cut the streets out of his life after all. I wasn't sure why that surprised me; maybe it was because we were thousands of miles away from home, and I hadn't expected to see one of his seedy friends here. Or maybe it was because I'd completely bought Hayden's story about wanting to leave all that behind. I'd thought Hayden was a diamond in the rough, waiting to be polished, but maybe he was *just* rough. Maybe finding out like this, before anything happened between us, was a blessing in disguise.

"Yeah…tomorrow." *When I fly by you and take it all.*

CHAPTER 13

Hayden and Hookup disappeared into Hayden's room. With the curtain drawn across the slider, I couldn't see anything, but maybe I could hear something, because I'd really like to know just what the *boys* had to talk about. Putting my ear against the glass, I tried to make out something useful. Mainly, all I could hear was my heartbeat—standing outside a hotel room obviously spying on the people inside was not exactly in my comfort zone. The guys were talking too low for me to understand, but from the tone, someone sounded angry. I hoped that was Hayden; I hoped he slugged the guy for interrupting our date.

Whoa, date? *No, definitely not.* We were just killing time, and I think I'd killed enough for one day.

When I got back to my hotel, I had trouble relaxing. Nikki texted me, probably wanting to go out, but I ignored her message. I didn't feel like heading out again. I just wanted to sit on my stiff bed and focus on tomorrow's race. *That's what really matters, not the mysteries surrounding Hayden.* He was just a means to an end. I needed to remember that.

I woke up early the next morning, the sky outside my window showing only the barest hint of a rosy glow. It was supposed to be gorgeous today—not too hot, not too cold, with clear blue skies for miles. The perfect day for a race.

There was an early-morning inspection of all the bikes entered in the race, so I got ready and headed to the track. It wasn't necessary for me to be there, since Nikki and the rest of the crew handled that, but I couldn't sleep anymore anyway; might as well do something useful with my time.

Nikki was already there and she looked far more rested than I felt. She did a double take when she saw me. "Wow, you look like shit. Feeling okay?"

Frowning, I tossed a rag at her. "I'm fine... bitch."

Nikki pointed to all the Cox Racing bikes awaiting prerace inspection on their respective mats. Upon arrival at the track, every bike was thoroughly inspected in an impound area, but before and after races, they were checked out on-site. Until the bikes were inspected, only two mechanics were allowed to be near them, and nothing was allowed to be modified on them afterward. Anything changed on a bike would be caught during the postrace inspection, and the fines, point deductions, and future race penalties were stiff. *No one* messed with bikes once they'd been given the okay. Well, in theory. Dad had decided that after Myles's "incident," no bikes were to be left alone. Myles was so positive Hayden was guilty that he had convinced Dad that the extra precautions were necessary. God, was Hayden guilty? The possibility that something might be going on and he might be a part of it made me queasy. *No, he wouldn't risk it, not even to win. He wants a better life.*

Distracting me from my thoughts, Nikki said, "Hey, can you keep an eye on these for a second? I'm gonna go find some coffee. Maybe some food too." She grabbed her stomach and hunched over, like she was being eaten from the inside out.

"Sure," I told her, nodding. "Bring me some too, will ya?"

She gave me a thumbs-up before she left. I waited there by the bikes for twenty long minutes, then I started getting bored. Sitting around doing nothing was not something I was good at. I liked action, movement. *God, Nikki, where the hell did you go for that coffee? Colombia?* I was spinning around on a swivel stool, waiting for either Nikki or the inspection officials, when the crew chief, John, walked into the garage area.

"You're here early. Good. Your father would like to speak to you." John was just as uptight before a race as my father often was. It was hard to believe they'd ever been my age.

I jerked my thumb at the row of bikes. "I have to watch the equipment."

John shrugged. "I'll keep an eye on them. Your dad is in his trailer."

Nodding at him, I made my way into the inner sanctum of the racetrack, the heart and soul of the event. Dad's Fifth Wheel trailer was resting in the Cox Racing area, and I climbed the few steps to the door, then lightly knocked. Dad's response was instant. "Enter."

For some reason, my heart started pounding as I opened the door. What if he knew I'd hung out with Hayden yesterday? What if he knew I'd ended up at his hotel room? "Dad? John said you wanted to see me?" I had to clear my throat halfway through my sentence. *Calm down, Kenzie. Control.*

Dad looked up from a table covered in paperwork and gave me a brief smile. Seeing it made me relax. "Yes, I just wanted to let you know that a new potential sponsor will be watching the race today. Watching *you* in particular. This could be a big account for us, Mackenzie, and you know how much we need the support right now." His eyes drifted down to the scattered sheets before him, and I knew by "support" he meant "money." *I know, Dad. That's why I'm betraying you by seeing Hayden.*

By the look on Dad's face as he frowned at me, he was unsure whether I was up to the task of impressing a high-profile sponsor. His apparent lack of faith in me was crushing, but I had a secret weapon he didn't know about under my belt. Thanks to Hayden and our late-night practices, I was well prepared for today. And tuning out the world, narrowing it down to just the two of us—that was how I was going to win. Hayden was my ace in the hole. "I'll do my best, Dad, just like I do every race."

Dad absentmindedly nodded, then he looked around his empty trailer. When he felt satisfied we were alone, he said, "Myles is still adamant about Hayden being dangerous... about the Bennetis being dangerous. I want you to keep your eyes open for anything weird today. If you feel like the slightest thing is off, you come to me."

That made ice shoot through my veins. Myles had said he would stay silent about my after-hours laps with Hayden, so long as he believed I was no longer seeing him. If his distrust of Hayden truly went so deep that he was still after my dad to do something... how much longer would he stay silent? Was our friendship deeper than his hatred? I hoped so. "Sure, Dad."

Dad's eyes narrowed. "I'm serious about this, Mackenzie. I've been looking into the stats for Daytona and Road America... and I'm seeing a pattern that concerns me."

"What do you mean?"

Dad sighed. "There was a meeting no-show, an engine burnout, a couple sick riders, illegal parts, and of course, Myles's wreck. All resulted in penalties that bumped Benneti's riders farther up the standings... Hayden being at the top."

I bit my lip so hard I almost punctured it. "Dad... that's racing. That stuff happens, it's completely normal." It couldn't be anything other than a coincidence. It was easy to start seeing trouble everywhere you looked if you were always looking for it.

Dad's steely eyes narrowed. "I've been around the sport long enough to know what's real and what's manufactured. Something strange is going on, and if anyone would sink to this level, it's Keith. So just... keep your eyes open, okay?"

"Okay. Well... I better get back to the bikes," I said with downcast eyes. Hayden's words from yesterday rang in my ears: *Their issues don't have to be our issues.* Did he mean that? Or did he say it just to throw me off track? *No, it can't be him.*

Peeking up, I saw Dad nod as he returned his gaze to the table. "Thank you, Mackenzie. Maybe it is over-the-top paranoia... but we can't afford for it to be anything more. Better to be cautious than sorry," he murmured, running a hand through his graying blond hair.

I left Dad's trailer feeling torn. I wanted to believe it was all random accidents—no, I *had* to believe that—because believing otherwise made me feel sick to the bone. I couldn't be conspiring with someone that twisted. But…there *were* things about Hayden that I just wasn't sure about. I really didn't know him all that well, and the people he called friends…His judgment clearly wasn't all that great. That was the only thing I *was* positive about.

When I got back to the bikes, I didn't see John there. Or Nikki. Someone else was there, though, kneeling down between my bike and Eli's on the end of the row. Was it an official doing an inspection? Had to be…but if it wasn't…shit. Getting ready to kick some serious ass, I stormed down the aisle. I stopped dead in my tracks when I recognized the disheveled dirty-blond hair. *Hayden.*

I felt like the world had just stopped spinning and I was trying to remain upright.

"Hayden?" I asked, my voice shaky with tension. "What the hell are you doing here?"

He zipped to his feet lightning-quick, then tossed on a carefree smile. "Dang it, you spotted me. I was…hoping to scare you."

My heart was pounding with dread. This couldn't be real. "What were you doing by my bike?"

He glanced down at my Ducati. "Hiding. But not very well," he added with a nervous laugh.

No, he wasn't. He wouldn't risk his career just to scare me; he wasn't that stupid. But now wasn't the time to demand answers. If John or Nikki came back…We couldn't be spotted together like this. "You shouldn't be here. You need to *go*," I said, looking around nervously.

Walking over to me, he grabbed my hand. "I know, but I can't stop thinking about yesterday. I couldn't sleep, and I just…I needed to see you before the race. I need to apologize. I feel like I chased you off, and that was the last thing I wanted to happen last night. You've got to believe me."

Did I? Well, I knew he'd wanted more to happen…same as *I'd* wanted more to happen. But it hadn't, and there was nothing that we could do about it now. Gently pulling my hand away, I told him, "You already apologized…and it's fine. But you need to go back to your area, before John or my dad come out here."

He sighed. "Yeah…I know." Twisting back to me, he lifted his eyebrows in an expression of hope. "Will you spend some time with me tonight, after the race? No distractions this time, I promise."

"Yeah…maybe." I shouldn't…but I wanted to.

His brows drew together. "Those are actually two different answers, you know. Which one is it?"

Turning him around, I pushed him toward the open bay doors. "It's a 'you need to go and we'll talk about this later' answer."

"Fine." He sulked like a child before walking away.

I shook my head at him, momentarily amused, but my heart never fully returned to normal once he was gone. What the hell had he been doing here? And where the hell were Nikki and John? The bikes were never supposed to be alone. Fear clenched my chest as I inched closer to my motorcycle. He hadn't been greasy, hadn't been dirty, and hadn't had any tools on him…so what could he have done? Nothing really. And why would he touch my bike anyway? Hurting me would only hurt himself. But if Keith had ordered him to do something…would he turn him down?

"Hey, Kenzie. The officials pass through yet?"

I turned around to see Nikki striding my way. "I'm not…I actually don't know."

She frowned at me. "What do you mean you don't know? You were here, right?"

Shrugging, I spat out, "John watched the bikes for a bit. They must have come while he was watching them." That's really the only reason John would have left them unattended. Maybe he didn't share Dad's concerns and he thought they were safe post-inspection. And they should be. My rookie year wasn't supposed to be laced with so much distrust. It hadn't been like this before Hayden's arrival.

Nikki's frosty eyes weren't warming any, so I nonchalantly changed the subject. "I thought you were getting us coffee?"

Both of her hands were empty. Dirty, but empty. Frowning, she shook her head. "Couldn't find any. You should probably go get ready. I'll find out if the bikes have been inspected."

Throwing on a smile, I told her, "Great! And…will you take a peek at mine again? I know you can't change anything, just make sure everything looks..." My voice trailed off as I suddenly realized that I couldn't flat-out ask her if my bike had been messed with. I couldn't explain why I suspected that it might have been—she couldn't know Hayden had dropped by to see me.

"Make sure everything's...what?" she asked, concerned.

There really wasn't anything I could tell her, except to admit that I was being overly cautious. "It's no big deal, and I know it's fine, it's just...sponsors are coming today, and I really need to impress the hell out of them."

Nikki's concerned expression instantly relaxed into a comforting smile. "Oh...yeah. But don't worry, Kenzie. Your baby is perfect." She patted my shoulder in support; she knew how important this race was for the family.

Damn. I couldn't ask her to look for something suspicious, so I was going to have to leave it alone and hope that Hayden hadn't done anything. Goddammit, I hated that I didn't know for certain that my bike was fine. I wanted to trust Hayden, but...could I afford to?

Things were off during my practice lap, which worried me. My bike felt different, but I was so wound up in my head that it could have just been me. I almost asked Nikki to prep my backup bike for the race, but she'd want to know why, and I couldn't explain. It had to be all in my mind anyway. There was nothing wrong here except for the fact that I was having doubts, and that was something I couldn't allow myself. Doubt was how people got killed in my line of work.

When we were all lined up in our grid boxes, I reminded myself over and over that I was fully prepared for this race. Nothing was going to stop me, and no fears or insecurities were going to hold me back. I was good at this, and I was ready.

I didn't turn to look, but I knew Hayden was in his designated spot, two places behind me; I could feel his eyes boring holes into my back. It gave me a sorely needed confidence boost to know I'd qualified ahead of him. I had an instant lead on him, one I never intended to lose.

Suddenly, the light I was staring at changed color; I'd been watching it so intently, I still saw a red glow inside the green. It reminded me of Christmas, which was what I felt today was going to be like for me.

As if we were all part of one sentient being, the pack of us surged forward. Determined to hold my position but careful to make sure I didn't dump the clutch, I released the restrained power beneath me and accelerated with the rest of my rivals. A part of me wanted to look back, to see where Hayden was in the pack, but I couldn't; the road ahead required all of my concentration. It was a little odd to be in front of him at the start—I was so used to chasing him. To fool my mind, I pretended the rider in front of me was Hayden. I even pictured him turning around and giving me a *come get me* head nod. Compressing my mouth into a firm line, I nearly maxed out the acceleration. *I've got you, Hayes.*

Time lost all meaning as I focused solely on the task at hand. Minutes could have passed, or days. I had no idea. I was high on life, lost in the moment of finally competing on my favorite track. Coming to Barber with my dad when I was younger, I used to disappear for hours in the vintage museum nearby, or I'd spend all day scouring the area, searching for all the different art sculptures. But now that I was actually *competing* on it, all of my previous memories paled in comparison.

With nineteen laps and fourteen turns, the track here constantly kept you on your toes. Between the twisting and turning, pushing and pulling, fighting for every inch while trying to not give anyone else a break, I was mentally and physically depleted by the time it was halfway over. Pulling strength from my countless hours of exercise, I pressed through the fatigue. When I saw the final lap flag being waved, a grin broke over my face. I'd kept my momentum up, and I was currently sitting in fourth place. All I had to do was maintain it for a little over two miles, and I'd be golden.

And that was when my bike wobbled.

I was so in tune with the instrument beneath me that I instantly felt the difference, and I knew something was wrong. Hayden, that son of a bitch. He *had* done something to my bike. He'd screwed me. But why? He needed me...we were partners.

Shocked, angry, and a little frightened, I slowed. Not by much, but it didn't take much at these speeds. Four people zoomed past me, Hayden included. Of the four, only Hayden twisted his helmet to look at me as he shot by. Was he gloating? Happy he'd gotten me? God, what an idiot I'd been to trust him.

When I finally made it over the finish line, the front part of my bike was vibrating so badly my teeth were rattling. Crushed, I kept my eyes glued on the scoreboard, waiting for the final times to be posted. I prayed with all my might that somehow I was magically still in fourth place, but I'd seen the racers flying by me. I knew the truth. Fourth was a fantasy.

My name and time flashed on the board. Eighth place, same as my Road America finish. Feeling like I'd been punched in the gut, I could barely hold back the tears of frustration and disappointment. I'd worked so hard, and I hadn't gained any ground in the standings. This wasn't how today was supposed to go. I was supposed to finish big, break a record, impress the sponsors...save Cox Racing.

Fury and betrayal were foremost in my mind when I returned to the garage. Nikki instantly approached me. "Kenzie, what happened out there? You were doing so great, and then..." Face pale, she looked over at my bike. "Something's wrong with her, isn't it? I missed something..."

I dug my fingernails into my palms as I paced. No, Hayden had fucked with me. He wasn't Keith, huh? No, he was so much worse. He'd made me begin to trust him, and he was going to feel the full force of my outrage when I saw him again. Spend time with him tonight? Did he honestly think I'd ever hang out with him again after this?

Dad walked into the pits then, a scowl on his face. "You almost had fourth place, Mackenzie. That would have impressed the sponsors much more than eighth. Why did you slow down?"

My internal fires still roaring hot, I snapped out, "My bike started shimmying...just like Myles's did at Road America. Thank

God I didn't crash." How the hell could Hayden have done that to me? Although I hadn't seen a flash of light like Myles had, hadn't heard a pop…

Dad's eyes went so wide, they were practically all white. His breath started coming harder, and he brought his hand to his chest, like he was in pain; he almost looked like he was having a heart attack. "What? Someone messed with you? Are you all right?"

I wasn't used to seeing him worked up over me, worked up over *anything*. Dad was always…level. Even when I'd slid out, he hadn't been scared, and I could swear that was what he was right now—terrified. Wanting to take it all back so he'd calm down, I said, "I'm fine, it was nothing."

Nikki shook her head. "Wait…you questioned me about your bike, Kenzie, and you seemed worried. I thought it was just nerves about the sponsors, but…did you know before the race started that something might be wrong with it?"

I wanted to rewind time; there was so much I would change. Panicking, words started tumbling out of my mouth. "No, I just, when I saw him with the bikes, I thought he might have—" Shit. I pressed my lips together to shut myself up, but not in time. I'd said too much.

"You saw who?" Dad asked, eyes hard. "Who did you see?" he pressed.

I shook my head. Fuck. *What do I say?* "I didn't…I didn't really see who it was…they took off so fast. But nothing appeared to be wrong with the bike, I just… " Damn it, why the hell had I opened my big fat mouth? This was going down a road it couldn't go. I needed to fix this, fast. Inhaling a calming breath, I told him, "It was nothing, Dad, my bike wobbled, that's all. I overreacted."

Not believing my denial, Dad's face darkened into an expression so menacing, it gave me chills. "No, you didn't overreact. Some strange person lurking around our bikes was most *definitely* something. It was Keith and his little punk. All of this started when he brought that bastard onto his team. And no one else in the league has a bone to pick with me but Keith—it was definitely him. That son of a bitch, I can't believe he'd go after my *daughter*."

He'd said that in such a low voice that no one besides Nikki and I heard him. I was grateful for that. With no proof, Dad couldn't really do anything to Keith. And if he said something to the officials without proof, Cox Racing would be the one who got in trouble. I didn't want that.

Letting out a long breath, I placed a hand on Dad's arm, trying to soothe him as well as myself. "It was just an issue with the bike. Something was loose. It happens—doesn't mean someone did something."

Dad's eyes narrowed as he looked down at me. "Don't be naïve, Mackenzie. You see someone around your bike and later you have problems? That means something. That means *everything*. Keith has gone too far this time. He won't get away with this."

He stormed away from me before I could say another word. Fear shoved the last remnants of rage from my veins. What the hell was Dad going to do?

Ignoring my crew and teammates, who were both congratulating and consoling me, Nikki and I hurried after Dad. Hopefully I could get to him before he did something stupid, like go to an official. While I was horrified over what he might do and what trouble it might cause him, it was surprisingly heartwarming to know that he was this worked up over my safety. Even though the situation was awful, it made me feel appreciated, validated...loved.

When I caught up to Dad, he was storming over to Keith's area. This was not good, not good at all. "Dad, no! Wait!"

Dad was on a mission, though, and my simple words weren't about to stop him. Pushing his way through multiple Benneti racers, he thundered up to Keith. "What the hell do you think you're doing?"

Bewilderment clear on his face, Keith looked around *his* area filled with *his* racers. Pulling down his too-large aviator sunglasses, he calmly said, "I think you're in the wrong place, Jordan."

Running up to Dad, I looked over to see Hayden watching the showdown with clear confusion in his eyes. I pulled on Dad's arm to get him to come with me, but he wasn't backing away from this fight. Not this time. Putting his hands on Keith's chest, Dad shoved him, snarling, "You piece of shit! You couldn't have my wife, so you had your punk go after my daughter!"

Keith lost his footing on his weak leg and fell to the floor. Everyone stopped and stared. Even though the hustle and bustle of the world around us was loud, I swear I could have heard a pin drop. Hayden broke through the crowd to help Keith to his feet. Ripping off his sunglasses, his cheeks flaming red, Keith shouted, "You've gone too far, Jordan! This is my area! You can't come here and—"

"And that's my daughter your thug messed with!" Dad made a move toward Hayden, but I grabbed his arm, holding him back. Hayden and I locked eyes; Hayden's were heated now. He was ticked. Not at me, though.

Keith's questioning gaze focused on me before turning back to Dad; Keith's eyes were dancing with anger too. "What are you talking about, Jordan? Have you finally lost your mind?"

Ignoring Keith's question, Dad shoved his finger into Hayden's chest. "I know you messed with Mackenzie's bike. I know you're behind this!"

Hayden's expression went from pissed to shocked, then back to pissed again. "Don't touch me, old man," he seethed, flexing his fingers.

Remembering what Hayden had done to his teammates when they'd cornered him, I tugged on Dad's arm. "Dad, we need to go. Now!" I hissed. Too intent on Hayden, Dad ignored me.

Keith seemed surprised and offended by Dad's outburst. "Unlike some people, Jordan, I don't need to tamper with racers to win." By the smug look on his face, it was clear he thought my dad was the one who was capable of cheating. My blood began to boil, which made it that much harder to hold Dad back. "I don't need to sink that low, Cox. I've got this little thing called talent," Keith continued. "It's something Vivienne often complimented me on."

Hearing my mother's name fall from Keith's mouth infuriated me. My father hearing it, however, completely shattered whatever slim hold he'd had on his control. "You son of a—"

He pulled back his arm to take a swing at Keith, and there was nothing I could do to stop him. Dad's fist connected with

Keith's jaw, making a sickening thud, and Keith fell to the floor again. Like hornets erupting from a crushed nest, the Benneti team swarmed into action. I heard someone shout for security, while others lunged at Dad. He pushed them off, then took a swing at Hayden. Hayden easily dodged, then set up his own punch.

"No!" I shouted at him. *If I ever meant anything to you...don't hit my father.*

Hayden snapped his eyes to me, then he slowly lowered his fist. My father took his second of distraction to strike at Hayden again, and this time he connected. Hayden took a jarring blow to the face that clearly staggered him. I rushed forward to help, but a hand on my arm froze me in place.

"Kenzie! Help me get your dad out of here!" I looked over my shoulder to see a pale-white Nikki scanning the scene with horror in her eyes.

Knowing she was right, I helped her disengage Dad from trying to hit...somebody. We each had to grab one of his arms to get him out of there, and he kept trying to go back, to "finish the job" as he said. He didn't settle down until we got him back to the trailer. I was shaking with adrenaline and shock when we got there. I had never seen my dad blow his top like that—*ever*. A new side of him had been exposed to me, and it wasn't pretty. It also made me wonder: How long could a person stay wound up tight before they exploded? Maybe absolute control wasn't all it was cracked up to be.

Dad looked sick when Nikki and I sat him on the couch. "I shouldn't have done that. I shouldn't have lost control. I shouldn't have...shouldn't have..."

I barely recognized my father. He'd always been so on top of things, so in charge of his emotions. But the thought of me being in danger, and Keith callously mentioning Mom, had unglued him. I wasn't sure what was going to happen now. There would be stiff repercussions for this; you couldn't punch someone here—at an *event*—and not be penalized, or fined, or worse. Benneti Motorsports might or might not have been involved with today's incident on the track, but it was Cox Racing who was going to pay.

Dad ran his hands down his face as he stood up and paced his office. "Damn it, I shouldn't have lost control. No one will believe me now..."

"Dad..." I didn't know what to say, didn't know what to do. I wanted to comfort him, I wanted to slug him, and I wanted to cheer for how he'd stuck up for me. I settled on gratitude, since it seemed like the most positive response. "I'm not sure what's going to happen now, but thank you for sticking up for me. I know you were just trying to protect me, and I'm... I'm so sorry this happened."

The residual anger in Dad's eyes immediately fell away. It was replaced with such profound despair that I was instantly sorry I'd said anything. "It's not your fault, Mackenzie. Nothing that happened today was your fault."

I was about to tell him it wasn't his fault either when someone started banging on the trailer door. "Jordan Cox? My name is Charles Collins; I'm with the ARRC. I need to have a word with you regarding an incident with Benneti Motorsports. Can you come out here, please?"

Dad closed his eyes and slumped over, like every bone in his body had turned to jelly; he suddenly looked about fifteen years older. Reopening his eyes, he quietly told Nikki and me, "Time to face the music. I'll speak with you both later."

Hoping this wouldn't go as badly as he feared, I nodded. "Good luck, Dad."

Looking utterly defeated, Dad shook his head. "There is no luck, Mackenzie. No luck, and no coincidences."

In the silence of his departure, Nikki put a hand on my arm. "I'm gonna go look at your bike... see if I can tell what happened." With a heavy sigh, I nodded and watched her leave. Closing my eyes once she was gone, I wondered how I could possibly keep my mind busy while I waited for answers.

A low voice disrupted my thoughts. "Kenzie? Are you okay?"

I opened my eyes to see Hayden standing in the open door. It felt so wrong for him to be in my father's office, but even still, a small part of me was glad he was here. I didn't really want to be alone right now. "You shouldn't be here," I told him, knowing it needed to be said.

He closed the trailer door, then stepped over to where I was. "Here is the only place I could be. Are you okay?" He put his hands on my forearms and examined my eyes; his left one was bruised and swollen. He was going to have one hell of a black eye tomorrow.

All I could read from his expression was concern, though. I didn't get it. My father had slugged Keith and then hit Hayden. Hayden should barely be able to look at me right now. "Aren't you mad?" I asked.

His lips compressed into a firm line. "I'm pissed. Your dad never should have laid a hand on Keith. But"—his expression softened along with his voice—"are *you* okay?"

His sincerity warmed my chilly heart, but I had concerns of my own, things I needed to know. Recalling everything that had happened made righteous anger shoot up my spine. *I trusted you.* I shoved him away from me. "What the fuck did you do to do my bike? And don't say nothing, because I know that's bullshit. I felt it—something was wrong."

Hayden sighed and I felt something in my chest crack. *He did mess with me.* "Look, Kenzie, it's not what you think..."

"Then tell me what it was, because right now, I don't see any reason why I shouldn't report you." Besides the fact that I would be fired once Hayden confessed how close we were, of course.

Hayden sighed again. "Okay, truth is...I wasn't there for you at all, but I didn't touch your bike, I swear. I just...had to check something. That's all I can say." His gaze turned distant, speculative.

Ice filled my veins. Disbelieving this was really happening, I took a step back from him. "All you can say? Is that supposed to make me feel better?"

Hayden shook his head as he approached me again. "I have your back, Kenzie, and I would never hurt you. Ever. You *mean* something to me. *That* is what should make you feel better."

It was a beautiful sentiment that he was sharing with me—one that made a tremor of delight flicker across my heart—but I couldn't risk my career on sentiment alone. "I fucked up with *sponsors* watching, Hayden. You know how badly my family needs them right now. Or...we did, anyway." My shoulders drooped as the reality of our situation pounded me. "I have no idea what's happening with my father right now. It could be over. He hit another team owner at an event. Shit. It's all over..."

Hayden's fingers were suddenly along my jaw, tilting my chin up to make me look at him. "It's not over until you let it be over, Kenzie. Keep fighting. Keep fighting, and don't ever stop." His eyes were passionate as they flicked between mine, and my breath completely stopped.

I thought he would drop his fingers, move away, tell me that he had to go—because there was no plausible way to explain this if someone came in here—but...he didn't. He just kept holding my face, kept sweeping his gaze across me, like he was searching for something. Approval? Rejection? I was such an emotional mess right now, I wasn't sure what I wanted him to do, but I needed him to do *something*.

"Hayden..." Just getting his name out was difficult. What did I want from him?

Hayden's face shifted with indecision as he studied me. Then he shook his head...and crashed his lips down to mine. My first instinct was to push him away, but my body was exploding with sensation and desire, and I couldn't. It was like we were racing again, like it was only the two of us in a crowd of thousands. I pulled him into me, wanting the rush, wanting the heat, wanting more...so much more. My fingers tangled in his hair, raked over his body, pulled at his hips. It was like I was a caged animal finally released; I couldn't get enough. I didn't even recognize myself as I ravaged him, and it felt so good to let go.

He was just as unrestrained, kissing me like he'd been dying to do it for years. His tongue found mine, and I groaned and clenched his shoulders. *Yes.* God, he tasted good, like cinnamon and seduction. I wrapped a leg around his body, pulling him closer. *More.* I could feel the length of him through his clothes, pressing against me, and I knew he wanted more too. *Yes, this is what I want, what*

I need. I don't care that we're rivals, that we're enemies, that we are completely forbidden. Let's just do this…

His hands were all over my body, clawing at my racing suit like he wanted to rip it off. The thought of being completely bare before him had me on the edge of another mind-shattering release. God, he just had to touch me, feel how ready I was, how much I needed him, and I would crumble to pieces.

But not here. Not like this.

I couldn't do this while my dad was out getting his ass handed to him by the officials—while he was possibly losing the business forever. It would be piling betrayal upon betrayal if I let Hayden take me *here.*

Hands on Hayden's chest, I firmly pushed him away from me. He was breathing heavier, his eyes glazed with desire. Swallowing to catch my breath, I told him, "You should go…before someone comes in here."

He tried to return his lips to mine, but I held him back. If he successfully reached my mouth again, I might not have the strength to turn him away. My body was already screaming to let him have his way with me, to submit to every erotic indulgence he might offer. But no, I couldn't listen. My head had to prevail right now—it *had* to.

As I tried to step away, Hayden pulled me back into his body. "I know I should care about that," he growled. "But right now, I really don't." His arms around me squeezed me tight. "I want you, Kenzie. Every goddamn time I see you, I want you. I want to feel your hands on my body, I want your legs wrapped tight around me, I want to hear you moan in my ear, smell the lavender in your hair. All I've been able to think about since that goddamn bull is what it would feel like to be inside you, to make you come, to tear down the walls you've built around yourself…to make you beg for more." He leaned closer, so his lips were almost brushing mine. "Racing gives me a high…but *you* make me feel alive."

That was too much for me. Threading my hands into his hair, I jerked his face down to mine. When our lips collided, a satisfied moan escaped me. God, he felt so good. As our hungry mouths attacked each other, he unzipped my leathers and started peeling them off my shoulders. Every place he touched me felt on fire, and I'd never wanted him more than I wanted him now. But I still couldn't do this here.

With a frustrated groan, I summoned every ounce of my remaining willpower and somehow managed to shove him away. Quickly, before my body could take over again, I moved behind my father's desk. I felt safer with a large piece of furniture between us. *But God, how I wish he would stride over here and throw me down on it.*

Startled by my own desire, I held both my hands up to him, stopping him before he even started. "I want you too. But we *can't* go there…and you know that. And that's why you're going to turn around and leave. Right now."

"Kenzie…" He closed his mouth and frowned, like he had no idea what to say to me. All I wanted him to say was goodbye. Regret was swirling within me, threatening to drown me, and I didn't want him to see me go under. We shouldn't have opened the box, shouldn't have tasted what was forbidden. Because one taste just wasn't enough…

Eyes full of mirrored pain, Hayden murmured, "Will I see you later tonight? Like we talked about?"

God, I'd never wanted to say yes so badly in all my life. But what left my mouth was "No."

I can't. And you can't either.

Hayden stared at me a second longer, then he turned and started for the door. As he was opening it, I found myself saying his name. When he looked back at me, I whispered, "Thank you for not hurting my father today. I know you could have, but you didn't…and that…means a lot to me." He probably could have taken my father out with one hit, if he'd been so inclined, but when I'd asked, he'd backed down. And he was on his way to sporting a black eye now because of it. I owed him for that.

A brief smile graced Hayden's face. "Every day I find there is less and less that I wouldn't do for you, Kenzie…and that scares the shit out of me."

He vanished before I could respond.

CHAPTER 14

The final verdict on my bike was that the normal wear and tear on the front forks had caused them to vibrate. It would have been fine for me to maintain my speed and there was no reason for me to slow down like I had. I'd overreacted, and all of us had suffered.

The officials decided to penalize every Cox racer in the event by adding thirty seconds to our time. That might not sound like much, but in our world, it was huge. I slipped from eighth to tenth. Eli and Ralph finished even farther back. They were both pissed, but there was nothing they could do, nothing any of us could do. Dad had stepped way out of line, and the organization was making an example of him.

In addition to the riders being penalized, Cox Racing was also slapped with a massive fine. Dad wouldn't tell me how much it was, but I knew it was a crushing blow to our already struggling business. To add insult to injury, with everything that had transpired, no sponsors in the crowd had stepped forward to align with us. And it was all my fault. I had sparked a chain reaction that could quite feasibly end Cox Racing. I felt sick.

When we returned to Oceanside, a cloud of darkness hung over everyone. You could almost see the despair hovering in the air above the Cox garages. No one knew what the future held for them anymore, and everybody was on edge.

Ignoring the thick bleakness swirling around my teammates, I headed upstairs to see my father. He hadn't said much once he'd gotten back from his meeting with the officials. Just briefly mentioned the speed penalty and the fine, then retreated behind a wall of stoic silence. He had to still be upset. Troubled at the least, torn apart at the most. Everything he'd worked so hard for his entire life was crumbling before his eyes. It was heartbreaking. I wanted to help him, I just had no idea how to do it now. Was racing well still enough to save us?

As I trudged up the stairs, I tossed around different comforting words I might say. All of them sounded horrible, lame, insufficient. I wanted to turn around and head back downstairs to the garages, but I knew I couldn't. Dad and I might not do heart-to-hearts, but I had to see this through; it was my fault. And if he was hurting, I needed to be there for him. Because after everything else was stripped away, after all was said and done, he was my father, and I was his daughter. And I wouldn't let him suffer alone.

After knocking on his office door, I waited for permission to enter. Once he gave it, I tentatively opened the door and walked inside. As I approached him, my heart started beating faster and my palms began to slick with sweat. I hated *everything* about the situation we were in, and I would have given anything for this meeting to be just another discussion about my lap times. I wished we could ignore the emotional part of the weekend and only talk about the racing. I could talk to him about *that* for days. But it was time to talk about something a little more serious, awkward as that might be for us both.

"Hey, Dad... How's it going?" I wanted to slap myself after I said it. *He's just gone through some sort of emotional crisis, and you ask him how it's going? Jesus, Kenzie.* "I think we should talk... about what happened this weekend. You were so... different. You scared me. Are you... okay?" I quickly added.

Dad finally looked up from his paperwork. He looked horrible, with large circles under his eyes and thick stubble along his jaw.

His normally perfect hair was in complete disarray, like he'd been stroking his hand through it nonstop. Definitely not okay.

Proving that we were cut from the same cloth, Dad completely ignored my question and my concern. "Ah, Kenzie. I'm glad you're here. I have a few things to discuss with you before you start practice."

By his professional tone, I might almost think today was just another day. Like nothing strange was going on, like he hadn't gone ballistic and attacked half of the Benneti crew. A large part of me wanted to let him shift the conversation and continue the illusion, but there was a secondary voice inside me that was screaming, *Avoidance isn't the answer!*

"Dad...you didn't...you didn't answer my question. You blew up at Keith. You *hit* him!" *And Hayden.* I kept that thought internal, though. Bringing up Hayden around Dad wasn't a good idea, especially when the memory of Hayden's lips on mine was still burning through my brain. I hadn't been able to stop thinking about him since that last intense moment in Dad's trailer. We'd finally admitted we wanted each other...we'd finally kissed. But our paths couldn't cross like that, and that one moment was all we would ever have. Even still...I hadn't talked to him since coming home, and a part of me was dying to know: Was I on his mind too?

Shaking that irrelevant thought out of my head, I continued. "You were screaming...wild...out of control. You've never... you've never been like that. *Ever.* So tell me the truth...Are you okay?" I hated that my words were fumbling, my heart was pounding, and sweat was oozing from every pore. I wished opening up were easier for me, but it wasn't. Every word leaving my mouth was a struggle.

Dad's expression was completely bland, like he was a machine working on autopilot. Looking down, he started shuffling through papers on his desk. "I'm touched by the concern, Mackenzie, but...I'm fine." Looking back up at me, he said, "Now when you get out there today, pay close attention to your positioning. You're still too high on the bike when you exit the corner. When you're rolling on the throttle, stay down as the bike rises."

I could only stare at him, dumbfounded. He really wasn't going to open up to me. At all. Was it any great surprise, then, that I was holding things back from him too? "Yeah... okay, Dad. I'll work on that."

Feeling like there was nothing left to say to him, I turned to leave. When I had my hand on the door to his office, Dad stopped me. "By the way... I'm going to make a public announcement tonight, but you're family... so you should know first..."

Twisting, I looked back at him sitting at his desk; for the first time ever, he looked tiny behind it. His composure finally cracked as he let out a long sigh. "I'm... I'm closing Cox Racing after this season. It's... it's over." The light in his eyes died after confessing that to me. It was like watching hope die.

Shock stole my breath, kept me silent for a solid ten seconds. I felt like I'd been hit in the head with a baseball bat, and my brain was vibrating. *No, this can't be happening.* This place was more than just a practice track to me. It was where we all talked shop, where we socialized, where we came together as a unit, where we worked out, where we played... where I'd grown up. I couldn't imagine it gone, couldn't fathom it in someone else's hands. And the team... who else would I race for if not my father? "Dad, no, you can't—"

He held up a hand to stop me. "I have to, Mackenzie. I've tried all I can... but the fine, and the bad press... lack of sponsors, lack of *wins*... there's just no digging our way out of this hole. It's too late. Best to just admit defeat... and move on." His shoulders hunched as he looked away from me.

His lack of belief in my abilities was devastating; for a second, my vision swam and my hearing buzzed. But he was right... my best finish so far was eighth. Not bad for a rookie year, but not good enough for what he needed. Still, I wasn't ready to throw in the towel. There were two races left. There was still time. "Dad... I can get you wins. Don't give up on me." My voice came out in a whisper.

Dad's eyes returned to mine. They looked empty. "I'm not, Mackenzie. I've already begun the process of finding you another team to race for next year. This won't be the end for you, I promise."

No, it was just the end for him. The end of his business, his legacy, his reason for getting up every morning. What would Dad do without Cox Racing? *And what will I do without him?* "Dad...?"

A sad smile graced his lips. "You should practice, Mackenzie. You'll need to stay on your toes to get the attention of a great team."

I had to leave. My eyes were watering and grief and disappointment were crushing me. Giving Dad a stiff nod, I hastily left his office and sped down the stairs. Away. I needed to get away. Bypassing everyone I knew, I ducked out of the garage and headed to the gate. Keeping my head down, I pulled out my phone. There was only one person I could possibly talk to about this. Without hesitation, I texted Hayden the news. *My dad is closing the business. He's quitting.*

Hayden's reply was quick: *I just arrived at the track. Meet me out back, by the weak spot in the fence.*

Making sure no one was watching, I headed out the inner gate. I looked over in time to see Hayden disappearing behind the curve of the wall surrounding the track. After making sure I was still alone, I followed him. The tears were falling down my cheeks by the time we met up near the chain-link fence with the semi-invisible door in it.

Hayden swept me into a hug before I could stop him. With his chest against mine and his strong arms sealing me into a tight embrace, the sudden sadness lessened. "God, Kenzie, I'm so sorry," he said into my hair.

His comment surprised me. "Why are you sorry?" I asked, stepping back so I could look up at his eyes. I'd expected curiosity, maybe sympathy, but never such deep concern.

He shrugged, and his gaze locked on mine so fiercely, I couldn't possibly have turned away. "I know what Cox Racing means to you and your family, how hard you've worked to keep it. I'm sorry it's being taken away from you."

My eyes stung again as his words hit me. A lifetime of memories relentlessly pounded against my brain: playing peekaboo in Dad's office, racing the track with my sisters on our bicycles, getting candy from the crew members…vague impressions of my mother's voice, her smell, her laughter, her love. These walls were saturated with my childhood, and letting them go hurt even more than I'd realized.

Sniffing, I shook my head. "I'm not ready to stop fighting, I just don't know what to do now. How do I fix this?"

Stepping back, Hayden began rubbing my arms; it felt like he was pumping life into me. There had to be a way to change things. It couldn't really be too late. "Is he closing now? Do you have time?"

Inhaling a deep, calming breath, I told him, "He's making an announcement tonight that he's closing Cox Racing at the end of the season. I have two races to turn things around." Maybe if I won one, or better yet, both of them, it would create a big enough media storm around me to change my father's mind. To give him hope to stick it out.

Hayden was nodding as he absorbed my answer. "Then we practice harder, longer. We don't stop until you're undefeatable." I wasn't sure how we were going to accomplish that, but I was moved by his willingness to help me. Especially since making it so I couldn't lose, as impossible a promise as that was, would also mean that he wouldn't win. *If only Myles and my father could see you now…they'd change their minds for sure.*

"Thank you," I whispered, hoping he understood just how deep my gratitude went.

His perfect face studied mine for long, silent seconds, and my pulse quickened under his penetrating gaze. It wasn't only desire fueling the steadily accelerating beats, though. No, it was something deeper…fonder. Something absolutely terrifying. Hayden's words in my father's trailer echoed through my brain as we stared at each other. *Every day I find there is less and less that I wouldn't do for you, Kenzie…and that scares the shit out of me.*

Hayden shook his head like he was waking from a daydream. A small smile cracked his lips, and I found myself responding in kind. "You're welcome, Twenty-Two. You said your dad was making the announcement tonight?" After I nodded, he said, "Then invite me over. We'll watch it together. Then we'll talk, strategize… drink. Whatever you want." His eyes drifted down to my lips when he finished speaking. *God, what do I want?*

His eyes lifted to mine again. They drove into me, igniting me like a lit sparkler being dragged across my skin. As I thought of where we were standing, of all the nearby buildings, people, and animosity surrounding us, suffocating us, all I saw were reasons why we couldn't get too close. But then the memory of his lips upon mine filled my brain, and I thought of how amazing it felt to be cocooned in his arms. I thought of how my mind shut off when he was near, how I stepped outside of myself. How I…grew…around him.

My internal disciplinarian was shouting at me to tell him no—it was too risky, too dangerous, it could lead to something impossible, improbable, and unwise. But surprisingly, the word that left my lips was "Okay." Then I rattled off my address.

Shit. What have I done now?

* * *

Hayden arrived at my house later that evening, about thirty minutes before the ESPN interview was set to air. My father had left the track earlier this afternoon to film the piece. I had to imagine he was back at home by now, most likely drinking heavily. I felt a little guilty that I wasn't going to be with him when the interview aired, but I also didn't agree with what he was doing. *I can still save us, Dad. Somehow.*

I opened the garage door to hide Hayden's bike the second I heard it in the driveway. His vehicle could *not* be spotted by anyone I knew; they might recognize it as Hayden's.

After I led Hayden into the house, he looked around my modest place with a small smile on his lips. "Not what I expected," he murmured, setting a bag on the island in the center of the kitchen.

"And what were you expecting?" I asked, opening the bag to find some boxes that looked like Chinese takeout. It smelled incredible. God, I was hungry, and thinking about the food distracted me from the fact that *Hayden Hayes* was standing in my kitchen.

Hayden seemed much more at ease. Hopping up on my counter, he made himself at home. "Something…grander, I guess," he answered with a shrug. "I mean, you *are* the daughter of a legend. I just assumed…"

His answer made me smirk. Turning to face him, I leaned back against the counter with my arms folded across my chest. "You assumed I lived like the princess you thought I was. But I'm not like that. I've always been…simple at heart. Dad too." A small laugh escaped me. "Actually, the only person in my family prone to excess is my sister Daphne. Her wedding budget alone could equal the GNP of a small country." That made me frown. Dad wouldn't skimp on Daphne's wedding to save the business. He'd still give her everything she asked for…and she'd still ask for everything. Because she didn't understand how dire things were. She might after Dad's interview tonight. If she stepped away from her bridal magazines long enough to watch it.

Hayden laughed, then sighed. The sound caught my attention, and I shoved Daphne to the back of my brain. By the look on Hayden's face, he seemed almost…troubled. "Your dad…what he was saying to Keith before everything went to shit…does he really think Keith is sabotaging racers?"

My jaw firmed as I pushed away from the counter. "I really don't want to talk about Keith right now. Not with what my dad is about to do, not with everything we're about to lose…" With a sigh, I shook my head and did my best to change the subject. "You hungry?"

"Mackenzie…"

From his tone of voice, I knew he actually wanted to talk about something deep, but that wasn't what I wanted from him right now. Not if it was about Keith. We could talk about me, we could talk about him, we could maybe even talk about us, but I did *not* want to discuss Keith. "Are. You. Hungry?" I firmly stated my question this time, so he would know that Keith was off limits.

Hayden looked about to argue, but then with a resigned sigh, he said, "Yeah…I'm hungry." Giving me a crooked smile, he added, "I couldn't decide between Thai and Chinese, so I got a little of both," as he hopped off the counter.

"Aren't they pretty much the same thing?" I asked, glad that he was willing to drop it.

His condescending expression spoke volumes. "No. Not even remotely. Unbelievable," he muttered, snatching the bag from the counter. As he began setting boxes on the island, he started telling me all the various differences between the two types of meals he'd procured. I tuned him out, instead watching the way his body moved under his clothing. That was by far more fascinating than the history of peanut sauce.

Hayden turned suddenly, open takeout box in hand. I snapped my gaze up, but not before he noticed I'd been checking him out. With a seductive curl of his lip, he stepped my way, closing the distance between us. Pulling a plastic fork twined with noodles out of the box, he murmured, "Try this, then you'll see what I mean."

Gaze locked on his, I parted my lips and let him push the food into my mouth. My eyes fluttered closed as the explosion of spices hit my tongue. "Mmm, that's good," I moaned after swallowing the last little bit.

"Yes, it certainly is..."

The heat in his voice made me open my eyes. He'd set the box down on the counter, and he was staring at me like I was dinner. Memories of our frenzied kiss flooded my brain, overwhelming my senses and lowering my defenses. *Wrap me in your arms again. Press your lips to mine. Take me, claim me, have your way with me. I'm waiting.*

"God, you're intoxicating," he whispered, his lips inching ever closer to mine.

"Am I?" I asked. He was the one making me feel lighter than air; just his presence made me dizzy.

His lips just missed mine, making me gasp. They trailed along my cheek, stopping just below my ear. "Definitely," he whispered, his breath hot against my skin. My body instantly kicked into overdrive. I was ready for him to do so much more than tease me.

He dragged his lips along my jawline, making me shiver so uncontrollably that he probably thought I was freezing. Desire surged to life as his mouth rounded my chin. *Yes. God, yes.*

Suddenly, a knock sounded on my front door. Hayden and I both froze, hoping silence would make the person go away. No such luck. A few seconds later, the doorbell rang, then I heard a familiar voice say, "You in there, Kenzie? It's Nikki, open up."

Damn it. Nikki wouldn't just go away if I didn't say anything, not with all my lights on clearly signaling I was home. No, if she really wanted to talk to me, she'd pound on my door, annoying my neighbors, ceaselessly call me on my phone, then eventually break a window to get inside. She could be relentless if the situation called for it.

Over my shoulder, I shouted, "Hold on, Nikki!" Shit. Now what?

There was a door in the kitchen that led to the backyard, and I started shoving Hayden toward it. Once he understood what was going on, he grumbled, "But what about my bike? It's locked in your garage."

Shaking my head, I told him, "You can get it later. Nikki can't know you're here." And hopefully she didn't want to go in my garage for some reason.

Hayden wasn't thrilled about being evicted, but he understood why he had to leave. Once he was safely outside, I hurried to the front door so Nikki wouldn't get too concerned over what was taking so long. As it was, she asked, "Everything okay?" when I opened the door.

Swishing my hand, I said, "Yeah, you just caught me in the bathroom."

Her brows knitted together as she stepped inside. "Really? It sounded like you were closer than that."

I mentally kicked myself, but Nikki didn't say or ask anything else, so I felt like she was letting it go. "Are you going to watch the interview?" she asked, tossing her stuff on the living room couch. "I was going to watch it at home, but I just couldn't. When John told us what was going on after your dad left this afternoon…I just couldn't believe it. He's going to shut us down? Like, seriously close the business?"

Shoulders slumping, I nodded. I don't think Dad had wanted John to say anything to the crew, but John had been pissed. John had stayed by Dad's side for so long, and Dad was throwing in the towel without even talking to him about it. He didn't think it was right. But it was Dad's business and Dad's business alone, and technically, he could do whatever he wanted with it. "Yeah...he's closing." *Unless I can somehow convince him not to.*

Nikki grabbed her stomach. "I need a drink for this." She headed to the kitchen before I could stop her. I was sure Hayden hadn't left any evidence behind, but as if I was afraid Nikki had developed some superpower that enabled her to sense things beyond the scope of a normal human, my heart rate started spiking in anticipation. I even held my breath as I watched her look around the room.

Lifting her eyebrow at me, she said, "Wow, hungry much? There's enough food here to feed a small army, which is so not like you. How are you holding up?"

Relaxing a little, since she didn't seem to have mutant abilities, I shrugged as I pointed at the food. "Well, I'm clearly stress eating, so..." *And lying out my ass.*

Grabbing some chopsticks, Nikki nodded. "Yeah, I get that. I've been snacking on pork rinds all day. I just can't believe this is happening." She swirled her chopsticks around a box of sweet and sour chicken with a forlorn expression on her face. "I have to be honest, I'm kind of freaking out, Kenzie. Aren't you?" she asked, looking up at me.

With a sigh, I walked over and grabbed a box for myself. "Yeah...I am." That much was true, at least. I couldn't imagine not racing for Cox, not going to the track I grew up at every day, not having that tangible connection to my mom's memory.

Nikki's eyes were sad as they swept over my face. "Is this really the only way? I mean, how much was he fined for hitting Keith?"

Throwing on a sad smile, I told her, "Dad won't tell me how much, but I'm assuming it's a pretty substantial amount. Then with my fine from that stupid interview, my sister's wedding, Jimmy leaving...It's just been one damn thing after another."

Nikki's lips twisted in anger. "It sucks. Your dad doesn't deserve... He might be a little tightly wound, but he's a good man, and a good employer. I'd hate for him to have to...I just hope he somehow bounces back from this and changes his mind. I love working for Cox Racing."

Yeah, me too. And that's why I won't stop fighting.

She looked so depressed about the prospect of having to leave us that I gave her a comforting hug. "It will be okay. Somehow...it will all be okay." Pulling back from her, I said, "The interview is about to start. Should I open some wine?"

She cracked a smile. "Yes, definitely."

After opening a bottle, Nikki and I gathered plates, glasses, and all the food boxes and headed to the living room. I made plates for us while Nikki found ESPN on the TV. The interview came on just as Nikki was sitting down on the couch beside me. I grabbed her hand when my father's somber face filled the screen. I'd seen him do major interviews like this before, but somehow it was surreal to see him on the screen, talking about his personal and professional downfall—because he couldn't talk about Cox Racing without bringing up Benneti Motorsports; even in death they were linked.

Strangely enough, the entire time my dad was spelling out Cox Racing's doom, I was thinking of Hayden and wishing he were with me. It made me feel guilty to want him there instead of Nikki. She was my closest friend, my confidante, my cheerleader, and yet, she wasn't enough to fill the void expanding throughout my chest. I needed a set of deadly green eyes to keep the misery at bay. *The business can't really be ending.*

But my father's clearly defined pronouncement stated otherwise.

"Well, Jordan Cox, you have the world's attention. What would you like us all to know?"

"Just this...I'm closing Cox Racing at the end of the season. For good."

For good? No, there was nothing good about this.

Nikki was weepy when she finally left for the night. I felt like I was barely holding on myself. Phone in hand, I debated texting

Hayden and telling him he could come back and get his bike. But if he came back, would I want him to leave? It was that realization that gave me pause. I didn't feel like being alone, but Hayden wasn't a good idea. I shouldn't have invited him over in the first place. And thank God Nikki hadn't discovered us. Even still, I hoped walking home hadn't sucked too badly for him. He lived with Keith, but how far away was that? I didn't know, and I really didn't *want* to know. Keith's home was the one place I couldn't—and wouldn't—go.

I was just about to text Hayden an apology when I noticed that the door from the kitchen to the garage wasn't entirely latched. Curious, I pushed it open and peeked inside. My truck was there, along with my bike…but Hayden's bike was gone. That little ass. He'd snuck back in and broken his bike out. While Nikki was here? And neither one of us had heard him. Damn, he was good…and that *wasn't* good. Why was I letting him in?

While I analyzed my thoughts on that question, my phone buzzed in my hand, alerting me to a message. Glancing down at the screen, I saw it was from Myles. My heart sank some that it wasn't from Hayden, then dropped to my shoes with dread once I read it: *Your dad is closing shop because of Hayden. Do you believe me now about him?*

I could practically feel Myles on the other end, staring at his phone, waiting for a response, and I knew only one answer would pacify him. If I said the wrong thing, Myles would tell Dad what I'd done, permanently burning a bridge between my father and me. And if Dad was mad at me, he'd never help me get on board with another team. God, I hated that that was my dilemma now…finding another team worthy of replacing Cox Racing. Everything was going so wrong.

Squeezing my eyes shut, I let out a long, soothing exhale that did nothing to make me feel better. Then I typed out a reply that made me feel sick to my stomach. *Yeah…I believe you.*

No, I didn't. There was just nothing else that I could say.

CHAPTER 15

For the next few days after Dad's announcement, my phone went off nonstop. Everyone was in shock, and they all seemed to think I could change Dad's mind. Theresa wanted to stage an intervention; she seemed to think Dad was having a midlife crisis or something. Daphne was concerned too, but she was still so singularly focused on the wedding that her worries were all a little self-centered; I'd had to reassure her at least three times that Dad had already paid for the majority of her grandiose affair, so she didn't need to stress about having to get married in his backyard.

As we all returned to our routines, I returned to my deception. I spent nearly every evening hanging out with Myles and Nikki, keeping up appearances and convincing them both that I believed the Bennetis were evil and Hayden was their instrument of destruction. It was surprisingly difficult to badmouth him, and to hold back from mentioning things that my friends didn't know. Like that he had been a foster kid, and he'd struggled for everything in his life, and Keith was giving him the chance of a lifetime. I wasn't sure if any of those facts would help his case anyway—they just made it sound even more likely that he was hurting people on Keith's behalf.

After my friends and I parted ways for the night, I would meet up with Hayden at the track. True to his word to make me unbeatable, Hayden and I worked out longer and harder than we ever had before. But as the days went by, all I felt was hopeless. Winning wasn't enough anymore. The immediate problem was that my family was strapped for cash. I needed money. A *lot* of money. I wouldn't get that racing, not all at once, not as quickly as it was needed. But how the hell could I earn a copious amount of money in time to change Dad's mind about closing down in three months? I had no idea, and it killed me that a solution wasn't showing itself.

"Come on, Kenzie!" Daphne slurred, shoving my shoulder to wake me out of my pity party. "Have fun! Relax! It's my bachelorette party, for God's sake. You can stress about life tomorrow, but tonight is about having fun. Drink up!"

I contained a sigh. This wasn't the first time she'd said this to me tonight. "I can't, Daph, I'm training for the race at Monterey. You know how important it is that I do well."

With an inebriated groan of annoyance, she whined, "That's weeks from now! I'm sure you can drink in your downtime."

Smiling at her, I lifted my glass of water. "Not if I'm your designated driver. Kind of goes with the job description."

Rolling her eyes, she tried to blow away a piece of the bright pink feather boa that had stuck to her lip. She didn't succeed, so I reached over and plucked it free. "Thanks," she said with a giggle, then she returned her attention to the penis straw reaching out of the blue drink in front of her; the glass was large enough to make a couple of goldfish a very nice home. It was her third.

The music in the club we were in was so loud, I could feel my brain vibrating. Daphne had six friends with her, all of whom had been keeping pace with the bride-to-be, which meant the remainder of my night was going to consist of me trying to pull the drunken gaggle from the club, herd them to Daphne's massive SUV, and then make sure none of them puked on the forty-five-minute drive home. It all sounded so tedious, I wished I *could* break down and have a drink. I had so much on my mind, though, I might not stop drinking. And one of us needed to be sober tonight.

God, I really wished Theresa wasn't in bed with the flu, so she could be here to help me. Being Daphne's keeper was no easy task. Not that she was being inappropriate or anything, but the bridal veil with a sparkling tiara made her an irresistible target for men. They seemed to think they could talk her into one last fling before she was officially taken off the market. Daphne had reserved the VIP section—complete with bottle service, $150 champagne, and a two-bottle minimum—so the leering was greatly minimized. Even still, the group of us was asked to dance at least every fifteen minutes.

I stayed behind with the alcohol whenever my sister got up to shake her stuff with some guy. The last thing I needed was someone drugging the drinks. By the time all the fruity blue things were gone and our mandatory bottles of overpriced champagne had all been consumed, I was on my last nerve. I should be training, not babysitting.

"Time to go, Daphne. Bar's closing." I figured if anything would actually get her butt out the door, it was alcohol deprivation.

"What? No... I'm not ready." She lifted one of the goldfish bowls to her lips, then tilted it back in a vain attempt to get one more drop.

I forcibly made her set it back on the table. "No. Time to go... Jeff is waiting for you."

Hearing her husband-to-be's name had a bigger impact. "Ohhhh, Jeffy! I love him," she said, leaning on me with a dopey smile on her face.

"I certainly hope you do," I muttered, struggling with her deadweight.

Lifting a finger at me, she said, "You need a boyfriend, Mackenzie. You should go out and find a guy like Jeff. Strong, sweet... hung like a horse."

Her girlfriends laughed like that was the funniest thing they'd ever heard, but I wanted to gag. I did *not* need that image in my head during family get-togethers. And besides, I kind of had someone in my life... he just wasn't someone I could talk about. And we weren't really anything. Except complicated.

After paying the bill and tipping the waitresses—with cash Dad had provided for tonight—I wrangled the drunk women and managed to get them outside. It was difficult. They kept wanting to wander off. I suddenly had a newfound appreciation for people with kids. But then again, kids listened when you yelled. Drunk people laughed, then did whatever the hell they wanted to.

The place where we'd parked was on the other side of a four-lane street. How I was supposed to get all of them across safely was beyond me. Holding my hands up so they'd focus on me, or try to anyway, I loudly stated, "Okay! When that light turns green, you're all going to follow me." One of the girls immediately started crossing the street. It was late at night and deserted, but still—I'd just told her what to do! Shuffling over to her, I snipped, "I said when the light turns green! Does that look green, Daisy?"

She shrugged and I clenched my fists in frustration. My sister owed me for this. Big time. The light finally changed color, and I urged them forward like a momma duck calling to her ducklings. "That's right, let's go. Stay in the lines, please."

As I glanced at the crosswalk signal to see if the light was going to change soon, I heard a familiar sound. Motorcycles. Motorcycles going full bore. I snapped my head around to stare in the direction of the sound, and there they were, coming straight for us. And it was clear from their speed they had no intention of stopping. Since we were too far to run to the other side, and the girls were too drunk to understand going back the way we came, I yelled, "Everybody! To me!" and held my arms open. Maybe if we were clumped together, the assholes would be able to dart around us.

The girls squealed, then practically tackled me. Over their heads, I glared at the two douchebags who were clearly racing. The black-and-silver bike didn't look at all familiar, but the other one...

I swiveled my head to follow as the bikes parted around our group. The person on a red-and-black Honda looked back at me before streaking onward. The bike, the helmet, the jeans, the jacket—there was no doubt in my mind who had just flown past me. *What the fuck are you doing street racing, Hayden?*

Some of the girls were crying now that the scary part was over with, but I was too riled up to comfort them. Pieces of the Hayden puzzle were starting to snap into place. His annoying late-night phone calls, and his vague answers about who was calling him. That son of a bitch! He hadn't given anything up. He'd lied to me!

"Okay, girls. We are going to run to the car, and you are going to get in as fast as you can!" I started pushing them toward the vehicle, since none of them wanted to move. They bitched and moaned about being shoved, but when I told them more bikes were coming to run them over, they finally started moving.

Once they were more or less settled inside the SUV, I started the car and peeled out of the parking lot. One of the girls screamed as we fishtailed around a corner. "Jesus, Kenzie! Slow down!" my sister screeched.

"I am going slow," I lied. "It just seems fast 'cause you're drunk."

She held a hand over her mouth. "Well, just…go slower then, 'kay?"

I nodded, but I had no intention of doing that. I needed to catch Hayden. I needed to know what was going on, and why he was risking his career to keep doing this. Why he was risking me…

I was barely aware of all the laws I was breaking as I tried to keep the tiny glow of Hayden's brake light in sight. When we got to a familiar sight, rows of cars, bikes, and crowds of people, I finally slowed down. Pulling to the side of the street well before the "finish line," I shut off the car and turned to my inebriated cargo. "Okay, I need to talk to someone for a second. All of you need to stay here. If you don't…well, there's a group of guys outside…with guns…and they might shoot you. So stay down and stay quiet." A few girls squeaked, one started crying, and my sister was wide-eyed and terrified. Oh yeah, I was going to hell.

When I opened the door, Daphne grabbed my arm. "What are you doing? It's not safe out there!"

Removing her hand from me, I gave her a reassuring smile. "It's okay, I have a bodyguard waiting for me. I'm locking you guys in. I'll be right back." Before she could protest anymore, I closed the door and armed the car—that way I would know if one of them opened a door. Hopefully, on the way back home, I could convince them all that this was just a bad dream. And hopefully none of them would puke in the car while I was gone.

Once my sister and her friends were taken care of, I stormed down the street in search of Hayden. That boy had some explaining to do. When I found him, he was next to his friend Hookup and the beefy guy from Road America and the bar. Hookup was handing Hayden a wad of cash, and as I watched the money change hands, it was like a flare had been lit in my face. *Money*. He raced for money…a lot of money, considering that all the bills I could see were hundreds.

Keeping my expression even, I stepped right in front of Hayden and waited for him to notice me. He was so absorbed in counting his cash, it took him a while. Hookup actually spotted me first. "Hey, Felicia lookalike. What brings you to my neck of the woods, girl? It's me, right? You haven't been able to stop thinking about me. I get that a lot," he said with a haughty sniff.

Hayden snapped his head up, and his eyes locked on mine; the healing yellow bruise around his eye seemed to darken as his face paled. "Shit," he muttered.

I lifted an eyebrow at that. Shit indeed. Shoving his money into the front pocket of his jeans, he held up his hands. "I can explain."

I pointed to the evidence. "No need. How much did you make?"

Hookup slapped his hands together. "Five grand, baby!"

My eyes widened. Five grand? For one race? And was that everything, or just Hayden's cut? "Damn…"

Hookup looked giddy; he must get a piece of the Hayden pie. "Yeah, and this was kind of a small one. Next time, bro, we'll double that." My startled gaze shifted to Hayden. Next time? How often did he do this? Hayden's eyes drifted to the ground, the guilt in them crystal clear.

Hayden's friend took his confused silence as an opportunity to hit on me. "So, pretty young thing. Are we going to be properly introduced, or would you like me to keep calling you 'Felicia lookalike'?"

He tried to slip an arm around me, but I shoved him off. "My *name* is Mackenzie, and I don't like to be touched."

He bowed, like I'd said my name was Queen Mackenzie. "Name's Tony, but everybody calls me Hookup."

"Why?" I asked, wondering if I really wanted to know.

With a Cheshire smile, he spread his hands wide. "Because anything you need, I can hook you up." He smacked the large guy beside him. "This here is Grunts."

I was about to ask why again when the man grunted at me. Okay, no explanation needed. "And you guys help Hayden with this…stuff?" I indicated the gambling going on around me. Another race was about to start.

"Kenzie…" Hayden whispered, but Hookup rode right over him.

"Yeah, we totally hook him up. Plan all his events, even those out of state. My sister Izzy helps too sometimes, when she can. She's got a kid, so she can't do all this late-night shit."

My eyes boggled as my mind spun. Well, wasn't he a fountain of information. I was about to probe for more, but Hayden grabbed my hand and started pulling me away. "Can I talk to you for a second?"

Glaring at him, I stated, "I think Hookup is doing just fine explaining things. You have something different to add?"

Mouth in a hard line, he nodded. "Yeah, I do…please."

He indicated down the street, and I reluctantly let him lead me away. "Fine." When we'd gone a few steps, I said, "You never quit this, did you? You told me I'd witnessed your last race, but that was just bullshit to keep me quiet, huh?"

Hayden sighed. "No, it wasn't. I really did think I was done. I *was* done. But—"

Yanking my hand away, I spun to face him. "But what? You realize what the officials will do if they catch you? It's not a fine. They'll ban you from the sport…*for life*. And everything you told me you wanted for yourself will go up in smoke." I snapped my fingers to emphasize my point. "Do you really want to risk that…for money? Are you really that shortsighted?"

"It's not about the money," he said, his eyes pleading. "I don't expect you to understand…but I don't have a choice."

Really? That was how he was going to play this? "You're right, Hayden, I don't understand. Care to enlighten me?"

Hayden scrubbed his sweaty blond hair into a sexy, rumpled mess. "Look, I'm really sorry you and your friends almost got run over, but I don't think now is the—"

"Start talking," I interrupted. "Or I start making phone calls."

It was a total bluff—I needed him too much to turn him in—but he seemed genuinely concerned that I would. "It's Izzy," he finally whispered.

I wasn't sure what I'd been expecting him to say, but that definitely wasn't it. "Izzy? The girl you said was like your sister? Why would she…?" A slice of that ugly jealousy returned. So he was risking his career…for a woman. I wanted to turn away, I wanted to run away. But I wanted answers more…so I stayed.

"It's not what you think," he quickly added. "It's Izzy's daughter, Antonia. You know…the kid you saw me with?" Now I was even more confused. What did her daughter have to do with *this*? Unless…"You lied about that too, didn't you? She *is* yours."

Hayden let out a heavy exhale as he shook his head. "No, she's not mine. Not by blood, but she's my responsibility. She's family." He looked back at his friends. "I *was* going to quit. I was going to get out, but Antonia…she got real sick a few years ago. Leukemia." His weary eyes swung back to mine. "We thought she'd beaten it, thought she was in the clear, but…it's back. And Izzy tries, but she's a single mom, she's barely staying afloat as it is, she can't afford…" He hung his head. "Do you have any idea how expensive it is to have a really sick child? Even with help from the children's hospital? Izzy can't work, not full-time, so…I do what I can to help her out."

Hayden lifted his eyes to mine, and our gazes locked. Holy shit. He wasn't risking it all for money…he was risking it all for a *child*. A sick child. Jesus. His selflessness blew me away. If only I could tell people about this, they'd see him in a completely different light. I knew I did.

As he stared at me, I felt like I should respond in some way, I just had no clue what to say. Even though I didn't have any kids myself,

I couldn't imagine the constant fear of losing a child. "I'm...I'm so...What she's going through...that's awful."

Hayden's lips compressed and a determined fire lit his eyes. "Izzy's entire life is that kid...and I can't let her suffer when I can help. Hookup, Grunts, and me...*this* is how we help them, how we've always helped them. I don't know any other way. At least nothing that isn't even more illegal than this is. So yeah, I know it's stupid, and I know I can't keep doing it or I'm gonna get busted, but Izzy, Antonia...the two of them are part of the only real family I've ever had. The only ones who've stuck by me through everything. I can't abandon them. I won't."

I could tell from his tone that this was something he was truly passionate about, and it made complete and total sense; I couldn't fault him for anything here. I mean, what lengths would I go to—what lengths *had* I gone to—to help my own family?

After a moment's pause, I told him, "I need to get my sister and her friends home. They're really drunk." I couldn't help but snort thinking about what I'd said to get them to stay put. "I told them if they stepped foot outside the car someone would shoot them, but honestly, I don't know how long that threat will really hold them. And I want to talk to you some more about this. Want to come over...to my house...tomorrow?" Those words were harder to get out than I thought they would be, and I was suddenly a bundle of nerves as I waited for his answer.

He chewed on his lip before giving it. "Sure." Then he smiled. "You really told your sister she'd get shot?"

I pressed my lips together to not smile, but I failed miserably. "Yeah...and I know...I'm burning for all eternity for that."

"Maybe not *all* eternity...This really isn't the best neighborhood. You might not be too far off the mark with your warning." I smirked at him...then started to worry about my sister's safety. Tossing my hand up in a wave, I told him goodbye and hurried back to the SUV. His response floated on the breeze. "See ya later, Twenty-Two." My heart thudded in my chest. Right...later.

When I got back to the car, I realized I hadn't needed to hurry at all. Everyone inside had passed out; they weren't going anywhere.

And thankfully, none of them had gotten sick. Daphne mumbled something about Jeff when I started the car, but that was the only sound she made the entire trip home. Dropping each girl off at her house and then trying to get her in the door was a painstaking process that I hoped I never had to repeat in my lifetime. My sister was the last stop, but thankfully Jeff was there to help me out. He laughed the entire time he helped me put Daphne to bed.

A pesky idea started nipping at my brain as I rode home on my motorcycle. A dangerous idea, a ridiculous idea, a brilliant idea. After I stowed my bike for the evening, I paced my living room; the thought wouldn't let me sit still for a second. Hayden was risking everything to help his family. It was time for me to do the same.

The next night, I opened my garage door as soon as I heard Hayden's bike in the driveway. My hands were clammy, due to both my idea and the fact that Hayden was in my house again. And there probably wouldn't be any distractions this time to stop the heat between us from boiling over into something…wonderfully disastrous. But no, that wasn't why I'd asked him here. Business, just business.

Hayden followed me into the living room after we'd safely hidden his bike in my garage. He looked like some damn Hollywood megastar in his frayed jeans and black leather jacket, and I reconsidered everything about this meeting being just about business. Would his tongue wrapped around mine truly hurt anything? I honestly wasn't sure anymore. But I knew it would definitely be crossing a line I couldn't uncross, and I didn't know if I was ready for that.

With his hands in his pockets, his chin down, and his eyes looking up at me with raw heat in them, it was hard to remember exactly why I'd invited him over. "You wanted to see me?" he asked, his voice low and seductive.

"Yes…" *God, yes.*

Hayden shook his head, and then his expression completely changed; he looked worried again. Pulling his hands out of his pockets, he took a step toward me. "Look, I know you're probably mad at me, and I'm sorry I lied, I'm sorry I kept this from you, but I don't—"

"I'm not mad," I stated, cutting him off.

His face twisted into adorable confusion. "You're…not? I figured you'd be pissed."

The surprise on his face made me smile. "No, I get it…you want to help your family. I do too…" I took a deep breath. *Here goes nothing.* "And that's why I want to enter the next street race *with* you."

I could almost hear a clock ticking down to an inevitable explosion as I watched Hayden's features morph into a stern look that rivaled my father's. "No," he said, finality in his voice.

It felt like the air had just been sucked out of the room. Seriously? Mr. Screw the Rules himself was going to tell *me* no? "That's it? Just…no? Now I *am* a little mad." Closing the distance between us, I poked a finger into his chest. "You're not the boss of me, Hayden. I want your help to get started…maybe even your…approval…but I don't need you to do this. And I *am* going to do it. Cox Racing needs money—a lot of it. *This* is how I can earn it. *This* is how I can save the family business."

Hayden rolled his eyes. Not swayed by my argument, then. Maybe he was annoyed that I wanted a slice of his pie. He needed the money too, after all. "I won't race directly against you, if that's what you're worried about—I don't want to take money from Antonia—but from the little I understand about street racing from Nikki, there are multiple events, right? Ones you don't participate in?"

Frowning, Hayden said, "Yes, there are different…" Then he waved his hand like he could brush away my dream. "But, Kenzie, think about what you're risking."

I sadly shook my head. "My family is done at the end of the year. I'm not risking anything."

Stepping toward me, Hayden put his hands on my arms. "You can still race for someone else, Kenzie. Don't throw it all away."

And that was when it hit me. No, I couldn't race for anyone else. I was tied to my father, shackled at the ankle, and if he drowned, then I drowned with him. “I don't want to, Hayden. If I can't race for my family...then I don't want to race at all. I'd rather quit than have someone else's name on my back.”

Hayden's hands tightened around my arms. I could tell that he was frustrated, but he understood loyalty, even ill-advised loyalty. “This isn't the way, Kenzie. People get hurt out there, sometimes killed. There are no rules, no safety nets, no caution flags to slow everybody down. It can get ugly. Fast.”

His fervent words made my heart pound, but I lifted my chin and put on my most defiant expression. “So can I.”

Letting go of my arms, Hayden raked his hands through his hair. “No, I'm not letting you do this.”

Rage shot right through me. “Why are you being such an unreasonable asshole about this?” I yelled.

Stepping close so he could peer down at me, Hayden yelled back, “Because I fucking care about you!” In a quieter voice he added, “And I won't lose you over some stupid street race.”

The fury inside me lessened with his words. *He cares about me...* “So help me, Hayden. Teach me what you know. Teach me the secret that will help keep me safe.”

With a sigh, he rested his forehead against mine. “There is no secret to keep you safe.”

Looking up, so I could see into his eyes, so that our lips were almost touching, I whispered, “I know...but teach me anyway.”

Hayden let out an aggravated groan. “Fine. Just because I think you'll try and do it without me if I don't, I'll help you. But for the record, I don't like it.”

Letting my lips brush his, I said in a low voice, “You don't have to like it...you just have to do it.”

A low sound rumbled from his chest. “There's only one thing I want to be doing right now...”

Feeling reckless, wild, carefree, and—for the first time in a long time—genuinely hopeful, I murmured against his skin, “Then do it...” Before I could consider whether my words were wise, Hayden pressed his lips to mine, and I was lost.

As his mouth consumed me, awakening every nerve ending in

my body, logic tried to rear its ugly head. *This is stupid, futile, pointless.* Hayden could never be an accepted part of my family, and I could never leave my family behind. As his tongue slid through my lips, flicking, then caressing, my mind self-destructed in an explosion of lust. *Fuck the future, I just want to feel alive right* now. And no one made me feel more alive than Hayden.

As I ripped off his coat, *Hayden* came alive. His hands were all over my body: my stomach, my back, my breasts. *More, I need more.*

As if he could hear me, he reached down and picked me up. I wrapped my legs around his waist and dug my fingers into his hair. *Yes, take me away from all of this. Far, far away.* Running his lips up my cheek, he panted in my ear, "Do you want me, Kenzie?"

I arched against his body, nibbled on his neck, answering him without saying the words. He let out a low, erotic noise that enflamed me, but he didn't move. And I knew he wouldn't until I answered him. Releasing my pride, I brought my lips to his earlobe. "Yes," I breathed.

He immediately started to move. Blindly stumbling through my living room while our mouths furiously reconnected, Hayden shuffled in the direction of the bedroom. When he found it, he walked us over to the bed, then threw me down on top of it. The sudden movement surprised me, ignited me, and my heart was beating as hard as if we were racing, as if we were jockeying for position. Looking up at him standing over me, the hallway light behind him casting an aura around him, I licked my lips in anticipation. *Yes, take your victory. Taste it, own it, claim it. It's yours...I'm yours.*

Crossing his arms, Hayden grasped the edge of his T-shirt and pulled it off his body, exposing miles of trim, well-defined muscles. I wanted them over me, on me. Wanted to run my nails down them and my tongue up them. I grabbed the edge of my own shirt, but Hayden stopped me with a word.

"No." When I bunched my brows in confusion, a slow, devilish smile formed on his lips. "That's my job," he murmured.

Holy shit, that was hot. My stubborn need to prove my independence momentarily battled with the throbbing wave of desire that his words provoked. Slowly my fingers released my T-shirt, and I relaxed back on the mattress. I didn't want to plan, didn't want to think, didn't want to dictate everything that happened here—I just wanted to feel. *Lead me, and I'll follow.*

"Good," he whispered as his eyes caressed my body. He slowly removed his shoes, then his socks, then his jeans. Seeing the outline of him straining against his boxer briefs made me squirm. Moving to the bottom of the bed, Hayden started crawling over me. He slid his hands up my legs as he went, and after a few inches, he stopped to place a kiss on my thigh. Even through the thick fabric of my jeans, it was exquisite. When he got to the tops of my legs and placed a kiss right between them, I cried out. Reaching down, I tried to pull him up my body. His smile still coyly seductive, he grabbed my hands and laced our fingers together.

"Not yet," he murmured. Then he brought my hands over my head and wrapped my fingers around a post in the headboard. "Hold on to this, and no matter what happens... don't let go."

My gaze was incredulous as I stared at him; his was confident, powerful, and seductive. My body trembled with excitement, and I realized I wanted to completely let go, wanted to let him command me. It was a heady feeling, one I wasn't used to—I'd always held on to control so tightly. My diet, my exercise routine, my daily schedule. Before Hayden, everything about me had screamed order. And all I wanted right now was to be screaming something else. I was positive Hayden could make me do that... if I let him.

Clenching the wood tight in my fingers, I closed my eyes and dropped my head back. *Yes... do whatever you want to me.*

He hummed an approving noise as he returned to my jeans. He popped open the button and I started breathing heavier. He unzipped them and I bit my lip and squeezed the wooden post so hard my knuckles were surely white. In one fluid movement, he had my jeans off. And then his hands and lips started over on their path up my legs. Once he was at the top again, I was moaning with need, just on the verge of begging. I felt his thumb graze me through my underwear and I gasped as my world begin to spin; everything was so intensified. I was drunk on him.

I felt his hot mouth hovering just above where I wanted him. *God, yes, kiss me there again.* "Mmm, you're so fucking wet," he murmured, his thumb coming out to touch me again. "Is this for me?"

He paused everything he was doing, and I knew he wouldn't move again until I answered him. "Yes…" As if to praise me for my answer, he swept my underwear aside and ran his tongue up me once, tasting me. I screamed out, "Yes, God, yes!"

Hayden's tongue returned to me, stroking me to a point where I couldn't form coherent words anymore. Then he stopped, and I could barely catch my breath. Him either. "Fuck, you taste good. I don't want to stop, but I can't leave half of you untouched…"

He started kissing his way up my stomach while he slid his hands behind me to unhook my bra. When he released the fabric, I gasped, then groaned. I'd never wanted a mouth on my nipples so much in all my life. I arched my back, begging him to explore me. His tongue burned a trail along my skin. When he finally reached my nipple, I bucked beneath him as the fire surged through me. *Why does everything feel so goddamn good?*

He groaned against my skin and he sucked and teased. His free hand ran up my underwear to cup my backside, and then his thumb started stroking me. It was too much, sensory overload, and I knew I wouldn't last long. I started panting as the sensation built. *So good, but I still need more.*

"Fuck, you're gorgeous," Hayden growled, then he ripped off my underwear and swapped positions, so his finger was rubbing my nipple, and his mouth was hovering over my exposed core. "I want you to come," he firmly stated, and then his mouth was on me. The intensity tripled and my entire body stiffened as the ecstasy burst through me so hard, I couldn't feel anything but bliss.

I was only partly cognizant of the noises leaving my mouth—curses, swears, moans and groans that seemed to last for days. As the high began to fade, alertness slowly returned and Hayden's face filled my vision. His eyes were wild with lust as he studied me. "God, you're fucking amazing when you come. Let go, baby. Touch me..."

My hands were stiff when I finally released the wood post, but when I slipped my fingers inside Hayden's underwear and felt him, the post was flimsy in comparison. A moan escaped me as my body started tingling again. "God, you feel good."

Hayden kissed my jaw, then my ear. "That's what you do to me. What you've always done to me..."

His caresses were gentle as he removed my shirt, my bra, his underwear. When we were both bare, he cupped my face. "If you don't want to take this any further, you can still say no. I'll get dressed and leave, no hard feelings." A half smile lit his lips. "What you've already given me is enough for tonight."

I worked my lip between my teeth as I considered leaving things like this. We'd already done so much, but was I ready to throw all caution to the wind? Was I ready to take that final leap with him? I wasn't sure, which probably meant I should tell him to leave. But with his body pulsing against my thigh, his rigid muscles finally under my palms, and the heated look in his eyes... I couldn't turn him away. I was already in too deep anyway... Look what had happened to Dad after years of bottling up his emotions. Maybe I *needed* this outlet. Maybe I needed Hayden for more reasons than I realized.

Running my hands up his back, I held him against me. "I want this... I want you."

That was all Hayden needed. His lips returned to mine, and he didn't ask me again if I was ready. His mouth ran down my neck while his fingers slid up my legs. I groaned in anticipation, delighting in the fact that I could touch him this time. As his mouth moved over my breast, I tangled my fingers in his hair. As his finger slid against me, I ran my hand down his chest, found the hard mass of him, and squeezed him tight. We both cried out, wanting more, wanting each other.

When I knew I wouldn't last much longer, I urged him to enter me. Removing my hand, he slowly pushed his way in. We both let out gasping noises of disbelief. Having a man inside me had never felt so good. It was like the electrified sensation when he touched my skin, continued all the way up inside me. Every inch he moved brought me closer to delirium. I was already feeling frantic with need, but Hayden kept the pace torturously slow and steady. The cries I let out were uncontainable, and eventually I *did* beg him.

"Oh God, Hayden, please, faster…harder…more."

"Jesus, Kenzie," he murmured in my ear. Then he gave me exactly what I needed. My earlier orgasm paled in comparison to the euphoria that I felt coming with him inside me. He released a second after me, calling my name as he tumbled over the edge.

Clutching him tight, I tried in vain to ignore the warmth of fondness spreading throughout my chest. *This doesn't mean anything, it doesn't mean anything…*

CHAPTER 16

When my heartbeat was no longer thudding in my ear and my breath was no longer rushing past my lips, reason started returning, bringing a tremendous amount of guilt and doubt with it. Had I just made a monumental mistake?

The silence in the room, broken only by Hayden's and my opposing inhales and exhales, was quickly unnerving me. He shouldn't be here. As absolutely amazing as it had been, it couldn't happen again. It wasn't only my career I was risking by being with him. Another instance like this, and my heart would be on the line too. And I'd rather risk something tangible, like a job.

My tumbling mind replayed the events of the last few minutes, both delighting and confounding me. A word Hayden had said stuck in my brain, and I repeated it before I could stop myself. "Baby…"

"Hmm," Hayden's tired voice responded from beside me.

Feeling heat in my cheeks, I turned my head and said, "You called me baby. You're not supposed to do that." I knew it was a ridiculous point of contention to bring up after everything we'd just done, but somehow, it seemed the only safe thing to talk about. I couldn't stand the silence another second.

Hayden chuckled, his lips curving into a grin that made me

want to kiss him again. The movement reminded me of all the places his mouth had been lately. That freaking talented mouth. A shudder passed through me. No, best not to think about it. "I did, didn't I? Should I apologize for that?" he asked, turning his head my way.

By "that," I knew he meant the sex more than the pet name. I really wasn't sure if he should apologize for either. "You should probably go," I whispered.

"It's almost dawn," he replied, frowning.

Turning my head to take in his relaxed posture as he lay beside me, I nodded. "I know, and that's exactly why you should go now. You never know who might drop by unexpectedly, and we're trying to save our careers, not shatter them to pieces..."

Propping himself up on his elbow, Hayden looked down at me. His expression was thoughtful. "Yeah... okay."

It hurt a little that he'd agreed with me so easily. But it really shouldn't. He was being smart by agreeing to leave. *So why the hell does it sting?* Pulling some hastily strewn covers over my body, I blurted something to quiet the confusion in my brain. "Well, good, because we've both got a lot on the line here..."

He agreed with me again, almost absentmindedly. "I know."

The stab of pain grew stronger. "Good... then you know that this... can't happen again." Sadness washed over me as I indicated the two of us. "This was a mistake."

His expression turned incredulous. "A mistake? The best sex of my life... was a mistake?"

His words warmed me and hurt me at the same time. Couldn't he see this was for the best? "We're already risking *so* much by racing... let's just save ourselves the trouble and not start this."

Anger was clear on his face now as he waved a hand over his bare body. "You do realize it's too late for that, don't you?" Yes. I did. God, how I did. Even now, I wanted to touch him, I wanted *him* to touch *me*. I wanted him to order me to lie still and let him satisfy me, over and over and over... But we weren't free to be those people. Not really.

"Can we just... not cross that line again?" I asked, my voice small. "Can we just keep things between the two of us about racing?"

Hayden's eyes hardened. "So you want me to ignore it when I remember what it feels like to be inside you? What your face looks like when you come? How you sound when I'm touching you? How wet you get when you're ready for me? How you taste...?"

My body started tingling to life, ready for another round. Just hearing him talking about it was making me wet, making me *want* him to touch me, tease me, taste me. *God yes, one more time...* "Yes..." My voice came out breathy, and I had to swallow the blossoming sensations so I could truly answer his question. "Yes. All I want you to do...is teach me to street race. Teach me to win."

Shaking his head, he got up off the bed. His muscles flexing and twisting as he moved did nothing to dispel my rising desire. *The sooner he leaves, the better.*

Putting on his pants, he said, "Okay...whatever. If that's what you want, then I'll leave and we'll act like this never happened. Not a problem." I had to bite the inside of my cheek to stop myself from telling him that what I really wanted was his mouth on me again.

As was typical after a night when I'd done something risky and dangerous that I knew my friends and family wouldn't approve of, I was a nervous wreck when I got to the track that morning. I felt like I had my sins stamped on my forehead for everyone to see—*slut, traitor, backstabber, gambler...idiot.* But I was only doing what I *had* to do. Or in one case, what I was too weak to resist. I didn't want to dwell on what Hayden and I had done, though, so I shoved it to the back of my mind.

Or tried to. Thoughts of being with him plagued me all day. His hard, flat muscles, his soft lips and wandering hands. The way he guided me, led me, teased me. The gentle touches that made me feel like a caged animal waiting to be released. The slow strokes that turned into wild frenzy. I'd never had anything like that, and I wasn't certain if I ever would again. I felt like pieces of me had been punched out and I'd always be incomplete.

"So, how was the bachelorette party Saturday?" Nikki asked while she arranged her toolbox.

"Fine," I murmured, not in the mood to talk. Staring out the open garage door, I studied the top half of the Benneti building, which I could just see over the track. Was Hayden over there right now? Was he thinking about our night too? Was he upset that I'd ended things? Or did he understand that we had to? Would he still show me how to street race?

"Where did you go? Bar, bowling…strip club?"

Still thinking about Hayden, I murmured, "Yeah."

Nikki stopped what she was doing and straightened to stare at me. "You did all three? Wow…no wonder you still look tired."

Shaking my head to clear Hayden from my mind, I told her, "It was a long night." Followed by another magnificent, long night. It was a weekend I would never forget.

While Nikki laughed, I excused myself to go work out. I needed the distraction. And also, now more than ever, I needed to be in tip-top shape. Myles was in the gym when I got there. He had another month to go on his cast, and his collarbone was far from healed, so he looked a little lost. Part of me wanted to avoid him—because knowing how he felt about Hayden, and knowing what I'd just done with Hayden last night, was too much to bear. But we were friends, and friendship came first.

"Hey, Myles," I said, climbing on an elliptical.

"Hey, Kenzie," he answered, his voice glum. "I wanted to keep my strength up, since I'm gonna have to look for a new team next year…but there really isn't anything I can do. I feel so fucking helpless." His dark eyes drifted to the wide windows that looked out over the property. Benneti Motorsports was practically the focal point of the view.

Holding my hand over the buttons of the machine, I tried to think of something vague and encouraging. "Everything is going to be fine, Myles, you'll see. Cox Racing isn't finished yet." *Not if I can help it.*

Myles looked at me with a hard expression on his face. "With that asshole out there messing things up for us, we might as well be." Swinging his crutch my way, he hobbled closer to my machine. "Do you finally see that we can't idly sit back anymore and let Hayden screw us?"

Myles's sentence was packed with double meaning, considering what Hayden and I had just done. I felt my cheeks heating and quickly grabbed my water bottle. After taking a swig, I told him, "We don't have proof, and Dad's already burned a bridge with the officials. If we say something—"

Myles interrupted me with a sigh. "I know. I just...I wish we had something on him...some kind of dirt we could use to nail him. And there's got to be some. There's no way that guy is squeaky clean."

Used to conversations like this, I gave Myles a look that I hoped was full of commiseration. "I know what you mean. But we don't have anything, so there's nothing we can do...Damn it." I really hated acting like I agreed with him, but what choice did I have?

At first Myles's expression turned even harder, but then he sighed again. "Yeah...I know. But if you see something we can use—*anything*—let me know. If we can stop him, Kenzie, we'll save Cox Racing."

He looked so hopeful that all I could do was nod. Great. There was nothing about Hayden that I could confess to Myles; I couldn't screw over Hayden without screwing over myself, and...I didn't want to screw him over. Myles was just going to have to continue to be disappointed and frustrated. And I was going to have to continue to feel really guilty about lying to him.

I stewed about that fact for the rest of the day. And no magical solution appeared to me when I was back at home. While I was eating dinner, Hayden texted with a time and a location to meet up. Relief flooded into me that he was keeping his word. I'd been worried that he'd change his mind. Nerves immediately replaced my calm. We were going to practice racing through the streets. Any last shred of innocence I possessed would be gone after tonight. But then again, maybe I'd given that up last night.

Way too damn early in the morning, I left my house to meet up with Hayden. Much to my surprise, he wasn't alone when I got to the meeting place. Boisterous Hookup and the quiet one, Grunts, were there too. Did Hayden not want to be alone with me now? For some reason, I found that really disappointing.

Parking my bike next to Hayden's, I watched Hookup and Grunts. They were standing on the sidewalk in front of Hayden's bike, and Hookup was engaged in telling Grunts a story. A car was parked next to Hayden, so clearly the pair weren't here to race.

Raising my visor, I turned to look at Hayden. Would things be weird between us now? After a moment of staring at me, Hayden raised his own visor. Seeing the heat in his emerald eyes stole my breath. *Yes, I think he has been thinking of me.* But I couldn't tell if his thoughts had been good or not. My mouth suddenly dry, I had to swallow before I could ask my question. "I thought we were going to be alone. What are they doing here?"

Hayden glanced up at his friends before looking back at me. "They run the show. If you want in, you have to impress them, not me."

My heart dropped to my feet as my eyes returned to the two men before me. Somehow I'd thought getting in would just require Hayden's okay…guess not. *All right. I can do this.* The pair didn't seem to notice I was here yet, so I revved my engine to get their attention. Hookup looked annoyed at being interrupted when his gaze fell my way, but then he smiled and clapped his hands together. "Felicia number two! How's it hanging, girl?"

I forced a smile to my face. "My name is Mackenzie, remember?" That wasn't bitchy sounding, right?

He snapped his fingers. "Right, right…Kenzie. So you want to join the big leagues, do ya?"

The world seemed to shift into slow motion. This was it. Last chance to reconsider. I gave him a stiff nod. "Yes. But I don't want to race against Hayden. I want to be put in a different event."

Grunts made some snorting noise as he crossed his beefy arms over his chest. Hookup looked at him and nodded, like he'd said something meaningful. "Yeah, I know, right?" Returning his eyes to me, he pouted. "Are you afraid to race against my boy?"

Narrowing my eyes, I revved my engine again. "I have my reasons, and they have nothing to do with fear."

Hookup looked intrigued, and he started to ask me something, but Hayden interrupted. “Come on, Tony, knock it off and let her show you what she can do.”

Hookup’s frown deepened as he met eyes with Hayden. “Fine, have it your way.” He smacked his hands together again, and a huge smile broke over his face. “Okay, first thing you should know is…there is no set course. Just checkpoints you have to hit along the way. Four of them, to be exact. During a real race, we’d have spotters at the points to make sure your ass isn’t cheating, but since this is practice, we’re gonna take your word for it.” He winked at me and I rolled my eyes. *Let’s skip the flirting, please; I’m not interested. In you.*

My unintentional addendum to that thought made me cast a quick glance at Hayden. Damn, he looked hot sitting on his bike. Was he really fine with last night? Or was he upset? Damn it, I needed to focus on this, not worry about him. This was important. This was my family’s ticket out of financial ruin. This was *everything.*

Hookup continued explaining where the checkpoints were, and I dragged my eyes back to him. The first three locations were going through town; the last one was the starting point. First person to cross all four points won. Simple as that.

“All right, girl, show us what you got,” Hookup said, winking at me again.

“Ready?” Hayden asked. His voice was tight and his eyes were void, like he was trying to be distant. Was he angry? I hadn’t meant to hurt him.

Not wanting him to see the pain in my eyes, I slammed down my visor and gave him a brief nod. Lowering his own visor, Hayden indicated for me to follow him, then led us to the crosswalk cutting through the quiet street. He stopped his bike with his tire almost touching the line, and I mimicked his position. There was a red light just in front of us, and that familiar feeling of anxious energy washed over me. Even though we weren’t on a track, I wanted to go, wanted to race him.

Hayden leaned over his handlebars, preparing for the moment

of release. I did the same…and then the light changed, setting us free. As if we shared the same mind, we both shot forward at the same time. It took me very little time to realize that street racing was nothing like racing on a track. On a specifically designed course, I followed all of my instincts, let logic carry me forward. But on the streets, logic had to be gagged and tied, and I had to ignore every instinct inside me. I first experienced the confusion when we hit a red light. I wanted to slow down and stop, but Hayden was going faster, not slower, and I had no choice but to follow suit; it hadn't been outright stated, but I got the feeling I had to beat Hayden, or come awfully damn close, to get an invite into this world.

Breezing through a red light felt so wrong that a wave of nausea swept through me. It passed, though, and the next time it happened, I felt a little less sick. It was super late at night, and most of the side roads were nearly empty. Everything was going to be fine, and no one was going to get hurt. I just had to keep telling myself that.

Hayden and I were neck and neck when we got to the first checkpoint—a coffee shop on the corner that I often frequented. Since we were racing through my hometown, I knew exactly where the second checkpoint—a little dry cleaner shop—was, and I knew a shortcut to get there. While Hayden kept going straight, I made a sharp right into a narrow alley. I wouldn't have been able to get through here in a car, but a bike was just fine. Breezing down the tight street, I emerged onto the main road just ahead of Hayden. I saw him look back in surprise, like he hadn't realized I was gone, then he hunched down for speed.

Laughing, I easily kept in front of him as we passed the second checkpoint. The third checkpoint was a Mexican restaurant on the far side of town from where we started. We had to cross a set of railroad tracks to get there, but at this hour, there shouldn't be any trains coming. As we got to a street that ran parallel to the tracks, I could see that my assumption was wrong. The lights of a train were barreling down the tracks in our direction; the train was going to hit the intersection before us, holding us up.

Slowing down, I debated finding another crossing. Hayden shot past me. Incredibly, he was increasing his speed, not diminishing it. Jesus, was he really going to try to beat the train? Was he nuts? But if he beat the train while I had to sit and wait for it...there would be no catching him. He'd win. And my only real chance of helping my father would evaporate.

Cursing the fate that had brought me to this point, I pushed my bike as hard as it would go. *Pretend the train isn't there. Pretend it's not outpacing you. Pretend it won't kill you if you don't time this right.* I was approaching the crossing too quickly, and yet not quickly enough. Letting out a quick prayer, I started a countdown in my head. *Three... two... oh shit, here we go.*

Hayden and I crossed the tracks so close together, we probably appeared to be one long bike to the conductor. The train's horn screamed at us, and the vibration from the metal beast vibrated my bike and rattled my rib cage...but it didn't hit us. Thank God.

I wanted to take a second to appreciate the fact that we weren't pancakes, but Hayden tirelessly blazed on to the next checkpoint. God, no wonder he was undefeated. He was fearless. And reckless.

At the Mexican restaurant, we turned around to begin the trek back to the starting point. Hayden was still in front of me, goading me on. I was right on his tail, though, and not about to give up now. Taking a chance, I chose a different road that I thought might be just a little faster. It was odd to no longer have Hayden directly in front of me, but if I imagined he was there, his taillight bright in my vision, I still felt that same energetic rush that came from chasing him.

Street after street, intersection after intersection, I pressed onward, trying to beat him to the finish. Every step of the way I was worried that he'd somehow already gotten there and his friends were making up their minds to seal my doom. *No, I need this too badly.*

Zipping around the last corner, I finally ended up back on the main street where we'd started. And Hayden was nowhere in sight. Shit. He'd finished. Even as my heart sank, I pressed on. I had to at least show them I was persistent. That had to count for something.

When my tires rolled over the crosswalk, I noticed that Hayden's friends were still here. Good. Hopefully I'd managed to impress them with my fortitude. As I slowed my bike, though, I noticed something odd about them. They weren't looking at me. They were staring—open-mouthed—at something just behind me. Wondering if a cop was on my tail—or worse yet, someone I knew—I snapped my head around to look. I was so shocked to see Hayden right behind me that I almost crashed my bike. *Oh my God! I beat him!*

Sliding my bike to a stop, I ripped off my helmet and raised it into the air. Hayden slowly stopped beside me and removed his own helmet. His face a mixture of annoyance and amazement, he slowly shook his head. "I can't believe you followed me over those tracks."

"There's nowhere you can go that I won't follow," I purred. I wasn't sure exactly what I meant by that, but at the moment I didn't care. If we were alone, I would have pulled his mouth to mine and begged him to take me to the brink again…but we weren't.

"Holy shit, man! She got you! She beat the unbeatable. She fucking beat Hayden fucking Hayes!" As Hookup ran up to us, Hayden's eyes turned smoldering, like he knew where my mind had drifted.

"Yeah…she got me…" he murmured. By the look on his face I was pretty sure he wasn't talking about racing anymore. I wanted him to lean over and suck my lip into his mouth. Then I wanted those marvelous lips to travel down my throat, down my chest, over my breast…Damn, just the thought of him in my bed again had me tingling with need. It was like he was forbidden fruit; I knew we couldn't go there, but I also knew how good being with him was, and I couldn't stop thinking about it. Was he having the same problem? Or was he still mad?

Luckily, Hookup ran between us, breaking the spell. Hand on my shoulder, he excitedly exclaimed, "Anybody who beats Hayden gets automatic entry to any event of their choice. Thursday is the next race. I'll call Hayden with the spot and the time." His expression suddenly turned sly after that. "I'm assuming you'll be with him." Before I could answer, he swung his gaze to Hayden. "You lucky son of a bitch! It's like you get to bang Felicia twice, man. Just don't let this one flip out and vanish. Bitch. Izzy's still pissed at her for bailing on her and Antonia like she did."

A myriad of expressions crossed Hayden's face while Hookup was talking. Irritation, anger, then sadness. "Yeah, well... Kenzie and I aren't like that. It's just... *racing*." He almost sneered the word, and an instinctive ball of anger tightened my chest.

Okay, he was mad. Well, I could understand that. The situation made me angry sometimes too, but it wasn't something either one of us could change, and taking it out on each other wouldn't solve anything. Relaxing my expression, I decided to simplify things by agreeing with him. "Yeah... just racing."

Hookup looked confused, like he didn't understand why two such similar people weren't "banging." "Okay..." He patted Hayden on the back in—I swear—consolation, then he took off and hopped into the car with Grunts. Seconds later the pair were gone.

With an awkward glance at Hayden, I wondered what to say now. The only thing that came to mind was "Thank you for doing this. I know you didn't want to... but it means a lot to me that you did."

I turned away, but looked back when I heard Hayden softly say, "I told you I would... and I keep my word." His voice was laced with so much wistfulness that it made my chest feel like a thousand-pound weight was sitting on it.

God, it would be so easy to forget everything between us and ask him to come over. And that would only make things so much harder. I could hide a secret racing partner from my father, hide illegal street racing, and probably even hide a secret lover for a time... but could I settle for a life of secrets? Hayden was forever linked to Benneti, which meant he could *never* be linked to me.

"Good night, Hayden," I murmured, and I was surprised to feel tears stinging my eyes. It shouldn't hurt already, but it did. I guess even once was too much.

CHAPTER 17

All day Thursday, I thought I might throw up, and when the sun finally set, I actually did. Even though I'd already raced through city streets with Hayden, I couldn't believe I was going to go through with this. I was putting it all out there to save the team I loved, and I hoped the risk paid off.

A different kind of nerves hit me when I got to the site of the race and pulled up beside Hayden's bike. So much had changed between us so fast, I felt dizzy and disoriented. What were we now? I had no way of classifying our relationship except unwise.

Hayden held his hand up in greeting when he saw me; he looked delicious in his leather jacket. He had on a white T-shirt, partially tucked behind a thick black belt. The large round metal buckle pulling it all together was like a beacon, calling out to my slowly accelerating sex drive: *Unbuckle me, undress me…undo me.* Shutting off my bike, I exhaled a deep, cleansing breath before removing my helmet. *Partners, just partners.*

Resting my helmet on the handlebar, I hopped off the bike and walked over to where Hayden was in a conversation with Hookup and Grunts. Hookup's grin was a mile wide when he noticed me. "Oh good, Felicia Two is here!"

Hayden immediately smacked him in the chest. "For the last time, that's not her name."

Hookup rubbed his chest; by the look on his face, you'd think Hayden had broken a rib or something. "Fine. Kenzie... Kenmeister... Killer Ken... Kenikaze."

It annoyed me, but I let the stupid nicknames go. Kenikaze was better than Felicia Two. Or sweetheart. "What's the plan?" I asked, hoping I didn't sound as clueless as I felt.

Hayden turned to me with a sad smile on his lips. He didn't appear to be angry anymore; I think I would have preferred it if he were. "All races are one against one, to draw less attention. You're entered in the first race of the night, against..." He searched the crowd, then pointed across the street. "Against that guy with the green Mohawk. He's a veteran, like me... so be careful." When he returned his eyes to mine, they were heavy with worry.

Tossing on an unconcerned grin, I did my best to act like all of this was routine. "I beat *you*. How tough can this guy be?"

Hayden's lips curved into a sexy smile that quickened my breath. "Very true," he murmured. Biting my lip, I turned my head to study my competition. Ignoring Hayden would be so much easier if I didn't find him so damn attractive.

The green Mohawk guy was with his crew, gathering bets and pumping up that side of the crowd. It was a little shocking to me just how many people had come out for this. It was so strange to think that until Nikki had exposed me to it, I'd had no idea this world really existed outside of movies. And now, not only was I a part of it, but I was about to make my mark on it.

Hookup explained the setup and where the checkpoints were. The race was taking place about thirty minutes east of Oceanside, and I didn't know the streets here as well as I knew the ones back home. The circuit moved around a lot, though, so I wouldn't always have the benefit of home field advantage.

Once Hookup was positive that I had some clue where to go, he told me, "You beat this guy, your cut is twenty-five percent of the pot."

That made me frown. "Twenty-five? What happens to the other seventy-five percent?"

Hookup's unhappy expression matched mine. "Organizers take fifteen, I take the rest. It ain't free to race, sweetheart. You lose, I'm out ten grand."

Surprise over the dollar amount made me momentarily forget that he'd just called me my least favorite name. "Ten thousand *dollars*? To enter *one* race?" Jesus.

Hookup nodded matter-of-factly at me. "Yeah, ten thousand *dollars*. Why do you think I tested you against Hayden? Had to make sure you were worth the investment." Holding his hands up, he shrugged. "But if you don't want to share with me, you're more than welcome to pay the entrance fee yourself. Assuming one of the organizers will even talk to you...which they probably won't. Bigwigs don't even come down here. You gotta know people...which is what I'm here for. Hookup *is* my name, after all."

His explanation halted any further comment. Sure, it was ridiculous how much of a cut Hookup was taking, but I didn't have that kind of money, or the connections he had. And if I won...well, it wouldn't be a bad start to helping Dad. And besides, I was sure Hookup used some of his earnings to help Izzy, so it wasn't *all* for nothing.

"It's fine," I quickly told him.

He nodded, like he'd expected that. "Don't be too discouraged. You'll also get a small chunk of the side bets, which Grunts and I handle for you. If you want to put some money down on yourself, we'd be more than happy to front you the cash." I immediately rejected his offer; I had enough pressure on me to win, no point in adding the potential to get very deep in debt on top of it.

Nervous energy pounded through my veins as I watched Hookup start taking outside bets. Grunts took my helmet and strapped a camera on it while I started pacing. Shit. This was actually happening, and I needed it to happen. I desperately needed to win. Hayden interrupted my restless movement by putting his hands on my shoulders. Squatting down a little, he looked me in the eye. "I know this isn't what you're used to and you're freaking out because you want it so much...but you can do this. Relax, and trust yourself."

"I really wish you'd stop doing that," I told him.

"Doing what?" he said with a smile.

"Getting inside my brain without permission," I answered with a frown. "It's really not fair, since I can't step inside your head."

With a rueful laugh, he looked away. "I wouldn't be so sure about that..." Returning his eyes to me, he lifted his scarred eyebrow. "But I didn't peek in your head this time. Your nerves are written all over your face. And you need to fix that, because no one will bet on you if you look like you're about to pee your pants."

Inhaling deeply, I shook my head. "I don't care about bets...I care about winning. I *need* this."

Hayden's face softened as he whispered, "I know. But the more people who bet on you, the more races Hookup will enter you in after this. You need to keep him happy if you want to keep racing. In a way, it's kind of like smiling pretty for sponsors and sounding great on camera. Legal or illegal, it's all part of the same game."

That didn't help my nerves at all; I sucked at both of those things. "Great. Good to know."

Hayden sighed as he studied me. "I'm not helping, am I? Hmm, I have an idea. Don't hit me..."

"Why would I—"

Before I could ask my question, Hayden's mouth was on mine. I was too startled to react at first, but then a warm, roiling heat started coursing through my body, obliterating every anxiety I had, and I voraciously kissed him back. My fingers moved to his chest, gripping his T-shirt in a desperate attempt to pull him closer. He slid his hands down my back, enveloping me in his scent, his feel, his sheer masculinity. The world around me melted into nothingness, and all that was left was Hayden, me, heat, lust, desire, and...some intangible force I couldn't even name.

His tongue slid along mine and I groaned with need. *Yes, more.* And just like that...he was gone. My lids felt like heavy weights were attached to them; opening my eyes was a struggle. When my vision finally focused, I saw Hayden staring at me with a wary expression, like a mouse trying to sneak around a sleeping cat. The realization of just what he'd done hit me so hard, I reacted before I could stop myself—I socked him in the arm.

Rubbing himself, he backed away with a scowl. "Hey, I said *don't* hit me."

"And I never agreed I wouldn't. You have no right to—"

Holding up both hands, he cut me off. "Are you still nervous?"

With the memory of his lips on mine…no, I definitely wasn't nervous anymore. I was something else entirely. "That still doesn't give you the right to do that." I tried to look menacing, but I didn't think I was pulling it off very well. The grin on his face confirmed that I wasn't.

"I know," he murmured. "That's what made it so much fun…"

Seeing his flirty humor return lightened something in my heart. Maybe we could retain some of what we'd had before we'd slept together. Although, with how much I wanted to pull him back to my mouth, I was doubtful. Luckily, Hookup approached us with news that the race was about to start before I could. "Hey, lovebirds. Time for Ms. Hot Shit here to strut her stuff."

"We're not lovebirds," I said, correcting him.

He smirked at me in answer. "Right…" Turning to Grunts, he said, "Hey, man, tell me…are throat inspections part of racing now?"

Grunts huffed an amused response and I grabbed my helmet from him. "Just show me where to go." I needed speed. Now.

Laughing, Hookup pointed over to the crosswalk being used as a starting line. My competitor was already there, waiting. After I joined him, someone in the crowd standing near the line shouted, "Next green light means go!"

My heart thudded in familiar anticipation, while a tiny voice in the back of my mind screamed, *This is crazy! You can't do this!* No…this wasn't crazy, this was a chance to win thousands of dollars, and I couldn't turn that down…I just couldn't.

The light changed color and when nothing but green filled my vision, I punched it. Mohawk boy beat me off the draw, but I was right on his tail. Since I didn't know the city that well, I stuck to

Hookup's suggestions. That got a little nerve-racking when Mohawk Boy veered left while I kept going straight. But Hayden had told me that going off course was sometimes strategic rather than an actual shortcut. He did it at times when there was no real advantage, but it got in the other rider's head, made them second-guess their choices. And doubt could sometimes make all the difference in a close race. I held firm to what I knew to be true, and lo and behold, when the Mohawkian appeared again, he was behind me.

And he stayed behind me for the next three checkpoints. At each one, a person holding a flashlight on the corner flicked the light three times to let us know they'd spotted us. After the last location, an espresso stand next to a gas station, we flipped a one-eighty and started heading home to the last checkpoint—the starting line. Mohawk got a surge of courage or adrenaline, for he pulled up next to me, leaving me in the lead by less than an inch.

Hayden had told me that the actual rules of the race were lenient. In fact, there were only two—don't start early, don't miss a checkpoint. Getting a little too…friendly…with your competitor wasn't a problem here. Just incredibly dangerous. As the last straightaway loomed before us, I let my bike drift near Mohawk's. Focused on his end game, he didn't move away from me. We were so close together now that I could have reached out and kicked him. Instead, I gave him a little kiss…with my bike.

The force of the movement jarred me, but I'd been ready for it. Mohawk hadn't. He minutely slowed down as his bike started to swivel, and I shot ahead of him. Yes! Now I just had to hold it for ten seconds…eight…six…three…one. As I crossed the line in front of him, a sense of wonder ran through me. *I won! Holy shit!*

A crowd surged around me when I stopped my bike, and Hayden's face was the first thing I saw when I tore off my helmet. He looked both upset and ecstatic. Throwing my helmet to Grunts, I hopped off my bike and into Hayden's arms. "I did it!" I squealed, squeezing him tight. It was only when his arms wrapped around me that I realized I'd hugged him. But I was flying high from my victory and it felt too wonderful to pull away.

Surprisingly, though, Hayden pushed me back. Holding my

arms, he scowled at me. "You nudged that guy? Are you insane? You could have wrecked, and there are no safety walls here, Kenzie."

At the moment it hadn't seemed like that big of a risk, not compared to letting everyone down, but now that the high was fading, I was beginning to see just how stupid that had been. "Undefeatable, remember? That's what I need to be. And I *was* careful about it...I swear."

Shaking his head, Hayden wrapped his arms around me again. "I've created a monster," he murmured.

"Shit yeah, you have!" Hookup exclaimed as he approached us. "We're celebrating after this. My treat. Well, not really, you assholes are buying your own shit, but you know what I mean. We're drinking!"

Hayden and I stepped away from each other and Hookup grabbed my shoulders. "Fuck, that was amazing. I'm kicking myself for not knowing about you earlier. Damn it. Well, here you go...your cut of the pot was five grand, plus another grand for side bets. Not bad, rookie." He reached into his pocket and handed me a thick wad of hundreds. I'd never held that much cash at one time. It was a heady feeling, and a little surreal. Six thousand dollars, instantly in my hand, and all I'd had to do was what I did almost every day. The relief and joy pouring through me made me feel like I was flying. I could actually do this. I could help my father and save the family business. Everything was going to be okay.

I found myself watching the next race with the discerning eye of a fellow participant. Critiquing routes, speeds, corners. It didn't even faze me to see the rider weaving in and out of traffic and blowing through stoplights like they were optional. I wasn't sure how it had happened, but somewhere along the way, I'd started seeing the entire world as one big racetrack.

Right before Hayden was set to go on his run, the last race of the night, I noticed a handful of people not watching anything that was happening. Instead, they were looking down side streets, occasionally chatting to someone on a walkie-talkie. Giving reports, from the looks of it, most likely keeping an eye and ear out for police. It was a chilling reminder of the true danger that came with street racing. Maybe more so for Hayden and me than anyone else here. But even still, I couldn't bring myself to leave early. I needed to see how Hayden finished.

The final minutes of betting were furious as the racers took their places, and I momentarily considered taking my six grand and placing it all on Hayden. I couldn't risk it, though, not even on an almost guaranteed sure thing like Hayden.

The light changed color and the pair were off with a roar of engines. I immediately ran to the van so I could watch the helmet cams. The guy Hayden was racing was good, and he pulled out in front. Hayden quickly caught him, then fell behind, then caught him again. I felt like biting my nails as I watched the high-speed back-and-forth action. This one would be close, that was for sure.

Hookup and Grunts were beside me, cheering for Hayden with loud, obnoxious screams, as if somehow he could hear them. "Come on, Hayes! Daddy needs a new pair of shoes, with a matching gold watch, diamond cuff links, and Escalade to go with it." Hookup smacked Grunts across the shoulder and he chuckled.

His materialistic comment pissed me off. Hayden was out there putting his career on the line to help a friend…to help Hookup's *sister*. Tearing my gaze away from Hayden, I looked over at Hookup. "So, your sister, your niece…do you help them out like Hayden does?"

Hookup looked annoyed by my question. "*Nobody* helps Iz out like Hayden. It's like he thinks he's somehow the kid's dad or something." He rolled his eyes, then quickly evened his expression. "Don't get me wrong, I throw her a bone here and there, but she's the one who went and got herself knocked up. Not *my* problem."

His callous attitude rubbed me the wrong way. "She's your family."

He shrugged. "Yeah, and that's why I help out every now and then. But the girl's gotta fend for herself at some point. Teach a man to fish and all."

Right. I wanted to tell him where he could shove his fishing parable. I hadn't met her, but Izzy seemed like a good person who was dealing with a horrible situation, not someone who was actively looking for handouts. Her daughter was sick, she was desperate to save her, and all Hookup seemed to care about was making money. I opened my mouth to voice my opinion, but something was happening on the screen and it distracted me. People were groaning, and throwing their hands up in disgust as I tried to figure out what was going on. Hayden's cam was still showing the road speeding by, but the other guy's cam was focused on the engine of his bike. It was smoking.

Hayden zipped across the finish line a few minutes later, and I wanted to cheer, but all I could think about was the rumor surrounding Hayden—on the streets, he never lost, and I was seeing the proof of that right now. He either had the best luck in town, or everyone he went up against was cursed. It was a frightening thought. But I had raced him before and won, and I'd come out of it unscathed, so it must just be good luck and bad coincidence.

Hookup and Grunts were congratulating Hayden, so I walked over and gave him my well-wishes too. His helmet was off and his smile was a mile wide. Hookup repeatedly socked him in the shoulder. "Twelve grand, man! That's your cut! I told you, when people know you're racing, the bets skyrocket. Everybody wants to beat my boy, but nobody fucking can! Now let's go drink! Meet you at Haven."

Hayden took his money from Hookup, then turned to me. "Want to?"

Biting my lip, I nodded. Between the risk and the reward, I was buzzing with vibrant energy. "Yeah, sounds good." Really good.

The entire group was dispersing, racers vanishing so quickly it seemed like they'd never been here at all. With a grin, I hopped on my bike and started heading somewhere…anywhere. Hayden followed me, and I couldn't resist teasing him. Standing up on my bike a little, I smacked my ass, then laid on the speed. *Race me or chase me, Hayden.*

He immediately took the bait, and we were neck and neck before I knew it. Hayden veered left and I followed him. I veered right and he followed me. Riding with him like this was the ultimate form of foreplay. Each turn was a caress, each acceleration a hard stroke. The air was cool on my exposed hands, sliding up my coat sleeves like Hayden's fingers. My breath was loud inside my helmet, echoing my rising passion back to me. I was on such a high, I couldn't think of a better way to top off tonight than to have Hayden's arms wrapped around my naked body. If I started us on a path to my house, would he follow?

But before I could, Hayden pulled in front of an abandoned warehouse lined with motorcycles. Some of them I recognized from the race; Hookup's car was there too. I could hear music thumping on the inside of the building, could feel the pulsing energy from my seat. Hayden removed his helmet, then walked over to me. "This…might not be what you're used to," he said, holding out his hand.

The excuse to touch him was too great, and I clenched his fingers in mine after slinging my helmet over the handlebar. "I find that I'm getting used to a lot of new things."

Hayden smirked. "I've noticed." His voice was low and seductive, and little hairs stuck up on the back of my neck. With a grin that could power this whole place, he pulled me toward the door. The world diminished, and all I saw was the curve of his smile. Until we got inside.

Three or four work lights brightened areas of the room, but in the places where darkness prevailed, every type of vice was being practiced: drugs, alcohol, cigarettes, sex—you name it, and it was probably happening. I wasn't sure at what age Hayden had entered this world, but I was positive it had been way too young to handle all this…excess.

In one corner of the room, seven or eight coolers shone under a light, and a couple of female bartenders were busy providing the thirsty crowd an assortment of beverages. On the other side of the room a couple of tables were set up, with clumps of people playing poker, and in the center of the far wall was an enormous set of speakers pumping out the rib-shaking sound.

Hookup and Grunts were standing near the cooler bar, getting drinks from a woman wearing a bra for a top, and Hayden led us that way. When we arrived, Hookup nodded in greeting, then had the girl pour two more of the mystery drinks; there were about six different liquors going into the cup and only a splash of cola to dilute the mixture.

While the woman worked, Hookup glared at Hayden. "Took you guys long enough. I thought you were both supposed to be fast."

Hayden rolled his eyes as he handed the girl cash for the drinks. "Some things are meant to be enjoyed slowly," he said, locking his eyes onto mine. A warm flush filled me; yes, some things definitely were.

We sipped our drinks at the bar, chatting with Hookup, Grunts, and some of the other riders. When our plastic cups were empty, Hayden tossed them in a garbage can and held out his hand again. "Dance with me?"

There were a handful of people dancing, but it wasn't exactly a club atmosphere in here. And most of the dancing—and I used the term loosely—was actually just rhythmic making out. But that drink had been strong, and I was still buzzing from the thrill of the race, and just the thought of having Hayden's hands on me… "Okay," I murmured, letting him lead me away.

He took me to a section of the room that was shrouded in darkness. The inky blackness was almost a palpable thing brushing against my skin, making my senses come alive. And then he wrapped his arms around me, pulling me close. As our bodies pressed together, something inside me opened. A tiny crack in my defenses, letting Hayden in when I knew I should be pushing him away.

Hayden ran one hand up my back while the other hovered tantalizingly close to my backside. Lacing my arms around his neck, I pressed myself closer and looked up at him with hungry eyes that I hoped conveyed what I was thinking. *Take me again, right here, right now. Maybe it's not too late…*

Hayden smiled at me as we slowly began to move. We weren't keeping time with anything but each other, and I was perfectly fine with that. "God, you were amazing out there tonight. I know I said

I didn't want you to do this—and I still don't—but I had a feeling you'd be good at it, and I was right," he said, his smile smug. "You're gutsy, fearless...but smart too. And so beautiful. You're a deadly combination, Kenzie, one who would drop any man to his knees." His expression turned so serious, so admiring, that my breath caught and my heart started pounding.

"Stop it," I murmured. We couldn't take it to that level. We just couldn't. Just being attracted to each other was hard enough.

"Stop what?" he asked, his face shifting into amusement. "Stop saying nice things to you?"

"Yes," I stated. "Because when you say things like that, it makes me want to do...things to you. And we can't...We said we wouldn't..." The harsh reality of my words hit me and I tried to squirm away from his embrace. I couldn't; his grasp was too solid.

"*You* said we wouldn't," he said, his voice heated with desire. "You're the one who said we shouldn't start this...after we already started it."

The passion in his eyes was captivating, intoxicating, and even though I wanted to cave, I had to at least try to stay firm; I was doing this for us...to make it easier in the long run. "And you *know* why we can't. There's no future here, Hayden, just a bunch of people we'll let down. You'll lose your job, I'll lose my father, and for what?"

"God, Kenzie, just shut up and let go," he growled, then he brought his mouth to mine. I moaned as his soft lips moved over me. When he pulled away, I was breathless. "For this, Kenzie. We risk it for this..."

He lowered his lips again and I met him halfway. He tasted too good, felt too good; I couldn't say no to the temptation after having had a piece of it. "Yes," I murmured into his mouth. *God, yes.*

I felt him moving us, but I didn't care where we were going. His lips were working against mine, his tongue was brushing over me, and his hand was finally firmly holding my ass. I was in a euphoric state of bliss that didn't allow logic to enter.

When I felt my back bump up against a wall, a groan escaped

me. Somewhere in the back of my brain, I knew we were in a warehouse full of people, but it was dark where we were, and everyone was preoccupied with their own carnal delights. No one would think twice about us making out against a wall.

His mouth transferred to my earlobe, and my eyes fluttered closed as he nibbled and sucked. As my hands tightened in his hair, he groaned in my ear. "You feel so good…I want to make you feel even better."

I wasn't sure what he meant by that, but I found out a second later, when he unbuttoned my jeans. I was three seconds from pushing him off me when he murmured, "Let me do this. Let me make you come, right here, right now."

Opening my eyes, I looked around the oddly lit building. No one was watching, no one cared, and with Hayden's body flush against mine, no one could see anything anyway. Before Hayden, I never would have considered doing anything like this, but now…I wanted more. Arching my back, I told him, "Yes…please."

He growled in my ear, then shoved his hand down the back of my jeans, the back of my underwear. I was so ready for him that when he slid his finger against me, I dug my fingers into his scalp and let out a loud cry as my head dropped back. "Oh God, Kenzie…you're so…Fuck…I want you. Come for me," Hayden groaned.

His finger started a slow circle that had me panting with need. God, he felt good. I wished it was more, wished it was his mouth, wished he was driving into me. Moving my fingers to his shoulders, I gripped him tight as I started shaking. I sought his lips, needing to drown my cries in his mouth before I alerted everyone to what we were doing.

His hips were grinding against mine, and the hard outline of him was teasingly pressing into me over and over. Not undoing his jeans took every ounce of willpower I had.

He moved a finger inside me and I broke contact long enough to whisper, "Yes, more…" He paused to shift positions and then he was sliding one finger inside me while simultaneously stroking my core. I was done. Gripping his neck tight, our mouths sealed together with passionate fury, I cried out in short bursts while the pleasure broke over me in a tidal wave of bliss.

We pulled back to stare at each other, and we were both panting. Eyes hazy with lust, Hayden carefully removed his hand from my jeans, then inserted a long finger into his mouth. His eyes closed as he devoured me, and when they reopened, they were hungrier than before. "Not the same as directly tasting you, but it will do. For now."

Jesus. How would I ever be strong enough to say no to him again?

CHAPTER 18

Every few days Hookup called Hayden with a new location, and every time I won a race—and that was most of the time—I hid the money in my house and pondered how I could subtly give it to my father. I couldn't just hand it to him; he would want to know where it came from, and I couldn't tell him that. I also couldn't just slip it into the business checking account—Dad was an excellent record keeper; he'd recognize something was off.

It was infuriating to have the solution to our problem in my hands and no way to share it with him. I'd have to be creative. Like I was being with Hayden. I'd managed to hold out on having sex with him for almost two weeks now. Not that we didn't fool around. The thrill that came from a great race often manifested physically between us. There was a lot of heavy petting, making out, and the occasional orgasm...but no actual sex. I was a little proud of myself for not caving. And *really* frustrated too. God, there were times when I would have paid him money to have him inside me...What we were doing was stupid, but adding sex to it would be so much stupider. Because no matter how often I allowed myself to ignore the truth, it was right smack in my face whenever I went to the family track.

Myles was grumpy whenever he visited and saw Hayden freely

walking around the Benneti side. Nikki was stressed about having to find a job somewhere else at the end of the season. Dad was busy trying to find another team worthy of having me. They were all a mess, a fact that was amplified when Theresa decided to have Daphne's bridal shower in the Cox garage. She said it was so everyone could participate, but I knew the truth—it was goodbye. They were all giving up. Except me.

More determined than ever not to accept defeat, I won my race that night. Hayden won his too, and like we did after most of our successful events, we ended up at some seedy abandoned building afterward, celebrating our victory with other racers. It made me feel a little guilty, allowing myself to be happy when everything back home was falling apart, but I was trying to fix that. And…I just couldn't say no when Hayden asked me to go with him.

I'd had a couple of strong drinks since getting here, and I was feeling good—loose, relaxed, and carefree. I wasn't thinking about how many calories I was consuming, wasn't worrying that I was overindulging, wasn't contemplating all of my many problems. I was putting all of that aside and living in the moment. And it felt so good to let it go, even if it was just for one night.

Hayden was giving me that look he gave me when he wanted more than just talking and drinking. God, I loved the way his eyes sparkled when he was horny. It set off something inside me, something primal and needy. I'd never get enough of him. Probably because I never allowed myself to *have* any of him. Just that one glorious time…

Leaning over so his mouth was almost touching my ear, he said, "There's a back room in this building. Want to go check it out?"

I knew exactly what that was code for, and I wanted it, had a deep, profound ache for it. Lifting my lip in a half smile, I slyly told him, "Sure…why not."

He grinned, then held out his hand for me. Hookup rolled his eyes as he watched us leave. Then he mimed jacking off and having an orgasm. Immature asshole. If we didn't need him to get entry into the races, I might have a conversation with Hayden about cutting him out of his life. He acted like a spoiled thirteen-year-old.

Hayden led us around back to a dimly lit hallway; whatever this place used to be, it was still connected to power. We looked around, but we didn't see a back room anywhere… just a bunch of boxes that made a sort of maze at the end of the hall. Hayden led us through them, and my heart started beating harder in anticipation. I couldn't wait to hold him, kiss, him, let him touch me… everywhere.

When we got to the last stack, Hayden pulled me behind it. The light was so scarce, I couldn't fully see him until my eyes adjusted. Once I was acclimated, the heat in his expression made my breath grow quick. "Have I told you tonight how incredibly sexy you are?" he asked.

Biting my lip, I shook my head. "No… not yet."

He crooked a smile at me that instantly had me tingling. "Let me show you, then," he said, opening his jeans.

I was squirming, I wanted to touch him so bad. Hayden stepped closer to me, pressing my back into the wall behind me. Taking my hand, he started leading me to him. "Feel me," he whispered in my ear.

A shiver washed over me as my fingers touched the hard ridge of him straining against his underwear. Damn. He was so ready for me. He had to be throbbing, had to be in pain. I should do something for him, for us. But no, that would be cruel. *Crueler than this?*

Ignoring my internal argument, I slipped my hand into his underwear and wrapped my fingers around him. Hayden let out an erotic noise that ignited my body. "Oh God, Kenzie, yes… Touch me." Knowing I shouldn't tease him when I couldn't follow through, I began stroking his body. His mouth found mine, and his kisses were frenzied with desire. "Yes, don't stop," he murmured.

I picked up the pace and he growled as he ran his fingers up my T-shirt to feel my chest. "Let's leave here. Let's go to your place."

He tweaked my nipple and I cried out, squeezing him harder. "No…" *Yes…*

Hayden pulled my hand away from him, then grabbed my wrists and held them against the wall. Looking exasperated, he panted, "Why not? How long do you want to keep doing this in places like *this*? In a bed, I could kiss every inch of you…run my tongue up you…tie you up…" he murmured, his mouth twisting into a crooked grin.

Damn…I wanted to say yes so badly my body hurt. As if he could sense that I was on the brink of changing my mind, he slipped a hand into my jeans and ran a finger over my pulsing core. "Fuck…how long do you want to keep wasting a perfectly wet pussy?" Leaning up, he groaned in my ear. "My cock could be buried inside you *right now*."

His words were dirtier than usual…and I loved it. I wanted more. "Oh God," I murmured under my breath.

"Exactly," he answered. "Instead of this, I could be plunging into you…over and over…until you come all around me…" His finger started simulating what he was saying and I had to struggle to hold on to my objection.

"Hayden," I whimpered. I couldn't take much more; I was going to explode if I didn't have him.

"Yes?" he said, his mouth teasing my lower lip.

I was just on the verge of telling him to take me home when someone started tromping through the box maze. "Hayden, dude, you back here? You guys done fuckin' yet? 'Cause I just found out something pretty amazing, and you should know about it." The intruding voice belonged to Hookup. *Are you freaking kidding me?*

Hayden instantly stepped back and fixed his clothes, and I instantly double-checked my own outfit. Jesus. My heart was about to burst out of my chest. Goddamn interrupting asshole. Or maybe I should be thanking him. That had been way too close.

Hayden's facc was clouded with anger when Hookup stepped around the corner into our hiding place. "What the hell is so important that it can't wait until we get back?" he snarled.

Touching his fingers to his chest, Hookup made a face like he thought we were adorable. "Aw, did I interrupt 'racing' time? So sorry about that, but I just had to tell you the good news, bro!" He looked like a little boy who'd just been told he was going to Disneyland. "You are both officially entered in the race this weekend. It's on!"

His raised both of his palms in the air, waiting for high fives. He didn't get them. Gritting his teeth, Hayden muttered, "That could have waited."

I was confused. Hayden and I had plans this weekend—important plans. "Wait a sec…*this* weekend? We can't this weekend. We've got a race this weekend."

Hookup slapped his hands together. "I know! 'Cause I got you in!"

Shaking my head, I held my hand up. "No, the ARRC race is this weekend. In Monterey."

Hookup nodded slowly, as if he were talking to a toddler. "Yeah, I know. The real race is after that shit."

Comprehension finally dawned on me, and I twisted to Hayden in surprise. "You race during official events?" Of course he did. That was why I saw Hookup and Grunts on the track sometimes. Or lurking in Hayden's hotel room. They were there to keep an eye on their asset. I was such an idiot.

Hayden gave me a sheepish smile. "Wherever Hookup can find a race is where I go, Kenzie. And you know why." I did. I completely understood his motivation for racing, which only made things harder. "Are you in?" he asked, and I got the feeling he was wondering about more than just the race.

Possible futures zipped through my mind—continuing this secret life with Hayden, always hiding in the shadows and back alleys. Coming out to my father, confessing everything, and watching him disown me. Losing it all—my dream, my lover, my career, my family. But the slim chance that I might hover on the line between worlds long enough to do some good had me nodding at Hayden. "Yeah…I'm in."

* * *

A couple of days later, we were several hours from home, in Monterey, California, preparing for the next big events—both the daytime and the nighttime ones. I wasn't sure which race I was more excited for. And I also wasn't sure which one would help Cox Racing more. The only thing I *was* positive about was that Hayden would be there for both of them, supporting me, pushing me... and wanting more from me than I was giving him.

There was an autograph session before the ARRC race, and the number of people there to see me was mind-boggling. I had been so sidetracked by the stress of trying to save the team that I often missed the fact that I was doing really well for my rookie year. In fact, if I kept on getting top ten scores, I'd be the highest finishing female... *ever*. And my fans were excited for me.

"You're the most inspirational racer on the track."

"I hope I ride half as well as you when I'm older."

"Can I have your number?"

That last one had been from a male fan. I signed his glossy photo of me with my name and nothing else. My love life was complicated enough.

After the signing, I had lunch with my father. He tended to eat alone now, since no one on the crew was happy about his decision to close at the end of the year. Some crew members had even left already. We were getting by on a skeleton crew that was desperately grasping at the razor-thin hope that Dad might change his mind. That he even *could* change his mind—being broke couldn't exactly be wished away or ignored. But it could be fixed, and that was what I clung to—my shield against the massive guilt tearing me apart.

Dad was already at his desk, eating a deli sandwich when I came in. "Hey, Dad, care if I join you?"

He gave me a partial grin. "Of course not, Mackenzie. You're a welcome change from John. The only thing he wants to talk about lately is investors. He seems to think merging with a third party could save Cox Racing." He sighed and shook his head. "I tried having a partner before... and you know how that turned out. No. When the storms come, you batten down the hatches and wait it out. But when the storms don't stop coming... you pack up what you can and move on."

"Dad... I..." *I can save you. I'm making a lot of money, and it's all yours. I'll be your partner*... I couldn't say it, though. I couldn't confess what I was doing.

Clearing his throat, Dad didn't give me the chance to finish. Pointing to the chair opposite him, he said, "Heard the latest gossip yet? There was a rider who missed the autograph session this morning. He's been gridded, but I don't think he'll even race. They say he got violently ill after the warm-up this morning. People are saying it's weird, since he was fine last night."

I knew what he wanted me to believe, but a rider getting sick before an event wasn't all that unheard of. "Dad, that doesn't mean anything."

Dad shook his head. "There's been other trouble this year too. Illegal parts here, bad spark plugs there, wrong tires... Riders who should know better are being penalized for stupid rookie mistakes. It's not natural," he finished with a grunt.

Only it was. It was all stuff that routinely happened during the course of a season, just usually not as frequently. "Dad... the officials are all over you after Barber. You can't—"

Pointing a finger at me, he cut me off. "All I'm saying is watch your back and watch your stuff."

I nodded. That much I could do.

After lunch it was time to race. Our positions on the grid were adjusted according to the sick rider's no-show. His vacant area was a radiating warning that I did my best to ignore. It was normal, routine racing. Hayden wasn't doing anything to mess with people, here or on the streets. It was coincidence, nothing more.

As we moved into our new positions, I found myself momentarily close to Hayden. Flipping up his visor, he told me, "Good luck out there, Twenty-Two." Then he winked, and I could tell he was grinning under his helmet. A schoolgirl flush rushed through me, making me avert my eyes. Seriously. I was a professional. A wicked smile shouldn't undo me.

The light shifted to green, and I surged forward. Corner after corner whizzed by, with me right on Hayden's heels. Aside from directly in front of him, this was my favorite place to be. Racing against him made my heart thud in my chest, made my breath come out in furious pants. God, I loved this.

Suddenly, smoke in the distance signaled a wreck somewhere

ahead of me on the track, and that feeling of contentment was snatched away. We were in too deep, though, and there was no way to avoid what was coming. All any of us could do was punch it and pray.

I followed Hayden through the wreckage of multiple crashed bikes. We made it through the eye of the needle, but I caught glimpses of a few riders behind me who weren't so lucky; they were sucked into the chaos and didn't emerge from the other side. Warning flags went up everywhere, and those of us remaining riders were forced to pit so the track could be cleared.

Fear tightened my chest as I examined the ripped-apart bikes. Save for a bit of good luck, I could have been out there in the wreckage. It was a side effect of my sport, though, one I'd made peace with a long time ago. But Myles and my father were inside my head, shouting at me that something was amiss, that none of this was as random and innocent as I wanted to believe it was. And if they were somehow right…then none of us were safe.

Once the track was cleared, we were allowed to finish the race. It was hard to get started again; I had so many swirling thoughts, fears, doubts, and worries for the wrecked riders. But I pushed all of that aside so I could do what I was meant to do: Race. Win. And maybe it was the lack of competitors, maybe it was my precision-point focus, but I smoked that course with a third-place finish. My highest ever, and a record for a woman on this track. Hayden finished second, his highest ever. And even though I had to sit through an interview after my finish, I was on top of the world.

I did it! *We* did it. Everything I'd done—everything Hayden and I were currently doing—it was paying off. Relief and joy coursed through me in waves. It wasn't too late to fix things. Dad would see that and change his mind. Everything was going to be okay. It had to be.

But when I saw my father, he wasn't excited for the future of Cox Racing…just happy to see that my own path was brighter. "This is great, Mackenzie. Finishes like this will go a long way toward getting you on a great team next year. Keep up the good work."

As he turned to walk away, I grabbed his arm. "That's it? 'This should get you on a new team'? What about *our* team, Dad? Don't you see how this can help us?"

He looked at where I was holding him, and I instantly released him. "No. What I see here is potential for *you*. Cox Racing is done. I already told you that."

* * *

I had a chip on my shoulder when I showed up at the assigned meeting place for the street race late that night. Hayden noticed immediately. "Hey. You…okay?" He studied my eyes, like he was trying to read the answer in them.

"Yeah," I told him. "Just trying to continue the fight when everyone else around me has given up."

Hayden smirked, and a knowing look flashed through his eyes. "I get that."

Yes. If anyone understood constantly fighting against impossible odds, it was Hayden. It filled me with peace to know that he truly understood me. It also filled me with fear. Sharing a bond with him meant sharing a piece of my heart, a heart he could potentially rip to shreds. But not making that connection with him was impossible. I couldn't ask the sun not to rise just because I didn't want to get burned. I'd just have to be careful, and Hayden probably felt the same way. When it came right down to the core of who we were, Hayden and I weren't all that different, and that only made it harder.

As if he'd followed the exact same mental path I'd taken, Hayden frowned. "I wanted to congratulate you on your race today, but there was never a good time. Keith was all over me, and my teammates…" With a shake of his head, he cleared his thoughts and smiled. "With everyone's eyes on me, I had to stay clear of the Cox camp. You understand?" I nodded. It was the same reason that had kept me from congratulating him—that damn Benneti/Cox Racing ban that kept us apart. Or was supposed to, anyway.

Hayden chuckled as he looked around the street rapidly filling with people. "Strange, isn't it? We have more freedom here, doing something that could feasibly get us arrested, than at our legitimate jobs. No matter how you try and make the world make sense, it just refuses to." Returning his eyes to mine, he murmured, "The universe is stubborn…just like a girl I know."

The smile on his face made a warmth bloom in my chest, and suddenly all the secrets we were keeping felt incredibly right. And then I heard Myles and my dad in my ear, whispering that something dark and sinister was going on, and Hayden was in the middle of it. The words tumbled out of my mouth before I could stop them. "Weird wreck today, right?"

A strange emotion flickered across Hayden's face, and he opened his mouth to speak…right as Hookup bounded to our side. "There are my star racers! Ready for this? It's gonna be a big one!"

Hayden smiled. "I've been ready all day," he said. I bored holes into the side of his face, but he wasn't looking at me anymore. Like I didn't even exist, his eyes were all on Hookup.

Not noticing the sudden tension between us, Hookup gave me finger guns. "You're up first, Kenzinator." I groaned at Hookup's never-ending nicknames for me, then went to find my bike. Since we were close enough to home, Hookup and Grunts had hauled our everyday bikes over in a trailer. It had been difficult to trust Hookup with my equipment, and if it hadn't been for Hayden assuring me it was fine, I never would have let him touch my motorcycle.

While Grunts got my helmet ready, I inspected my bike. It seemed fine, but it was always good to double-check. I could feel someone hovering nearby while I worked, and when I peeked my head up, I saw Hayden staring at me; his expression was dark and his eyes were intense. "You might be right about the wreck. It *was* a little…weird. But racing is unpredictable, and sometimes weird things happen…" His eyes lost focus for a second. When he came back to himself, he shot me an untroubled smile. "Good luck out there, Kenzie."

He left before I could respond, and a pit of dread formed in my stomach. *Sometimes weird things happen*? He sounded like he was making excuses…but for what? Or was he just saying what I often said—that our sport was dangerous, and sometimes crap happened. Shit. I didn't know for sure just what he'd meant by that. And I hated not knowing.

While I tried not to read too much into anything and just take the encouragement as it was offered, Grunts approached me with my helmet. It was time to line up for the race. My heart was thundering as I pulled up to the line. *Sometimes weird things happen.* Right. That was why I practiced diligence and control, so I could avoid the weird things. But I raced better when I let go, when I imagined Hayden was beside me and I let everything else fall by the wayside. I couldn't be cautious *and* fearless. I had to choose which path to take, which philosophy to embrace. And if I was going to make a difference to my family, there was only *one* option—close my eyes and leap.

The light turned green and I took off like I had nothing to lose and everything to gain. In most cases, I think my sheer determination would have been enough, but my competition this race was just as crazy as I was, and unfortunately, he had a slightly better bike. I could have easily taken him on my official racing motorcycle, but this was my street bike, and it wasn't quite as high powered. By the third checkpoint, I was a good two feet behind the other rider. I was going to lose.

Then something on the bike in front of me flashed, and the rider almost instantly lost control. We were approaching a corner when it happened, and he slid out and crashed into the side of a Dumpster. I couldn't believe it! Accelerating, I hurried to the final checkpoint—the finish line.

Everyone in my "crew" was cheering and jumping when I won, and Hayden wrapped me in a huge hug the second I hopped off my bike. It was only later, when we were drinking in celebration, that I realized I'd only won because my competition had had something…weird…happen to his bike. Like Hayden said, sometimes weird things happened while racing, but they seemed to happen around him more than anyone else. It was too frequent to be coincidental…which meant it wasn't. And now the weird things were happening to me too. I was benefiting from something nefarious, from something unnatural. Hayden was the only person I could think of who would want to see me win. And I had no idea what to do about that, because right or wrong, I desperately needed to keep winning.

CHAPTER 19

Over the next several weeks, Hayden and I kept secretly racing, and I kept winning. Actually, I hadn't lost a single race since before Monterey, even though there were some races that I never should have won. It was unnerving to know some secret force was helping me, and a part of me felt so dirty, like I was stealing. But I needed the money, so I stayed quiet and didn't voice my fears or concerns to anyone.

There was no one I could talk to anyway. Except Hayden, and since he might very well be the one behind it all, he wasn't an option. The dilemma made me feel more tangled up than I'd ever felt before. Because if Hayden really was the reason I was succeeding, then he was also the reason Myles was done for the year. I was betraying one of my best friends every time I talked to Hayden. Every time I joked with him, smiled at him...kissed him. I was a horrible person. While I got ready to head to the practice track, I wondered how long I could keep balancing on this very thin moral line. And which side would I land on when I inevitably fell off?

Myles was stomping around the garage when I got there. His leg was healed now, but his temper wasn't. Or his determination to make Hayden pay. It was an added stress I didn't need...because

I wasn't entirely sure that Hayden *shouldn't* pay for what had happened to Myles.

Glancing at me, Myles snapped, "I can't believe it's been months, and that douche still gets to ride."

"That's because he can't be banned without proof he's doing something wrong, Myles." God, I hoped my face wasn't giving anything away; the guilt was eating a hole in my stomach.

Myles scowled. "He's guilty of something, and I won't rest until I figure out what."

He stormed out the door, and the remorse inside me tripled. I hated the fact that I couldn't truly support Myles in this—I hoped he never got dirt on Hayden; I needed him…and I wanted him to stay. If only Myles could just let the whole thing go. Ruining Hayden's career wouldn't help his own anyway, and stewing on it was slowly poisoning him. But I understood why he couldn't. If someone took racing away from me, even for just a year, I'd be a basket case. And like Myles, I probably wouldn't stop until I'd had my revenge.

Nikki came in just as Myles was leaving. "What's eating him?" she asked. Then she sighed. "It's Hayden, isn't it? I keep telling him to drop it and move on, and he keeps digging his heels in deeper."

She slowly shook her head, like she didn't understand. Sadly, I did, and that was why not being firmly on Myles's side killed me. "Yeah. He's desperate to get dirt on him, to get him banned from racing."

Nikki got real quiet, then she said, "I think it's time we told Myles about the street racing."

My heart started thudding so hard, I heard the ocean pounding through my brain. "What?" I squeaked. *Does she know what Hayden and I are doing?*

Nikki swallowed, like she was nervous. "Remember? Hayden was at that race…the one I dragged you to. I know it will paint us in a bad light, me especially…but I think we should tell Myles about it. And I seriously doubt Hayden has stopped doing it, so Myles might be able to catch him. I've still got contacts, I can find out where the next race is." Her face fell. "Myles will be pissed at me for betting on that crap…but he'll get his dirt on Hayden, so he'll get over it."

Shit. Shit. Shit. Yes, he would definitely get his dirt on Hayden, and he'd also get dirt on *me*. And once Myles figured out that I'd been lying to him and conspiring with the enemy—and occasionally getting down and dirty with him too—he would write me off as a friend and tell my father about everything I'd done. In his anger, he might tell the officials too. My career would be over, and Cox Racing would be history. I couldn't let that happen. "I wouldn't, Nikki. Myles…we've had long conversations about street racing before. He really hates it, almost more than my father does. He thinks anyone who participates in it is practically…subhuman. I don't think he would forgive you."

God, I sucked. But my words didn't seem to have the intended effect. Nikki's face went pale, but her expression hardened, like she was bracing herself for that fate. "If he can't get over it, then…I guess I'll just have to deal with that. But I've got a way to help Myles, and I'm not going to sit back and do nothing while one of my best friends slowly goes insane. It was a stupid idea anyway. All of it was stupid. I never should have gotten sucked into that world."

You and me both. Fuck. How could I possibly salvage this? I couldn't stop racing—I was too close to having enough money to make a real dent in the business's debt. Hayden couldn't stop racing—that little girl needed him too much. We both needed time.

Knowing she wasn't going to like this, I told Nikki, "Okay, but don't say anything to him yet. Can you wait until after the last race in Jersey?"

Nikki looked like I'd just asked her to make sure my bike failed. "What? Why?"

Holding back tears of frustration and shame, I told her a small, incomplete version of the truth. "I can't explain why, but I'm better and faster when I'm racing against Hayden. I *need* him to be in the race if I'm going to save this team. Please?"

Nikki studied my face for long seconds before saying anything.

And when she did, I was bombarded with relief. And guilt. "Yeah, okay, Kenzie. I'll wait until the season is over."

When I met up with Hayden later that night for another street race, I knew I needed to tell him about what had happened with Nikki. We both needed to get out of illegal racing after Jersey, or everything was going to blow up in our faces. It would be hard to leave that kind of money behind, especially for Hayden, but it was for the best. We couldn't keep trying to belong in both worlds. Well, I knew I couldn't. I was alienating my friends and family, lying to almost everyone I knew; I was starting to feel like a stranger in my own skin.

"Hayden...I..."

Before I could tell Hayden anything, Hookup approached us. And he was excited. "Mad Mackenzie! You are not going to believe the news I got for you!"

And you probably won't believe the news I've got for you: I'm quitting, and taking your best rider with me. "What news?" I asked, feeling hollow inside.

"Prepare yourselves for this...The L.A. Mondo is back!"

He said it like I was supposed to know what the hell he was talking about. "What's that?"

Seeing that I wasn't impressed, Hookup frowned. "The L.A. Mondo? The biggest street race on the West Coast?" When my face didn't change, he rolled his eyes. "Fucking rookies. The L.A. Mondo is the biggest and best. Everybody wants in, but hardly anyone can afford it. Just the best of the best make it. The entrance fee is one hundred K."

My jaw nearly hit the floor and Hookup finally smiled. "One hundred thousand dollars to enter?"

Jesus. If I actually won that race I'd have more than enough to save Cox Racing. "I want in," I told him. And even as I said it, all thoughts of putting aside this seedy world right now left me. *One big score, then I can get out.* And never look back.

Hookup bumped my fist. "Damn straight I'm getting you in." He turned to Hayden, who had his calculating eyes on me. "What about you, H? You're in, right?"

Hayden studied me a moment longer before shifting his gaze to Hookup. "You know what that money could do for Izzy and Antonia. They wouldn't need any more for a long time…so of course I'm in."

I was so relieved to hear him say that. If Izzy wouldn't need money for a while after he won—and I was sure he'd win—then he wouldn't need to street race. One more event, and then we'd both be done. And when Hayden was semiretired, I would warn him about Nikki telling Myles all about his illegal career. He probably wouldn't risk street racing at all after that, and then we'd both be safe…and Myles would be chasing a shadow.

* * *

The race was the night before my sister's wedding. Probably something I should have considered before I'd said yes. But "the Mondo" was my ticket out, so saying no wasn't an option. And besides, racing hours didn't conflict with wedding schedules. I could easily do both. I'd be really tired, but I could catch up on sleep after I'd solved all of the family business's problems.

After an uneventful wedding rehearsal followed by an extended dinner at a vastly overpriced seafood restaurant, I killed a few hours at home, then headed to L.A. My excitement grew as I rode. This could be it. Everything I needed to save everything I cared about. It was potentially the answer to my prayers. If I could win.

The bright lights of the city showed themselves, and I smiled as I made my way to the meeting place. I was so close to a solution to Cox Racing's problems that I was shaking with excess energy. It took me a while to find the out-of-the-way street that held the starting line, and Hayden was already there by the time I found it. Waving me down, he indicated a small space beside his bike to park. There were so many people here, I felt like half the city had turned up.

Nerves were eating at me as I pulled up beside him, but once I saw his beaming smile, they began to subside. I was a good rider, and I'd gotten considerably better since racing with Hayden. He might have started out as the secret to my success, but regardless of what I'd told Nikki, I was a force to be reckoned with on my own.

"Hey, Twenty-Two, are you ready?" he asked, running a hand through his messy blond hair.

I nodded. "This could change everything for us, Hayden. We could be legit. We could leave this world behind. We could be..."

My voice trailed off as my thought died. Whether we won or lost tonight, it didn't change the fact that we couldn't actually be together.

Hayden's smile fell a little, as if he understood what I'd been thinking. It instantly returned, though. "Yeah, this is the one we've been waiting for. An answered prayer..." His voice grew reverent, and for a second, I wasn't sure if we were still discussing the race. *Is that what we are to each other? An answered prayer?* That thought felt so right, it scared me.

We were staring at each other, lost in thought, when suddenly Hookup tossed his arms over our shoulders. "This is it, lovebirds! The big kahuna! The one that will place me on the path to greatness." He lifted his hands and mimed an explosion. "My name in lights, known as the greatest manager in the state." The way he said "manager" made it sound like "pimp." It made my skin crawl a lot more than it probably should have.

"Hayden and I are still the ones who need to win. It's our talent that gives you that...greatness."

Hookup's smile was so smooth, I could have ice-skated on it. "That was implied. Your greatness equals my greatness. And vice versa. We're a team."

I resisted the urge to tell him that I already had a team. That the entire reason I was doing this in the first place was to help *my* team. As if he knew I was about to bite, Hayden grabbed my elbow. "When are we up?"

Hookup nodded to the street, where a pair of riders were making their way to a crosswalk. "You're up after these losers."

While the riders positioned themselves, a flurry of last-minute betting happened around me. I heard people shouting their bets to

Grunts, who wrote each one down in a book. My eyes popped as I heard the numbers being tossed about. Five grand. Ten. Twenty. It was an obscene amount of money to place on happenstance, and it made me wonder…I usually avoided the side bets, but with the amount of money to be made tonight…maybe I should place a bet this time?

On a whim, I turned to Hookup and said, "Place fifteen grand on me. And fifteen on Hayden."

Hookup smiled and relayed my order to Grunts. "What are you doing?" Hayden hissed in my ear.

"Doubling my money," I told him. Then ice water flashed through me. If Hayden was hesitant, then maybe I shouldn't be so confident. I quickly turned back to Hookup. "Wait, I changed my mind. I don't want to bet."

With a megawatt grin, Hookup shook his head. "Sorry, sweets. A bet laid is a bet played. You're in the books."

Anxiety chewed at my gut as I mulled over what I'd done. Sure, I had enough to cover the amount if I lost the bet, but I needed every penny to give to my father. I'd just have to win. That was all there was to it.

The active betting stopped, and the riders at the start line hunched down in preparation. Once the light changed to green, they'd take off. Wondering what my potential profit might be tonight, I turned to Hookup to ask him if he had any idea. My question was evaporated by a strange squealing sound cutting through the night. When I spun around to see what was going on, I saw lights zipping around a corner, turning onto the street. Bad lights. Blue and red lights. Cop lights.

"Hayden," I murmured, turning to look at him. I felt like everything was happening in slow motion, like I had turned to ice. No…I couldn't get busted, couldn't go to jail. It couldn't end like this.

Hayden's eyes widened as he spotted the danger. Then he grabbed my shoulders. "Drive hard, drive fast. And don't stop until you get home. I'll meet you there."

Stubborn refusal to leave without him gripped me, but Hayden shoved me toward my bike before I could object. "Go, Kenzie! I'm right behind you. I promise."

He headed for his bike, so I took his word for it. Slamming on my helmet, I straddled my bike and started the motorcycle. Throwing it into gear, I lurched forward, onto the sidewalk full of scrambling people. I tried to go around them as carefully as possible, but even still, I clipped a few. I couldn't take the time to care, though. I needed to get out of here.

When the sidewalk led me to an alley, I hit the gas as hard as it could take it. As I flew down the cracked concrete, I heard the sirens kicking on. Multiple sirens from multiple cops. And from the fluctuating sounds—some closer, some farther—it was clear they were following people; someone was going down tonight.

I couldn't slow down to see if Hayden was behind me. I just had to hope that he was. I didn't know the roads well, and as I darted from alley to side street, to yet another vacant alley, I quickly became lost. I could feel people behind me, but I was still too scared to turn and look. My heart was pulsing so fast, it felt like someone was conducting "Flight of the Bumblebee" inside my chest. It wasn't supposed to turn out like this. Tonight was supposed to be the answer to all my problems, not the beginning of them.

Suddenly the alley I was racing down spilled out onto a street I knew. Thank God, escape. Not stopping to make sure the coast was clear, I punched it across two lanes of traffic, then turned left. I heard vehicles honking, screeching to a stop, but no one hit me. My breaths were frantic as I tore along the road. I could have just gotten myself killed, and wasn't that worse than losing everything? I wasn't sure.

Regardless, I made myself slow down and scan the street behind me. No cops were chasing me. Oh thank God, no cops were chasing me. My relief didn't last long, though. I didn't see Hayden. Shit. I couldn't leave him behind to get caught, no matter what he said. Wondering if I'd completely lost my mind, I made a U-turn and raced back to the alley I'd escaped from.

I had absolutely no clue how I'd retrace my path to find him, and raced blindly down streets that seemed vaguely familiar. All I knew for sure was that they were leading me back toward the epicenter of danger, not away from it. Every cell in my body was telling me to stop, telling me to quit this insane plan and give up…but I couldn't leave Hayden behind.

Just when I was positive I was lost in this godforsaken city, I glanced down a side street and saw Hayden zip across the opening. A motorcycle cop followed closely behind him a few seconds later. Shit, shit, shit. *What do I do? Leave him, or help him?* It really was no question at all. Thick or thin, we were in this together.

Squealing my back tire, I quickly turned the bike around and headed back the way I'd come. Hayden was on a street running parallel to mine. I raced to get ahead of where I thought they might be, then turned left onto a side street that would intersect with theirs. If I timed this right, I'd cut between Hayden and the cop, possibly confusing the officer long enough for Hayden to get away. But then, of course, the cop might come after me…

When I reached the crossing, I slowed down and hoped that this worked. I breathed a quick sigh of relief when I saw Hayden fly by, then I punched it. Praying I didn't smack into the cop, I pushed my bike to the max. I cut in front of the pursuing police officer with only inches to spare, and as I looked back, I saw the cop slam on his brakes, then fishtail to a stop. I didn't wait around to see how long it took him to recover.

Forward. Ever forward. *Please don't let him come after me.*

It felt like an eternity passed, but finally I pulled onto a street I recognized. And even better, this one had signs for the freeway. I just wanted to get out of the city and leave all of this behind. With a silent prayer, I looked around to see if Hayden had found this street too. I exhaled with relief when I spotted him not too far behind me, and thankfully, alone. Had we actually done it? Actually escaped? I couldn't believe it, and I was buzzing with anxious energy. I needed to slow down and act natural, though. We needed to act like we weren't running. And that meant we had to obey traffic laws.

My hands were shaking when we stopped at a red light. I felt like police were going to descend on us from every angle. I wanted to run so badly that just sitting there was pure torture. I looked over at Hayden to distract myself. Nodding at me in reassurance, he held a hand out like a stop sign; clearly he understood my desire to keep fleeing. Thank God he was okay. Thank God we were both okay.

Hayden seemed to remember something and looked around. There was traffic crossing in front of us—all normal cars and trucks, no cops—and no one behind us. While I watched, perplexed, Hayden hopped off his bike and quickly removed some sort of sticky-looking, magnetic-lined black plastic film from his license plate. I couldn't tell from my angle, but I had a feeling that officer chasing him hadn't been able to read his plate at all...which meant he was safe. Jesus. Where had he gotten that thing? And when the hell had he put it on his bike?

Hayden rolled the film up and slipped it into his jacket as he straddled his bike. I could only stare at him in wonder. Just when I thought I'd seen it all, he managed to surprise me. Now if only we could get all the way home without him needing that thing again.

The rest of the drive home was thankfully uneventful, but adrenaline was still rushing through me when we pulled up to my house and hid our bikes in my garage. Goddammit. That had been way too close. When we got into the kitchen, I couldn't calm down. I felt like a thousand needles were under my skin, continuously pumping me full of caffeine. I was jittery, anxious, and on edge. But most of all, I was relieved. We'd done it, we'd gotten away.

"Oh my God, Hayden. Oh my God! We could have been...we were almost...Shit!" Yanking my hair out of its messy ponytail, I started pacing back and forth. Too close. Much too close.

Hayden watched me with an incredulous expression on his face. "You came back for me. I told you not to. I told you to go straight to your house and not look back. But you came back. Why?"

"Because I couldn't let them take you away," I said. "You're trying to rebuild your life...trying to save a little girl. You don't deserve to go to jail for that." Something in the back of my brain told me that wasn't the real reason I'd returned for him. *His pain is my pain.*

Stepping forward, Hayden grabbed my arms. "You'd gotten

away," he growled, his voice intense. "You were free, and you put everything back on the line. For me. Why?"

"I already told you why," I cried, trying to get away. Saying he meant something to me, that I...had feelings for him, wouldn't do any good, wouldn't change anything between us. It would only make things harder. Didn't he understand that?

Apparently he didn't. "Not good enough," he stated. I could tell he wasn't going to back down an inch, not until I told him the real reason I'd risked it all. "Just tell me," he whispered. "Stop holding it in, Kenzie."

I was lost under his penetrating gaze, and all my reasons to keep him at arm's length vanished in a puff of smoke. "Because I care about you," I murmured, my voice barely audible. I almost heard a door creaking inside me as I admitted that. My heart was opening, letting him in. *Tell him the rest—that you can't stop thinking about him, that you worry about him...that you love him.* God...I did love him...but I couldn't admit that. It would only hurt us both to tell him.

"You care about me? How?" he asked, his tone soft.

I tried to say something, tried to somehow explain how I felt without really saying it, but that was impossible, and the words stuck in the back of my throat.

Hayden smiled, like he understood. "There was once a time when I thought that keeping shit in would make it go away. I was yanked around so much when I was a kid that nothing felt stable, nothing felt real. Izzy and Hookup...and Felicia...they gave me solid ground for the first time in my life. Then Felicia...she took it all away again when she left without a word, and I swore...I swore I'd never let *anybody* in again. And I tried to keep you out. God knows I tried. But I needed you, then I started to like you...and now...now I'm in love with you, and it's too late for me to keep holding it all in."

My mouth dropped open as a shudder went through me. *He loves me?* "Hayden, I..." Words failed me, and my sentence died. *He's in love with me...and I'm in love with him.* We were a tragedy waiting to happen.

Smiling wider, Hayden said, "I love you for everything you are, and everything you do. And I understand it doesn't change anything. In our case, love might not be enough. But that doesn't alter the fact that I feel that way, and neither does *not* telling you that I feel that way. Keeping the feelings to myself won't save us any pain. Nothing will save us, Kenzie. We're doomed. And I love you. And I don't regret a thing."

A sob hitched in my throat. Every word he was saying felt like goodbye. A torturous, painful farewell that would change me forever. "Stay. Stay with me tonight. Don't go…"

He ran a finger across my cheek, then over my lips. "Nothing could drag me away from you right now."

His mouth replaced his finger and I hungrily consumed his lips. Everything felt so powerful, yet so final—like we were opening and closing a door at the same time. It made me frantic, needy, and I started pulling off his jacket right there in the kitchen. "I want you," I murmured, running my fingers down the firm muscles of his chest. "Take me to the bedroom."

A low noise escaped him as he moved his mouth to my ear. "I will take you in *every* room," he whispered; I instantly wanted him to make love to me right there on the kitchen table. *Yes…*

I started tugging at his shirt, wanting it off. He helped me, pulling the fabric over the back of his head. Once his skin was bare, I brought my mouth to his collarbone and moved my fingers to his jeans. *I need more.*

Hayden stopped me. "It's your turn," he said, unzipping my jacket. When that fell to the floor, he trailed his fingers along the skin just above the waistband of my jeans. I tried to rip my shirt off, but again he stopped me. "Let me," he whispered. Then he slid his hands up my ribs, taking my shirt with them. He bent down to kiss every inch of exposed skin, and when he got to my breasts, he kissed each peak through my bra. Electricity shot through me, igniting me.

Removing my shirt, he dropped it on the floor. "You're so beautiful, so perfect." Slowly, he ran his fingers along my shoulder, grabbing my bra strap and taking it with him. The calculated deliberation of his movement was excruciating. We'd only just begun, and I was already dying for him to be deep inside me.

He kissed my bare shoulder as the strap fell away, then he started on the other one. When the bra finally fell to the floor, he brought a hand up to cup my breast and a shudder of expectation passed through me. Then he closed his mouth around my nipple and stroked it with his tongue. A loud groan left my mouth, followed by some incoherent plea for more.

A rumbling noise of approval vibrated my skin as Hayden teased me. Then his fingers found my waistband and started undoing my jeans. *God, yes.* I helped him shove them down my hips, helped him remove my boots, my socks. We were completely uneven when I was left in only my underwear and he was still half-dressed, but I didn't care. I wanted to be bare before him. "Where do you want me?" I panted, my thumbs in my underwear, ready to rip them off if he commanded.

Hayden's eyes closed for a fraction of a second, as if my words had been a stroke of my tongue over his cock. I loved the thought of satisfying him on every level. I wanted him to be happy... all the time. Because he meant... so much to me.

He focused on me again and his hands went to my hips, over mine, and he helped me slink my underwear to the floor. "Hop up on the island," he murmured. Breathing heavily, I did what he asked without question. I would do almost anything he wanted right now, so long as we were together. "Lie back and close your eyes," he said.

The Formica was cool but invigorating against my skin. I never kept anything on the island, preferring it bare and open, accessible when I needed it. I'd just never imagined needing it in this way. A row of spotlights dangling from the ceiling threw hot circles of light against my skin; it was almost like I was on display for him. Arching my back, I closed my eyes and waited for my lover, my soul mate. *Touch me, Hayden. I am completely yours.*

I heard him removing his clothing and I squirmed, feeling restless with pent-up energy. Then I felt him place my legs over his shoulders, and I started to breathe so hard, I thought I might pass out. He began placing tender kisses up my thigh but then I felt him pause, heard an erotic exhale leave his lips. "You're so fucking gorgeous," he murmured. "So ready, so wet. God, I bet you taste good…"

With that, he ran his tongue up my core. The shock wave that radiated through me made me cry out, and I had to grip the edges of the island to stop myself from holding his head there. "Shit, yes, you taste good," he panted. "Oh God, Kenzie, I need you so much." There was something about the tone of his voice, some serious edge of pain, panic, and fear, and I knew he wasn't talking about sex. *I need you too.*

"Hayden, please," I begged. *I don't want to think about the bleakness of our future, I just want to savor the moments we have.*

His mouth returned to me, his tongue stroking my core while he sucked, teased, and pleased. He was firm, aggressive, commanding, and still, it wasn't enough. I let go of the counter to hold his head to me; I couldn't let him go. *I don't want to ever let you go.*

The painful need inside me grew to a precipice, and like he knew it was coming, Hayden slowed his movements, coaxing me to the end instead of pushing me. Euphoria crashed around me like a storm, and I couldn't contain my joy. And just as the crest started fading, I felt Hayden pull my hips closer to the edge. Then he was filling me, and I gasped as he started stroking me toward something amazing again. I rocked my hips against him as he slammed into me. His noises were frantic, needy, like he was on the verge of climaxing. I was almost there again too. Just a little more.

"Fuck," he murmured. His fingers swirled over a nipple, then trailed down my stomach. When he got to where we were joined, he moved his thumb in small circles over my core. "Come with me, Kenzie. God, please come with me." I could tell by his voice that he was close, and his thumb running over me was exactly what I needed to get there.

My body stiffened as the ecstasy washed over me again. I clutched the hard surface above my head as a loud, passionate "*Yes*" escaped my lips. I felt Hayden coming a second later, heard his own erotic groans as he released, and I felt utterly and completely whole.

As the surge of bliss began to fade into the background, as our breathing returned to normal and our hearts slowed, a feeling of despair started sneaking up on me. How many times could we make love like this before we truly had to part ways?

Removing himself from me, Hayden handed me a dish towel from nearby, then pulled me into his arms. He held me close, like he also knew this couldn't last. A contented sigh escaped me as I wrapped my arms around him. *Yes, this is what love should feel like.*

Hayden kissed my head before picking me up and carrying me to the bedroom. He laid me on the mattress in the dark room and helped me get under the covers. When we were both buried under blankets, I turned to face him. Pulling his mouth to mine, I wished with all my heart that I could keep him. That we could remain here, in this bed, and let everything in the outside world slip away.

As our lips moved together, I felt that same wish in the force of his kiss. We were both trying to hold on to something that couldn't be contained. We'd each lose something far too important by being together. It was a price I couldn't pay, even though I loved him.

Hayden sighed into my skin, a sound conflictingly full of happiness and sadness. He ran his fingers through my hair as he held me tight to his chest, and a heavy dread fell over us both. Because now that we had both fallen…the true pain would begin.

CHAPTER 20

I woke up to the feeling of a tongue swirling around my nipple. It wasn't a bad way to wake up, but it was definitely disorienting. It took me a solid minute to remember what had happened last night—the disastrous race, fleeing the cops, the heated moment with Hayden in the kitchen, making love on the island...Hayden admitting he loved me, finally admitting to myself that I loved him too.

Pushing aside the emotional pain we'd experienced last night as we'd fallen asleep in each other's arms, I threaded my fingers through Hayden's hair and allowed a satisfied hum to escape me. We were fated for disaster, but at least we had this moment together. And it was a good one.

Seeing that I was awake, Hayden started moving his lips up my neck. "Hey," he said, his voice low and seductive. "I'm glad you're up."

"It's not like you left me much of a choice," I answered, angling my head so he could kiss all the way up my throat.

A low laugh escaped him as he nibbled on my earlobe. "What can I say? I like mornings." I couldn't help but smile. I liked mornings too, but for a whole new reason now.

Hayden placed a line of kisses along my jaw as his fingers moved up the inside of my thigh. I wasn't sure if I was ready for him yet, but his finger against my skin was light and gentle, and before long I was breathing harder, wanting more.

He moved on top of me, then slowly slid inside. We both let out long, relieved exhales. "Making love to you feels so good…I don't ever want to stop," he said, giving me a soft kiss. I started to agree, but he moved his hips and I groaned instead.

The pace he kept was slow, steady, and unhurried. We cherished every sensation, every thrust, every pulse of pleasure. I was torn between wanting that epic climax and never wanting to stop feeling this good. But eventually, I couldn't contain the explosion. It was going to happen no matter what I did, and now that it was upon me, I didn't want to stop it.

Grabbing Hayden's hips, I pulled him into me. As my cries grew frantic, more urgent, Hayden dropped his head into my shoulder and started to stiffen with his own release. "God, yes, Kenzie, now…come with me."

His angle as he came was perfect, and the explosion of bliss instantly hit me. I clawed at his hips as it overwhelmed me, buried me, consumed me. I would never be the same after making love to this man.

Hayden slumped against me, breathing heavily into my ear. I clutched him tight, desperately trying to hold on to the euphoria, desperately trying to ignore the fear that this might be our last time together.

"Oh God," I said, trying to lighten the mood. "Why weren't we doing this from the beginning?"

Hayden laughed as he nuzzled my neck. "I tried to tell you, but you wouldn't listen. Your stubbornness holds you back."

"My stubbornness is part of the reason we race so well together," I retaliated.

Lifting his head so he could look down at me, Hayden crooked a sexy smile. "True enough," he murmured. Leaning down, he gave me a soft kiss, then rolled over so he could withdraw himself. I sighed as he left me, and Hayden looked back with an amused grin. "I'd be happy to do that again, but I think I need a drink first. I'm a little dehydrated." I smacked his shoulder in answer... but I didn't tell him no.

He left the room bare naked, and I waited just a half second before wrapping a sheet around myself and following him. When I caught up to him in the kitchen, he was slipping on his underwear. The room was strewn with clothes and memories. I wouldn't be able to set anything on the island again without thinking of Hayden.

Opening a cupboard, I grabbed a glass and handed it to Hayden. While he walked over to the faucet to get some water, I studied the evidence of our lovemaking. My eyes washed over his jacket and a piece of last night popped into my head. "That thing you put over your license plate, it kept the number hidden, right?"

Hayden nodded while filling his glass. "Yeah... Hookup's invention actually. You were already gone, but he peeled one off and slapped it on my plate before making a run for it. He always said he kept a few on him just in case of a bust. I thought he was crazy for being that paranoid, but I guess he wasn't." He frowned, then shook his head like he was shaking off a bad thought.

Just as Hayden started taking a sip of his water, his cell phone started ringing. Setting the glass down, Hayden made his way over to his jacket and found his phone; by the annoying alarm ringtone, we both knew who it was.

"Hookup, hey... you okay?" Cringing, Hayden pulled the phone away from his ear. Even from where I was standing I could hear Hookup's annoyed voice. "Yeah, I see you've been calling all night. I was kind of... busy. Sorry. Kenzie and I are fine, though. We made it." A flush crept through me as Hayden's eyes met mine. I hadn't heard his phone ringing. Guess we'd gotten carried away.

Hayden listened to Hookup talk for a little while, then asked, "Did everyone make it out?" His face suddenly went pale and his lips parted in surprise. "Grunts got picked up? Is he...? Are you getting him out? Are they pressing charges? Did he have the book on him?"

White-hot dread shot through me. I'd made a bet. My name was in that book, both as a bettor and a racer. I was double fucked if

Grunts had it on him. Hayden closed his eyes; I didn't know what that meant. Then he quietly said, "It was coded, right?"

He sagged in relief and I was finally able to breathe again. Jesus Christ. My life had actually flashed in front of my eyes. "Okay, yeah. Let me know when he's home."

He hung up the phone and I started panicking. "Grunts was caught? Is he going to jail? Am I going with him? Was my name in that book?" I frantically looked around my kitchen like the cops were about to bust in.

Shaking his head, Hayden walked over to me and put his hands on my shoulders. "It's fine, everything is fine. They were only able to bust him for evading police. There wasn't enough proof of anything else, and the betting book is all gibberish nonsense. Grunts is the only one who knows how to read it. The cops just wanted to scare us. They've got nothing."

I shoved him away from me. "Well, it worked, I'm scared. I can't do this, Hayden. I can't lose everything like that. My family, my career, my freedom? It's too much…I can't ever race again. I'm out. Hookup can hate me for life, but I'm done."

Understanding on his face, Hayden soothingly said, "Okay, Kenzie. I'll tell him you don't want to do it anymore, and I'll make sure he leaves it at that."

Using one hand to hold my sheet in place, I cupped his cheek with the other. "You have to quit too. It's too dangerous. You have too much to lose." Dropping my hand, I slowly prepared to tell him the worst part of all this. "I…have bad news. Something I thought wouldn't matter, because I thought we'd both have enough money after winning that damn race to quit with a clear conscience. I thought we'd wake up today done with that life."

Hayden frowned as he studied me. "What news?"

Biting my lip, I wished I didn't have to tell him about my friends' plan. He'd always dislike them after this. Not that all of us being friends was really an option anyway. "Nikki and Myles…they…" I paused for a deep breath, then let it all out in a rush. "Myles blames you for getting hurt and being out this season. He wants you gone. He's obsessed about it. Nikki was there the night I first saw you street racing. She's going to tell Myles what she knows, and she's going to help him…try to catch you doing it…so you'll be banned from racing." Shaking my head, I hoped he would listen to reason. "I bought us time—she won't tell him until after the race in Jersey—but you can't go back, Hayden. You really will lose everything…so you might as well quit now. Why tempt fate?"

Hayden worked his jaw, and I could see the anger he was struggling with as he tightened his muscles. After a moment of silence, he slowly shook his head. "I can't give it up. You know that. But thank you for telling me about…your friends. If I know someone's looking for me…I can hide my plates, keep my face covered, use a fake name…but I can't quit while Izzy needs me, while *Antonia* needs me. And I'm sorry if that bothers you."

My eyes began to sting as hope failed me. "You can't straddle both worlds forever, Hayden. You'll slip up, or you'll get hurt…"

Grabbing my hand, he softly said, "I have to try, Kenzie. I have to keep fighting for as long as I can, and I know you understand that." I opened my mouth, but there was nothing more to say. I did understand, but that didn't make me any less afraid for him.

While I tried to find words, Hayden smiled and said, "I really would love to take you back to bed…but don't you have a wedding to get ready for?" He nodded his head at the clock on the wall.

"Oh shit. I'm supposed to meet my sister at the salon in an hour. She will literally hunt me down and kill me if I'm late."

Hayden laughed, then let me go. "Wouldn't want that."

There was a wistfulness in his eyes that tore my heart. "I'd take you with me if I could…you know that, right?" I said.

He nodded, his smile soft yet sad. "Yeah, I know."

I hated seeing that look on him, hated feeling the same way. "What are you going to do today?" I asked, trying to change the subject.

He shrugged. "I thought I'd go to the track. It's pretty quiet on the weekends. It's nice to be there…alone." Knowing his teammates were assholes and he was basically on his own over there made a slice of anger go right through me. He shouldn't be an outcast on his own team.

Hayden frowned as he watched me process. "You okay?" he asked.

With a pain-filled exhale, I nodded. "Yeah, I just…" *I wish you didn't have to keep street racing. I wish your team accepted you. I wish my father would accept you. I wish you could celebrate with my family today.* "I wish things were different," I finally said.

Leaning down, Hayden gave me a soft kiss. "I know. I do too. Will I see you tonight? After the wedding?"

With a sad smile, I nodded. For now, we would pretend things between us could actually work. It was the only way *we* could keep fighting.

* * *

Hours later, when my hair was spritzed and styled and my makeup was garish and overdone, I felt better…and so much worse. I'd given up the illegal racing, washed my hands clean of the sin. The miasma of guilt that had come along with the forbidden activity was gone, and I felt like I could finally breathe around my family again. But grief had swept in once the guilt was gone, and its weight was almost unbearable. Were Hayden and I done as well? Because I couldn't keep dating him behind my father's back any more than he could keep racing behind Keith's back. Technically, the two of us had been finished before we'd even begun.

And my father…without the street racing, I had no real way to help him. Even winning the ARRC championship wouldn't be enough. Not anymore. I could only better my own position with another team, and it felt so wrong to focus on my dream and leave Dad's to die. But I had to accept that I'd failed in trying to save him—to help get him back on solid ground, I'd hoped to earn around $200,000, but I'd only made a little over a third of that amount, and that wasn't enough. I had to let Dad's dream go. And I had to let Hayden go. I had to let everything go.

A troubled sigh escaped me for the thousandth time, and Daphne shot me an annoyed look. Resplendent in a tight white mermaid-style wedding dress that was adorned with what had to be ten thousand shimmering seed-pearl beads, my sister radiated beauty and elegance. Her long blond hair was swept up away from her neck, with hundreds of tiny loose curls spilling from it. A tiara was artfully crafted into the design; the princess of the family was finally getting her moment to shine. And she didn't want anyone ruining it, especially me. "It will be over with soon, Mackenzie. Just try not to fidget when you get out there, okay? You looked like you had to pee during rehearsal yesterday."

I wanted to say something snarky in reply, but I just didn't have it in me. We were waiting in a "staging area"—basically a private garden area next to the main garden where Daphne was binding herself to one man for the rest of her life. But Jeff was a good man, and he adored my sister, did everything he could to make her happy, even when she was being ridiculously overbearing. He was the exact right match for her, and the fact that they had found each other—were allowed to date each other—and were now getting married made me a little sad.

Daphne and Jeff's wedding was taking place outside at the base of a bridge crossing over a meticulously landscaped koi pond. The fountains on each side of the bridge were dyed with the wedding colors—bright orange and vibrant red. Rows and rows of pristine white chairs were decorated with red and orange roses, while professional violinists were in a corner playing traditional wedding songs. On the far side of the pond, out of view of the crowd, was a cage holding a pair of doves. They were going to be released later in the ceremony, at the crest of the pivotal moment, when the bride and groom turned to face the crowd as husband and wife. Not at all over-the-top.

From where I was waiting, I could see the chairs beginning to fill up with family, friends, and acquaintances of my sister and her soon-to-be husband. Dad was waiting with us, to walk Daphne down the aisle, and Theresa was a bridesmaid, same as me, but the rest of our immediate family was sitting in the front row—both sets of grandparents, aunts, uncles, and a couple of cousins. Behind them, in the next two rows, were members of Cox Racing, including John, Nikki, and Myles. It warmed me to see that Daphne had invited every single one of them. Even though Cox Racing was ending soon, the crew and riders were family.

I tried to get Myles's and Nikki's attention so I could wave hello, but they weren't looking my way. Nikki was gorgeous, as she always was at social events, but she was chewing on her nails; she only did that when she was nervous. And while Myles looked great in his suit, his face was so stony, I could probably place him among the statues scattered throughout the gardens and no one would know the difference. What was up with them?

While a new anxiety started eating at me, Theresa tapped my shoulder. When I looked back at her, she shook her head, making her blond curls dance. "I wouldn't let anyone see you yet. Bridezilla will be pissed." She grinned as she glanced at where Daphne was talking with the wedding planner; it looked like she was bitching the poor woman out for something. Turning back to me, Theresa leaned in and whispered, "Do you think she picked out these dresses just to torture us? Mine weren't nearly this bad."

She was almost right about that. The gown Theresa had shoved me into had been a formal southern gown that looked like a *Gone with the Wind* parody, but at least the color had been nice. Daphne's dresses were a horrid shade of tangerine that was supposed to coordinate with the koi in the pond. And as if the color weren't bad enough, it had a gigantic foot-wide red bow right above the ass. It was quite possibly the ugliest piece of material I'd ever seen. But somehow, with the way my mood was shifting, it was fitting.

"Yeah, I think this is payback for giving all her dolls haircuts when I was seven."

Theresa laughed at my comment, then her gaze grew fond. "I can't wait to see what you pick out for your wedding."

A knot tightened in my stomach so suddenly that I almost bent over. That wasn't my future. Not with Hayden, at least. I rapidly blinked to clear away the sudden watery haze obscuring my vision. "You honestly think I'll get married? I barely have time to shower, let alone date."

Theresa laughed again, and suddenly Daphne was by our sides. "What's so funny?" she asked, then her bright blue eyes turned uneasy. "Is something wrong? Is it the music? Chairs? Flowers? What?"

Theresa and I each put a hand on her shoulder while Dad came over to stand behind her. "Everything is fine, Daphne. You can relax now," he assured her.

Daphne didn't look very assured, but she nodded. As I looked between my father and my sisters, the knot in my chest turned to an ache. "I wish Mom was here," I whispered.

I heard Theresa sniff as Dad's eyes locked on mine. Giving me a wistful smile, he said, "She's here, Mackenzie. Trust me…she's here."

The instant water in my eyes threatened to spill over and ruin my makeup. Then I happened to look over at Daphne. She was waving her fingers in front of her eyes, desperately trying to dry them before her mascara ran. Her face was a combination of sadness and fury. It made me laugh.

Directing her heated gaze at me, she snapped, "No emotional comments before the ceremony, Kenzie. Jesus! Are you trying to kill me?"

I burst out laughing, and even though she glared at me, the lightened mood felt good. I just hoped it lasted.

The ceremony finally began and I walked with my assigned groomsman to the base of the bridge. When the violinists played the wedding march, the entire crowd stood for Daphne. I teared up again as I watched Dad walking with her. For the first time in a long time, he looked genuinely happy, almost carefree. And full of love and pride for his daughter. I hoped he felt the same way about me, and prayed he never found out about all the things I'd been doing. Would he understand that I had done it for him? Would it matter? A betrayal was a betrayal.

My mood darkened again as the wedding progressed. It didn't help that the ceremony was more than an hour long, with flowery poems, pages of quoted scripture, and *two* full songs. When it was finally over and Daphne and Jeff were walking down the aisle as husband and wife, I almost cried in relief. My feet were killing me in these uncomfortable heels, and my mind was shifting back to all the things I couldn't have. I needed a drink. Maybe several of them.

A circle of tents were set up on the far left side of the gardens, holding food for the reception and enough alcohol to flood Oceanside. While Daphne and Jeff kept everyone busy in a seemingly endless receiving line, I darted to the bar. The second I stepped in front of the nicely dressed bartender, someone behind me said, "Two whiskeys, straight. Actually, make them both doubles."

I looked over my shoulder to see Myles standing there. Now that I was finally seeing him up close, he seemed worn out. Ragged, like he hadn't slept at all. "Hey... you okay?" I asked.

Myles shrugged. "I don't know, Kenzie. I honestly just don't know anymore."

Having his hard gaze directed at me made ice water fill my veins. "What do you mean? What's wrong?"

Myles didn't say anything right away, just grabbed the glasses from the bartender and handed me one. He took a sip of his potent drink, then shook his head. "I need some answers, Kenzie. Truthful ones."

My heart was hammering now. "About what?" I asked. I brought the drink to my lips and let the burning whiskey generously coat my mouth. It was horrible and wonderful at the same time. *It's okay, he doesn't know anything.*

Leaning in close, Myles murmured, "Hayden. Are you sleeping with him too, or is it *just* about street racing?"

I immediately choked on the liquid fire coursing down my throat. And that made my objection to his claim sound pitifully weak. "What? What... are you... talking about?" My eyes were watering as I coughed and sputtered, but that was nothing compared to the panic flaring in my chest. *He knows. How the fuck does he know?*

Nikki rushed up to us then and started patting my back. "Jesus, Myles. What happened to being subtle?" With a glare, she handed my drink to him, then started pulling me away from the bar. Myles followed a step behind us. As I looked over at her, I saw that she seemed just as weary and bedraggled as Myles. Oh God...what was going on?

Nikki's worn face was filled with a lot more compassion than Myles's. "I'm sorry, Kenzie. I know you told me to wait to tell him about the racing, but I couldn't. He was so upset, he wanted something on Hayden so bad, and I knew..."

"She knew what you'd been up to!" Myles shouted.

Some people around us heard him, and I felt dozens of inquisitive eyes beginning to train on me. Shit, I was going to be sick. Nikki glared at Myles again, then shook her head at me. "I didn't know what you were up to, I swear. But Jesus, Kenzie...what the hell have you gotten yourself mixed up in?"

Stopping in my tracks, I held both hands up to them. "I don't know what you're talking about," I stated in a low voice. It was a lie, and yet it was the total truth too. I couldn't talk to them about anything until I knew what they knew.

Myles was immediately in my face. "We saw you. We went to the race in L.A. last night, and we *saw* you."

I felt the color draining from my face. Yes, I was definitely going to be sick. "Oh..."

Myles's eyes turned to ice. "Yeah...oh. After Nikki told me about the racing, and told me about the huge race in L.A., I knew exactly how I was going to get Hayden. I just had no idea I'd be trapping you too. You have no idea how shocked I was to see you there, Kenzie. With *him*." Lifting his phone, he began to show me a slideshow of photos. The world, the bikes, the racers lined up at the crosswalk, Hayden standing alone by his bike, and then lastly, me...standing with Hayden, getting ready for my turn. He had proof. I was fucked.

"Don't show this to my dad," I begged.

Myles let out a rueful laugh. "I feel like we've had this conversation before, Kenzie. This is the part where you beg me not to say anything, then I let you convince me you've changed your ways, then you go behind my back and fuck the enemy!"

He yelled that, and everyone around us heard him. My gut twisted into sharp knots. "No...I'm not..." I was. And I had. And there was nothing I could say to defend myself. Tears of shame started streaming down my cheeks.

Hearing me still trying to deny it made Myles so mad his face turned bright red. "You still can't be honest, can you? He's the reason I wrecked, Kenzie! The reason I missed an entire season. He could have fucking killed me! Don't you care about that?"

"Of course I do. Just let me explain..." I tried to put a hand on him to calm him down, but he yanked his arm away from me.

"Don't fucking touch me," he snapped; he was shaking with anger now.

Nikki tried to soothe him, but all the yelling had finally gotten my father's attention. My stomach turned to lead when I saw him storming our way. "Mackenzie? Myles? What the hell is going on here? I could hear you two arguing all the way from the receiving line." He aimed that statement at Myles. Seeing that Myles was two-fisting it, Dad grabbed the drinks from his hand and set them on a nearby table. Hands on his hips, he shifted his stern gaze to me. "Someone start talking. What's going on?"

I couldn't speak fast enough, and Myles beat me to the punch. Holding up his phone, he told my dad, "Your daughter has been illegally street racing with a Benneti racer. Hayden Hayes, the asshole who sabotaged my bike. And as if that wasn't bad enough, I'm pretty sure she's sleeping with him too."

And just like that, my world imploded. I couldn't save myself, couldn't save Hayden, couldn't save anyone.

Myles's face went pale white, like he'd just realized what he'd said. He tried to pull his phone away, but it was too late—my father snatched it out of his fingers and started flipping through the photos; his eyes darkened with every shot.

When Dad finally got to the last picture, he coolly handed the phone back to Myles. "I see," he said, his voice cold and detached...emotionless.

Feeling desperate, I grabbed my father's arm. "That's not what happened. That's not what *is* happening." *Yes. Yes, it is.* Shaking away the truth, I told him, "Hayden was just my ticket into the race. He showed me the way, but it was just *me* racing. He didn't want to help me, but I threatened him to make him do it. Because I wanted to win enough money to save Cox Racing. To help you." Feeling like my heart was being split in two, I sobbed, "All I wanted to do was help you save the business, Dad. And I have. I've got almost eighty grand at home, and it's yours. All yours! Let's go now and get it. Please! Let me show you! Let me help you!"

Dad's eyes widened when he heard how much money I had, and even Nikki and Myles sucked in disbelieving breaths. Then Dad closed his eyes and pressed his lips together so tightly, they turned white. When he opened his eyes again, his voice was edged with tightly controlled anger. "We will talk about this later, after your sister's wedding reception." He turned, walked away, and didn't look back, and I knew I'd just lost him. I felt it inside the deepest part of my soul. My father was gone. And possibly my future. And maybe even Hayden's.

Nikki was the first one of us to talk. "You really won eighty thousand dollars?"

With dead eyes, I directed my answer at Myles. "Yes, I did. To save Cox Racing. That's all I was trying to do, Myles. And you just destroyed…everything."

Regret in his eyes, Myles shook his head. "I didn't mean to. It just slipped out. I was so mad…and I'm so sorry…" Holding up his phone, he started doing something on the screen. "Here, I'm deleting all the pictures. There's no proof now. You and Hayden…you won't get in trouble with the officials."

Wiping smudged mascara off my cheeks, I told him, "We'll still get kicked off our teams. No proof is needed for the Benneti Ban," I said, my voice warbling. "We were seen together off the track…that's proof enough for Keith and my dad…who actually *did* see the proof before you deleted it. And you know what, if Dad brought this type of accusation to the officials about his *daughter*…even without proof they'll probably believe him. You might have just destroyed my career, Myles."

Myles looked away, and grief crashed into me. It was really over. I'd be fired at the least, banned at the most. Hayden would probably get sucked into my downfall…if he was lucky, he'd only be fired. And if that happened, would anyone else take a chance on him? I'd been trying to do something good, and now everything was destroyed…and all because of Myles's vendetta. "Did you two call the cops?" I whispered. "Did you bust us?"

Myles and Nikki looked at each other before looking at me; both of them had pale faces and guilty expressions, and I knew what they were going to say before they said it. Nikki's eyes turned glossy, like she knew this confession would permanently alter our friendship. "We didn't know you were going to show up. When we arrived and saw what was going on…when we saw Hayden…you weren't there. You didn't get there until after we'd called the cops…and then, it was too late to stop it…and we were both so…"

Myles picked up as her voice trailed off. "We were pissed, Kenzie. We felt like you'd betrayed us…so we didn't warn you. We left you there, right before the cops showed up, and I'm…so sorry," he whispered. "I feel really shitty about that now."

Nikki glanced at Myles. "I felt really shitty about it then, and I debated driving to your house a million times to make sure you made it, but I felt so guilty, I couldn't even call to check on you." Her eyes glistened as she sniffed. "We should have warned you…We should have talked to you. We should have handled all of this so differently."

Myles sighed and looked at the ground. "I just wanted to get Hayden so badly…"

"Well, you didn't get him," I snapped. Anger and pain and grief swirled within me so violently, I couldn't separate them anymore. "Hayden got away scot-free." Barely. Myles's eyes glinted with deadly heat. Even now, he wanted to punish Hayden. He always would, and I would always get caught in the cross fire.

Myles opened his mouth, and I knew he was going to say something I didn't want to hear at the moment. And there was nothing else to say, really. The damage had already been done. Despair nearly choking me, I told them, "Last night was my *one* chance to make enough money to bail out Cox Racing for good, and you both took that from me."

Nikki immediately stepped toward me, arms outstretched like she wanted to hug me. “Kenzie…I’m so—”

Stepping away, I raised a finger. “Don’t. I can’t right now.” *You took Cox Racing…and you took Hayden too.*

Turning around, I started walking away. I heard both Myles and Nikki calling my name, but I ignored them. I was roiling with emotions—I could feel the tears resurfacing—and I wanted to be alone when I completely fell apart.

CHAPTER 21

After the wedding planner helped me retrieve my bag from the dressing room, I hastily made my way to the parking lot. When I was finally inside my truck, I considered calling Hayden and telling him everything was over. I couldn't bring myself to do it, though. I couldn't crush him before I'd even told him how much he meant to me. And I couldn't stomach the thought of losing him; of the two things I was about to have ripped away from me forever, Hayden was the one that would leave the biggest hole in my heart. Just thinking about never seeing his emerald eyes, crooked smile, or messy helmet hair had me struggling to breathe. Not being able to race with him, talk to him, let down my walls and let myself go with him…I couldn't bear it. I couldn't tell him it was over yet, because if I stayed silent, maybe we could squeeze in one last night together.

One night that will never be enough. I couldn't hold back the grief after that thought, and laying my head on the steering wheel, I released every ounce of pain inside me with racking sobs.

I wasn't sure how long I cried, but eventually the tears all dried up. My head was pounding, my throat was so dry it was sticking to itself, and my heart…that felt like it would never function properly again. I did what I could to focus on something other than the pain, but it wasn't working. All I could think about was how much everything hurt—from deep inside my heart to the tips of my fingers, I ached.

Glancing at my lap, I noticed there were tearstains all over the gown Daphne had made me wear; it almost looked like I'd been caught in a rainstorm. I suddenly felt guilty. I should be out there celebrating Daphne's wedding with my family, not here, hiding and mourning. I wasn't sure I could fake happiness right now, though. Or be near my so-called friends. Or be near my dad. He was furious at me, and he had every right to be.

Deciding that I owed it to my sister to support her no matter what I was going through, I cleaned up my face and cracked open my door. When I put a foot down on the gravel parking lot, I noticed someone coming my way. My heart leaped into my throat as I watched my father approaching my truck.

Stepping all the way out of the truck, I took a deep breath and prepared myself. At least I could accept my fate with grace. Face stern, Dad stopped when he was directly in front of me. "What are you doing out here?" he asked, flicking a glance at the empty cars around us. "You missed the toasts and the cake."

"I needed to pull myself together," I told him. My voice was scratchy but, thankfully, steady.

Dad nodded, like he approved that I'd chosen to do it in private. "And have you... pulled yourself together?"

"Yes." As much as I was going to, at any rate.

"Good. Then we should probably... talk... about what you've been doing," he said, discomfort in his voice. "And we might as well get it over with now... while we're alone."

As my gaze fell to the ground, a heaviness blanketed the air. It was full of awkward tension that felt like sandpaper against my skin. Dad and I were horrible at opening up to each other. Or maybe it was just me. *I* was horrible at opening up to people. Hayden was the only one who'd truly cracked that seal, and it had taken him a while to do it. But Dad wanted to know what was going on with me, and I had no clue what I was going to tell him. Continue on with my lie, or confess it all? Either way I was pretty sure he was going to fire me. If not for street racing, then for that damn Benneti Ban.

Hayden and I never would have had to hide hanging out together if it weren't for that ban. And I never would have begun the process of lying and keeping things from my family. Myles might think differently about Hayden if he'd been allowed to socialize with him. Nikki too. And maybe even Dad. They might have seen what I saw if they had gotten to know him. Everything might be different right now if that ban didn't exist. And it existed because of Keith…and my mom.

Before the affair, there hadn't been a ban in place. Keith just didn't like my dad for getting him injured. But after Mom slept with Keith…God, the shit had hit the fan. I still didn't understand how that had happened. How could Mom have betrayed Dad like that? Was Dad reminded of that incident every time he looked at Keith? A nonstop log fueling the Benneti Ban fire? Would Dad be more tolerant if Mom were still alive?

Lifting my eyes from the ground, I peeked up at Dad. He was looking everywhere but at me, and I knew exactly what was going through his mind—he wanted to ask me about Hayden, about street racing…he just didn't know where to start.

Clearing my throat, I decided to break the ice between us by asking him a question I'd been wondering for years. "Dad…were you and Mom…happy?"

Dad seemed genuinely shocked by my question. "Why would you ask that?"

"I was just thinking about Mom…and Keith." A throb pulsed through my skull as anger surged through me. "Why would she…? I mean, how could she…?" My voice trailed off as my thought died. I shouldn't have brought this up. Dad was going through enough as it was.

Surprising me, Dad smiled. "How could she step outside our marriage?" I could only nod in response, and Dad's small smile shifted into a sigh. Shoving his hands into his pockets, he quietly said, "There was a time, Mackenzie, when I asked myself that question every day. I suppose the problem started after the wreck with

Keith that...ended things for him." Closing his eyes, he shook his head. "It was a stupid mistake, one I never should have made. I misjudged our distance, rubbed his tire as we were coming out of a corner...We both lost control, but he hit the wall at just the right angle with just the right force..." He paused as the memory swept over him, then opening his eyes, he continued, "Well, I'm sure you've seen the video. It was just a freak accident, but Keith has never seen it that way, and he's never forgiven me. We were best friends, brothers, on top of the world together. I didn't think anything could ever come between us, and then it did. Keith was looking for a way to hurt me after that wreck...and he found one."

As Dad dissolved into the past, sadness clouded his features; it made me ache with sympathy to see it. "It's strange what the mind holds on to. I sometimes forget your and your sisters' birthdays, I sometimes forget my *own* birthday, but the day I found out about Keith and your mom...it's like it happened yesterday. I don't think I'll ever forget it, even though I wish I could."

He paused and his eyes grew glossy. The sight would have typically had me finding an excuse to leave, but I touched his arm in support instead. A small smile lightened his expression, and I was glad to see it. "I'd come home from the track late, which was pretty typical of me at the time. Your mother was usually asleep when I got home, but that night...she was still up. She was pacing our bedroom, and her eyes were puffy, like she'd been crying recently...that was pretty typical too."

Bewilderment went through me as I tried to process what Dad was saying. She was sad? Frequently? In all the stories I'd heard of Mom, no one had ever mentioned that she'd been so unhappy. I'd assumed she'd been unsatisfied—why else would she have had an affair?—but never outright depressed.

Seeing that this information was new to me, Dad explained. "Your mom...she was never really the same after she had kids." He held up his hands to stop the sting of his words. "Don't get me wrong, she loved you guys more than anything, but she was...different. Sad...all the time. We figured out later she was suffering from pretty severe postpartum depression. That's what the doctors called it, at least, but back then, all I knew was that she cried a lot, and nothing I did seemed to make her happy." His gaze drifted to his feet, and his hands came out of his pockets to run through his hair. "I didn't know what to do, so I spent more and more time at the track." His eyes flashed up to mine, defensive. "That was necessary, though. Keeping the team afloat has never been an easy task."

I nodded as if I understood and sympathized, but with every word, I felt like my childhood was changing, diminishing. Parents were supposed to be perfect, idyllic. But they weren't. They were just...people. Fallible, like everyone else.

Dad gritted his teeth, and his eyes turned hard. He was getting to the worst part of the story. "Keith...that coldhearted bastard... he swooped in when Vivienne was at her weakest, her most vulnerable. He took advantage of her pain, her loneliness, and he tried to turn her against me, tried to convince her to leave me...just to pay me back for taking his career."

His hands squeezed into fists so tight, his knuckles turned white, and I thought if Keith were here, Dad would gladly punch him again. After a moment, he relaxed his hands and his expression. "They both hid the affair from me for months, until Viv couldn't take the guilt anymore and came clean. That night I came home and found her pacing the bedroom. She said she couldn't live a double life anymore...she had to let me know what she'd done."

His expression turned reflective as he remembered the worst night of his life, and his eyes went from wet to nearly spilling. I'd never seen my father cry before. Ever. Anger ate at me as I watched him try to subtly brush the tears away. "How could she do that to you? Even depressed, how could she sleep with *him*?"

Dad sighed. "It wasn't entirely her fault, Mackenzie. I'm not trying to misplace blame here, but it was partly my doing. I knew she was hurting, but I didn't know what to do for her...so I ignored her and what she was going through. Keith...he gave her the attention she needed, he listened to her problems, he did and said all the right things...while I buried my head in work. I hid while she cried...and that wasn't right."

His eyes turned despondent as age-old guilt filled him. It pierced my heart to see it. "Neither was cheating on you, Dad," I softly said. "She crossed a line she shouldn't have crossed. That was her choice, and you're not to blame for it." I bit my lip, then made myself ask, "How did you ever forgive her?"

A sad smile played across Dad's lips. "Lots of therapy. And patience. And understanding. And communication. Vivienne was hurting, and when she reached out and I wasn't there…she grabbed the next best thing. It took me a long time to forgive her, but eventually we got through it, and came out the other side much stronger." His expression instantly turned to stone. "Keith, on the other hand…I will never forgive him for what he did. To me, to Vivienne, to you girls…to our entire family. The two of us were brothers once…He should have known better. Things between us will *never* be right."

It was no great surprise that Dad despised Keith. I hated him too, now more than ever. The *only* good thing about Cox Racing ending was the fact that Dad would finally be free of him. We all would. "Why did you stay at the track so long? Why didn't you sell the minute you knew about the affair?"

Dad looked out over the parking lot. "I don't think I can explain it properly…there were too many reasons. Pride. I didn't want Keith to think he'd driven me away, didn't want him to think he'd won. Practicality was another reason. The track was perfect for what I needed, and sharing the expense of it with another owner was necessary. But…I think the real reason I stayed there was because…" His eyes drifted back to mine. "That track holds all of my most precious memories. My children grew up there, took their first steps there. You rode your first motorcycle there. I proposed to your mother in my office…I swear I can still smell her perfume every time I go in there." He sighed again. "Even now, after everything, if I could keep Cox Racing alive, I would. Deep down, I really don't want to close, Mackenzie."

Heartbroken for him, I eagerly beseeched him to change his mind. "Then don't. Take my money. Get a loan. Get a new partner…something. There has to be another way, Dad, there just has to be."

With a warm smile, he shook his head. "I can't get another loan, and while eighty grand is a good start, it's only fixing a small dent in a much bigger problem. And as for another partner…aside from John, I haven't found anyone who wants to merge with me…and John can't afford it. Trust me, Mackenzie, I've done the math. There *is* no other way. It's time for both of us to let the past go." His smile slipped. "It's time for us to let that part of your mother go. But the track isn't the only place her spirit resides. She's in all you girls…especially you." His gaze turned wistful. "You look so much like her, it hurts me to look at you sometimes. It's a good pain, though. It really is."

I had to swallow about ten times in a row after that. Dad looked uncomfortable for a moment, then he continued. "I'm really not good with emotional stuff like this. And unfortunately, I have to be your boss first, not your father, so sometimes, I do purposely pull away, and I'm sorry for that. I just want you to succeed. I want you to live up to your full potential, and not settle for anything less than extraordinary." Reaching out, Dad placed his hand on my arm. "I can't afford to say it as often as I would like to…but I'm extremely proud of you." Frowning, he let his hand fall away. "And that makes what you've done so much worse. Street racing…? What the hell were you thinking?"

I was instantly battered with joy and sorrow. I'd finally heard the words I'd wanted to hear all my life…and they were laced with pain, because I'd betrayed Dad and our family legacy by partaking in something illegal and sordid. I felt sick. "Are you going to turn me in?" I whispered.

Dad ran a hand down his face. Pausing to massage his temple, he let out a fatigued exhale, like the weight of the world was on his shoulders. "Myles told me he deleted the photos, so I have no proof to back it up with…but…if I accused my daughter, the officials just might…" He paused to study me and my heart started racing. *Is he saying yes?*

After another second, Dad shook his head. "No, I'm not turning you in, Mackenzie. Without proof, any decent lawyer could get you racing again, so it's not worth my time or reputation." He cracked a small smile after he said it, and I knew he was actually happy to have an out. He followed the rules, because that was the kind of man he was, but he didn't want to see racing get taken away from me.

Relief flooded into me, and Dad frowned at seeing it. "But please tell me that you at least understand how wrong what you did was."

I did understand, and that was what made it all so hard. Shaking my head like I could shake away the guilt, I told him, "I do, I just couldn't resist the money. You were so despondent after the fine for hitting Keith, and we were in debt so deep, I knew winning just wasn't enough anymore. Doing something drastic seemed the only way to save us."

His gaze turned stern after hearing my plea. I'd seen the same look in his eyes when I'd done something wrong on the track and he was about to correct me. "I appreciate the gesture, I really do, but it was stupid. There is *no* protection for you on the street. No caution flags, no inspections, no pit stops. But there *are* stoplights, pedestrians, and other motorists who aren't aware that they're obstacles in a high-speed race. Not only is it forbidden, Mackenzie, but it's incredibly dangerous. You could have been killed, and I don't want to bury another woman I love because of a stupid accident."

He slowly shook his head, and his expression grew heavy with grief. It made it hard to keep looking him in the eye, and I let my gaze drift to his chest. "I'm sorry, I didn't think of it that way. I just...wanted to save the legacy," I said, peeking up at his face.

Dad's lips slowly curved up as he let out a quiet huff of disbelief. "The legacy is *you*, Mackenzie. Don't you get that?"

My eyes watered. I'd never looked at it that way either. "I...I'm sorry."

Dad's expression hardened as his calculating eyes studied me. "Yes, I believe you truly are sorry. But that's the only part of this street racing story that I believe. What you told me earlier...I don't buy it. There is no way you came up with this plan all on your own, and there is no way that Hayes kid offered up the information simply because you asked. What's *really* going on with you and that Benneti boy?"

I immediately wanted to lie. I wanted to protect Hayden and tell Dad that nothing was going on. That everything I'd said about Hayden being innocent and me threatening him to get into street racing was true. But my father had just poured his heart out to me, and I couldn't lie to him. "He's not what you think, Dad. He's a good person, and he has his own reasons for being a part of that world, reasons that are just as good as mine."

Dad grunted in disapproval. "His reasons don't matter, Mackenzie. You can't be with him—in *any* way. And you definitely can't trust him. He lives with Keith, did you know that? He depends on him for *everything*. And if Keith tells him to slice your tires, he'll do it. Without hesitation."

"No, he won't. He—" I snapped my mouth shut so fast I bit my tongue. *He loves me and I love him, and he would never hurt me.* I couldn't say that, though. Dad would be furious that our relationship was that serious, and it definitely wouldn't help change his views on Hayden; it might even deepen his distrust of him. And sadly enough…Dad might be right. While I didn't think Hayden would ever hurt me, I wasn't so sure about everyone else. I was certain Hayden had helped me win on the street, which meant it was also quite possible he'd helped Myles lose. I had no real idea how deep his loyalty to Keith went. Would he ignore a direct order? I didn't want to find out.

Dad's face hardened, like he knew exactly what I was thinking. "He will, Mackenzie, and that's why…I have to do something to put a stop to this."

I felt like the ground had opened up and was about to swallow me whole. This couldn't be happening. "You're actually going to fire me?"

I thought for sure he was going to say yes, but instead, he shook his head. "There's only one race left in the season, and after that, Cox Racing is finished. Firing you at this point would be meaningless."

He wasn't going to punish me by prematurely ending my time with Cox Racing? "Then what are you going to do to me?" I asked, not sure if I wanted to know the answer.

Dad's stony expression didn't change. "Nothing. So long as you never see him again."

My heart started pounding as his words sank in. He was going to let me get away with fraternizing *and* street racing? So long as I cut out the man who drove me, moved me, touched me, consumed me. Even as much as loving him scared me, even though I knew it was pointless, futile, and…even if I had doubts about Hayden's methods and loyalties, being fired sounded so much easier than letting him go. "And…if I did…see him again…what would happen?"

With an annoyed growl, Dad's hand came down to smack the side of my truck. "Damn it, Mackenzie, don't push my buttons. Don't make me sacrifice our relationship to save you."

His voice was strained at the end, clearly pleading, but the threat still wasn't clear to me, although the fear climbing through my veins was beginning to freeze me solid. "What are you talking about? What would you do to me if I kept seeing him?"

Dad's shoulders sagged, and he seemed to age right before my eyes. "If I feel I have no other choice to save you from yourself, then…I will ruin your career. That's how much I love you."

For one painful second, my heart stopped beating. "Excuse me?" I must have misheard him. That was the only explanation.

His face sad but resigned, Dad said, "You heard me correctly, Mackenzie. Stop seeing that boy, or I will make sure no other team hires you. Not even Benneti."

A dark laugh escaped him, but I didn't find any of this amusing. "You…can't be serious."

"I've never been more serious," he stated.

Rage surged through me so fast I felt light-headed. "You can't do this to me. You don't even know him. All you know is what other people tell you about him, and they're wrong," I hissed.

Dad paused a moment to collect his thoughts before he answered me. "I know you've changed. The girl I knew wouldn't have risked her career and her life street racing. The girl I knew wouldn't have lied to her friends and family. And the girl I knew wouldn't be hiding in a parking lot instead of celebrating her sister's wedding. Face it, you're not the same person, Mackenzie... because of him."

Everything he was saying was true, but none of that had been Hayden's fault. I'd made my own choices, awful as they were, and most of them had been born of desperation—to help my family. I tried to think of something that Dad couldn't argue with. All that came to mind was "I'm a better racer because of him."

Dad looked away before returning his eyes to me. "This might not make sense coming from me, but one thing I've learned over the years is that... racing isn't everything."

He wasn't going to see it my way, so I might as well lie. What could it hurt at this point? Tossing my hands out to the sides, I quickly stated, "I'm *not* with him. It's just how I said it was. I used him, that's it. Hayden means nothing to me." Just saying it made a sharp jolt of pain reverberate inside my chest, like I'd torn out my heart and it was limply hanging by a thread.

I was certain Dad didn't believe one word of my denial, but he smiled anyway. "Good. Then we don't have a problem."

No, we didn't have *a* problem, we had a hundred problems. "Tell Daphne congratulations for me. I'm going home now."

Dad's expression shifted, and I could see the disappointment in his eyes. I wasn't sure how he'd expected me to react to his ultimatum, but he had to have known I wasn't going to like it. He was going to ruin my career? Because he thought I could do better than Hayden? Because in his mind, Hayden was just a punk who did Keith's bidding. He didn't know Hayden's hopes, Hayden's dreams, didn't know about Izzy and her sick daughter. Dad hadn't bothered to look beneath the surface... and he never would. It really was "him or me" with Dad, all because of who Hayden raced for. Goddammit. Why the hell did Hayden have to be a Benneti?

I started to get back inside my truck but paused when I heard my dad say, "I know you don't understand right now, but you'll thank me one day, Mackenzie. I promise."

One day I would understand him blackmailing me? I highly

doubted it. Sliding into my seat, I slammed the door, found my keys, started my truck, and left him there, alone.

As I drove away, fatigue started creeping up on me. That entire incident with Dad had been draining. I had no idea how a conversation that had started out so heart-wrenching had left me so angry. I'd never felt closer to my dad than when he'd opened up to me about Mom, but now…it was like he'd dug a wide chasm between us, with only a rickety rope bridge connecting the sides. And I didn't know if I wanted to cross over to his side…or hack the bridge to pieces.

I tried to stop thinking as I sped down the highway. The past was too painful, the present too bleak. Dad had mentioned sacrifice, but that was exactly what he was asking me to do. Sacrifice Hayden, sacrifice my career, or sacrifice my relationship with my father. How was I supposed to choose which one of those things I could live without? It was like asking me which limb I wanted removed. There were no good solutions to this problem. Either Hayden or my father was going to be hurt by my decision. And so was I. Either way, I was screwed.

When I got to my house, I immediately crawled into bed and stayed there; I only left to use the bathroom and brush my teeth. Maybe that was how I'd survive this. I'd stay in bed, hiding from my life. I just needed a day of not thinking, not deciding. If I refused to make *any* decisions, then nothing could hurt me.

I thought my plan was foolproof, until around ten at night, when my doorbell rang. Blurry-eyed and lethargic from doing nothing but sleep all afternoon, I groaned at the obnoxious sound but didn't get up. That was when the doorbell started going off repeatedly, like someone was pressing the button over and over. I threw a pillow over my head to drown out the sound. When my late-night visitor started playing "Jingle Bells" with the doorbell, I finally tossed off the covers and got up.

I cracked open my door and wasn't too surprised when I saw Hayden peering back at me; he'd wanted to come over tonight, after the wedding. Freshly washed with perfectly disheveled hair and a light layer of stubble along his jaw, he looked a hell of a lot better than I currently did. He was mouthwatering, and all I wanted to do was crawl into his arms. And that was exactly why he shouldn't be here. I hadn't made a decision yet; I hadn't even tried.

Putting his hand up on the doorframe, he inclined his head as he studied me. "You okay? You look like you were wrestling a bear…and lost."

Frowning at his comment, I shook my head. "It's late, Hayden…you should go."

I tried to close the door, but he put his hand on the wood and stopped me. "You haven't answered my question yet, and this isn't late for us."

Sighing in defeat, I opened the door all the way. "You shouldn't be here. If someone sees your bike…" I supposed that didn't matter anymore. What the hell was I going to do?

"Then unlock your garage so I can put my bike inside. Unless you want me to break in?" He shrugged. "I don't mind doing it that way…but it would be a hell of a lot easier if you just opened it."

I hesitated, then stepped back so he could enter the house. Once Hayden was inside, he silently studied me while I closed the front door. The edge of his open leather jacket looked so inviting; I just wanted to slip my hands inside and feel the taut muscles of his stomach, sides, back; feel him wrap his arms around me. I wanted to pretend nothing had changed, even though everything had.

Instead of moving toward the kitchen, Hayden continued to stand there, staring at me. Just when I was about to ask him what he was waiting for, he raised an eyebrow and said, "You still haven't answered my question. Are you okay?" I opened my mouth but he stopped me by putting his finger on my lips. "Before you answer, don't try and blow me off by telling me you're fine, because you look like hell, and I know you're not. Just tell me the truth. Tell me what happened."

Glaring at him, I yanked his finger from my mouth. "I look like hell? Thanks, just what every girl wants to hear."

Hayden's face firmed as he stared me down. "Quit deflecting. What happened, Kenzie?"

With a sigh, I ran my hands through my hair. What to tell him, what not to tell him? Did I end things now? Or did I keep it going a little while longer? Both options felt impossible. "I was just…debating…things."

That was true. It was also vague and ominous. Hayden's expression shifted to one of concern. "Things about us?"

I gnawed on my lip to stop myself from answering him. I wasn't ready for this. At seeing my hesitation, Hayden let out a weary exhale. "Okay…it's about us. Maybe I can help you figure it out." Bending down, he looked me in the eye. "Keep it simple, Kenzie. How do you feel about me?"

Answering him felt like making a decision, so I tried to evade the question. "What does it matter how we feel about each other? There's no future here."

"It matters to me. You already know I love you, Kenzie. You're everything I never knew I wanted. And I know we can't…" He frowned. "It's complicated between us…but that doesn't mean it's impossible. I'll hide my bike in your garage every night if it means I get to be with you." Leaning forward, he gave me a small kiss; it felt like an explosion going off in my brain, and my heart felt like it was growing and dying. Pulling back, he whispered, "So how do you feel about me?"

You're everything to me. But I can't throw my family away for you, and it kills me that I have to choose between the two men I love the most.

In my silence, Hayden reached up and stroked my cheek. "Kenzie," he murmured. "Talk to me…open up to me. You don't have to say you love me if you don't feel it, just tell me what you *do* feel." His lips briefly touched mine again, and I felt the walls inside me bursting open. I wanted to tell him everything I felt for him, I wanted to risk everything to be with him. I wanted to be his everything, and I wanted to tell him he was the only one who had ever made me feel this alive.

"I…"

I love you. So much, I don't know how I could possibly live without you. And that terrifies me.

My words caught in my throat, immovable. Hayden kissed me

again, maybe hoping to loosen them. Then his kiss deepened, and a soft groan escaped him. His hand shifted to my backside and he pulled me closer, until we were firmly together. As we should be.

His lips moved to my ear. "Kenzie...please...talk to me."

Closing my eyes, I stopped thinking and let my heart make the decision for me. "I want to be with you. I want to be yours, and I want you to be mine. I...I love you too."

The weight of indecision was gone when I opened my eyes. I felt free. I'd done it. I'd chosen. And now I had to live with that choice. But with Hayden by my side, I could get through anything. And my father...he had to come around eventually. If he could forgive Mom for cheating on him, then in time he could forgive me for this. We would just have to keep it quiet until I'd found a new team to take me on. It would do Dad no good to blacklist me if I'd already been hired.

Feeling lighter than air, I giggled as I threw my arms around Hayden's neck. He was laughing too, and looked happier than I'd ever seen him. We would find a way to make this work. Threading my fingers through his hair, I spoke between tender kisses. "Let's get your bike inside so you can make love to me."

With a groan of approval, he scooped me into his arms. "That is the second-best thing I've heard all night."

We hid his bike as quickly as humanly possible, and minutes later we were in my dark bedroom. A pulse of desire shot through me, hard and heavy. I couldn't speak, I couldn't think, I just needed his lips on mine. Our kiss was hungry and frantic, and I ripped off clothes while I pushed him backward, toward the bed. When I was just as naked as he was, I debated leaping into his arms so I could make love to him standing up. I couldn't wait another second.

Maybe sensing my desperation, Hayden gently pushed me back. "We have all night," he murmured. Tenderly grabbing my hand, he led me to the bed, then slowly pulled me on top of it. "You said you wanted to make love, and I want to show you just what that means."

I frowned. "I know what making love means."

"Do you?" he asked, a smirk on his lips. Then his hand ran over my hip. The feel of his skin on mine was so wondrous, I closed my eyes. Lying by my side, he pulled me into him. As his legs wrapped around mine, his hand ran up my back, over my shoulder, and lightly down my breast. I gasped at the sensation. While he peppered me with soft, tender kisses, he whispered, "I want to worship you. You deserve to be worshipped."

With all the things I'd done lately, I wasn't sure if I agreed, but his body against mine felt so amazing that I wasn't about to argue. His legs gently rubbed against me while his hand traveled over my stomach, my hip. He massaged wherever he touched, and I had the odd feeling of an ache releasing while a different, much more intense one started building.

Rolling me onto my chest, he ran his hands over my back. It was heaven. Then his lips drifted down my spine. Also heaven. His fingers traveled down my legs, probing, massaging. As his mouth worked its way up my back again, he let a finger teasingly slip between my thighs. A cry escaped my lips as a shock wave of pleasure burst through me. He left his fingers there, stroking my core, as he pressed his chest against my back and kissed my shoulder.

"I want you to feel nothing but amazing, because *you* are nothing but amazing," he murmured in my ear.

When he turned me over onto my back, all coherent thought fled from my mind, and all I felt was desire. And love. Hayden's lips started trailing down my neck, my chest. Soft kisses played across both breasts, over both nipples, then down to my stomach. By the time he reached my thighs, I was squirming with need, panting with lust; I felt like a caged animal, like I was going to tear the bed apart if he didn't touch me where I needed him. His words calmed me. "We have all night. I'm going to make you feel good over and over."

He softly licked my core, and my eyes rolled back into my head. *So... good.* Then he slowly worked his mouth against me, and that hazy oblivion took me over again. Nothing mattered but how amazing he felt.

I was still in that fog of euphoria when he worked his mouth back up to mine. Placing soft kisses on my parted lips, he pressed the tip of his cock against my entrance. "Look at me," he whispered.

I opened my eyes to find him staring at me. Then he cupped my cheek. I saw so much love and tenderness in his gaze that I almost didn't care about making love to him anymore. *This* was enough. But then he pushed into me, and the feeling of oneness, of rightness, intensified. His mouth opened, but he didn't close his eyes or look away. We were completely locked, heart and soul, as our bodies joined.

His hips began to move in a slow rhythm, and it was a struggle to maintain the leisurely speed, but the feeling of him moving within me was more powerful, more profound, than any time before. Inexplicably, I felt tears stinging my eyes. "Oh God," I murmured, clutching his back and pulling him into me in an all-consuming hug. I never wanted this to end.

Hayden clutched me to him as he drove a little deeper, a little harder. Clenching my hand, he rested his forehead against mine. As our pace naturally increased, he started kissing me, long and deep, searing passion lacing every movement. The pressure began mounting quickly, and I knew there were only seconds left in this life-altering connection. My head dropped back as I moaned his name. "Hayden…"

His hand squeezed mine, and that was all the assurance I needed to let go. A cry escaped my lips as the orgasm crashed through me. Hayden's free hand returned to my cheek, coaxing me to look at him. While I rode out the bliss of my explosion, Hayden went through his. Right before he peaked, he murmured, "I love you. God, I love you."

I wrapped my arms around his neck and pulled his mouth to mine while he came. *I love you too.*

CHAPTER 22

The next three weeks were incredibly difficult for me. My father routinely asked how things were going. He always left the question vague enough that we could be talking about anything, but I saw right through him. He wanted to know if I'd ended it with Hayden. I answered him with almost the same words every time: *Don't worry, Dad, I'm doing what you asked.*

But I wasn't, and I felt so horrible about it that I'd started avoiding being alone with my father as much as I could. My stomach was so constantly tangled that I might as well resume street racing. At least that way, my frayed nerves would be making me money. Not that that really mattered anymore. Cox Racing was finished.

In addition to feeling guilty about outright lying to Dad, I was also being hounded with apologies from my best friends. Nikki and Myles both felt awful about what they'd done, Myles especially, since he'd been the one to let the truth slip out to my father. They texted, called, and harassed me nearly every day. Anger had helped me keep my distance at first, but the emotional roller coaster I was on was slowly wearing me down.

Sitting down on a stool one afternoon, I watched Nikki tuning up my bike, and I debated whether I could talk to her before the guilt and regret ate me alive. I wasn't one to willingly open up, though—Nikki usually had to drag my problems out of me—but I was tired of being alone; the emotional island I'd stranded myself on was sinking.

"Hey... Nikki?"

She immediately dropped her wrench and spun around on her stool to look at me. It had been a while since I had initiated our conversations... or actively participated in them. Nikki had been getting a lot of one-syllable answers lately. "Yeah, what is it? Do you need something? Do you want something? Thirsty? Hungry? Horny? I can't really help you with that last one, but I could ask around."

Her enthusiasm to help me made me laugh, but remembering my problems made me sigh. Had there ever been a time when life had felt easy? Glancing around to make sure we were alone, I asked her, "Can we talk about something?"

Nikki immediately nodded. "Oh, thank God! Is it about what happened at the wedding? Because Myles and I are so sorry. We never meant for any of that to happen, and it's been killing me that I don't know what your dad said to you. He hasn't told anyone. Even John doesn't know." Eyes wide, she quickly added, "Not that I've been asking around or anything."

With a sigh, I shook my head. "No, it's not... well, maybe it's connected. But before I tell you anything, you have to swear on our friendship that you won't say a word of this to anyone. And I mean it, Nikki... you can't tell anyone, not even Myles." I would tell him myself... when I was ready.

Nikki immediately made an X over her heart, and I opened my mouth to spill my guts, but nothing came out. I'd held this in for so long, it was difficult to talk about it. Inhaling a deep breath, I fought through the awkward tension squeezing me to pieces. I could do this. "I... I'm in love... with Hayden." Even while I was cringing, waiting for her to kill me, a sense of relief rushed through my body. It felt so good to finally talk to someone about him.

Nikki looked at me like I'd just smacked myself in the forehead with her wrench. "You're...? With Hayden...? Hayes?"

Her stunned expression made me want to laugh, but my reality was too painful for joy. "Yeah, I know... It shocked me too."

"How did that even happen?" she asked, mystified.

With a sad smile, I began confessing all the secrets I'd been hiding for so long. "At first, it was just racing. I wasn't doing well enough to make my father happy, and like I told you before, Hayden and I really do race better together, so... we started breaking into the track at night to practice together. I got my best times with him, when everyone else was asleep."

Nikki's mouth dropped to the floor. "You broke into the track?" she hissed.

A small laugh finally escaped me at her reaction. "Yeah. I even picked the lock a time or two." She just stared at me blankly, like she didn't even recognize me. With a weary exhale, I shook my head. "I didn't know he was still street racing until Daphne's bachelorette party... when he almost ran me over." I smiled at the memory, then frowned. "It seemed like the only way to save Cox Racing at the time, so... I begged him to let me do it. He didn't want me anywhere near it at first. He was really worried about me getting hurt... we even fought about it. But it was a price I had to pay to save the business, or try to anyway, so I told him I would do it with or without him."

Nikki nearly fell off her stool. "You've always been so... controlled, so by the book... so regimented. It's like you're telling me you're secretly a porn star or something. I just can't quite wrap my head around it."

I rolled my eyes at her comparison, but I understood what she was saying. It had been so gradual, I hadn't even realized I was changing. Not really, anyway. "Somewhere along the way, I... started having feelings for Hayden. They were just physical at first. God, I was so attracted to him... But the more I got to know him, the deeper the feelings went. And the entire time, I knew we were doomed. I knew it didn't make sense to fall for him... but I did." Feeling tears prick my eyes, I locked gazes with her. "I'm so in love with him, Nikki. I'm in love with him, and my father is going to ruin me if I don't stop seeing him. He told me he would make sure *no* team took me next year if I didn't let Hayden go, and I believe him. But I *can't* stop seeing Hayden—I feel so alive when I'm with him, more like who I'm really supposed to be. I can't give him up, and I'm screwed because I can't." I frantically wiped at the big fat tears rolling down my cheeks.

Her face a mixture of sympathy and surprise, Nikki rolled her stool over and gave me a hug. "Shit, Kenzie...I had no idea." Pulling back, she frowned. "Why the hell didn't you tell me earlier?"

Drying my cheeks, I shook my head. "Because...you know it's not easy for me to...talk about things like this. I'm not comfortable with emotional stuff. And then on top of all that, Hayden's...forbidden, and everybody here hates him, Myles and my dad especially. I was worried that if I told you, you would have told someone else, and I would have been fired."

She opened her mouth to defend herself, and I interrupted her. "Don't even try to deny that you suck at keeping secrets." She cringed, then nodded, and I let out a weary sigh as I continued. "In the beginning, I convinced myself you'd talk about it, and word would get out, and everything would be ruined. But actually...I think I just didn't want to hear that I was being stupid, that I was making a huge mistake. I didn't want to be talked out of my plans. Didn't want to accept what was happening. And then I fell for Hayden, and it was too late..."

Nikki's expression softened as she wiped some tears off my cheeks with a clean section of her rag; I hadn't even realized I'd started crying again. "Do you really love him enough to risk your career for him? As long as I've known you, racing is all you've ever cared about."

A smile brightened my face. "It sounds crazy to admit it out loud, but...yeah...I'd rather give up racing than him." Nikki smiled, and her eyes sparkled like she was about to cry, she was so happy for me; seeing the acceptance eased my pain considerably.

She moved her arms like she was going to hug me again, but I stopped her by grabbing her forearms. "I'd really like to keep both, though, so I need you to keep your word and not say anything to anyone. This is serious, Nikki. So long as my dad doesn't know I'm still seeing Hayden, he won't sabotage my career."

Nikki stared at me for long, silent seconds before finally nodding in agreement. Tossing my arms around her, I pulled her in for a tight hug and thanked her for staying silent, for listening to my problems, and for being such a good friend. My heart was still a tormented mess when I left her, but I found that I could breathe a little easier after sharing my stress.

Calling it an early day, I headed for my everyday bike. My phone chirped at me while I walked. It was a message from Hayden: *Meet me at our spot out back.*

I knew he meant the hole in the fence, but I couldn't do it. I'd been avoiding meeting up with Hayden almost everywhere outside of my house—no late-night practices, no bars out of town, no cheering him on at street races. With the stakes so much higher than before, I couldn't risk *any* meeting that might get back to Dad. But since I didn't want Hayden to know about the chaos going on with Dad and Myles, I had to keep my real reason for being extra cautious hidden. Because if Hayden knew Myles had figured out the truth and told my dad, and the only reason my dad hadn't said something to Keith was because he hated him too much to talk to him—a fact that might change if Dad thought I was still seeing Hayden—Hayden would be as much of an emotional wreck as me. And I didn't want to do that to him. Not right before the last race of the season.

Peering over at the Benneti side of the universe, I saw Hayden in his leathers, standing in front of the garage door, phone in hand. He was looking my way without appearing like he was looking my way. With an inward sigh, I texted him back: *Can't. Meeting Daphne for lunch.* Lying to him was even worse than lying to my dad, but I couldn't take the risk of being seen with him. Hayden responded with a frowny face and a guilt-reducing laugh escaped me. *Coming over tonight?* I asked.

Of course. I'll be late, though. I have a race.

Clenching my phone, I debated asking him not to go. Maybe if

I promised him enough sexual favors, he'd stay with me tonight instead. But Izzy and Antonia would suffer, and I didn't want that any more than Hayden did. I just wanted him safe. And since the street racing circuit wasn't a secret anymore, it didn't feel safe.

Be careful. Please?

I always am, sweetheart. And yes, now that you actually are *my sweetheart, I can call you that. And if you don't like it, you'll just have to spank me later. Or I could spank you…*

With heated cheeks, I covertly flashed a glare his way. *Don't tempt me, Hayes.* Even from the distance between us, I could see him laughing, and it warmed my heart. If I could keep balancing on the fine tip of all my multiple deceptions, then maybe everything would be okay, and maybe this wouldn't all blow up in my face.

So I wouldn't be a complete and total liar, I called Daphne and asked her to go to lunch with me. She'd mellowed out a lot since the wedding, so it was much easier to be around her. Surprisingly enough, she wasn't mad that I'd skipped out on most of the reception. She'd gotten a little tipsy during the toasts and hadn't cared about much after that.

Daphne and I had a nice quiet lunch. Afterward, I drove home and changed into my swimsuit; the ocean sounded great right about now. After attaching my board to my truck, I headed to my favorite secret spot. I parked in the reeds, then lugged my board down to the ocean. It was early afternoon during the middle of the week, with about an hour left before school let out, so the beach was empty except for me. It felt like my very own private slice of heaven.

I rode in a handful of waves, then noticed that I was no longer alone. Hayden was standing on the shoreline, watching me just out of reach of the water. Trudging through the shallows with my board, I walked to the edge of the waves. "What are you doing here?"

His eyes scanned the front of my suit, and my body instantly began to tingle. "Well, when I showed up at your house and you didn't answer—I got through 'Jingle Bells' *and* 'We Wish You a

Merry Christmas' and you didn't come out to kick my ass—I figured you were here."

A grin crossed my lips, but it instantly shifted into a frown. He shouldn't be out in the open like this with me. "You should be at the track, getting ready for New Jersey this weekend."

"No, I should be making love to my girlfriend." His finger started tracing the neckline of my bikini, instantly sending my body into overdrive.

"Hayden," I murmured, not sure if I wanted him to stop…or keep going.

He lifted both hands into the air. "You wouldn't meet with me at the track, and I have something for you. I couldn't wait until tonight to give it to you." He reached into his jacket and pulled out a small jewelry box. My eyes widened and my heart started thumping. No. He couldn't be doing what I thought he was doing. Not yet; it was far too soon. Although, maybe Dad would completely lose the upper hand if Hayden and I were married…But shit, I was too young to get married.

"What's that?" I asked, my voice tight.

Hayden looked at me funny for a second, then shook his head. "No, no…it's not what you think."

He opened the box and I looked inside. Nestled in the velvet was a ring, but it was more like a cocktail ring than any sort of engagement ring. Three thin loops of sterling silver were intricately woven together to make a beautiful two-inch-long infinity symbol that would run from joint to knuckle. The edges were polished and gleamed in the sunshine. It was simple yet stunning. "Oh my God, Hayden…It's beautiful."

I started to slip it on my right hand, but he stopped me. "Look inside the band…I had it inscribed." Bringing it close to my face, I tried to make out the tiny letters. WITH ALL MY HEART, MAJOR ASSHAT.

My eyes flashed to his, and he crooked a grin. "Didn't think I'd ever noticed your phone, did you?"

A flush started creeping up my chest, and his gaze drifted to my breasts. "Jesus, Kenzie, you're killing me."

I laughed as I slipped the ring onto my hand. It fit perfectly. "I'm surfing, it's just a swimsuit."

With a look that said I might as well have told him a bike was just a bike, he murmured, "It's a bikini." His hand reached out and he brushed a thumb across my nipple. "A nice bikini…" His other hand reached around behind me to slip down the back. "A *very* nice bikini."

Having his skin touching mine was too much, and a groan escaped me. God, now that I was letting myself have him, I couldn't get enough of him. "Let's go to my place," I breathed.

Removing his hands from my body, Hayden grabbed my surfboard and tossed it on the sand. Then he picked me up and set me down on top of it. "Let's stay here," he growled, urging me to lie back on the board.

My eyes scanned the beach, but it was still deserted. "I don't know, we're out in the open…"

I couldn't finish my objection. Hayden had pulled down my bikini bottoms, just enough to put his mouth on me. My vision swam. All I could see was trees and rocks, all I could hear was the surge of the ocean, and all I could feel was the bliss of his tongue caressing me. It was a perfect moment, and I didn't want to stop it. Even if someone did show up, I probably wouldn't push him away. I couldn't.

As his mouth continued to move against me, his hands massaged my breasts and squeezed my nipples. And then his mouth moved to my neck and he was over me, whispering in my ear how much he wanted me, and how amazing I was. I unzipped his pants and pushed them down enough so he was free.

The rightness of being with him washed over me as he plunged deep. I grabbed the board beneath me with both hands, felt my new ring digging into the fiberglass as he drove me toward a quick release. Yes, this was worth it. This was what I wanted. More than anything, *he* was what I wanted.

* * *

Saturday morning, we were making final preparations for the last race of the season at New Jersey Motorsports Park in Millville, New Jersey. I couldn't believe the final race was already here. The end of an era, the end of Cox Racing. No matter how I finished, things would be different after today. Dad would close his doors and never reopen them. I would have to start taking a serious look at other teams, and strip my bikes of all their colors and sponsors. It was a fresh start in some ways, and Hayden wouldn't have the fear of his career being cut short once I was no longer a member of Cox Racing, but being here at the last event felt more like a funeral than a celebration.

Everyone else I ran into was excited, though. There was only a thirty point difference between first and tenth place. The championship was close, still open to anybody, and there was a feeling of hope in the air—no one was clinching anything this year.

The mandatory meeting between all the owners and racers was uneventful—no one was late, no one was sick. The only thing stressful about it was the quiet rage buzzing between Keith and my dad, but that was normal. Both of them always looked like wild stallions temporarily being held under control, and it was clear that if they were left alone in the room, the enforced peace wouldn't last for long.

I also felt like I was being held in check, barely holding on to the reins of my body. Hayden was standing just behind Keith, and try as I might, I couldn't take my eyes off him. Just being in an enclosed space with him, even a space crowded with random people, was making it hard to breathe, hard to focus. Whenever I managed to pull my gaze away, I felt the heat of his stare on my skin. And whenever I did look his way, our gazes locked tight. His expression was carefree and casual, but his eyes spoke volumes. *I want you. I need you. I love you. Let's go somewhere private so I can show you.*

But I couldn't cave here and allow our nightly visits to continue. Not when we were surrounded by gossiping racers who might let something slip to Keith or my father. We were effectively cut off from each other until we were back at home. It was torture.

My father watched me like a hawk throughout the entire meeting, and when we were finally freed for the afternoon, he grabbed my arm to keep me next to him. Irritated, I bit out, "I was just going to ask Nikki if she needed help setting up. If you don't believe me, you can call her in five minutes."

From the way his eyes narrowed, I could tell Dad didn't like my tone. Behind him I could see Hayden watching us with a concerned expression on his face. Hayden still didn't know that Dad knew about us...and that Dad thought we were firmly in the past. Hayden was probably worried that I was in trouble for something. I would be, if Dad knew the truth.

Releasing my arm, Dad told me, "This is the last race, your last chance to impress people. Two teams have approached me about picking you up, and they're both good teams—Excess and YTK. Do well today, and you might have a shot with them."

I knew both of those teams, and Dad was right, they were good. They were also both based on the East Coast, which meant I would be living thousands of miles away from Hayden during the training season...and for me, that was most of the year. "Those two are my best options? So you want me to live in North Carolina or Virginia? I'll be on the other side of the country from you. From everyone I care about."

Dad's lip quirked, and I knew he was wondering just who I cared about. "Don't be dramatic, Mackenzie. It's part of the job. A part you haven't had to experience up until this point, since you came into the sport with connections. But trust me, everyone pays their dues, and they pay them gladly, because there are thousands of people who will take their place in an instant if they aren't willing to sacrifice for it." He turned as if he was finished, but then he looked back at me. "This is the way it will be, Mackenzie, or it won't be any way at all."

He walked away after his ominous words, and I clenched my hands into tight fists. Hayden was still watching the exchange, still curious and worried. I was seething as I felt Dad's trap closing around me. So, this was his master plan to keep me from Hayden? Place me on a team on the other side of the country from him? Had that been his goal all along, or was it just a precaution, in case

I hadn't followed his command about never seeing Hayden again? Dad had screwed me, either way. If I wanted to move forward, one way or the other, I would have to do it without Hayden. Because it was clear from Dad's last remark that if I turned down either of the two teams he'd picked out and struck out on my own to find one closer, he'd begin the process of blacklisting me, and I was positive that he still had the power and influence to do it. Dad was painting me into a corner, then building a wall around that corner to keep me fenced in. There was no way out of this trap, not if I wanted to keep racing. One day I would understand, my ass. *Fuck you, Dad. I will never understand this.*

Glancing over to the other side of the room, I saw Hayden giving me *I want to talk to you* eyes, but I couldn't talk to him about this. I couldn't talk to him about anything while we were here. I faked a brief smile, hoping that would placate him for now. He didn't seem to buy it, but Keith was calling for him, and Hayden had no choice but to follow.

When I finally left to return to my so-called team, I was still infuriated. I ran into Myles along the way, looking soulful and apologetic; it didn't improve my mood one bit. He had flown out with the crew to schmooze for a new team too, but unlike me, Myles was free to make arrangements with any team he wanted. He just had to convince them that he was healthy, and that missing almost an entire season hadn't hurt him in any way. Normally, I would have helped him out however I could, but right now, Myles was about the last person I wanted to see.

He started walking my way, and I immediately spun on my heel and started walking the other way. Hurrying to catch up to me, he shouted, "Come on, Kenzie. Don't do this! Someday you're going to have to talk to me, it might as well be today." I'd made peace with Nikki, but I hadn't gotten there with Myles yet; his betrayal went so much deeper, and hurt so much more.

I wasn't in the mood to try to fix it now, so I walked even faster. Catching up to me, Myles grabbed my arm. Glaring at where we were connected, I snarled, "Let me go, Myles."

Letting his fingers fall from my arm, he tossed his hands out to his sides. "Then talk to me. I said I was sorry a million times, Kenzie. What more do you want?" he asked, looking exasperated.

Between the conversation with Dad and the look on his face, I couldn't hold back my anger anymore. "Because of you, Dad is sending me three thousand miles away next year. I was trying to keep my family together, and instead, I'm being driven away. And there is no apology that will make up for that fact!"

Myles's eyes widened as he gaped at me. "Three thousand…?" His eyebrows bunched in confusion. "You don't have to go where he sends you, Kenzie. Come with me. I'm going to talk to a couple teams today, and one of them is based in California. I'm sure they'd take you. You're amazing."

My eyes pricked with angry, pain-filled tears. "I can't. Dad won't let me deviate from the path he's chosen for me. If I try…he'll ruin me."

His earlier shock was nothing compared to how he looked now. Looking around, he leaned in and whispered, "Is this because of Hayden? Because I said you guys were hooking up? I'll tell him I was wrong. That I was just guessing, and I was wrong."

For the first time in a long time, his comment made me smile; there was no joy in the movement, though. "I appreciate that, Myles, I really do…but it's too late. He believed you, and it's too late. And besides…you were right. I *was* hooking up with him. I love him and I can't be with him." Not without paying a very hefty price.

The look on Myles's face was a mixture of anger, disbelief, and pain. But then, finally, he seemed to decide that our friendship was what mattered here. "I'm…so sorry, Kenzie. I can't say I understand…but I'm sorry you can't be with him."

I could feel the tears building, and I did *not* want to cry here. "If you truly are sorry, then you won't breathe a word of that to anyone." Myles clenched his teeth together so hard, I heard them grinding, but he nodded. Once I had his word, I immediately excused myself. "I'm going to go talk to Nikki, check on the bikes. The race is starting soon."

Myles looked like he wanted to hug me or something, so I left him there as quickly as I could. All this emotional weight being put on me right before the race wasn't helping things at all. But I supposed the race didn't really matter anymore—my fate was already sealed, regardless of my standings.

When I got to the garage where the bikes were being held, I looked around for a crew member. The place looked empty, but someone had to be here. "Nikki? You in here? I need to talk to you… You're not gonna believe what my dad just said."

No one answered me, but a telltale clang of metal hitting the ground told me where she was. Hoping she had some sort of advice for me, I moved in her direction. "Dad's really crossed the line this time, and I have no idea how I'm going to—"

I lost my voice as I turned a corner and saw something I never thought I would see. Hayden was crouching beside one of my bikes. He had a wrench in his hand and he was fiddling with the engine. Oh my God…he really *had* been the one tampering with bikes. And now he was messing with mine…

Hayden's face went deathly white when he snapped his eyes to mine. "Holy shit," I muttered, slowly backing away.

Dropping the wrench, Hayden shot to his feet. "It's not what you think, Kenzie."

He took a step toward me and I held a hand out. "No, it's worse. I was contemplating throwing it all away for you—my career, my family…everything. And you've been messing with riders? My father and Myles were right all along… " My vision started fluctuating, my heart started racing. I was going to pass out. Or vomit. Maybe both.

Hayden violently shook his head. "No, they're not right about me. I'm not doing anything, I promise."

He grabbed my forearms to keep me from running away, and I was too stunned to yank free. "I thought they might be right," I said, dazed. "After I kept winning on the street, even when I shouldn't have won…I thought maybe they were right. And I really didn't know how to feel about that. But I never thought you'd hurt me. I never thought you'd mess with *me*."

I finally snapped out of it enough to yank my arms free. Hayden looked like he was beginning to panic. Running his hands through his hair, he repeated, "I'm not doing anything. Please, Kenzie, you've got to believe me. I said I'd never hurt you and I meant it." He tried to put his arms around me and I pushed him away.

"Then what the hell are you doing here?" I yelled. I felt like the cement beneath me was turning into quicksand. Everything I'd believed was wrong.

"I'm trying to fix something!" he shouted, then he pulled some sort of device from his pocket.

"What is that?" I asked, feeling cold all over.

He curled his fingers around it in a tight grip. "Something that shouldn't be on your bike." There was anger in his voice and rage in his eyes. "I promise I'm not involved with what's going on, Kenzie."

My heart began to thud. "But something *is* going on…and you have *something* to do with it, don't you?"

Closing his eyes, he gritted his teeth. "I can't…I wasn't sure…" When he reopened his eyes, they were worn, haggard. "I can't explain, I just need you to believe that I would *never* hurt you."

"Would you hurt Myles, though? *Did* you…hurt Myles?" My throat felt so dry, every word was hard to say.

Hayden's face fell, like he'd been hoping I wouldn't ask that. "Not intentionally," he whispered.

The walls that Hayden had been coaxing open inside me snapped shut so hard, I hunched over from the blow. Hayden stepped forward, like he was going to help me, and I raised my hands again to hold him back. "Get away from me."

"Kenzie, please…"

My entire body started shaking. "No…I don't want to hear it—just get the hell away from me."

"Goddammit, Kenzie, don't do this. Let me explain!"

Rage, pain, and betrayal were swirling within me so ferociously that I knew if he didn't leave, I was going to pick up a screwdriver and start pummeling him with it. "Leave me the fuck alone!" I yelled.

Expression tight, he started backing away. "Fine, I'll go. We'll talk about this some other time."

"There is no other time between us, Hayden. We're done." The anger in my belly kept that statement from hurting, but I knew it would catch up with me later. I didn't have a choice, though. I couldn't trust him, that much was clear now, so I definitely couldn't throw away everything to be with him.

Hayden opened his mouth to say something, then we both heard the door to the garage being opened. Looking frustrated, Hayden glanced at me before turning and running out a second door in the back corner of the room—a door that had been locked this morning.

John walked in a few moments later, a thirty-two-ounce cup of soda and a tray of gooey nachos in his hands. He stopped when he spotted me standing among the bikes. "Mackenzie…I was just…" He sighed. "Don't tell your dad I left the bikes alone. My wife won't let me eat this crap, and she's got everyone spying on me for her. Events like this are the only time I can indulge…"

My only response to his explanation of why the bikes were alone was a wave of my hand. I didn't care. About anything. Everything was over.

As I prepared myself for the race, every single part of me felt numb. I couldn't believe that after everything I'd done to keep him, it was just…over. I debated going to my father and telling him everything I knew about Hayden. I debated contacting the officials and squealing about what I'd just seen. And I even debated not racing, and just letting the season end. But the thought of actually doing any of those things made me feel sick, so I didn't. Instead, I spent an exorbitant amount of time staring at the ring Hayden had given me. As I mentally traced the three looping infinity symbols, I wondered if he had ever been honest with me. Had I meant something to Hayden, or was I just another race to conquer?

My cell phone went off four times in a row as I stared at the silver ring in my hand. Since I was positive it was Hayden each time, I let every call go to voice mail. Whatever he felt he had to say to me, whatever weak-ass excuse he'd dreamed up, he could leave it in a message. And maybe five years from now, when I no longer felt enraged with betrayal, I'd listen to it. Better make that ten years from now.

"You okay, Kenzie? You usually answer your phone when someone calls it."

I looked over my shoulder to see Nikki staring at me with dark eyes full of concern. I hadn't had a chance to tell her about the most recent trap my dad had set for me, but now it seemed pointless to be upset about it. Going to a team on the other side of the country sounded like a great idea. "Yeah, it's just…it's the last time I'll be racing for Cox Racing. I'm trying to take it all in."

The truth of that statement didn't hit me until I said it out loud. Then it just about knocked me over. Pain squeezed my chest as I let the finality of it flow through me. It was the end of my family's business. From now on, no matter where I ended up, I would be racing for a stranger.

Nikki looked equally upset. "I know what you mean. Cox Racing was the only team I wanted to work for when I was in tech school. Then when I graduated and got the job…it was like a dream come true. And now it's over. I still can't believe it."

The crack in my heart that Nikki had unknowingly opened was eating away at my shell of numbness. I'd never get through the race if I let my emotions take over, so shoving them into the background, I told her, "I'll worry about all that tomorrow. Today, I just want to do the best I can."

Nikki threw on a proud smile while my thoughts churned. "You're gonna knock 'em dead, Kenzie. Every team will be trying to snatch you up. I just hope I end up somewhere close to you. And Myles."

A tear fell from her eye, and she quickly brushed it aside and busied herself with work. Setting the ring inside my bag, I did the same. It hurt too much to think about everything I would soon be leaving behind—my family, my friends…my home.

A little while later, I was in the grid box waiting for the lights to change. I tried to keep my focus straight ahead of me, tried to ignore every rider around me, but I couldn't control myself any longer. I glanced over at Hayden, a couple of spots behind me, and butterflies swirled in my chest, making me feel like a giddy child again. But these butterflies had wings tipped with razor blades, and each flutter sliced me open. I couldn't see his expression through his helmet, but I felt like I could hear him in my mind. *Don't end this yet. Let me explain.* There was nothing to explain, though. He was guilty, plain and simple. I forced my eyes to the front, to my future, whatever that might be now.

When the light changed and the bikes around me started roaring to life, I took off. And even though I was in front of Hayden, I was pushing hard to get away from myself more than anyone else. I didn't want to miss Hayden, but I already did. I didn't want to think about him one way or another, but I couldn't stop picturing our many moments together. I was in the middle of a race, for God's sake; I didn't have time for this shit! Why couldn't I just shut my feelings off and go back to a time when I didn't know Hayden existed? I'd been happy then, blissfully ignorant of all the feelings he would pull from me, of all the pain he would cultivate. But I might as well ask the concrete to not be so hard, ask the ocean to not be so wet, or ask the sky to not be so vast.

Why did anyone put their heart out there, where it could, and most likely would, be ripped to shreds? There was a gaping hole inside me, an emptiness that even living out my childhood dream couldn't quite fill. Like an eclipse, I was sunny and bright around the edges, but dark and hollow in the center. *It hurts. So much.*

I needed to stop this and focus. I still had a job to do. Leaning over my bike, I allowed myself to pretend that this was the first race, and I had a bone to pick with him. *Beat Hayden, beat everyone.* I shoved my heartache to the back of my mind, and a flood of endorphins rushed over me, drowning me in the thrill of the moment. The powerful engine roaring with life propelled me forward. The road raced beneath my feet, the bike hummed with need and energy, and the landscape blurred past at a dizzying pace in my peripheral vision. Yes. This was peace.

Lap after lap, turn after turn, I focused only on the road and passing the person in front of me. Riders and colors merged into one, and suddenly, everyone I chased was the same person—

Hayden. I didn't worry about what that meant as I dipped lower in the turns, my knee pads barely skimming the ground. I pushed myself and my bike to the absolute limits, and all I heard was the blood rushing through my ears and my breath, loud in the enclosure of my helmet.

It was a tight race, and a little after the halfway mark, there was still no clear leader. At least fifteen of us were closely clumped together, fighting it out for the top spot. This one was going to go down to the wire. The group of us were heading into a series of S-curves. Arranged like ducks in a row, we moved almost as one through the turns...but then, all hell broke loose. Somewhere near the front of the line, a bike went down. Or maybe two or three went down. I couldn't tell. All I knew was that I was caught in the line of ducklings with nowhere to go—bikes were in the road, blocking it. We were all too close together and moving too fast to stop in time. Our only hope was to somehow avoid becoming a part of the pileup by swerving, but there were too many of us for there to be any hope that we wouldn't crash into one another. Rider upon rider was getting tangled up in the chaos. Bikes wobbled, lost control, spinning, tumbling, and sliding across the asphalt. Riders were thrown from their vehicles, and more than a few were run over by the next bike to hit the disaster area.

Everywhere I looked I saw carnage—bike parts, hazy smoke, and unseated riders; I couldn't see a clear path anywhere. With only microseconds to make a decision, to correct my course, to do something to save myself...I froze. I pictured myself smacking into a bike, tumbling over and over, bones snapping, the weight of other bikes and riders crushing me until I couldn't breathe...

This was it. This was how my life was going to end.

I love you, Dad, you ridiculously stubborn, devoid-of-emotion man. I love you, Daphne, I love you, Theresa. I love you, Myles, Nikki. I even love you, John, in a way. But mostly...Hayden, I love you so much.

My heart thudded in my chest as my life and loves flashed before my eyes. Then suddenly, a rider zipped in front of me, cutting me off and waking me from my indecision. On instinct, I shifted to avoid colliding with him, and managed to escape the wreckage in the one small clearing remaining on the far right side of the track. As I passed clean through the chaos, I risked a glance back to see who my crazy savior was. In knocking me off course, they'd taken my doomed path. And they'd accelerated to get around me…so they'd hit with ten times the force.

When I was safely away from the carnage I slowed and stood up on the pedals, hoping to see something, anything. There was only one person I could think of who might walk through fire for me…but it just couldn't be him. Please, God, it couldn't be.

It was hard to see through the riders trying to stand, through the twisted metal of warped bikes. And then, like in a scene from an apocalyptic movie, an empty bike slid free from the wreck and tumbled to a stop in front of me. My heart seized in my chest as the bold black numbers spelled out my worst fears—43. Hayden. No…Why would he do that? He'd blasted through the gates of hell to spare me an unimaginable fate. He'd sacrificed himself for me, and I knew, without a shadow of a doubt, my life would never be the same after this.

CHAPTER 23

The track was pure chaos, and I was quickly swept up in it. Rescue vehicles rushed into the madness while all the riders were ordered to go to the pits. When I was as close as the officials would allow me to stand, I watched in terror as metal was shifted and pinned riders were exposed. As they were pulled away and hauled off on stretchers, I couldn't help but imagine myself in the carnage. It should have been me, not him.

Looking around, I spotted a few members of the Benneti crew standing nearby. Keith and his team were huddled together, faces pale, arms wrapped around shoulders in support. They looked terrified, and it wasn't for the bikes, it wasn't for the standings, it wasn't for the glory. No. It was for their people, trapped, hurt, and possibly maimed or dead. *Please God, don't let Hayden be dead.*

From somewhere behind me, I heard Nikki yelling my name. Like a plow cutting through snow, she split the crowd to get to me. When she was within arm's reach, she pulled me in so tight, I couldn't breathe.

"Thank God you're okay. I saw you going straight for the bikes, then I lost you and all I saw was smoke and chaos. You didn't come back to the pit…I didn't know if you made it out…" She squeezed me hard as she drew in a shuddering breath. I was having trouble breathing, but I didn't pull away.

When Nikki finally let me go, I tried to wipe my cheeks dry. It was impossible; more tears just kept coming. Why couldn't I stop crying? "God, it was awful, Nik," I sputtered. "I was going to hit the wreck... and then he... he made me swerve. I found a clearing, but he didn't. He..." A racking sob took over me and I couldn't finish speaking. *He watched out for me. He saved me. He loves me, and I love him. I should have trusted him, I should have believed him. And now it might be too late to tell him I'm sorry.*

"Who are you talking about, Kenzie?" she asked, eyes wide with concern.

"He... took the hit for me. He loves me..."

Comprehension suddenly sparkled in Nikki's eyes. "Oh God... it was Hayden, wasn't it? Hayden... saved you?"

Nodding incessantly, I took a step back from Nikki and returned my attention to the track. It was mostly clear of people now, if not debris. I still didn't see Hayden anywhere. Had I missed his rescue? Goddammit. Looking back, I told her, "I need to find him. I need to know Hayden's okay."

I made a move toward the track and Nikki grabbed my elbow. "Wait, Kenzie, your dad is looking for you. If he finds you down there asking about Hayden... he'll flip, you know he will."

I didn't care. I needed to find out if Hayden was still *alive*. "He saved my life, Nikki, and I'm going to make sure he's okay. If that violates Dad's rule... then I guess I'm about to violate it. I'm not going to ignore someone who just risked *everything* for me. My father taught me better than that," I added, raising my chin.

Nikki gave me a sad smile as she let me go. "I hope you find him," she whispered, and from her tone of voice, I could tell that what she was really saying was "I hope he's worth it." *He is.*

Officials tried to shoo me off the track when I got close, but I ignored them. Somebody here had to know something, and I wasn't resting until I found that person. Most of the people remaining were rescue personnel and investigators trying to figure out what happened. None of them knew Hayden, let alone knew what had happened to him. Being in the dark was frustrating, and I felt like I was about to rip somebody's head off if I didn't get a decent lead soon.

And that was when I ran into Myles. Seeing a familiar face nearly made me cry with relief. Finally, someone who knew who I was talking about. Myles could point me in the right direction. "Have you seen Hayden?" In my panic, I grabbed his shirt and pulled him into me.

Myles threw his arms around me. "Kenzie…Jesus, I'm so glad you're okay. It looked like a war zone out there."

I hugged him back just as fiercely as he held me, then the uncertainty got to me, and I pushed him away so I could look him in the eye. "Hayden. Please tell me you saw him."

Myles pressed his lips together, and an expression passed over his face that chilled me to the bone. It was a look of compassion and pain, and also indecision, like he wasn't sure if he should tell me something. I thought I might start hyperventilating if he didn't. "Myles…please, I know you don't like him, but I need to know if he's okay. Did they take him to a first aid station? Do you know where it is?"

Myles shook his head. "I saw them putting him into an emergency vehicle…but I heard the medic tell the driver to go straight to the hospital. I don't know what's wrong with him, but…he wasn't moving. At all. I'm so sorry, Kenzie, but…he got hit pretty hard…"

His words struck me like a cannonball to the chest. Straight to the hospital? That meant it was serious. Life-threatening serious. Jesus. Turning away from Myles, I started running. I wasn't even sure where I was running to or how I would get there, but I didn't care. *This can't be happening.*

Somehow, I managed to pull myself together enough to get my keys, find my rental car, and drive to the closest hospital. Hoping I was at the right place, I sprinted to the nurses' station and slapped my hands down on the counter. "I need information on Hayden Hayes," I told the nurse at the desk, breathless. "I think he just came in with a group of injured motorcycle riders. Can you tell me if he's okay?"

The nurse scanned my outfit; I was still in my racing suit, my sponsors proudly splashed all over my body. "Are you his wife?"

I nodded. "Yes." Whatever got me through the door.

She looked down at her computer, then frowned. "Hmm..."

"Hmm, what?" I asked, trying to read her screen.

She cocked an eyebrow at me. "This says he's not married."

Even though I was relieved I was at the right place, my eyes started shimmering with building tears, and my voice warbled when I spoke. "Please, I just need to know what happened, if he's okay." The floodgates released and my tears spilled over. "He saved my life, I just need to know he's okay."

The nurse's face turned sympathetic. "I'm sorry, I can't tell you anything, but...there's only one elevator between the operating room and the recovery rooms. If you were to wait there...well, who knows what could happen." She pointed down a hallway.

Hope exploded within me; it was blinding, like a flare sparked in my face in the darkest of night. Operating room...recovery room. That meant he was alive...and he might survive whatever was being done to him. I hated that he was being cut open, hated not knowing what they were trying to fix, but at least I had direction, and direction was better than nothing.

"Thank you," I murmured. She handed me a tissue, and then I was off...to wait some more. I paced while I waited, and every time the double doors leading into the restricted area opened, my heart started pounding. It was never him, though. I was just about to go back and beg the nurse for details when the doors opened and I saw a familiar head of messy blond hair.

I rushed to his side. "Hayden!" As I peered over the edge of the bed he was being transported on, I studied his face—bruising, a few cuts, but he still looked as perfect as ever. He was really out of it, though; his eyes fluttered open, but the gorgeous green gems never stayed visible long.

"Kenzie..." he murmured, before closing them again.

The nurses pushing him along tried to get me to step back, but

I was too busy examining the bed, examining his body. I couldn't tell by looking what was wrong with him. Could he move? Could he walk? Was he all messed up inside?

"Is he okay?" Surely they'd be pushing him to the ICU, not the recovery rooms, if he was truly in trouble. Right?

One of the nurses gave me a stern look like she wasn't going to say anything, but then her face turned sympathetic. Maybe she could tell I was hanging on by a thread. "Broken wrist, a few cracked ribs, a hairline fracture to his femur, a bit of internal bleeding, but he'll be fine. He was very lucky, from what I've been told. It could have been a lot worse."

That stopped me dead in my tracks. He was okay. Taking only a brief second to recover from that shock, I hurried in with them when they all stepped into an elevator. I wasn't losing Hayden again.

I wasn't allowed in the recovery room, though, so again…I waited. I was so sick of waiting. Keith showed up while I was killing time. I kept out of sight while he talked to the nurse, and prayed that I could get in to see Hayden without him knowing. I had to make sure Hayden was okay, but I didn't want to ruin his career.

Finally, I saw Hayden being wheeled into a private room. Keith was distracted with a group of reporters, so I took the opportunity to sneak inside. Hayden was completely awake now, and smiled when he saw me. "Twenty-Two…you're okay. Thank God."

Tears stung my eyes as I nodded. I went to grab his right hand and saw it was casted. "Yeah…thanks to you."

He nodded, then cringed. "Good," he said through clenched teeth.

They were giving him medicine for the pain—they had to be—but he was still hurting. Seeing him in pain made me feel even worse. "I'm so sorry, Hayden."

Suddenly, his eyes were sharp, intense, and focused. "Don't be. I would do it again in a heartbeat. A thousand times over if necessary…anything to keep you safe."

I didn't know what to say to that, so I dried my cheeks and sat on the side of his bed. Neither of us spoke for several long minutes, and the silence was as suffocating as the pungent smell of antiseptic. I had so much to say, I didn't know where to start. Knowing I didn't have a lot of time before Keith showed up, I jumped right into it. "How could you do that? How could you push me out of the way and sacrifice yourself? You scared the shit out of me." My voice shook so badly, the words were almost unintelligible.

Hayden understood me, though, and let out a long sigh. "Because the thought of you hitting that pile...scared the shit out of *me.* And I don't handle fear well. Or the thought of losing you. I...know we can't be together. I know your dad thinks I'm a demon, and you think Keith is the devil. I know you've got questions about me, about what I was doing, but...the simple fact is, I love you. And I would do *anything* to protect you."

I knew he was telling the truth; I saw it in his eyes—the absolute adoration, the feeling of *I'll love you forever and I'll never get over you.* I felt the same way, and I wanted him to know that. "I love you, Hayden. More than I wanted to, more than I thought possible, and honestly...more than I was comfortable with. But I'm so glad I fell in love with you. I finally feel...complete."

Hayden's expression was glorious, like he'd just heard something he'd been waiting his entire life to hear. But little by little, his joy faded. "I feel that way too...which only makes the fact that we can't be together so much worse."

Scooting closer to Hayden on his bed, I grabbed his good hand. "We *can* be together, Hayden. And I want us to be together. I want to be with you more than I've ever wanted anything, and I don't care if that means my father ruins my career. I don't want to race at all if I can't race with you."

Hayden looked confused. "What do you mean...ruins your career?"

Knowing I had to tell him everything, I let out a long, cleansing breath. "My father found out about the street racing...found out about us. Since Cox Racing no longer exists after this year, threatening me with being fired wasn't enough for him. Dad...he told me that he'd make sure no one else hired me if I kept seeing you."

Hayden was stunned silent, then he exclaimed, "No. He can't do that! He can't steal your future because of me. I won't let him."

His sweet attempt to stick up for me made me smile. Then my smile fell. "It doesn't matter anymore. The replacement teams he found for me are both on the East Coast. I'm not going to ride for a team based thousands of miles away from you, and Dad won't let me ride for a local team...so I'm not riding anymore. It's as simple as that." Bittersweet relief filled me as the decision firmed in my mind. This was how it had to be.

Hayden's face clouded over as he tried to sit up straighter. "You can't do that. It's your dream."

It was. And leaving it behind was like slicing off a piece of my soul. But I could live with a segment of my soul missing. I couldn't live without my heart. "I'll be fine. We'll be fine."

Sighing, he shook his head. "Maybe he wasn't serious. I mean, he wouldn't actually do that to his own daughter, would he?"

I kept my face as blank as possible. "Yes, he would. He used the threat as motivation for me to end things with you, but I didn't listen. Dad doesn't bluff, he follows through. And once he finds out we're together, that I'm staying here in California with you and not going back east to ride for one of the teams he picked for me, my career will be over."

Hayden let out a weary sigh as he looked away. "I'm so sorry. I never wanted that to happen."

"I know," I whispered.

Looking back at me, his eyes suddenly sad, he said, "Why would you give it all up for me? I'm not worth it, Kenzie."

Carefully bringing my legs up onto the bed, I cupped his cheek. "Yes, you are. *You're* everything I never knew I wanted, and I love you. I'm giving up racing because racing is the only thing I can live without. I can't live without you."

I slowly lowered my mouth to his and cherished the soft warmth as we connected. Desire and passion instantly sizzled my skin, and I wanted more, so much more. A lifetime of more. We'd have to wait, though; Hayden was in no shape for intimacy. But as soon as he *was* ready, we would be together—in the open, defying the odds. Since I was a civilian now, there was no ban in place preventing us from being together. With me no longer racing, there were no more reasons for us to be apart. No good ones that I could think of, anyway. But still, before we went any further…I did need answers about what I saw him doing before the race.

When we broke apart, I searched his face. "If I'm going to give up the only job I've ever wanted…"

Hayden took my brief pause to interrupt. "Kenzie, I don't think you should—"

I lifted my eyebrows and kept talking like he hadn't spoken. "…then I need you to tell me exactly what you were doing with my bike. You said you were fixing something. What?"

Hayden sighed and closed his eyes; he looked exhausted, and I didn't know if that was because of the painkillers he was on or what he was about to tell me. "Before I say anything, I want you to know that I was clueless about all of this." He reopened his eyes with a frown. "No, that's not entirely true. I had my suspicions, but I didn't want to know…so I didn't ask."

"Didn't ask what?" I whispered, suddenly feeling nervous.

"Myles and your father are right about the bike tampering, they were just wrong about me being the one doing it," he stated.

My heart was thumping in my chest now. "Was it Keith?" I asked, venom in my voice. Whoever was responsible for messing with the bikes was probably the reason Myles had gotten hurt. And Hayden too. Jesus, was that wreck today accidental or intentional? Either way, Keith seemed like the most likely suspect. Although that didn't explain how I had done so well during the street races. Keith hadn't known about that. If Hayden hadn't helped me…then who had?

Hayden shook his head. "No, not Keith…Hookup."

His name reverberated around the room, and my mind spun as pieces starting falling into place. The rumor, my wins, the incidents at the track…"Why would he…? How did he…? I don't understand."

Hayden sighed as he studied his cast. "It took me a while to put it together myself. I haven't confronted Hookup yet…but I know he's the one doing all this. Him and Grunts. I've seen them before, sneaking around the track during ARRC events; then one day, I watched Hookup put a device on a bike. I wasn't sure what it did or why he was touching stuff, but during the race that bike had problems, and I knew he'd somehow messed with it. Probably some remote trigger that affected something small enough that it didn't get noticed. And then, once it was triggered, it was gone, so no proof."

His face suddenly turned somber. "I should have said something to someone...should have done something to stop it once I was sure it was Hookup, but Hookup...he's my ticket into street racing. I need him to help Antonia, so I had to keep my mouth shut. But even without that...we're so tightly bound together, if he goes down, I go down. He'll make sure of that." Clearing his throat, Hayden tried to give me a reassuring smile. It didn't reassure me; my gut felt like he'd punched a hole in it. "I started searching bikes after that, though, trying to minimize the damage he was doing, but I never knew which ones he was going to hit, so most of the time I didn't find anything."

I instantly recalled the thing Hayden had showed me. "Until today...when you found something on *my* bike." Shit. Hookup had targeted me, and if it weren't for Hayden's diligence, I would have been at the epicenter of today's wreck.

Hayden's face reflected my realization. "Yeah...that son of a bitch. He's been complaining ever since you stopped racing for him. I didn't think he'd do anything to you out of respect for me, but apparently he doesn't respect me as much as I thought."

"Why would he tamper with bikes?" I asked. It made no sense to me.

With a sigh, Hayden said, "He's a compulsive gambler, always has been, always will be. He was affecting the outcome so he could make money. And I'm the one who invited him into this world. God, I feel so stupid. I never questioned why I always won on the streets. Never questioned the malfunctions during close races...the odd things that seemed to always give me the edge I needed. I should have known something was up back then, but I needed the money, so I turned a blind eye."

I put a soothing hand on his arm. "Hey, I did the exact same thing, Hayden. I knew I shouldn't have won some of those events, but I wanted the money so badly...I just accepted it." A small smile curved my lips. "But then again, I thought it might be you doing it, and I was really torn for a while. In the end, I decided it wasn't you, so I didn't say anything. Or...I hoped it wasn't you, so I didn't say anything."

A matching smile brightened Hayden's expression. "It wasn't me." He frowned. "Well, I guess that's only partly true. I am the one who brought Hookup into this world. Into your life...and now he's gunning for you."

"He didn't get me, though. You stopped him. And saved my life," I added, squeezing his arm.

Hayden's expression didn't change. "He got someone else instead, and look how many people were hurt this time. No, I ignored the lucky coincidences because I didn't want to deal with the truth. And then, when I couldn't deny what Hookup was doing anymore...I didn't do everything in my power to put a stop to it, because I still needed him." He shook his head in anger. "But he's gone too far, and I'm done with him, done with him and Grunts. You were right, I can't straddle the line anymore. I love my friends, but they aren't worth dying for...not like you."

My entire body flushed with heat, and leaning over, I pressed my lips against his and kissed him with all my might. I poured every ounce of emotion I felt for him into that kiss—the heat, the fire, the love. Somehow, over the course of the last several months, he'd become my entire world, and it filled me with such relief to know he hadn't been the one behind the multiple wrecks, accidents, and incidents. He hadn't been behind anything sordid, except the street racing, and he was letting that go. I wasn't sure what that meant for Izzy and Antonia, but I knew it only meant good things for Hayden. He was free. And so was I.

Hayden looked unsure when we pulled apart, though. Stroking his cheek, I asked him, "What is it?"

He cringed, like he was in pain again. "It's killing me that you're giving up racing." Sighing, he shook his head. "I can't believe I'm going to say this, but I can't let you quit for me, Kenzie. I know what it means to *me*, so I know what it means to you...and I can't let you give it up."

Pulling back from him, I frowned. "I don't want to live on the East Coast, and that's the only choice my father has left me with, so I'm not just giving it up for you. It wouldn't be the same racing for another team anyway." A long exhale left my lips. "I wanted to save the family business, but I couldn't. My father was right...it's time to move on."

My words didn't alleviate his worry. "You'll end up hating me," he quietly stated.

Throwing on my brightest smile, I shook my head. "No, I won't."

His brows drew together, and he didn't say anything else, but I could clearly hear the words *Yes...you will* echoing around the room. Not liking that ominous imaginary voice, I ravaged him with my lips again. He couldn't tell me we were doomed if we were actively making out.

After a few long, lingering, perfect kisses, I moved my mouth to his ear. "I can't wait to get you back in my bed."

Hayden groaned, then hissed in a sharp breath. "This is going to be the longest recovery period ever. When can I go home again?"

I laughed, then shrugged, because I really had no idea. The only thing I knew for certain was that when he did go home, he'd be going home with me.

* * *

It was difficult to leave Hayden's room, but with Keith hovering nearby, I knew I couldn't stay long. And besides, I knew we'd be together again soon. Nothing was keeping us apart anymore.

A soft smile was on my face as I quietly left his room. My good mood vanished the second I stepped into the hallway outside. My father was standing there, looking angrier than I'd ever seen him; even his altercation with Keith seemed calm compared to the heat in his eyes now. "Dad? What are you doing here?"

My father clenched his hands tight; his entire body was shaking with restraint. "Myles and Nikki. They wouldn't tell me where you were at first, but I eventually got it out of them."

Knowing he'd probably threatened them in some way, I cringed, then sighed. "What did you say to them?"

Stepping forward, Dad ignored my question. "Are you testing me, Kenzie? Is that what this is? Because I meant everything I said. I *will* ruin your career before I let you be with him." He pointed toward Hayden's room; his finger was shaking with barely controlled rage.

"He saved me, Dad. He pushed me out of the way, he took the hit for me." I pointed back to his room as well; my finger was a lot steadier. "Hayden is the reason I'm not in that room."

A mixture of emotions rippled across Dad's features—anger, uncertainty, hate, and, surprisingly enough, gratitude. For a moment, he was at a loss for what to say. Hayden doing something positive for me was probably beyond the realm of possibility for Dad. I might as well have told him a superhero had swooped down and lifted me to safety. "Mackenzie…everything happened so fast, you can't be sure—"

I cut off his argument with an icy glare. "He saved me, Dad."

Dad's expression shifted into rigid disapproval. "He might have… helped you…for some reason…but that doesn't change anything. He doesn't get a pass for one good deed. You still can't date him."

I inhaled a deep breath. Might as well get this over with. "Yes, I can. I'm an adult, and I'll make my own decision about who I spend my life with. I love him, and he loves me. We're going to be together, whether you like it or not."

As I stared at Dad, I could practically see the steam coming from his ears. Then he closed his eyes, and exhaustion swept over him; he suddenly seemed old and frail, like life had smacked him down one too many times. "Please…don't make me do this, Mackenzie."

"You're not doing it, Dad. I am. I'm done. I quit." Walking past him, I murmured, "As you once told me, racing isn't everything."

CHAPTER 24

My heart was pounding against my rib cage as I drove back to the track. I'd done it. I'd cut ties with my father, my family, and my career. I'd thrown away everything I'd ever wanted for a boy I'd known less than a year. It made absolutely no sense, and yet I didn't regret my choice. I had to live my life *my* way, and not how my father wanted me to live it.

The track was still chaotic when I got there, and everywhere I turned people were rippling with emotion. Most wanted answers, some wanted blood. Of the twenty-four riders entered in the event, ten had been involved with the wreck in some way, and four were in no condition to return to the track today. No one had died, from what I could tell, but at least one rider probably wouldn't ever race again. It was heartbreaking; Hookup's greed had hurt so many people.

Since so many bikes and riders were injured, the officials decided to call the race as complete. Everyone's positions were logged at the time of the wreck, which made even more people angry. The officials were determined to get to the bottom of what happened, and consequently they were all over the riders and crew. I was hustled into a meeting with them almost the second I stepped foot on the track, and when I left the interrogation, I was drained, and not entirely sure that I'd done the right thing.

I'd kept quiet about everything I knew, everything Hayden had told me at the hospital. I hadn't been sure that telling the officials about Hookup wouldn't somehow come back to hurt Hayden—he was the one who'd given him access into this world, after all. Would he be punished for his small part in Hookup's crime? I didn't know, and that had kept me silent.

Later that evening, the officials released their final statement on the wreck. They said that multiple overheated engines were at the root of the problem; a pair of bikes had gone down at almost the exact same time, and in almost the exact same way. Many people felt that it was too similar to be a coincidence, but no one had any clue who would be stupid enough to do such a thing. No one knew anything for certain, except Hayden and me.

When I got back to the hotel after a long afternoon of shuffling between the track and the hospital, I saw Myles and Nikki sitting at the hotel bar. They both seemed subdued as they sat silently at a circular table, staring into drinks that looked untouched. I thought about ignoring them and going to my room, but honestly, I was tired of fighting with people. And I could use a drink; today had been one long, emotional roller coaster.

Myles gave me a tentative smile when I sat between him and Nikki. "Hey, Kenzie…did you see where you ended up in the scoring?"

I shook my head. I'd been too absorbed in other things to find out. And really, I think I'd subconsciously been avoiding the results. Since racing wasn't going to be a part of my life anymore, my final standing didn't really matter. Or at least, it wasn't supposed to matter. *God*, I was going to miss racing.

Myles's grin grew wider as he leaned forward. "With the race being called early, you ended up in third place. Fifth overall. That's a record for a female finish…and for Cox Racing. You know how long your dad has been trying to get into the top five. Not bad for your first year, Kenzie." He held up his drink in a toast.

"A record? Top five…? No one at Cox Racing has done that since Dad retired. Not you, not Jimmy…I never thought…Oh my God…" I hadn't realized how well I'd done. My focus had shifted from winning races to winning money halfway through the year, and I'd lost a bit of that drive to succeed. It struck me now, full force, and tears of joyful sorrow pricked my eyes. Now that it was over, now that it was too late…it finally meant something to me again.

Seeing that I was getting emotional, Nikki rubbed my back. "Hey, it's okay, Kenzie. This is the first of many records for you. In fact, I bet you blast this one out of the water next year."

Sniffing, I wiped my eyes dry. "There is no next year. I quit racing. Today was my last day." I supposed my glorious finish was a hollow victory anyway. Hookup had dinked around with the standings so much…who knows where I would have finished if this year had been a typical year. But still…I was in the record books. I'd done it. And now it was over. The reality of it all was crushing.

Both Myles and Nikki looked like I'd socked them in the gut. "Quit? You can't…" Myles's voice trailed off, then he let out a low curse. "Is this because of us? Because we told your dad you went to the hospital to see Hayden? Was he mad when he found you?"

"Mad" didn't seem like a big enough word to cover it. "Furious," more like. "No, it's not because of you guys. I quit because I want to be with Hayden, and Dad won't let me do that *and* race. I had to make a choice between the two…so I did." And no matter what Hayden said, I wouldn't let it tear us apart. It was my decision, and I stood by it.

Nikki looked like she was about to cry. "Are you mad at us for telling your dad? Did we fuck up again?"

I smiled as the melancholy began to lift. I was gonna be okay. "No, I'm not mad at anyone anymore. I'm done with rules and bans and fear. I'm through with hiding how I really feel, and…I love Hayden. We're going to be together…hopefully you guys will be okay with that."

Feeling worried that they'd reject me like Dad had, I anxiously looked between the two of them. Nikki seemed okay with everything, but Myles frowned. "And what about what he did to me, Kenzie?"

"It wasn't him, Myles. It was—" I stopped myself before I said anything about Hookup. It was safer for Hayden if I kept that information to myself. "Hayden's guilty of a lot of things, but in this, he's innocent. He didn't touch your bike. He was actually trying to help stop what was happening. And you'll just have to take my word on that."

Myles narrowed his eyes at me. "You know something."

I flicked a glace around the bar to make sure no one was within earshot. "Nothing I can freely talk about, and I'll deny knowing anything if anyone asks. You'll just have to trust me on this one," I said, raising an eyebrow pointedly at him.

Myles sighed, then nodded. "I trust you. I don't know if I trust *him* yet…but I do trust you."

"Good," I said, slinging an arm around each of them. "Because I don't think I could handle losing my two best friends on top of everything else. I'd go nuts for sure."

Nikki laughed, then sighed. "I can't believe it's all really ending…The three of us at Cox. Your dad closing shop. Myles and I moving on. You…retiring. It all seems so surreal. This wasn't how I pictured your rookie season."

Me either.

"Hey," I said, turning to face her. "Not everything is changing. I'll still be in Oceanside, and the three of us will still go out. Even if we're not all working together, we'll stay close. Deal?" I asked, holding a pinkie out to each of them.

They both clasped fingers with me and we all shook on it. "Deal," they said in unison.

The remainder of the night was peaceful for me. Even though my future was hazy, I felt secure in the fact that I wasn't alone. I had Nikki, I had Myles, and I had Hayden. And that was enough. It had to be.

When my friends headed to the airport to go home the next morning, I went to the hospital to see how Hayden was doing. When I walked into his room, I immediately spun on my heel and made to leave. It was too late, though—I'd been spotted. "Cox? What the hell are you doing here?"

Keith Benneti was standing beside Hayden's bed, leaning on his crutch, looking shocked and pissed. He swung his gaze to Hayden and scowled; I swear, both Keith and my father had mastered the disapproving glare. "Care to explain to me what a member of Cox Racing is doing in your hospital room, Hayden? I thought I explained the rules clearly and concisely. No fraternization, period."

All the blood drained from Hayden's face as he stared at his mentor. "Keith…I can explain…"

Realizing that Hayden was in danger of losing his job too, I immediately stepped forward to try and defuse the situation. "I'm not a member of Cox Racing anymore. I quit."

Keith snapped his gaze back to me, and an amused fire danced behind his eyes. It sickened me to see him happy—this man had caused my family so much pain—but I ignored the bile rising up the back of my throat. It was Hayden's happiness that mattered to me right now, and I wasn't going to let this stupid ban burn us both. "You…quit?" he asked, his mouth widening in a smug smile.

Swallowing the indignation, I straightened my shoulders. "Yes, I quit. I'm no longer a member of Cox Racing, and really, Cox Racing is dissolving as a company in a few weeks…so either way, the ban no longer applies to me. I'm free to be here, same as you."

Darkness swirled in his eyes after I said that, but it quickly evaporated into glee. A curt laugh escaped him. "You quit your father's team right at the end of its pitiful existence? Wow, and people say I'm an asshole. Damn…that must have killed him. And if it didn't…well, I have no doubt that seeing his daughter screwing a Benneti will put him one step closer to the grave." He swung his meaty hand in Hayden's direction. "Sure. If you really want to fool around with my best rider, then go ahead. I've got no problems with you, so long as you're an *ex*-Cox." Laughing, he limped over to me and put his hand on my arm; it took a lot of willpower to not pull away. "Just be gentle with him for a little while. I need him in tip-top shape next season. Top five next year, Hayes. You mark my words."

With that, he walked out of the room, leaving us alone. It was almost incomprehensible to me that Keith was okay with Hayden and me being together. Although this wasn't truly acceptance on Keith's part, more like retaliation. I couldn't quite wrap my mind around it. In a daze, I walked over to Hayden's bed and sat beside him. "Did he give us permission to date…just to piss off my dad?"

Looking stunned himself, Hayden nodded. "Yeah…I think so. He's really not as bad as you think," he quickly added, searching my face.

Giving him a soft kiss, I shook my head. "We'll just have to agree to disagree on that one." Keith's stipulation—*so long as I you're an ex-Cox*—rang in my ears, causing a surprising flash of anguish to wash over me. I was no longer a member of Cox Racing. No one was. Shaking off that painful thought, I shifted the conversation. "Did he tell you where you ended up finishing?"

"Sixth. You?" he asked, a small smile on his face.

"Fifth," I said, my smile uncontainable. My ranking still stunned me. I just wished I'd truly earned it and not been handed it by Hookup's unwanted "help."

I thought Hayden might be upset that I'd finished above him, but by his expression, he only seemed happy for me. "Really? That's amazing, Kenzie."

His compliment made a bizarre warmth travel through every inch of me; it didn't exactly match hearing praise from my father, but it was damn close. Dad hadn't said a word to me after our confrontation in the hospital. He hadn't even commented on my amazing finish. "Yeah…I guess I broke the record for a female. And a record for Cox. No one's done it since my dad retired." And Dad should be proud of me for that fact, not avoiding me.

Leaning over, Hayden grabbed my cheek and pulled my mouth to his for a soft kiss. "That's great, Kenzie…and sad, all at the same time." He sighed as he searched my eyes, maybe gauging how I was doing. I was fine. Sort of. "So what are you going to do, now that you're not racing?" he asked.

"I really don't know. Track journalist, maybe."

Hayden gave me a wry smile. "You hate interviews."

"I hate answering questions," I said, raising a finger. "Asking them might not be so bad." Frowning, I dropped my hand. "I just…I still want to be a part of the world." I couldn't imagine not going to events, not smelling the exhaust fumes, not hearing the revving engines, not feeling the excitement of the crowd, the anticipation of the racers.

Hayden cracked a smile as he stared at me. "You could always model," he said with a crooked smile.

I gave him a bright grin in response. "And I could always break your other wrist too."

Hayden laughed, then grabbed my hand with his good one. "You'll figure something out, Kenzie. I know you will." I nodded at his comment. Yeah, I would find a way to move on. I had to. After a second of silence, Hayden softly said, "You know…you could probably work for Keith? You're an amazing rider. I bet he would hire you, no matter what your dad says to the other teams. You know Keith doesn't give a shit what your dad thinks."

I considered that for a moment before I answered him. "Yeah, that's true…and yeah, Keith probably would take me just to hurt my dad, but…" A rough exhale left me. "I'd rather never get on a bike again than race for that man. I know you like him, but I really can't—"

Hayden interrupted me with his lips on mine. "I know," he said when we pulled apart. "It's okay. Like I said, you'll find something. Something that works for you."

I gave him a soft smile, then lowered my head to his shoulder and snuggled into his side. Something that worked for me…that wasn't racing. Seemed like an impossible combination—racing was all I'd ever wanted to do with my life—but I wasn't giving up hope yet. I mean, look how far Hayden and I had come. If we could somehow find a way to work things out and be together, then anything could happen. My dream wasn't over yet.

As I was enjoying a moment of peace with my boyfriend, someone knocked on Hayden's door. A few seconds later, a pair I hadn't expected to see stepped into his room: Hookup and Grunts. Grunts looked like he always did—an emotionless rock of a man. Hookup had both hands over his eyes. "Yo, H-man, you decent?" He cracked his fingers to look at Hayden and his amused expression faded. "Oh hey, Felicia Two…didn't know you were here."

I immediately jerked upright on the bed, making Hayden flinch in pain. "What the hell are you doing here?" I asked.

Face clouding over, Hookup folded his arms over his chest. "Could ask the same of you, quitter. Here to lead Hayden on, then leave him high and dry? Like you left me?"

"I didn't..." I forced myself to take a calming breath. "I was done; it had nothing to do with you personally. But you trying to sabotage my bike was most definitely personal!"

Hookup's face shifted into a picture-perfect look of confusion. "What the hell are you talking about?" He turned to Hayden. "What the hell is she talking about? What did you tell her, dude? You didn't do that thing again, did you?"

That age-old doubt began to crawl across my skin, but I squeezed Hayden's hand and pushed it back. Hookup was just trying to save his own ass. Hayden's eyes narrowed as he studied his friend. "Game's over, Hookup. I saw you messing with bikes, but I fixed Kenzie's before you could screw her over too. I'm in here because of you, man. You fucked me over. I thought we were friends, but I guess I was wrong."

Grunts took a step forward, but Hookup put a hand on his chest to hold him back. "This...sport you chose is dangerous, dude. You knew that going into it. I just came here to make sure you were okay, but this..." He indicated the bed with his hand. "*You* did this, not me."

Hayden squeezed my hand so hard I felt something pop. "So you're really not going to take *any* blame for this? People got hurt, Hookup. Kenzie almost got hurt!"

Hookup's lip twitched, like he was amused I'd almost ended up in a bed beside Hayden. Asshole. With a shrug, he told Hayden, "How can I take blame for what *you* chose to do for a living? I told you it was a waste of time. I told you you could make more money racing for me. You're the one who insisted on being all respectable and shit. You're the one who fucked *me* over, Hayden. If anyone should be pissed, it's me!" His face was red with rage by the end of his rant.

"Unbelievable," Hayden muttered. He made a move like he was

trying to stand, and I put a hand on his shoulder and gave him a warning glare. He was not going to get into an altercation with this thug in the hospital while he was supposed to be resting. Hayden shifted his eyes to me, but he relaxed back onto the bed.

Returning his eyes to Hookup, he spat out, "We're done. Don't call me, don't text me, don't drop by. I'm done racing, I'm done trying to be your friend. From now on...you don't exist to me." Looking back at me, he softly added, "I'm done straddling both worlds."

"You selfish son of a bitch!" Hookup said. "You think you can just walk out on *me*? I've saved your scrawny ass more times than you know. You were just a lost, punk kid before I found you, before I gave you a purpose. You think you belong in your fancy world, racing your fancy bikes? That's not who you are, and you know it. When these people eat you up and spit you out, you'll be begging me to come back, and fuck if I'll let you. Come on, Grunts. We're done here."

He twisted to leave, and Hayden called out his name. His real name. "Tony!" When he looked back, Hayden said, "I know what you did, and I have proof that you did it. If I ever see either one of you near a track again, I'll have the cops on you in an instant, and you won't be able to talk your way out of what I've got on you. Oh, and don't think the threat of taking me down with you will change my mind. It won't. I'll happily go to jail to see you behind bars."

Hookup glared at Hayden, and if looks could kill, I'd be single again. He stormed out of the room with Grunts right behind him. My thudding heart took a solid ten minutes to calm down, and even then, I still felt shaky. Hayden rubbed my back, like he understood how worked up I felt; maybe he felt the same way, and he was just hiding it better.

When I finally felt like Hookup wasn't hiding around the corner, waiting to jump out and attack us, I whispered, "Do you really have proof that will put him away?"

Hayden let out a breath, and judging from the heaviness of it, he'd been holding it for a while. "Just the thing I found on your bike. I don't really have a way to tie that to Hookup... but he doesn't know that."

With wide eyes, I twisted to look at him, "Will that threat really stop him?"

He gave me a reassuring smile. "Yeah, I think so."

I didn't feel as reassured as he wanted. Frowning, I asked, "Will he come after you... to eliminate that threat?"

Hayden's smile twitched with doubt. It was subtle, and I only saw it because I'd been watching for it so closely. He shook his head. "No... he's not stupid; he won't risk messing with me. I'm not exactly helpless," he added with a wink.

Remembering him laying out three Benneti assholes, I knew he was right, but still... I had a horrible feeling Hookup didn't play fair, and if he decided to come after Hayden, Hayden wouldn't know it... until it was too late.

* * *

Hayden and I came home from New Jersey a couple of days later, and I spent most of my newfound free time taking care of him in his apartment above Keith's garage. I never in a million years thought I would be at Keith's home, and a part of me felt like just breathing the air here was betraying my family. Seeing where Keith lived up close and personal was so surreal. Especially one afternoon when Keith walked over in just his boxers to check on Hayden. I could have gone my whole life without seeing that.

Whenever I was at Hayden's, I mothered the hell out of him; it annoyed him to no end. "You don't have to wait on me hand and foot, Kenzie. I have crutches, I can fend for myself. I could even drive over to your place so you wouldn't have to see Keith as often."

With a bright smile, I brought a spoonful of soup to his lips. "You can't get back on a bike yet. And besides, this is too much fun. I'm not ready to give it up."

Hayden groaned, and I shoved the spoon in his mouth. Once

he swallowed, he apologized. Again. "I'm so sorry, Kenzie. About everything. You should be celebrating your amazing finish with your family...not stuck here taking care of me."

With a sigh, I rested the spoon on Hayden's tray. "It's not your fault, remember? And I'm not stuck here. I want to be here. I want to be with you. I'm exactly where I belong."

Hayden smiled and I leaned over and kissed him. When we pulled apart, he asked, "Has your dad spoken to you yet?"

I knew he wasn't going to like my answer, so I was reluctant in giving it. "No. I've called him a few times, but he hasn't picked up. And my sisters... Well, Theresa is ignoring me too, but Daphne chewed me out. Said I broke Dad's heart." That was surprisingly hard to admit to him, and to myself. I had never wanted to hurt Dad, never wanted to hurt anyone. I just wanted to be free to make my own choices, to follow my heart.

Hayden wrapped his arm around me. "Hey, it will be okay... somehow. I promise."

I nodded, but I wasn't sure that was something he could promise. My entire family was pissed at me, and that kind of anger didn't go away overnight. I just had to show them that Hayden was a good person, a person worth caring about. I had to give them time. Then they'd forgive me... maybe.

A few days later, Hayden was done with being cooped up and pampered. We started going out and being social. We even hung out with Myles and Nikki, which was a little odd for everyone. Hayden did his best to keep things light and breezy, and for their part, Myles and Nikki were surprisingly friendly, although I did see Myles wince a few times, like he was slowly being tortured. They also kept looking over their shoulders, like they were doing something wrong and any second they were going to get caught. I supposed that was a remnant of the Benneti Ban. But Cox Racing didn't exist, so the ban didn't either. Everything was over.

"So what are you guys going to do for the next season?" I asked them while casually sipping on a beer.

Myles took a gulp of his drink before answering. "I signed on with Stellar Racing... so I guess I'll be teammates with Jimmy again." He looked disgruntled by that fact. "But Eli and Kevin signed on too, so I won't be completely alone."

A pang went through me as I thought about Myles being so far away. Stellar was just outside of San Francisco. "Well... at least you're still in California. We can still... meet up." He nodded, but both of us knew the visits wouldn't be frequent, especially while he was training. "What about you?" I asked Nikki.

She let out a long, sad sigh. "Nothing yet. I just can't... I don't know. I don't want to leave. I like it here." She looked around the table, and I could clearly see what she really meant was that she liked it here with us, but that was already going to change with Myles breaking off on his own. Her leaving was inevitable, and it wouldn't surprise me in the least if she followed Myles to Stellar.

Hayden brought my hand to his lips and gave the back of my knuckles a soft kiss. Being allowed to publicly display our affection for each other was weird... and wonderful. Smiling, I kissed his cheek. Myles cleared his throat, and I looked over to see him cringing. He hadn't adjusted to this new reality yet. "So... what are you going to do, Kenzie?" he asked.

Keeping my gaze locked on Hayden, I told Myles, "I don't know what I'll be doing... but I know I'll be just fine doing it."

Myles made a gagging noise and I quickly snapped my attention back to him. "If that was some subtle reference to your sex life, I don't want to hear it, Kenzie. I really don't."

Tossing a coaster at his face, I laughed, "No, it wasn't. I just meant... whatever happens, I'll be okay."

Myles silently studied Hayden and me leaning against each other for a moment, and then finally a slow smile spread across his face. "Good, I'm glad to hear it. You deserve happiness." Raising his glass, he looked around the table and said, "To Cox Racing. Gone, but never forgotten."

His words constricted my chest, and I squeezed Hayden's hand tight as I lifted my glass. Yes, definitely never forgotten.

Hayden was quiet after dinner, speculative, and when he reached my truck in the parking lot, he swiveled on his crutches to face me. "Do you mind if we don't go home right away? There's someone I'd like you to meet."

My heart started pounding, because I knew exactly who he meant. I still asked, though. "Oh yeah, who?"

Hayden flashed me a killer smile, like he knew I didn't really need to ask. "Izzy and Antonia. I kind of…talk about you a lot…and Izzy's getting sick of the fact that she doesn't know you yet. As she put it, the two of you should be besties already." He rolled his eyes, but I saw the fondness in his expression.

My palms instantly started sweating. Meeting Izzy was sort of the equivalent of meeting Hayden's parents. Throwing on a smile that I hoped looked calm, I said, "You talk about me?"

Hayden laughed as his gaze fell to the ground. "Yeah. At first, I'd only tell her that you were my training partner. I never even mentioned that you were a girl. But Izzy's smart, she figured it out pretty fast." Peeking up at me, he said, "She knew I loved you before I did." That made my smile turn genuine. Hayden kissed me, then let out a sigh as he shook his head. "There were so many times I wanted to push you away, but Izzy got on my case not to. She said I needed to let people in again, give them a chance…" Clearing his throat, he let out a rueful laugh. "She's kind of a know-it-all jackass…but she's family."

My grin was uncontainable. "I would love to meet her."

Minutes later, Hayden was packed in my truck, giving me directions to Izzy's apartment. When we got there, I helped Hayden out of the truck. He locked gazes with me, and my breath froze in my chest. God, he had engaging eyes. "She's in four-A," he murmured, pointing to our left.

Giving him a peck on the lips, I nodded, and we began heading that way. Nerves started building with each step, but with Hayden hobbling along beside me, I pushed them back. Izzy had fought for us before we were even an "us." I had no reason to be afraid of her.

Hayden knocked on her door, and when it cracked open, a child peeked up at us. The little girl had beautiful, big brown eyes, but they were worn, sunken, and weary; she'd clearly seen too much in her short life. They sparkled when she spotted Hayden, though.

"Uncle Hayden! You made it!" she squealed, throwing open the door. The sight of her bald head was shocking, and a piece of my heart tore open as I watched Hayden lean over and squeeze her tight. *No child should be sick like this.*

"Of course I made it, Bookworm. I told you I'd be here, so I'm here." From the firmness of his statement, it was obvious he would never break a promise to this girl, no matter how much it cost him.

Izzy appeared from behind her daughter, and the resemblance to Hookup was striking. She seemed way too young to be a mom. She probably was.

Her eyes turned glossy as she examined the aftermath of Hayden's wreck. "God, Hayden, you look worse than you described. Now I feel like a jerk for not visiting you. But Antonia was… Well… I've had my hands full."

Hayden walked through the door and gave her a one-armed squeeze. "I told you not to worry about it, I'm fine. Kenzie's been taking excellent care of me."

He looked back at me and winked, and I couldn't help but smile. Fondness on her face, Izzy turned to me and indicated inside. "Kenzie, it is so good to finally meet you. Hayden's told me so much about you… and wow, Tony was right, you *do* look like Felicia." She cringed after she said it and flashed a glance at Hayden. "I'm so sorry… It just slipped out."

Hayden frowned at Izzy, but I waved off his concern as I walked through the door. "It's fine… I'm sort of used to it," I said with a forced smile on my face. It turned genuine as I watched Hayden trying to tickle Antonia with his good hand.

Izzy smiled at them as she closed the door behind me. "Be careful with her, Hayden. She just got out of the hospital; I don't need you sending her back." Hayden lifted his hand in surrender, and Antonia took the opportunity to tickle him. Izzy laughed, then twisted to me and said, "I don't know what I'd do without Hayden. She's so happy when he's around."

A sorrow-laced joy spread over me as I watched Antonia dissolve into a giggle fit. "She's beautiful," I told Izzy.

She nodded, and her matching brown eyes grew moist. "Yes, she is." Swallowing, she quickly swiped under her eyes and tossed on a smile. "We were just about to have hot fudge sundaes. Join us?"

Even though I was stuffed from dinner, I nodded. "Sounds great."

Sitting down with Izzy, Antonia, and Hayden was surprisingly… easy. I felt like we all fit together, like I'd known Izzy and her daughter for years. Izzy was sweet and welcoming, Antonia was quick-witted and funny. And tired. She didn't eat much of her dessert, but she wouldn't leave the table until the rest of us were done.

When the last of our bowls were empty, she grabbed Hayden's good hand. "Uncle Hayden! Read me a story!"

Hayden grimaced, but it was clear he was joking. "Really, Bookworm? Shouldn't you know how to read by now?" He tossed a frown Izzy's way. "I'm disappointed, Iz. I thought you'd teach her how to read before you taught her how to walk."

Izzy chucked a napkin at his face while Antonia whined, "Please? You do the voices better than Mommy."

Hayden smiled at me, then carefully scooted away from the table. Grabbing his crutches, he told her, "Okay, fine. But you have to listen with your eyes closed. You look like you haven't slept in weeks, kid." Antonia brightened, but Hayden was right; she looked exhausted.

The pair of them shuffled off to Antonia's room, Hayden faking complaints the entire time. Izzy shook her head at him once he was out of sight. "That girl has got him wrapped around her little finger. He's so protective of her, always has been. Probably 'cause of how he grew up." Turning to me, she said, "He told you about being bounced around the foster care system, right?"

"Yeah…he mentioned…some of it," I answered.

Izzy indicated the living room couch, and we went over to sit down on it. "He never seemed to be able to find a family that stuck, so he attached himself to Tony and me…and Felicia, of course. The four of us, we did everything together. Thick and thin, hell or high water, we were family. We had each other's backs…"

Her expression turned sad. "But that was then, this is now…and things are different." Before I could ask her if she was okay, the wistfulness suddenly shifted to an almost childlike glee. "Hayden's gonna kill me for saying this, but he really likes you. Won't shut up about you, which is why I feel like I already know you." Putting her hand on mine, she added, "I can't wait to be best friends."

I laughed at her comment, but I had the feeling she was right; considering how warm and welcoming as she was, and how much she meant to Hayden, we were bound to be close too. I now had another sister... one who was actually talking to me at the moment.

Izzy and I chatted for a few minutes, until Hayden came back into the room. His expression somber, he told Izzy, "She went out like a light halfway through the story. She... okay?"

Izzy gave him a smile that was surprisingly reassuring; I had a feeling she'd perfected it over the years. "She's as good as she can be for today."

Hayden sighed as he made his way over to sit beside me; Izzy's eyes were reflective as she watched him. When he was settled on the couch, she leaned over her knees and said, "So... Tony was here earlier. He's really pissed at you, Hayden, but he won't tell me why. He just keeps cursing and calling you..." Pausing, she shook her head. "I made him leave because he wouldn't stop swearing in front of Antonia. It was upsetting her."

Hayden looked down at the cast on his wrist. Antonia's name was scrawled across it in big black letters. "It's nothing, Izzy. It will blow over."

"Bullshit, Hayden. Tell me the truth; I don't like being lied to." Her eyes got fiery after that. Izzy might seem frail, but she was tough.

Hayden closed his eyes and took a deep, calming breath. When he reopened them, he lifted his cast and said, "Tony is the one who did this to me."

All the color drained from her face. "What?" she whispered.

Hayden lifted his good hand. "Not directly, but... he's been hurting people, Izzy. Good people. And I got caught in the cross fire." Glancing at me, he went on to tell Izzy everything that Hookup had done. He finished his story with "He's out of control, and I can't be a part of it anymore."

"What do you mean, you can't be a part of it?" Izzy asked, but from the sadness in her eyes, she knew what was coming.

Hayden worked his lip, and it took him a few seconds to answer her. When he did, I could tell he was nervous. "I told Tony... I told him I'm done street racing, told him I'm done being friends... told him I'm done with all of it. I can't live in both worlds anymore, Izzy. I want more..."

Izzy's forlorn gaze fell to the coffee table, and Hayden reached over me and put a hand on her arm. "Hey, that doesn't mean I'm done with you or Antonia. I'll still be around. And I'll still help out, however I can, I promise. It's just... not going to be large bags of cash anymore."

Izzy laughed and Hayden smiled. Then he added, "I just can't have Hookup in my life. He's toxic, and you should... you should seriously consider whether or not you want him around either."

Her expression changed, and she no longer appeared child-like to me. She seemed far too old for being so young. "I know my brother's into bad stuff, Hayden. I've learned to stop asking, and just accept that he's... on a different path than me. But he's family, and I can't just write him off like that."

Hayden nodded. "I know. I just thought I'd throw it out there. Be careful around him, Izzy. I don't want to see you go down with him. You or Antonia."

Izzy nodded, then she looked between us and smiled. "I never thought I'd see the day when Hayden Hayes went straight. I thought for sure you'd follow Tony..." She paused to press her lips together, and when she opened them again, there were tears in her eyes. "I'm so proud of you, Hayden. And I'm so glad you got out."

Hayden grabbed her hand and squeezed it tight. "I'll get you out too, Izzy. I promise." His eyes locked with mine and a silent question passed between us. I nodded in answer. *Yes, I'll help you. I'll help Izzy and Antonia in any way I can.*

CHAPTER 25

Hayden's recovery went well, although he routinely complained that healing was a slow and tedious process, and he preferred things to be fast and exciting. The doctors had told him to stay away from racing for at least eight weeks, but he only made it five and a half before the burning itch to be back on a bike had him returning to the track. With his leg and his wrist still in casts, he couldn't do much, but he wanted to be near his bike. I sympathized. My two Ducatis were now taking up space in my garage, next to my everyday bike, and I stared at them at least twice a day.

Even though I knew it would be difficult on me, I went with Hayden to the practice track. I told myself it was just to make sure he took it easy, but I knew that wasn't entirely it. I wanted to see my old stomping grounds. I braced myself for the emotional pain when we stepped through the inner gate into the main area of the track, but even still, I was so stunned when I saw it, I couldn't move.

Being at the track when every trace of my family's business was gone was more surreal than being at Keith's place. Everything here was the same, and yet completely different. The Cox Racing name had been removed from every single sign, and the buildings across the way from Benneti's buildings were completely vacant. A large

FOR SALE sign on the outside of the Cox garage was the only decoration; a heartbreaking reminder of what I couldn't change. Nikki had cried the day she'd cleared all her stuff out. I'd cried after she'd told me about it. All of this felt so…final. A legacy had died, and I hadn't been able to do anything to save it. I'd failed, in so many ways.

Tears in my eyes, I turned my back on the remnants of my past, and moved toward my future—with Hayden…on the Benneti side of the track. It was odd to be on Benneti turf. I didn't think I would have been able to do it at all if Hayden hadn't been there, holding my hand and squeezing my fingers in encouragement every few seconds; he understood just how difficult this was for me. It was really hard to shake the feeling that I was surrounded by the enemy.

The garage bay doors were open, and darting into the first one, Hayden made a beeline for his bike. He was intercepted by a pair of burly riders that I recognized as the two assholes who'd threatened him into washing their bikes and bringing them beer in return for staying silent about me. Expecting the worst, I instantly tensed. Hayden did too, and his grip around my fingers became painful.

"Rodney, Maxwell…how's it going?"

The pair scrutinized Hayden like they were scanning him for weaknesses. Since his wrist and leg were bound in fiberglass for a few more weeks, he had two glaringly obvious frail spots. They surprised me by smiling, though. "Hayes…that was one nasty-ass wreck you survived. Glad to see you're not dead." With that, they smacked him on the back and continued on their way.

Hayden seemed amused by the turnaround, but not shocked, like I was. "They like you now?" I asked. "Because you could have died?"

Hayden shrugged. "Guess getting smeared over the concrete moved me up a notch in their eyes. And I suppose they finally don't believe the rumor about me messing with bikes, since I was the one who got taken out. It's not like I would sabotage myself…" He frowned after he said it, and Hookup's face flashed through my mind. No, Hayden hadn't done it, but one of his closest childhood friends had. Asshole. His carelessness could have killed somebody, could have killed *Hayden*. I hoped he took Hayden's warning seriously and left us the hell alone.

With a beaming smile on his face, Hayden gave me a tour of Benneti Motorsports. A pang went through me at just how similar it was to Cox Racing. The décor was a little different, the colors were different, but if I squinted just right, it felt like I was back at Cox. It made a vicious stab of homesickness go through me, and I had to blink my eyes several times to stop the tears.

Hayden noticed. Stopping, he turned to face me. "Is this too much? Do you want to go?" His eyes flickered in the sunlight streaming through the wide windows, the green changing from radiant to translucent as clouds covered the shifting rays.

I tried to smile, but it felt forced to me. "No, I'm fine. It's just… so strange, and a little sad. I can't help feeling like I shouldn't be here…like I'm somewhere I don't belong."

Hayden cupped my cheek and locked gazes with me. "I know exactly how you feel. When I first stepped into this world, I felt like…like I was trying on shoes that were way too tight. Everything pinched, and every part of me felt uncomfortable. Do you know what changed that for me?" he asked, smiling.

"No…what?" A genuine grin lightened my heart as I thought about what his answer might be.

Stroking his thumb over my cheek, he murmured, "You. I ran into you, and all of a sudden, I was distracted, annoyed…and driven. And I forgot all about how foreign it felt here…how lonely." I laughed at the memory of how we used to be, and Hayden's expression turned fond. "I know things didn't turn out how you wanted them to, but if you'll let me, I'll help you. I'll distract you, annoy you, push you…Whatever you need from me, I'll be here for you."

He leaned in to touch his soft lips to mine. As we shared a tender kiss, someone a few feet away let out a loud groan. "Oh God…is this what I'm gonna have to put up with all the time being your mechanic, Hayes? Because this was *not* covered in the training seminar."

I broke away from Hayden. “Nikki? What the hell are you doing here?”

Nikki laughed, then rushed over and flung her arms around me. After a quick hug, she pulled back and said, “I took a job with Keith. Don’t be mad, I just couldn’t leave here…” Her dark eyes shifted to the windows, where they overlooked the track that held countless memories for both of us.

The tears threatening to escape again, I brought her back to me for another hug. “I’m not mad. I’m glad you’re here. I’m *so* incredibly glad you’re here.” Over her shoulder, I saw Hayden watching the two of us with joyful eyes. Once again, he didn’t seem surprised; he must have known she’d taken a job here. I wanted to smack him for not telling me, but I was too happy that I had two friends here. The Bennetis seemed a lot less evil now.

That was, until the supreme commander of Benneti Motorsports showed his face. “Hey! Cox’s kid!” We all three looked over to see Keith thundering our way. There was a limp to his walk and a crutch under his arm that made him look eerily similar to Hayden. With the addition of a pot belly and muttonchops, of course.

When he got close enough, Keith pointed a meaty finger at me. “You need to call your father and order him to sell his side of the track to me. My real estate agent said he won’t accept any offer I make him. *Any!* This is absolutely ridiculous. He disbanded his team, blacklisted his daughter…what the hell does he care if I own the track?” I opened my mouth to say something, but Keith didn’t let me speak. “He’s holding on to the only thing I want, out of spite. I really shouldn’t be surprised by that. Asshole.”

I felt like Keith was subtly referencing my mother with that jab, and a flash of white-hot anger rushed up my spine. It cooled when the words “blacklisted his daughter” floated through my brain. Had Dad done it? Had he called around and made me unhirable? Feeling icy defeat settle around me, I told Keith, “I’m sorry, I can’t help you. My father isn’t talking to me right now, but I’m sure he can’t hold on to the property forever. He’s lost too much…” *The business, his daughter…*

Shoving down the pain, I told Keith something I had thought

I never would. "I'm sure he'll need the money soon, and then he won't have a choice but to sell it to you."

A slow smile spread over Keith's lips, chilling me even more. Nodding in approval, he slapped a hand on my shoulder. "I knew there was a reason I didn't mind having you around."

He shuffled off and I fervently wiped at my shoulder. God, I needed a shower.

When I got home that evening, I tried calling my father. Like every time I called him, it went straight to voice mail, and as usual, I hung up before leaving a message. How long was he going to avoid talking to me? I debated driving over to his place and confronting him, but Hayden had come home with me, and I didn't want to leave him. And...I wasn't ready to face my father yet. Feeling his disapproval and disappointment in the silence between us was one thing, seeing it on his face was another.

Putting my phone away, I debated what I should do. Keith's words were stewing in my brain, slowly poisoning me. I really wasn't sure if I wanted to race for anyone besides Cox Racing...but if I tried, would I even be *able* to get on another team? Or had Dad really stolen that from me? *Only one way to find out, I guess.*

After getting Hayden settled on the couch, and laughing when he frowned at my babying him, I started making a list of teams that I could race for. I started with the ones based closest to me, then worked my way out a couple of states; that was as far away as I wanted to be from Hayden.

"What are you doing?" Hayden asked, curious.

Setting down my pen and paper, I gave him a long look before answering. "I know I said I was fine not racing, and I am...but you were right when you said it was my dream, and I need to at least *try* to find another team to race for." Surprise hit me after I admitted that to him. I had initially just been curious whether Dad had followed through with his ultimatum, but after my confession, I realized it was more than that. If there was a way I could race *and* still be with Hayden, it would be the ultimate dream come true. And throwing in the towel without even asking around would be a stupid waste.

"Good," he said, giving me one of his hundred-watt smiles. "The last thing I want is for you to resent me because you gave up racing to be with me. You belong on the track, Kenzie. It's in your blood."

Smiling, I made myself comfortable on his lap. He was right, racing *was* in my blood. And I felt homeless and unsettled without it. I'd thought the feeling was just because Cox Racing was gone, but I was realizing it went deeper than that. Now I just needed someone who would give me a chance.

* * *

Two and a half months after the accident, you wouldn't know from looking at Hayden that anything had happened to him. He was healed, he was perfect, he was mine. And currently, he was naked.

We were rolling around the queen-sized bed in his apartment. Turning me onto my back, Hayden pinned my arms above my head and grinned at me with a devilish smile. "Gotcha," he whispered.

Biting my lip, I squirmed beneath him. "So what are you going to do with me?"

Those absorbing jade eyes I loved so much studied my face, and the playful curve of his lips turned adoring. "Never let you go," he answered.

His mouth lowered to mine, and the soft kiss he placed upon me stole my breath. Yes, I could definitely spend eternity wrapped in his arms. "It might be hard for you to race like this," I whispered.

His lips moved over to my neck, then traveled up to my ear. Every spot he touched sizzled with need. *Do that again.* He gently sucked my earlobe into his mouth, then breathed, "I'll get used to it."

Groaning, I tried to wrap my arms around him, but he held me tight. I snapped my gaze to his, and his engaging half smile returned. Before I could complain, he released my arms, then he twisted me to my side and kissed down my shoulder. I arched against him as he nestled against my back.

While he placed tender kisses down my side, he struck up a quiet conversation. "Have you heard back from PT Racing yet?"

With a defeated sigh, I told him, "Yeah…and they said almost the exact same thing as everyone else. *We hate to have to tell you this, since you're a very talented rider, but we just don't have any openings on our team at the moment.*"

As the new season approached, I found it harder and harder to accept that my career was over. And while no one would admit to the real reason they were rejecting me, I knew the truth…Dad had called in some favors and made sure none of them took me. Maybe he wanted me to come crawling back to him, beg for his help in getting a job. After I dumped Hayden, of course. "There's still one team I haven't heard back from, though," I added. "Myles's new team, Stellar Racing."

Hayden paused, and I could feel his guilt in the silence. Finally he murmured, "I'm sure they'll say yes. And they're not too far away, which is good." His lips pressed against a ticklish spot along my ribs, making me clench my stomach. He chuckled at my reaction and then continued along his southerly path. When he got to my ankles, he pulled my top leg back, then began kissing along the inside of my bottom leg.

"Yeah…" I groaned. The anticipation of where his lips might lead him had me breathing heavier. *What were we talking about?*

When Hayden got to my knee, he paused and asked, "Do you regret your decision?"

He'd stopped kissing me and his tone was more serious than before, so I forced my brain to reactivate. Looking down at him peering up at me, I saw unmistakable concern on his face. Reaching down, I cupped his cheek. The stubble along his jaw was heavier than before. We were making up for lost time now that he was in tip-top shape again, and we hadn't come up for air a lot lately. "No…of course not." Even though my life was completely different from what I'd thought it would be, and even though I missed racing more than I'd thought I would, I didn't regret choosing Hayden. My only regret was that my father couldn't accept and support my decision.

Not wanting to think about my hazy, uncertain future, I leaned up and sucked on Hayden's bottom lip. He made a satisfied noise, then shifted me back to my side and started over with his slow-paced seduction. He didn't ask me any questions this time, and I was squirming with desire long before his magical tongue slid between my legs.

"Oh God... Yes," I murmured, holding his head in place. He made a noise so erotic, I almost came instantly. As it was, I was on the brink, torn between letting myself go or saving it until he was inside me.

Wanting us to be satisfied simultaneously, I pushed him away. He was breathless when he looked up at me; his eyes were glorious as they burned with desire. Feeling worshipped, confident, and completely needed, I urged him to lie back, then straddled him. His eyes fluttered closed as I pushed him inside me. Mine closed too; there was nothing in this world that felt better than the two of us uniting.

We slowly began to move together, and every nerve ending in my body screamed in approval. I was so worked up, I was already on the verge of releasing, but I wanted this to last, wanted us to experience it together. Opening my eyes, I stared down at the man who had somehow claimed my closed-off heart. Watching the euphoria flicker across his features was mesmerizing, and it opened something deep inside me. I felt closer to him than I ever had before. We were competitors, friends, lovers... and soul mates. He completed the part of me that I hadn't even realized was missing.

"God, I love you," I murmured, my voice thick with emotion.

Hayden's eyes opened and locked on mine. "I love you too," he panted, reaching for my face. As he pulled me toward his mouth, he added, "So much... so goddamn much."

Our mouths moved together as seamlessly as our bodies, and as I felt the pressure building and my release starting, I grabbed his face, kissing him harder. "God, Hayden... I love you..."

I barely got the words out before bliss exploded throughout my body in a wondrous wave of pulsing pleasure. Hayden only got out "I..." before he stiffened and cried out with his own release.

We rode out the sensation together, our unity amplifying it into something beyond a mere physical act. We were connected in every aspect: body, mind, and spirit.

Hours later we stumbled out of bed and headed to the track. Keith had an announcement today that he wanted everyone to be there for. I didn't need to go, since I wasn't a member of the team, but I wanted to see Nikki...and honestly, I had nothing better to do with my day. I was living off my street racing earnings for now, but if Stellar Racing didn't take me—and God, I hoped they took me—I might have to look for a day job just so I didn't die of boredom.

We drove our street bikes through the inner gate of the practice track and I looked over at the Cox side, like I always did. I supposed one day I'd stop doing that...years from now. Pulling my gaze away, I focused my attention on the Benneti side. There were a bunch of people already there, standing around the three garage bay doors. Multiple tables were set up in front of the doors, each of them piled with snacks and refreshments. Some of the crew had beers in their hands, others had heaping plates of food. Were we celebrating something, or had Keith decided to have a party for no reason? Shit. Had he finally talked Dad into selling?

We parked our bikes a ways from the crowd, then took off our helmets. As we got closer, I saw Nikki standing next to another mechanic; she had a paper plate with a piece of cake on it. Nikki was wearing her red-and-black Benneti jumpsuit, another sight I still hadn't gotten used to. She spotted Hayden and me just as my cell phone rang. I stopped to pull it out of my jacket pocket, and Hayden stopped with me. Looking at the screen, I saw that it was Stellar Racing—my last hope for a local team. Flashing my eyes up to Hayden's, I said, "It's them...Myles's team. They must have an answer for me..."

Hayden grinned, as if he already knew what they were going to say. "Answer it," he encouraged.

Taking a deep breath, I connected the call, then brought the phone to my ear. "Mackenzie Cox." The voice on the other end was bright and bubbly...but their message was the same as everyone else's: Thank you, but no thank you. That was it, the last haystack, and just like all the others, this one didn't have a needle in it. No one was going to take me. No one nearby, anyway, and I didn't want to go too far from Hayden. Not after everything we'd gone through to be together. It just didn't seem right. No. I would find something else, something that worked for me…for us. "Thank you for your time," I told them, before hanging up.

As I slipped my phone back into my pocket, Hayden's face fell. "What did they say?"

Even though I felt like a door was permanently shutting in my face, I tossed on a smile. "Same thing everyone else said…no."

Hayden frowned. "I'm so—"

I cut him off before he could finish. "Don't. We both knew it was a long shot. I mean, they did just hire a bunch of ex–Cox employees, after all. Now, let's go get some cake. I'm starving."

Hayden was still frowning, but I didn't want to hear about how bad he felt, so I left him there and headed for Nikki. She was frowning too as she looked me over. Then she handed me her slice of cake. "Here. You look like you need this more than me."

"Thanks," I said, taking the plate and immediately shoveling a chunk of cake into my mouth. It wasn't a job, but it was Bavarian cream. That made up for some of it.

Nikki looked like she was about to ask me what was wrong, so I beat her to the punch. "Keith make his big announcement yet?"

She shook her head. "No, I think he was waiting for Hayden." She looked over at him right as he caught up to us. He had a soulful look in his eyes that pierced my heart. I didn't have time to be sad, though…and I didn't want to discuss my fate, the fate I'd chosen.

"You've got to try this," I said, shoving a forkful of cake into his mouth.

He started to look annoyed, then the taste hit him and his eyes fluttered closed. Oh yeah, that was the power of Bavarian cream. As Hayden chewed his cake, I debated whether I should confront my father. He still wasn't answering my calls or returning them, and I'd stopped calling him a while ago, but maybe it was time for that drop-in now. Maybe if I told him to his face that he was being childish and meddlesome, and he needed to let me live my life in the way I saw fit, then he'd change his mind and call in some different favors. Doubtful, but there was always a slim hope he would see reason. It was either that, or I completely gave up and called it quits on racing...for good. And being in this garage—smelling the oil and grease, seeing the bikes and components all around—I just wasn't sure if I could accept defeat. Not without one final battle.

As I was mapping out the conversation in my head, Keith walked out of the garage bay door and into the crowd hovering around the food. Strangely enough, Keith was with a rider in full racing leathers, complete with a black helmet with the visor down. Odd. And dramatic. The rider was wearing Benneti colors, though, so I quickly surmised that Keith's announcement was that he'd hired someone. Great. I couldn't get a job to save my life, and I'd just stumbled into a congratulations party for someone else. Perfect. In my resentment, I avoided looking directly at the rider. *I shouldn't be here.*

Keith held his hands up over his head once he was outside, and the noise of idle chitchat dwindled to silence. "Everybody, thank you so much for being here. And in such a timely fashion too..." His eyes narrowed as he shot a glare at Hayden. Guess we'd spent a little too much time exploring each other this morning. Oops.

I saw Hayden flip his hand up in a friendly wave, like Keith was merely acknowledging him and not chastising him. Keith shook his head at Hayden, then told the crowd. "As you know, I've got exciting news. Benneti Motorsports has just acquired a new rider. And boys, your new teammate will blow you out of the water..."

He looked over at the rider and they obligingly took off their helmet. My jaw dropped to my chest when I noticed something I should have observed immediately. The new rider was a girl.

She looked about my age but was smiling at the crowd with a calm assurance that made her seem older. This was a woman who wasn't easily intimidated. I wasn't sure who she was, but I was a little startled by how much she looked like me: same dark, wavy hair, same deep brown eyes; we even had the same basic bone structure.

She looked more like my sister than my *actual* sisters. Seeing a doppelgänger of myself was a little... unnerving.

Hayden seemed affected as well. From beside me, I heard him let out a long exhale followed by very quiet words. "Oh... shit."

Curious about his reaction, I turned to look at him. "What's wrong? Do you know her?"

Before Hayden could respond, Keith announced her to the group. "Everyone! I'd like you to meet our newest superstar, and Benneti Motorsports' first and only female rider: Felicia Tucker. And take it from me when I say that this girl here can ride. She is going to obliterate every female record there is." Locking eyes with me, Keith added, "Move over, world; there's a *new* girl in town."

Felicia. Hookup's oft-repeated comments about how much I looked like Hayden's ex flashed through my mind, blinding me. No, it couldn't possibly be the same girl. She'd left, and no one knew where she'd gone. This was coincidence. Had to be. Only... Hayden wasn't acting like she was a stranger.

Felicia's eyes were drilling holes into Hayden as she acknowledged the crowd. "It's an honor to be a part of the Benneti Motorsports team, and I can't wait to get to know all of you better." Her raptor-like gaze hadn't left Hayden's, and ice formed in my belly. No, this couldn't be happening.

Feeling like I was dreaming, I slowly swiveled to look at Hayden. He was pale as he stared right back at Felicia. "Felicia?" I asked quietly, my voice sounding shaky. "*Your* Felicia?"

Hayden turned to me slowly, and his eyes were the last thing to move away from her. Settling his gaze on me, he roughly swallowed. "No, not mine, not anymore... but... yeah... same girl."

I felt like the air around us had turned thick with trepidation; inhaling was a struggle. I could tell Keith had hired her to get back at me because my father wouldn't sell the track to him. Had he hired a female rider in a deliberate attempt to undermine what I'd done this year, or had Keith known that Hayden had once had a connection with this woman? As I turned to stare at Felicia, she shared a brief conspiratorial look with Keith, and I knew in an instant that she'd told him everything about herself. Keith had known she shared history with Hayden when he hired her. And it was obvious from the multiple glances she was giving Hayden as she moved through the crowd of eager men practically salivating to meet her that she wanted that history to continue. Her sultry eyes were clearly shouting, *We're not done yet.*

Over my dead body, bitch.

Damn it. This was not what I needed right now. Looking back at Hayden, I narrowed my eyes at him, handed my cake to Nikki, and then started walking toward my bike. I couldn't be here for this; Hayden reuniting with his old flame was not something I wanted to witness.

The tears started to form before I was even three feet away. But then, I heard boots pounding on the cement, running to catch up to me. Startled, I looked over to see Hayden by my side. Grabbing my hand, he laced our fingers together. Giving me a calm, reassuring smile, he said, "Where we going, Twenty-Two?"

I stopped and stared at him, dumbfounded. "Are you serious? Your ex reappears as your new teammate, and you're asking me where *we're* going? Don't you want to stay and talk to her? Ask her why she disappeared on you? Ask her where she's been all these years? Ask her what the hell she plans to do now that she's back in your life?"

My words were getting faster, and my heart was accelerating to match them. Stepping into me, Hayden grabbed my face and kissed me, hard...in full view of anyone who might be watching. And the feeling of eyes burning into my back told me someone was most definitely watching.

When we pulled apart, Hayden left his hands on my cheeks. "You're the one I love. She's my past, and yes, seeing her shocked me at first, but *you're* my present and my future. Where she went, what she wants, why she's here...it doesn't matter to me. Where *you* want to go right now, that's all that matters to me. *You're* all that matters to me. So tell me, Kenzie...where do you want to go?"

God, wasn't that the question of the day. Where did I want to go? I wasn't sure, but it filled me with relief and joy that he wanted to come with me. I smiled as I answered him. "Let's go for a drive up the coast... and just... see where we end up."

Hayden nodded, then leaned in to give me another kiss. When we separated, he whispered in my ear, "Race me?"

Grinning brightly, I whispered back, "Race me or chase me, Hayes."

ABOUT THE AUTHOR

S. C. Stephens is a #1 *New York Times* bestselling author who spends her every free moment creating stories that are packed with emotion and heavy on romance. In addition to writing, she enjoys spending lazy afternoons in the sun reading, listening to music, watching movies, and spending time with her friends and family. She and her two children reside in the Pacific Northwest.

You can learn more at:

AuthorSCStephens.com
Twitter @SC_Stephens_
Facebook.com/SCStephensAuthor